K. Piper

PETER LOVESEY AND PETER DIAMOND

BLOODHOUNDS

SO-BEA-311

"A challenging . . . test of wits. . . . The plot quickens . . . getting trickier at every turn. Watch out for red herrings."
—**Marilyn Stasio, New York Times Book Review**

"Intelligent . . . delightful. . . . A colorful. . . amusing diversion."
—**Washington Times**

"A witty . . . elegant procedural."
—**Los Angeles Times**

"A feast for every mystery fan. . . . The novel parodies Agatha Christie, Elmore Leonard, and Georges Simenon all at once. . . . Lovesey gives us twists and surprises worthy of his illustrious predecessors."
—**Pittsburgh Post-Gazette**

*Winner of the Silver Dagger Award from the Crime Writers Association and the Critics' Choice Award

more . . .

"Lovesey is at the top of his form in BLOOD-HOUNDS . . . the fourth, and probably best, Peter Diamond novel."

—*Detroit Free Press*

"Lovesey lovingly pays homage to the 'golden age' of the genre in this playful, clue-laden book."

—*Denver Post*

"Entertaining. . . . A witty takeoff on the always titillating 'locked room' mystery."

—*Booklist*

"An extraordinary combination of classic puzzle with a contemporary police procedural; an immensely satisfying work by one of Britain's foremost mystery novelists."

—*Houston Chronicle*

"Lovesey spins a tale rich in character and sharp humor."

—*San Antonio Express-News*

"A fine novel. . . . Lovesey pays homage to the classic puzzle sleuths, but adds his unique blend of characterization and wit, and comes up trumps in his entertaining novel."

—*Herald* (Rock Hill, SC)

"A great story line . . . entertaining . . . [with] delightful and unique characters. . . . The only flaw with this novel is that it is over much too quickly."

—Southern Pines Pilot (NC)

"Wanting to know how Diamond figured out the puzzle kept me reading far into the night. . . . An ideal book for a mystery fan on a cold winter day."

—Roanoke Times (VA)

"Fans of John Dickson Carr shouldn't miss this brilliant homage to their master."

—Meritorious Mysteries

"Another wonderful chapter in one of the top crime fiction series being written today . . . expertly surrounded by clear, intelligent prose."

—Deadly Pleasures

"BLOODHOUNDS is a paean to crime and detective fiction, past and present; a shining tribute to a genre too often considered less than literary. . . . Disarmingly charming and utterly brilliant, it is surely destined to become a classic."

—Star Press (Muncie, IN)

BLOODHOUNDS

PETER LOVESEY

THE MYSTERIOUS PRESS

Published by Warner Books

A Time Warner Company

MYSTERIOUS PRESS EDITION

Copyright © 1996 by Peter Lovesey
All rights reserved.

Cover design by Jackie Meyer
Cover illustration by Mel Grant

The Mysterious Press name and logo are registered trademarks of Warner Books, Inc.

 Mysterious Press Books are published by
Warner Books, Inc.
1271 Avenue of the Americas
New York, NY 10020

Visit our Web site at
http://warnerbooks.com

A Time Warner Company

Printed in the United States of America

Originally published in hardcover by The Mysterious Press.
First Printed in Paperback: September, 1997

10 9 8 7 6 5 4 3 2 1

BLOODHOUNDS

THE FIRST RIDDLE

THE CHALLENGE

CHAPTER ONE

D ETECTIVE SUPERINTENDENT PETER DIAMOND WAS SUF-
fering in the rear seat of a police car scorching toward
Bath along the Keynsham bypass with the headlamps
on full beam, blue light pulsing and siren wailing.

"You want to look out for idiot drivers," he shouted to his
driver.

"Everyone can hear us coming, sir."

"Yes, but they don't all do what you expect." If this went
on much longer, his heels would make holes in the carpet. He
was only aboard because he'd been giving evidence in court
at Bristol and happened to ask the driver for a lift back to
Bath. The emergency call had come over the car radio soon
after they drove off. Sheer bad luck. "You said this one is a
bank."

"Yes, sir."

"Do you have a bank account, son?"

"Yes, sir."

"At this branch?"

"No, sir."

"Well, then."

"It's an emergency call."

"It happens all the time," Diamond told him, still compet-
ing with the siren. "Some poor chump goes into the red, and
the manager bites his leg off. They're sharks. They send you

a letter telling you you're two pounds overdrawn and then slap on a ten-pound charge for sending it."

The conversation didn't develop. The siren defeated it. Diamond tried not to look at the dizzying blur of green that was all he could see of the trees beside the road. Only that morning, sitting in court, he had seriously thought police work in Bath was a doddle. When they approached the roundabout that linked Bath Road and Broadmead Lane he closed his eyes.

They came to a screeching halt outside a branch bank on the A4 in Saltford.

"Looks like we're the first," Diamond said without a trace of pleasure in the achievement. "Who's that wally in the doorway, do you reckon—one of ours, or one of theirs?"

The man was wearing a gray pinstripe three-piece and waving to the police car, so the balance of probability was that he was friendly. He came over while Diamond was still in the act of levering his large body out.

"Routledge," the pinstriped gent introduced himself. The voice had a fruity quality, a definite hint of the plum. "Chief Clerk." He actually offered to shake hands—as if Diamond had called to open an account. "You got here very quickly."

"What's the state of play?"

"Well, the manager, Mr. Bellini, is dead."

"Dead?"

"Shot through the head," the chief clerk said in the clipped, matter-of-fact tone of a British actor suppressing his emotion in a film about the war.

"You mean that? Is the gunman still in there?"

"Er, no."

"Any witnesses?"

"Witnesses? No, it happened in Mr. Bellini's office."

"People must have heard the shot," said Diamond.

"Oh, that's for sure."

"And seen the man come out."

Routledge gave the matter serious thought. "I don't think

they could have done. You'll have to ask them. I think they ducked behind the counters."

Diamond's brain was grinding through the information he'd been given. "If no one saw the gunman come out, how do you know he isn't in there still, with Mr. Bellini?"

Routledge gave a shrug and a self-effacing smile. "Well, as a matter of fact, officer, I shot him myself. Forgive me for speaking plainly. Mr. Bellini was a total plonker."

CHAPTER TWO

THE CHURCH OF ST. MICHAEL WITH ST. PAUL, BUILT JUST before Queen Victoria came to the throne, stands at the point where Broad Street meets Walcot Street, close to the Podium and the Post Office. The writer John Haddon in his *Portrait of Bath* described it as "a good eye-stopper," a summing-up that is difficult to better. The spire is one of the tallest in the city. The south front, necessarily slender because of the tapered piece of ground it occupies, is said to have been inspired by Salisbury Cathedral. Unhappily Salisbury Cathedral doesn't sit well in the center of Bath. Narrow lancet windows, buttresses, and pinnacles do not blend easily with Georgian or mock-Georgian pediments and columns. The nicest thing that has happened to St. Michael's in recent years is that the stone cleaners were called in. A century and a half of grime has been removed, and now the color of the building matches adjacent buildings even if the architecture does not.

At ten to eight on a rainy October evening a woman in a yellow PVC raincoat approached from Broad Street, taking care to block her view of most of the building with her umbrella. The scale of St. Michael's intimidated Shirley-Ann Miller. She was not a churchgoer. The only time she had braved the inside of a church in the past ten years was for a Nigel Kennedy recital at Christchurch during the Festival some years back. The adolescent crush she'd had on the punk violinist had lasted well into her twenties. This evening she was drawn by another enthusiasm, and it had to be a strong pull to get her here, for the meeting was to take place in the crypt.

The main doors to the church were locked. Shirley-Ann toured the outside searching for another entrance, doubts growing as to whether she had been misinformed. On the Walcot Street side she found a set of descending steps behind railings. She took off her glasses and wiped them dry, looking for some kind of notice. At the bottom of the steps was an arch-topped door that definitely led under floor level. She released the catch on the umbrella and gave it a shake, took a deep breath, and stepped down.

Prepared for flagstones, cobwebs, and tombs, she was reassured to find that the way into the crypt was clean and well lit. There were doors leading off a short corridor, and she could hear voices from the room at the end.

She always felt nervous meeting people for the first time, but that had to be overcome. She pushed open the glass door to her right and stepped inside. It was like a private health center, warm, light and carpeted, with not a coffin in sight. The cream-colored walls had travel posters. Everything was so immaculate that she was concerned about marking the oatmeal carpet with her wet shoes.

The man and woman she had overheard stopped speaking and stared at her. To Shirley-Ann in her jittery state, the woman appeared a dragon empress, sixtyish, with a broad, powdered face with emerald-green eye shadow that toned with her peacock-blue high-necked oriental dress. Jade earrings. Heavily varnished nails. The rest of her was more European; permed blond hair and fleshy orange lips pursed in disdain.

The man was as awesome in his way as the woman. His black beard looked as if it came from a joke shop; it didn't match the silver hair on his head. Shirley-Ann found herself wondering if the beard was attached to his red-framed glasses, and if the whole thing lifted off in one piece.

Since neither of these people spoke, she introduced herself.

They just stared back, so she felt compelled to announce, "I do hope I'm not in the wrong place. Are you the Bloodhounds of Bath?"

How toe-curling it sounded.

The man didn't answer directly, but said, "Do you want to become a member, then?"

"I was told there might be room for me. I adore detective stories."

"I wouldn't admit to that if I were you." He cautioned her as if he were giving legal advice. "Some of the group won't be at all happy with such an admission. We have to define our tastes most scrupulously. You would be better advised—if you must give anything away at this stage—to say that you are a student of the crime novel, wouldn't she, Miss Chilmark?"

The dragon empress twitched her mouth and said nothing.

The man went on, "The term *crime novel* embraces so much more than the old-fashioned detective story." He took a measured look at the stone pillars of the crypt. "We're a broad church here."

Shirley-Ann realized that this last remark was meant to be witty. She managed a semistifled laugh, and then said, "I didn't mean just detective stories."

"What did you mean?" he asked.

She was beginning to think she had made a ghastly mistake coming here. "I said the first thing that came into my head."

"Not always wise. Should we call you Miss, Mrs. or Ms.?"

"I'd prefer you to use my first name, if that's all right."

"Perfectly all right with me," the man said in a more friendly tone. "I'm known to everyone as Milo. I don't much care for my surname. It's Motion, and I was called deplorable things at prep school. On the other hand, Miss Chilmark is always addressed as . . . Miss Chilmark."

Miss Chilmark explained in a voice that might have announced the programs in the early days of television, "There have been Chilmarks in the West Country for seven hundred years. I'm not ashamed of my surname."

"How many are there in the group?" Shirley-Ann asked. It had to be asked. If there weren't any others, she wasn't staying.

"The Bloodhounds? We're down to six. Seven, if you join," Milo informed her. "We've had a goodly number over the years, but they don't all persevere. Some die, some leave the district, and some are out of their depth. Are you well informed about the genre?"

"The what?"

"The crime fiction genre. What do you read?"

"Oh, just about everything," said Shirley-Ann, not wishing anyone to think she was out of her depth. She felt marginally more comfortable knowing that there were other Bloodhounds than these two. "I devour them. I've been through everything in the library and I have to go round charity shops for more. I'm always looking for new titles."

"Yes, but what are they? Whodunits? Police procedurals? Psychological thrillers?"

"All of those, all the time. Plus courtroom dramas, private eyes, espionage, historicals."

"And you like them all?" asked Milo dubiously.

"I read them all, even the dreadful ones. It's a compulsion, I think. I like them better if they're well written, of course."

"It sounds as if you could contribute something to the group," he said.

"Why not?" she said generously. "I have hundreds to spare."

Milo felt the beard as if to check that it was still attached and said, "I meant a contribution of opinions, not books. We're not all so catholic in our reading. We tend to specialize."

Miss Chilmark was moved to say, "Personally, I require some intellectual challenge, and I don't mean an impossible plot set in a country house between the wars. Have you read *The Name of the Rose,* by Umberto Eco?"

Shirley-Ann nodded.

She wasn't given time to say any more.

"A masterly book," Miss Chilmark enthused. "Full of wonderful things. Such atmosphere. Such learning. What a brilliant concept, placing a murder mystery in a medieval monastery. And the mystery—so intriguing that you don't want it to end! A map, a labyrinth, a distorting mirror, and brilliant deductions. Of course everyone else has climbed on the bandwagon since. These stories that you see everywhere, about the monk in Shrewsbury—"

"Brother Cadfael?" said Shirley-Ann.

"That's the one. Transparently inspired by Eco's great work."

"I think you could be mistaken there," Shirley-Ann gently pointed out. "The first Cadfael book, *A Morbid Taste for Bones,* appeared some years before *The Name of the Rose.* I know, because I read it when I was recovering from my appendix operation, in 1977. *The Name of the Rose* came out in 1983, the year I got a frozen shoulder."

"That can be agony," said Milo.

"Oh, but I'm sure it was available in the Italian," said Miss Chilmark with a superior smile.

"I should check your facts before you take her on," Milo muttered.

Shirley-Ann said no more about Brother Cadfael, but she had privately vowed to find the truth of it at the first opportunity.

There was a timely interruption. Another of the Bloodhounds came in, unfastened the silk scarf from her head—it looked like a Liberty design—and shook her hair. Blond and short, this was hair of the springy, loose-curled kind that needed no combing to look neatly groomed.

Shirley-Ann's hand automatically moved to her own head to tidy the crow's nest she knew was there. Hers would never cooperate.

Milo introduced the newcomer. "This is Jessica, our expert on the female investigator. Give her a chance and she'll reel off all their names."

"Lovely!" Shirley-Ann was relieved to discover that the Bloodhounds weren't all over sixty. "Let me try some. V. I. Warshawski, Kinsey Milhone, Sharon McCone, Jenny Cain."

"Let's hear it for the Brits," countered Jessica with a wide smile. "Cordelia Gray, Jemima Shore, Anna Lee, Penny Wanawake, Kate . . . Kate . . . Val McDermid's character, em . . . Oh, what's my brain doing?"

"Kate Brannigan," Shirley-Ann said almost apologetically. "You read McDermid?"

"She reads everything, apparently," said Milo without spite. "She's going to keep us very well informed. I'm extremely wary of disclosing my special interest in such company."

The remark, and the arch way it was said, caused Shirley-Ann to wonder if Milo was gay.

Jessica removed her black Burberry raincoat and dropped it on a table at the side of the room. She was dressed dramatically in a black top and leggings, with a white satin sash. "Where's the chair?"

Milo looked puzzled, and no wonder, since ten padded chairs were arranged in a circle in the center of the room.

"Chairperson," Jessica explained. "Polly."

"Late for once," said Milo. "And so is Rupert."

"Rupert is always late," said Miss Chilmark. "I'm quite willing to take the chair for the time being if you wish to begin." She strutted across to the circle and sat down.

"That one would love to take over," Milo confided to Shirley-Ann. "It's her ambition."

Jessica said, "Let's give Polly a few more minutes. She'll be all flustered if she thinks she held us up."

"Which is why we should start, in my opinion," said Miss Chilmark from the circle.

No one else moved to join her, and that seemed to settle the matter.

Jessica asked nobody in particular, "Is Sid here? Oh, yes."

To Shirley-Ann's amazement a man in a fawn raincoat confirmed his presence by stepping into view from behind a pillar and lifting a hand in a gesture that might have been intended as a friendly wave, except that the outstretched fingers and the startled eyes behind them suggested Sid was warding off a banshee attack. He must have been in the crypt before she arrived. He said nothing, no one took any more notice, and Shirley-Ann felt rather embarrassed for him.

"You must be local. Am I right?" Jessica inquired of Shirley-Ann in the charmingly assertive tone cultivated English women use to show that they ignore certain things.

"We have a flat in Russell Street," Shirley-Ann answered. "That is, Bert—my partner—has the flat. We've been together almost six months. He's local, born and bred in Bath. I'm afraid I'm not. I only arrived in the city last year."

"Don't apologize for that, my dear," said Jessica.

"Well, I do feel slightly ashamed among people who have been here for years. You see, I work with one of the bus companies, on their tours."

"You're a guide, and you only came last year!" said Jessica with a peal of laughter. "Good luck to you. Where are you from? You sound like a Londoner."

"Islington, originally."

"And your partner's a Bathonian. Well, you'll get all the gossip on the city from him, I expect. What does he do?" She was drawing out the information in a way no one could object to.

"Bert? He works at the Sports and Leisure Center. He's often out in the evenings, so the Bloodhounds would fit in quite nicely for me—if you'll have me. Who runs it?"

Milo pitched in. "We're totally informal," he claimed, though the evidence so far suggested otherwise. "Two or three of us—that is to say, Polly Wycherley, Tom Parry-Morgan (now dead, poor fellow) and I—discovered a mutual interest in crime fiction through a dinner at the Pump Room a few years back, when the writer P. D. James was one of the speakers. We happened to be sharing a table, you see. Polly is one of life's organizers, as you will discover, and she made sure that we all met again. Periodically we've been traced to our lair by other Bloodhounds."

"That's how you join," added Jessica.

"Now I understand the name," said Shirley-Ann. "And is there a fee?"

"We chip in enough to cover the hire of the room," said Milo. "We used to meet in pubs at the beginning, but some of the ladies decided a meeting room would be more civilized."

"That isn't true," Miss Chilmark called across from the chair. "We were asked to meet somewhere else after Rupert misbehaved himself in the Roman Bar at the Francis."

"We could have gone to another pub," said Milo.

"You know it would have been the same story."

The information-gathering had not been entirely one-sided. Shirley-Ann did some mental addition and realized that she now knew something about all the Bloodhounds. Six, Milo had said. Three women: Polly, the Chair, famous for her organizing skills, but liable to be flustered if late; the Eco devotee, Miss Chilmark, ambitious to take over; and Jessica, the expert on the female private eyes. She was grateful for Jessica. And the men: Milo, probably a civil servant by his pedantic manner, and possibly gay; Sid, who hid; and Rupert, who misbehaved in pubs. Good thing she hadn't come here to look for male companionship.

"Rupert's all right," Jessica told her. "I think it's mostly role-play with him. He claims to have met all sorts of famous people. But he stops us from getting too stuffy and parochial. He's deeply into what he calls 'Crime Noir'—authors like James Ellroy and Jonathan Kellerman."

"Will he be coming tonight?"

"I expect so, but not before we start. He likes to make an entrance."

Shirley-Ann wasn't yet convinced that she would tolerate Rupert as blithely as Jessica did.

A voice from the door said, "So sorry, everyone. What will you think of me? I dropped my car keys down a drain, and I've been trying to hook them up for the past twenty minutes." It had to be Polly Wycherley, and the poor dear was flushed with the experience, or her embarrassment. Her breathing sounded asthmatic. She raised the average age of the group closer to sixty, but there was a reassuring softness and mobility in her features. Short, chunky, silver-haired and wearing a pale green Dannimac coat, she was Shirley-Ann's idea of a favorite aunt.

"Did you get them back?" Milo asked.

"Yes—thanks to a kindhearted taxi driver who saw me on my knees by the side of the road. It happens quite often, apparently. Not to me, I mean." Dimples of amusement appeared in her cheeks. "I could tell you what to do if it happens to you, but I've wasted enough time already. Listen everyone, I've got to wash my hands. Why don't you begin without me?"

"Good suggestion," said Miss Chilmark. "Sit down, ladies and gentlemen."

"We can wait a few more minutes," said Jessica quickly.

"Yes, let's wait," Milo chipped in.

Miss Chilmark's eyes narrowed, but she said no more.

"What's the program tonight?" Shirley-Ann asked Milo.

"I'm not sure. We leave that up to Polly. We're not too rigid about the way we run it. One thing you should be prepared for: We take turns to talk about a book we enjoyed recently."

"Don't you dare mention *The Name of the Rose*," murmured Jessica.

"I hope I don't have to go through some initiation rite."

Milo's eyes sparkled. "A secret ceremony?"

Jessica said, "Black candles and a skull? What's that club that writers belong to? The Detection Club."

Polly reappeared, and there was a general move toward the circle of chairs. The Bloodhounds didn't look as if they went in for secret ceremonies.

CHAPTER THREE

"COME IN, PETER, WE'RE WAITING WITH BATED BREATH," said the Assistant Chief Constable.

"What for, sir?"

"You don't know?"

With distrust, Diamond eyed the amused faces around the oval table in the conference room. This was the evening when the ACC's monthly meeting of high fliers took place upstairs in the "eagle's nest" in Bath Central Police Station.

"For the story of your latest arrest. How you nicked the Saltford bank clerk."

"Am I being ever so gently sent up?"

"Good Lord, no. We want to share in your satisfaction. You let it be known in no uncertain terms that a decent murder hadn't come your way since you were reinstated as head of the squad. Now this falls into your lap."

"I wouldn't call it a decent murder," said Diamond. "Two little men in a bank. One gets on the other's wick, so he shoots him. It isn't worth the paperwork."

"Has he confessed?"

"In seventeen pages—so far."

The ACC commented, "That *is* some paperwork. It isn't so straightforward, then."

"He has a list of grievances going back six years."

Several sets of eyes met in amusement across the table. No

one said it, but Diamond was well known for having grievances of his own, and one of them was the amount of form-filling in modern police work.

"Where did he get the gun?" someone asked.

"Right between the eyes," said Diamond.

"I meant where—"

"We haven't got to that yet. About page twenty-five, I should think."

"Don't despair, Peter," said the ACC—a relative newcomer who hadn't really earned the right to call anyone by his first name yet. "Keep taking the statement. Your bank clerk may turn out to have been a serial murderer."

Polite smiles all around.

Diamond shook his head and said, "A good old-fashioned mystery will do me. I don't ask for bodies at every turn. Just one will do if it presents a challenge. Is that too much to ask in Bath?"

"Anytime you feel like giving up . . ." murmured John Wigfull, head of the murder squad until Diamond's recall. Wigfull now functioned as head of CID operations, and he wasn't a happy man either.

The ACC sensed that it was time to get down to business, and for the next hour Wigfull, rather than Diamond, was in the hot seat. The main item on the agenda was crime prevention and Wigfull had taken over Operation Bumblebee, the publicity campaign against burglary. It was a new baby for him, but he'd done his homework, and he managed to talk convincingly about the reduction in the crime figures. "It's an outstanding success however you measure it, sir," he summed up. "And of course all the break-ins reported go straight into the hive."

"The what?" said the ACC.

"The hive, sir. The computer system operated by the Bumblebee team. We analyze the results and decide on initiatives to sting the villains."

"So computer technology has a major role here?" said the

ACC, worthily trying to head off a veritable swarm of bee references.

Diamond stifled a yawn. He wasn't in sympathy with computers any more than he was with bee-based PR campaigns. His thoughts turned to poetry, of all things. This was totally unlike him. He hadn't read a line of verse in years. Yet a phrase mugged up years ago for a school exam was stirring in his memory. What the devil was it? An illustration of some figure of speech?

The discussion of Operation Bumblebee persisted for another twenty minutes. Everyone else around the table seemed to feel it was a chance to make an impression on the new boss, and the squirm factor steadily increased, with talk of getting the buzz on burglars and how the entire station was humming.

Then that elusive phrase surfaced clear and sonorous in Diamond's mind. He spoke it aloud. "The murmur of innumerable bees."

The room went silent.

"Onomatopoeia."

"I suppose it is time we brought this to a close," the ACC said, after a long, baffled stare at Diamond.

CHAPTER FOUR

*I*N THE CRYPT, THE BLOODHOUNDS WERE IN FULL CRY.

"The puzzle is the thing," Milo Motion bayed. "The challenge of the puzzle. Without that, there's nothing."

"You said it!" Jessica rounded on him. "There's nothing in those books except the puzzle, and if the puzzle's no good you feel cheated at the end. Most of those so-called classic detective stories are flawed. Agatha Christie went to preposterous lengths to mystify her readers and she's reckoned to be the best of them. Take the plot of *The Mousetrap*."

"Better not," Polly Wycherley gently cautioned her. "Just in case any of us hasn't seen the play."

Jessica jerked her head toward Polly in annoyance, and the flounce of the blond curls drew an envious sigh from Shirley-Ann. "Have a heart, Polly," Jessica said. "How can we have a serious discussion if we aren't allowed to analyze the plots?"

The reason why Polly was everyone's choice as chairman was made clear. She explained evenly, but with a distinct note of authority, "Jessica, dear, we all love discussing crime stories, or we wouldn't be here, but another reason for coming is to get recommendations from each other of marvelous books we haven't read. Don't let's rob any book of its mystery."

"I deliberately mentioned *The Mousetrap* because it isn't a book," Jessica pointed out.

"Yes, and we appreciate your restraint, but just in case some of us haven't seen the play . . ."

"Is that a ruling from the chair?"

"No, we don't go in for rules," Polly said serenely. "If you want to criticize the puzzle story in general terms, my dear, I'm positive that you can do it, and still make the points you wish to."

"All right," offered Jessica. "What I'm saying without mentioning any titles—"

"Thank you, dear," murmured Polly.

"—is that in order to mystify people, *really* fox them, I mean, writers were forced into concocting story lines that were just plain silly, like one very well-known whodunit in which the person who tells the story is revealed as the killer in the last chapter."

"The last chapter but two, if my memory serves me right," put in Shirley-Ann.

Jessica widened her eyes. "I can see we're going to have to watch what we say in future."

Shirley-Ann felt herself reddening and was relieved when Jessica softened the remark with a smile.

Milo was not smiling. "What's wrong with the narrator doing it?"

"Because that's a trick," said Jessica. "A piece of literary sleight-of-hand. She had to go to absurd lengths to make it work. I mean, the writer did. This is so difficult, Polly."

"It didn't trouble me," said Milo. "And it didn't trouble millions of other people, judged by the success of the book you're talking about. It's still in print after seventy years."

"Is that how long ago it was written?" said Polly, dangerously close to offending the principle she had recommended a second or two before. But it seemed she was only steering the discussion in a less adversarial direction. Her piloting couldn't be faulted.

Miss Chilmark, the dragon empress, who had been silent up to now, waded in. "There's really no reason why a puzzle story shouldn't have other merits. I can think of a work with a wonderful, intricate puzzle that is intellectually pleasing as well as theologically instructive. A novel of character, with a respect for history . . ."

"Any guesses? I never got past page forty-two," murmured Jessica, unheard by Miss Chilmark, who continued to rhapsodize on the merits of *The Name of the Rose* until she was interrupted by the barking of a dog.

"This will be Rupert," Jessica informed Shirley-Ann.

"With a dog?"

"The dog isn't the problem," said Milo.

As it turned out, Milo was mistaken. The dog was a problem. Everyone looked toward the door, and a large brown mongrel, perhaps a cross between a setter and a German shepherd, stepped in and sniffed the air. It had a thick, wavy coat gleaming from the drenching it had got, and it trotted directly to the center of the circle and shook itself vigorously. Everyone was spattered. There were shrieks of outrage, and the meeting broke up in disorder. A chair was overturned, and Polly's handbag tipped upside down. The dog, excited by the commotion, rolled on its back, got up, and barked some more.

Miss Chilmark cried, "Somebody take it outside. My dress is ruined."

The owner appeared, a tall, thin, staring man in a black leather jacket, dark blue corduroys and a black beret, and rapped out a command.

"Marlowe, heel!"

The dog wagged its tail, gave another shimmy, and distributed more moisture.

"It takes no notice of you whatsoever," Miss Chilmark complained. "You ought to have it on a leash. Or, better still, leave it at home."

"That's a flint-hearted attitude, if I may say so, madam," Rupert replied in an accent redolent of one of the better public schools. "Coming here is the high point of Marlowe's week. He's merely doing what dogs do to dry themselves."

Milo said, "And what about all the other things dogs do? Are we going to be treated to those? I can't bear the suspense."

"What have you got against dumb animals?" said Rupert. "How would you like to sit here in a sopping wet coat?"

"How would you like it if I sent you the dry-cleaning bill?" Miss Chilmark riposted.

"Call yourselves Bloodhounds, and you panic when a real dog turns up," Rupert said, with a grin that displayed more gaps than teeth.

Polly Wycherley judged this as the proper moment to restore order. "Why don't we all go back to our seats? Then Marlowe ought to settle down. He's usually no trouble."

"The chairs are wet," Miss Chilmark objected. "I refuse to sit on a wet chair."

A cloth was produced, the seats were wiped, and the meeting resumed with Marlowe in disgrace, anchored by a lead to his master's chair leg, and forced to lie outside the circle.

Shirley-Ann was intrigued that Rupert could appear so indifferent to the chaos he and his dog had just inflicted. He sat between Polly and Milo in a relaxed attitude with legs crossed and his left hand cupping his chin. It was a face without much flesh, dominated by a beak of a nose and dark, deep-set, alert eyes overlapped by the front edge of the black beret.

Polly said, "We were having quite a fruitful discussion about the predominance of the puzzle in the classic detective novel."

"Tiresome, isn't it?" Rupert took up the challenge at once. "Totally unconnected with the real world. All those eccentric detectives—snobbish lords and little old ladies and Belgian refugees looking for unconsidered clues. Absolute codswallop. In the whole history of crime in this country, real crime, I defy you to name one murder that was solved by a private detective. You can't." His owlish eyes scanned the circle. "You can't."

"That doesn't put me off," Milo gamely answered. "I don't want my reading too close to real life."

"Or real death," said Jessica.

"Exactly." But Milo had missed the point.

Rupert laughed and displayed even more gum. He was quite a ruin, but extremely watchable. "Fairy stories for grown-ups."

"Why not?" said Milo. "I like a little magic, even if it turns out to have been a trick."

Shirley-Ann chimed in, "That goes for me, too."

Rupert gave her a pained look. "Another one suffering from arrested development. Hell's teeth, I'm seriously outnumbered now."

Polly sounded a lighter note. "When some of us heard P. D. James at the Pump Room a few years ago, she said she must have had the mind of a crime writer even as a child, because when she first heard the nursery rhyme about Humpty Dumpty, her thought was 'Did he fall, or was he pushed?'"

Even Rupert smiled, and then went straight on to the offensive again. "And they all live happily evèr after?" he pressed them. "Is that what you want from your reading?"

"A sense of order restored, anyway," said Shirley-Ann. "Is that the same thing?"

Milo remarked, "I like the loose ends tidied up."

"So that you can sleep easy, knowing that all's right with the world," Rupert summed up with heavy irony. "Do you people ever read the crime statistics? Do you know what the clear-up rate is? Has any of you ever had your house burgled?"

"Yes."

Heads turned abruptly, for it was Sid who had spoken. He was so inconspicuous that even a single word was quite a bombshell. Having let it fall, he lowered his eyes again, as if the flat cap resting on his knees had become more interesting than anything else in the room.

Shirley-Ann was intrigued to know what Sid was doing in

a discussion group like this if he was so reluctant to join in. He plainly didn't wish to say any more. He avoided eye contact. His posture, his whole behavior, seemed to ask the others to ignore him, and that was what she herself had done up to now. She prided herself on being observant, so Sid obviously had a special talent for self-effacement. Not to be defeated, she regarded him minutely. Probably in his early forties, she guessed, with a more powerful physique than his bowed shoulders suggested. Slightly hooded blue-gray eyes, of which she had seen only glimpses, so her power of observation was not so faulty after all. Small, even teeth. Nothing in his looks could justify such shyness. Perhaps he felt out of his element socially. The clothes didn't give obvious clues, except that they were what you expected a man twenty years older to wear. A white shirt and black tie under the raincoat. Was he an undertaker, perhaps? Not a policeman, for heaven's sake? Dark blue trousers, probably part of a suit. Black, well-polished laced-up shoes. The workingman's raincoat that he wouldn't be shedding, however warm the surroundings. And the flat cap on his knees. You poor, pathetic bloke, Shirley-Ann summed up. You're not enjoying this one bit, so why are you here?

Rupert had been slightly thrown by Sid's observation. "The point I was about to make—I think—is that the sort of thing you people enjoy doesn't deserve to be called a crime novel. The only crime novelists worthy of the name are writers you've probably never heard of, let alone read. Ellroy, Vachss, Raymond—the ones bold enough to lift stones and show us the teeming activity underneath. Not country houses, but ghettos where young kids carry guns and murder for crack and even younger kids are sodomized. Corrupt cops taking bribes from pimps and beating confessions out of luckless Irish boys. Rape victims infected with AIDS. Squats littered with used syringes and verminous mattresses and roaches feeding on stale vomit."

"I don't have the slightest desire to read about stale vomit," said Miss Chilmark. "You get enough of that on the television."

"Precisely," said Rupert. "You switch channels and watch some sanitized story about a sweet old lady who makes nanas of the police through amateur detective work. The same formula week in, week out."

"As a matter of fact, I hardly ever watch television these days," Miss Chilmark told him loftily. "I don't know why I still keep the set in my drawing room."

Rupert's eyes glittered at the mention of Miss Chilmark's drawing room.

Polly cleared her throat and said, "Did anyone wish to say any more about the classic detective story?"

"Is that what we were discussing?" Milo said with a disdainful look at Rupert. "You could have fooled me. Yes, one of us obviously has to speak up for the story that challenges the reader, and as usual, it's me. I put it to you that the Golden Age writers between the wars brought the art of mystification to perfection. Regardless of what some of you were saying just now, I could name a dozen novels of that time, and probably more, that for the brilliance of their plotting stand comparison with anything written in the last half century. You may talk about the intricacy of a le Carré novel or the punching power of your hard-boiled Americans, but for me and for many others the test is whether the writer has the courage to lay out a mystery—a fair puzzle with clues—and say to the reader, 'Solve this if you can'—and then pull off a series of surprises topped by a stunning revelation at the end."

"But at the cost of many of the other merits one looks for in a decent novel," said Jessica with more restraint than Rupert.

"Such as . . . ?"

"Character, pace, sharp dialogue, and, above all, credibility. The books you're talking about were excellent in their time, Milo, but they were never more than pleasant diversions."

"Pastimes," suggested Shirley-Ann, and got a nod from Jessica.

"That's a word you don't hear so much these days," said Polly abstractedly. "Pastimes. Nice word."

Milo was not to be overridden. "Of course, the most basic and fascinating form of detective puzzle is the locked room mystery."

Rupert groaned and slid down in his chair with his long legs extended.

Milo ignored him. "The master of the locked room mystery was John Dickson Carr. The 'hermetically sealed chamber'— as he called it—was a feature of many of his finest novels. I don't know which of you has read *The Hollow Man*."

Shirley-Ann gingerly raised a hand. The only other reaction came, surprisingly, from Sid, who gave a nod without removing his gaze from his flat cap.

Milo said, "In that case, I shall definitely bring my copy with me next week. Quite apart from being one of the most entertaining detective stories ever written, *The Hollow Man* has a famous chapter devoted to locked room mysteries. Dr. Fell, Dickson Carr's sleuth, holds up the action to deliver a lecture on the subject that is a delight from beginning to end. Am I right?" He looked toward Sid, who gave another nod.

"Yes, why not?" Milo went on. "I shall read it to you next week, and I'll warrant that Dr. Fell will make some converts among you, even if I can't."

Rupert confided loudly to Shirley-Ann, "He's hooked on this hogwash, poor fellow. We'll never get him off it. Belongs to the Clue Klux Christie and the Daughters of Dorothy L. and the Stately Holmes Society. Quite mad. They think of themselves as scholars, these people. Believe me, my dear, the only fan club worth joining is the Sherlock Holmes Society of Australia. They meet once a year, get totally plastered, fire guns in the air and sing, 'Happy Birthday, Moriarty, you bastard, happy birthday to you!'"

Shirley-Ann felt some sympathy for Milo. He had been outnumbered even before Rupert's arrival.

Polly nudged the tiller again. The best way to focus the discussion, she said, might be to move on to the part of the evening when members spoke about particular books they had read recently. Miss Chilmark offered to begin, but the resourceful Polly remembered that Milo had somehow missed his turn at the previous meeting, so he went first. His announcement that his chosen text was *The Hound of the Baskervilles* was received with an enormous, deeply embarrassing yawn. For a moment no one escaped suspicion. Then the dog, Marlowe, lying on his side, yawned again, and there were suppressed giggles.

Undaunted, Milo made a spirited claim that *The Hound of the Baskervilles* refuted the arguments leveled against the classic detective story. The power of Conan Doyle's setting and the drama of the plot far outweighed the whodunit puzzle, which was revealed long before the final chapters.

Rupert went next, after first admitting that he, too, admired much of Conan Doyle's work, but found *The Hound* one of the least satisfying examples. He spoke about an Andrew Vachss novel, *Blossom,* based on a real case about the tracking of a sniper who murdered teenagers for sexual kicks. Vachss, he told the Bloodhounds, was a New York child abuse lawyer who drew on genuine case histories and whose books unashamedly crusaded on behalf of young victims. They were written in anger, with a missionary zeal.

The evening was drawing on, Marlowe had given up yawning and was whimpering intermittently, and Miss Chilmark could be constrained no longer. Milo objected that they had often before been lectured on *The Name of the Rose,* but Rupert, his face radiant with mischief, pointed out that it was a multilayered book. He gave Marlowe a push, and the dog rolled on his back and went quiet. Miss Chilmark was allowed to continue on the understanding that she would talk about aspects she had not touched on before. To her credit, she had some insights to offer on Eco's use of the monastery library, symbolically and as a device to enhance the mystery. All this did take longer than anyone else's contribution, and as a consequence Shirley-Ann wasn't called upon.

"Care for a drink?" Jessica asked her when the meeting closed. "The Moon and Sixpence is just across the street."

She wasn't used to pubs, and said so. The only thing she knew about the Moon and Sixpence was that there was a plaque on the wall outside stating that it was the address from which the world's first postage stamp had been posted. This piece of philatelic history was open to dispute; there was *another* notice making a similar claim for the postal museum higher up the street. They were currently exhibiting the famous stamp, on special loan from its owner. Shirley-Ann knew next to nothing about stamp collecting, but she'd been highly amused one Sunday morning at discovering the conflicting statements. Trivia of that kind fascinated her.

Jessica pointed out that it was still raining, so they might as well take shelter in the pub and see if it stopped. "That is, if your partner isn't expecting you, or something."

Shirley-Ann was flattered to be asked. She'd placed Jessica in a more sophisticated league than her own. Obviously this chic creature had never once seen the inside of a charity shop, the source of most of Shirley-Ann's clothes. Jessica, she felt sure, was one of that select breed of women who dressed out of the classiest boutiques—where the sales staff started by showing you to a chair and serving you with coffee in bone china cups. It had emerged during the meeting that Jessica was assertive and resourceful and confident at dealing with men. Shirley-Ann told her that Bert wouldn't be back from the sports center for at least another hour.

So they skirted the front of the church and nipped across Broad Street and through the cobbled passage to the Moon and Sixpence. "Some of the people here are far too hearty for my taste," Jessica confided as they went in. "I prefer the crowd across the street in the Saracen's Head, but there's one drawback."

"What's that?"

"The Saracen's is Rupert's favorite watering hole. He dives straight in there after Bloodhounds. Rupert can be fun, but in small doses, as I imagine his wives discovered."

"Wives?"

Jessica held up the four fingers and thumb of her right hand.

Trade was brisk in the bar of the Moon and Sixpence. It took them some time to get served. "You don't know who to blame most," said Jessica in a carrying voice. "The blokes piling in like a loose scrum or the barmaids who refuse to catch your eye." Promptly they were served with their halves of lager. Jessica spotted a corner table just vacated by a middle-aged couple.

"I brought Sid here a couple of times," she told Shirley-Ann.

"The quiet man?"

"Yes, silent Sid. He's slightly better at communicating one-to-one. The poor guy's impossibly shy."

Shirley-Ann said, "I noticed Polly is very gentle with him."

"She mothers us all. What a bunch!"

"Why did Sid join if it's such an ordeal?"

"Someone told him he should get out and meet people, or he might easily flip his lid. He reads crime, so he found his way to us. It must have taken incredible guts to come down those stairs the first time."

"What sort of crime?"

"The lot, like you, everything from Wilkie Collins to Kinky Friedman. And he knows what he likes. He's quite an authority on John Dickson Carr, the writer Milo was on about."

"Does he ever say anything about himself?"

Jessica laughed. She had the whitest teeth possible. "Does he ever say anything? I think he might loosen up in thirty years if I worked at it. He does security work, I gather. Not

M16. Just a glorified night watchman. That's when he gets his reading done, I expect."

"He isn't married?"

"Doubt it. I haven't asked." Jessica took a sip of lager and gave a penetrating look. "You said you aren't?"

"Married?" Shirley-Ann shook her head. "Bert and I live together, and that's enough for the time being."

"How did you meet?"

"I joined a self-defense class he was running."

"And he got through your defense?"

She smiled. "No trouble. How about you?"

A sigh from Jessica. "I'm cash and carried, as they say. Nine years. Barnaby works in ceramics. Well, that's the way he tells it, and it sounds impressive. Actually he makes those miniature houses. You know? About this high. They sell quite well. People will collect anything. They finish up with a whole village on top of the telly." She spoke of her husband without warmth, Shirley-Ann noted. She'd had no difficulty sounding warm over almost everything else she'd mentioned.

"And do you have a job yourself?"

Without conceit Jessica told her, "I manage an art gallery in Northumberland Place. It's called the Walsingham, but really it's mine."

"Gracious. I've passed it hundreds of times."

"Come in next time. I won't sell you anything, honest to God. I might even offer you a sherry."

"You must know a lot about art."

"Just certain things I specialize in."

"Modern?"

"Contemporary. You have to be careful over terms. I don't deal in abstracts, which is most people's idea of modern. I'm a shop window for some talented young artists who can actually manage to produce landscapes without zip-fasteners across the middle, or bits of newspaper pasted onto them."

"Local artists?"

"From all over."

"Do you paint?"

"God, no."

"But you obviously know what's good."

"It's ninety percent bluff, darling." Jessica bent her right hand and inspected her long fingernails. "What did you make of the Bloodhounds, then? A rum lot, aren't we?"

"I enjoyed the discussion," Shirley-Ann answered with tact.

"You'll get weary of it. We have that argument about escapism versus realism every week in some form or other. The puzzle versus the police procedural. Country houses versus mean streets. It's never resolved. Never will be. Milo and Rupert are at opposite poles. I'm somewhere between, I suppose, but I refuse to give support to either of them."

"I expect it's amicable."

Jessica dissented by letting out a breath and vibrating her lips at the same time. "I wouldn't count on it. They're capable of murder, both of them."

Shirley-Ann laughed.

"I'm serious."

"You can't be."

She put her hand lightly over Shirley-Ann's. "Darling, if ever I've met a group of potential murderers anywhere, it's the Bloodhounds. It wouldn't take much. They've read about killing, come to terms with it in their minds. I mean, aren't we all participating mentally when we read a crime novel?"

"I'm not sure," said Shirley-Ann. "I've never thought of it like that myself."

"We're the experts, we people who read them steadily. We know all the plots. We've read the gory bits. We know what the police look out for. If anyone could do the job and get away with it, one of us could."

From across the room came a peal of laughter. Someone had reached the punch line of a joke. It seemed well timed. Shirley-Ann looked to see if Jessica was smiling, but her face was serious.

CHAPTER FIVE

ON THURSDAY, ANOTHER MEETING WAS HASTILY arranged. Putting on his glasses and picking up a file, the new Assistant Chief Constable said, "Gentlemen, I'm sorry about the short notice, but this is a matter of some urgency. You'll recall that we had an encouraging report from Mr. Wigfull only last Monday evening on crime prevention here in Avon and Somerset." He nodded toward Wigfull.

"Sir?" said Wigfull brightly.

Peter Diamond, seated opposite, surprised himself by recalling another verse from long ago: "How doth the little busy bee improve each shining hour." Wisely he didn't speak it aloud.

The ACC was thinking along the same lines. "This has Bumblebee written all over it. Yesterday we received a tip-off that a major crime is being planned in Bath. A theft. Just out of interest, I wonder if any one of you could name the most valuable piece of property owned by the city."

"A building?" said Tom Ray, the Chief Constable's staff officer.

"Portable property."

"Something in the Roman Baths, sir?" suggested Wigfull, his whiskers positively twitching with the challenge. "A gold torque?"

"Not so ancient as that."

"Precious metal in some form?"

"No."

"An antique object?"

"You could describe it as such, but antiquity is not what makes it so valuable."

"A work of art, then?"

The ACC bestowed a smile on Wigfull. "You're almost there. Anyone else with a suggestion?"

It was apparent from the faces around the table that there would be no takers except Wigfull.

"I don't know a lot about art, sir. Where is it housed? In the Pump Room?"

"The Victoria Gallery." Sensing astutely that he had reached the limit of his officers' knowledge of fine art, the ACC unveiled the truth. "It is Turner's painting of the Abbey. A watercolor. Anyone been to see it?"

Total silence.

He added, "It's worth over a million."

"One picture?" said Tom Ray, rolling his eyes.

"J.M.W. Turner was probably the greatest painter our nation has ever produced. This was one of his earliest works, completed before he was twenty-one."

"Hope it's insured," said Diamond.

The ACC gave him a shocked look. "We're not giving anyone the chance to steal it."

"Isn't the gallery guarded by Impregnable?"

Impregnable was the private security firm entrusted with the safety and security of the mayor, the officers, and all the public buildings of Bath. Among the police, there was an unending series of jokes about Impregnable.

"Yes, but that doesn't mean we abdicate our responsibility."

"Good Lord, no," said Wigfull. "If the Turner was taken, we'd get stuffed by the press, not Impregnable."

"Who's Deep Throat?" asked Diamond.

"Deep who?"

"Your source, sir."

"That's uncertain," the ACC admitted. "The tipoff reached us by an indirect route. A CID officer in Bristol—Sergeant Plant—seeking information on another matter, picked it up from one of his snouts."

"I like it," said Diamond, his belly quivering with amusement.

"What?"

"Sergeant Plant, our plainclothes man. Who was the snout—Mr. Grass?"

The ACC reddened ominously. "You'd do well to take this seriously, Superintendent. Plant is a promising young officer."

Diamond made an effort to contain his amusement by thinking about the list of jobs waiting to be done in his new home in Weston. This meeting shouldn't drag on much longer if the Turner was the only topic.

"The point is," the ACC resumed, "we have the opportunity to prevent a major theft. I'm ordering a review of security at the gallery. Mr. Wigfull, the Bumblebee team will be responsible. You can liaise with Impregnable. We're not trying to score points here. The painting is kept upstairs in the permanent collection. Check the windows, the roof, all points of access. See that the alarms are functioning and the guards are aware of the threat. Art thieves are among the most professional of all the criminal fraternity."

"Right, sir," said Wigfull. "If you don't mind my asking, is the prime objective to scare them off?"

The ACC hesitated. "Well, I see this as an exercise in crime prevention, don't you?"

"Absolutely, but . . ." His voice trailed away.

"What's your point, then, John?"

Wigfull picked his words judiciously. "I may be out of order, sir, but it seems to me that we have the opportunity of, er, staking out the gallery and pulling in these villains."

"Ah." The ACC's response was flat, still uncommitted.

"If so, it might be wise not to make a show of strengthening the security."

"You think so?"

"We don't want them getting suspicious."

"You're thinking of setting a trap?"

"With the Bumblebee team and a few others, I could catch them in the act, sir."

"Good thinking." Wigfull's plan had got the nod.

"I'll need officers I can rely on, sir, preferably people I know. As we were told that the murder squad isn't overburdened at this time—"

At the mention of his murder squad, Diamond jerked forward in his chair. "Hold on. How long will this pantomime go on for? I can't spare men to sit in an art gallery for weeks on end."

"It might improve their minds," said Tom Ray.

"You're not busy," said Wigfull. "You may not have a murder in the next month."

"I may commit one," muttered Diamond.

He had little chance of defending his empire. It was decreed by the ACC that four of the murder squad should be seconded at once to Operation Bumblebee. Wigfull picked them himself. He had the gall to pick Inspector Julie Hargreaves, Diamond's best detective.

"I can't release Julie."

"I need a woman," insisted Wigfull.

Tom Ray said, "Tell us something new."

Wigfull gave him a fish-eyed stare and said, "She'll be just right for this. She can sit behind the desk and sell postcards."

"Terrific," said Diamond. "Would you like her to dust the picture frames as well?"

CHAPTER SIX

ON FRIDAY, THE PAPER HAD A NEWS IN BRIEF ITEM AT THE foot of page two about the murder of the Saltford bank manager and the magistrates' court appearance of the chief clerk. Stephanie Diamond spotted it by chance when she was looking for the weather forecast. The *Guardian*'s layout always defeated her. Peter wasn't mentioned by name, but now she understood why he was working so late these evenings. He'd muttered something about a meeting as he'd climbed in beside her the wrong side of midnight. Most of his time at work seemed to be spent in meetings or filling in forms.

She timed his breakfast to perfection, lifting the two lightly coated eggs from the pan and placing them on the slice of fried bread beside the bacon and tomatoes just as he came downstairs. The pampering he got at breakfast helped him through the day. She reckoned it was a fair trade for the cup of tea he brought her in bed these chilly October mornings. She couldn't move a muscle without her fix of tea. And he often cooked dinner when he was home.

He reached for the paper and glanced at the football results. Missed the item on page two. Then he yawned.

"Any chance of an easier day today?" she asked him.

"Every chance," he said bleakly.

She felt a stirring of concern. "You haven't done anything rash?"

"Like what?"

"Like resigning again?"

He smiled faintly. "No. It's just gone flat."

"What do you expect in Avon and Somerset? The Himalayas?"

He cut into a fried egg. "I'm not ambitious. I'd settle for the Mendips, but all I see is the Somerset Levels. Take that murder that happened on Monday. The genius who did it walked up to me, shook my hand and confessed."

"That must have helped your clear-up rate."

He didn't answer. Statistics had never appealed to him.

"You can't have it all ways," Stephanie remarked. "We live in a gorgeous old city. It's going to be quiet. If you want serious action, you'd better start applying for jobs in Glasgow or Manchester, but don't ask me to come."

"Thanks." He put some more food in his mouth. "But you're wrong, Steph. Avon and Somerset isn't short of villains."

"You mean they're all in the police."

He grinned.

Stephanie said, "Which villains, then? Local farmers protesting about the bypass?"

"Professionals, I'm talking about. The smartest piece of shoplifting I ever heard of happened in my patch."

"In Bath?"

"Bristol. Didn't I ever tell you? They did one of those ultraexpensive dress shops."

"A boutique?"

"Yes, in Southmead. It was a night job. I don't know how many thousand quids' worth of designer gowns. They didn't break in, didn't smash anything, didn't leave any prints, didn't even set foot on the premises. We never caught them. Took us a long time to work out how it was done."

"If they didn't break in, they must have had a key," Stephanie guessed.

"No."

"Then it was some kind of inside job."

"It wasn't."

"Didn't set foot in the shop, you said?"

"Didn't need to."

"I give up. How was it done?"

"They worked through the letterbox with a twelve-foot boat hook. Dragged the display racks across the floor and tugged out the dresses one by one. Even the owner said she had to admire their cheek."

The kettle boiled, and he made instant coffee for them both, his thoughts on the day ahead. There were still three or four hours of form-filling for the Crown Prosecution Service. The chore couldn't be delegated. All his best people were on Operation Bumblebee now.

Stephanie turned up the volume on the radio. Diamond finished his breakfast in silence.

On BBC Radio Bristol some harbinger of gloom was wittering on about the traffic. If Steph was first downstairs she generally switched on the local station. When Diamond was forced to listen to anything at all in the morning he found it easier to tolerate the more po-faced Radio Four.

The short interval after he'd eaten and before he got up from the table was when Steph found it easiest to broach things she was planning. This morning, it was more of a confession she had in mind. "I don't think I told you," she began, not entirely honestly, because she knew for sure that she hadn't raised the subject until now. "A few weeks ago, soon after we moved in properly, when you were at work and I was trying to get some more of those damned tea-chests unpacked, I heard a noise behind me. Gave me a fright. It was this little cat, no more than a kitten really, playing about with the newspaper we'd wrapped the plates in. You'd think he belonged here." Steph saw an ominous look in her husband's eye and talked on rapidly. "I'd no idea where he came from. Naturally I asked around. Pete, he was a dear little thing with enormous ears and feet for his size and just a few stripes in the middle.

I tried the people who were here before us, but they didn't know. In the end I did the right thing and took him up to Claverton."

"The home for strays?" Diamond said. "Yes, you did the right thing, Steph."

She nodded. "They get a lot of animals brought in. I didn't like leaving him really, being so young."

"Too young to care, probably."

"Oh, I don't know about that. Anyway, the young girl there said she'd let me know if he was claimed."

"And was he?" Diamond asked hopefully.

"Er, no."

"And where is he now? Still there?"

"I went to see him yesterday."

"To Claverton? What did that dingbat say?"

She swung around defiantly. He'd gone too far this time.

But Diamond wasn't insulting the people who took in strays. He got up from the table and reached for the radio. The speaker was well into some item: ". . . so if any of you geniuses listening out there can make better sense of it than we can, call me now. I'll give you the number presently. Is there something we ought to know? Is it like a Valentine message? Is it in code? Is it a cryptic crossword clue? I tell you one thing, for sure. It had better not be some wise guy trying to slip a commercial into BBC local radio or we're all in shtuck. No, my money is on a good, old-fashioned riddle. I understand we're not the only radio station to have received it. And the same message was sent to the local press. The whole region is going to be racking its brains over this. Let's prove that Radio Bristol has the most intelligent audience. We can crack this together."

"Give it to us again, then," said Diamond, and you would think he had been heard, the response was so quick.

"I'm going to give it to you one more time before we move on to the sports news. Make sure you have something to write it down. Ready?

" '*J.M.W.T.*
Surrounded by security.
Victoria, you challenge me.
I shall shortly come to thee.'

"Got it? Chew on that for a bit. Must move on now. Sports news coming up next. But I kid you not, listeners, the message was received this morning, early, but early, and we have no idea what it means, or who sent it. What or who is J.M.W.T.? Who is Victoria when she's at home? Over to you."

Diamond reached across the table for the pen and the *Guardian,* placed ready for Stephanie's daily assault on the quick crossword. He made a note in the margin.

Stephanie remarked, "You're always telling me puzzles are a waste of time."

"Crossword puzzles, yes," he said, tearing off the scrap of paper and pocketing it.

She said, "About this kitten. I know if you saw it, you'd be captivated."

He said abstractedly, "Yes."

"Then you don't mind if . . ."

He said, "Anything you say, my love. Got to get off to work now."

At Manvers Street Police Station he found a worried John Wigfull in the communications room. The big black mustache was drooping ominously.

"I suppose you've heard," Wigfull said.

"Depends what you mean."

"This message about the Turner. It's all over the city. The radio. The papers. People are phoning in."

"I did catch something on the radio while I was having breakfast. There's no doubt in your mind, then?"

"J.M.W.T.," said Wigfull. "Turner's initials. And the mention of the Victoria Gallery. 'I shall shortly come to thee.' I'd say that's pretty conclusive. I'm up against a nutter."

"Sounds like a poet to me."

"Same thing."

"A public relations expert, anyway," said Diamond. "He's used the local media to some effect."

"Is it just a stunt?" Wigfull asked, as though Diamond in his infinite wisdom might be able to confirm the fact. "If you're aiming to steal a picture, you don't broadcast it to all and sundry."

"Is the picture still in place?"

"Yes, thank God. I spoke to Julie Hargreaves a few minutes ago. She's at the gallery. I keep checking with her. Up to now, everything is in order."

"What's the problem, then?"

"No problem. Just that I'm bloody annoyed. First I get the tip that someone is about to stage a robbery and then, when I put a team in place, this message goes out, all over the city. Someone is doing his best to run rings around me."

Diamond suppressed the smile that wanted to come. "No chance you can spare Julie for a couple of hours, I suppose? I'm a bit pushed collecting statements of this Saltford incident. I've got all those bank clerks to interview. Julie does it so well."

"Sorry," said Wigfull. "She was assigned to me."

"If I went down to the gallery I could look at the security for you. I'm sure you've got it under control, but sometimes another pair of eyes will spot something."

"Do you think so?" Wigfull's eyes betrayed a flicker of uncertainty.

He parked illegally in Bridge Street under the statue of Queen Victoria that stands in a niche high up in the gallery's facade. For a Georgian city, Bath commemorates Victoria's name quite generously, with a park, a bridge, several streets, a pub and a burger bar, as well as the art gallery. Considering that Britain's longest-reigning monarch shunned the city for the whole of her reign, she scarcely deserved so much. She was brought there for a brief visit as a young girl, before she was Queen, and the story goes that while she was standing on the hotel balcony she was deeply offended to overhear someone remarking how thick her ankles were. Bath was struck off her visiting list forever.

Glancing up at the old killjoy as he got out of the car, Diamond weighed those words he had heard over breakfast: "Victoria, you challenge me. I shall shortly come to thee." Did the message mean what Wigfull had assumed, a threat to plunder the gallery of its Turner, regardless of the extra security? Or might it be interpreted another way?

It was not impossible that the cryptic message didn't refer to the owner of the thick ankles at all, but to some living Vicky who had a connection with the Turner. A curator? A gallery attendant? For God's sake, Diamond, he chided himself, it's Wigfull's problem, not yours.

A local journalist he recognized as from the *Bath Chronicle* was at the corner of Bridge Street, by the entrance, waiting to hear the latest. So much for the puzzle the whole region was supposedly racking its brains to solve.

"Are you on this case, Super?"

"What case?" Diamond rapped on the door, annoyed by that "Super." The gallery wasn't open to the public yet, but the security team would be inside.

"The Turner. Has it been knocked off?"

"I've no idea what you're talking about."

"Come on, Mr. Diamond. I've got my job to do, same as you."

"Nothing to my knowledge has been knocked off," said Diamond.

"It's still there?"

"Far as I know."

"You must be taking it seriously. You must be worried that they mean to have a go."

"Do I look worried?"

He heard the sound of bolts being withdrawn. One of the

great wooden doors opened a fraction, and part of a face was briefly visible, followed by the sound of static from a personal radio. The door opened widely enough to admit him. The reporter said something about cooperation, and then Diamond stepped inside, and the door slammed in the face of the press, if rather more heavily than the constabulary intended.

The last time Diamond had seen the black-and-white marble tiled vestibule was when the lower floor had been in use as the public library. Now both floors were used as galleries, and the permanent collection was upstairs. He was escorted up the stone staircase past some paintings of rustic scenes, most of them featuring sheep, or what were intended by the artists to pass for sheep, but could have been giant, cream-colored rats, or armadillos. Landscape painters, he decided, weren't on the whole successful with sheep.

Not the sort who spent his leisure hours looking at art, he'd never ventured up here before, and it was grander than he expected. At the top of the stairs was a tiled area surrounded by columns supporting the dome of the building, the underside of which was decorated in gilt with the signs of the zodiac. He stepped into the gallery, and was surprised by its size. It was a fine example of Victorian pomp, big enough for a ballroom, some fifty feet high, with a copy of the Parthenon frieze extending right around the walls below the glazed, arched roof that extended the length of the room. There were no windows. The pictures in their ornate gilt frames were attached to maroon-colored walls, and some were displayed on purpose-built units along the center of the room.

"Safe as the Bank of England, I would have thought," he remarked to Julie Hargreaves, who had got up from behind the attendant's desk to greet him. "I suppose he could try a *Rififi*-style entry from the roof."

A look of incomprehension crossed Julie's face, and he realized that the film *Rififi* must have been made before she was born. Not for the first time, he had to remind himself that his best support in the murder squad was female and not much over thirty. Julie was a colleague he could rely on absolutely. She was as bright as a brand-new coin, and it was a measure of her professionalism that he disregarded her good looks. He hoped it wasn't a measure of his advancing years.

"It was a film," he informed her. "Maybe you saw one called *Topkapi*? Same method of entry . . . No? Never mind."

"Two men spent the night on the roof," she told him.

"Two of ours?"

She laughed. "I hope so. There are two more up there now."

"I take it that the picture is still in place?"

"I expect you'd like to see it." She led him across the gallery to one of the display units in the center. "It's not so big as I imagined."

He looked at the fixings before he examined the painting. The Turner was secured to the wooden unit with nails driven through small metal plates projecting from the back of the frame. A thief equipped with a crowbar wouldn't take long to achieve his purpose, but no system has been devised that will withstand that kind of assault. Galleries are better employed installing alarm systems and strong locks.

As for the painting, he was less than impressed. It was a muted watercolor, a view of the Abbey from across the churchyard at an angle that to Diamond's eye was distorted, making the West Front outrageously taller than it is. He'd often sat on one of the wooden seats in the yard and looked at the building from that direction. Bath Abbey projected a sort of charm, but it had never pretended to be lofty. It wasn't as if the painting had other merits to compensate. He could see nothing remarkable in the pale blue and yellow ocher coloring or the brushwork. The total effect reminded him of a dull Sunday. Toward the bottom of the picture was an empty sedan chair with two attendants beside it, and elsewhere the artist had tried to add some interest by including several figures of women in long skirts.

"Would you hang it in your front room?" he asked Julie.

She smiled slightly. "I think it ought to be here, where everyone can enjoy it."

"Be honest. Turner may have painted some wonderful pictures, but this one is crap."

She said, "There's a lot worse. There's one on the wall over there called *The Bride of Death* that gives me the creeps. It's really depressing."

He told her that he was reclaiming her from John Wigfull, and the relief on her face was obvious. She preferred real people, even if it meant statement-taking, to looking at Victorian deathbed scenes. She called up one of the sergeants on duty downstairs and instructed him to take over in the gallery until her replacement arrived.

CHAPTER SEVEN

POLLY WYCHERLEY SAID OVER A CUP OF CAFÉ AU LAIT, "You didn't mind meeting here, I hope? It's one of my favorite places. I always think of dear Inspector Maigret here."

The call had come unexpectedly, before 8:30, when Shirley-Ann was in the shower and Bert was about to leave for work. He'd handed her the mobile phone and a towel and followed up with an intimate fumble that had made her squeak in protest. What it must have sounded like on the other end of the line she dreaded to think. Anyway, it hadn't stopped Polly from suggesting coffee at Le Parisien in Shires Yard.

Not knowing what the weather would do on a mid-October morning, Shirley-Ann had put on a pink trouser suit overprinted with what looked like large blackberry stains. She had bought it for a song last May in the Save the Children shop in Devizes, along with the white lamb's wool sweater that she was wearing under the jacket. Polly was less colorful, in a dark mauve padded coat. As it turned out, there was some fitful sunshine, so they sat under a red-and-white umbrella at one of the marble-topped tables outside. Faintly, from the interior of the café, came a song just recognizable as "J'Attendrai."

Polly was right. This little sun-trap tucked away between Milsom Street and Broad Street could have been lifted from the Latin Quarter. Le Parisien and the Café René existed side by side, and the waiters really were French. "To be truthful, I think of Rupert Davies lighting his pipe. You wouldn't remember him, dear. You're too young. It was in black and white, on Monday evenings."

"Television."

"And that elegant Ewen Solon, who played Lucas, his sidekick. A dreamboat in a porkpie hat. Soigné." Polly gazed wistfully across the yard. "I could have forgotten I was married for Lucas." She pulled herself together. "I wanted to talk to you about Monday night."

"The Bloodhounds?"

"Did you find it off-putting? We weren't at our best, and I didn't want you to go away thinking you wouldn't bother another time."

"I enjoyed myself immensely," said Shirley-Ann, and meant it.

Polly didn't seem to have heard. "Rupert really is the limit, with that dog. He's a much nicer man than he appears, but he makes no concessions to what I think of as decent behavior. He thinks we're all terribly bourgeois and deserve to be shocked, but that's no reason to let the dog misbehave." Her hand shook as she lifted the coffee cup.

"It didn't bother me at all. Really."

It seemed that Polly identified so closely with the Bloodhounds that the incident upset her personally. But as the conversation went on, recapitulating the meeting, it became clear that she was agitated about something more than Rupert's dog. She skirted the matter for some time, retelling the story of the club's beginning over that dinner at the Pump Room in October 1989, even using the same phrase about the deceased founder member, Tom Parry-Morgan: ". . . now dead, poor fellow." Then she started recalling the names of people who had joined, stating the reasons why some had left, as if it was important to stress that they hadn't all been put off by Rupert. "There was Annie Allen, a very old lady who gave up because of the cold evenings; a young chap who was more interested in films than books. Now what was his name? Alan Jellicoe. Another man, Gilbert Jones, was out of his depth, I think, and lasted only three weeks. The Pearce sisters found that the evening clashed with lacemaking when the evening classes started up." The list continued: Colonel Twigg, who wandered in by mistake, thinking it was about crime prevention; Marilyn Slade-Baker, the delinquent girl, whose probation officer stopped her from coming; the Bentin family, just visiting from Oklahoma. More names followed.

Shirley-Ann wasn't counting, but upward of fifteen had dropped out, and that seemed a high figure. Of the surviving six, Polly and Milo had been the founders; the formidable Miss Chilmark had joined soon after and bored everyone with *The Name of the Rose* ever since; then Rupert had arrived one evening looking like a convict after two weeks on the run; shy Sid had been introduced by his doctor; and Jessica had joined only last year. "You could write a thesis about our reasons for sticking with it," she summed up. "All sorts of motives."

"What's yours?" Shirley-Ann asked.

Polly seemed derailed by the suddenness of the question. "I haven't really asked that of myself. I have my own thoughts why the others continued to come. I suppose I like being at the center of something. The others seem to regard me as the mainstay. And I do enjoy crime novels."

"And Milo? Why does he come?"

"For the companionship, I suspect, though he is the sort of man who joins everything he can. He's a long-standing member of the Sherlock Holmes Society, and Lord knows how many other clubs. The Agatha Christie, the Dorothy Sayers, the Edgar Wallace, the Saint. He belongs to them all, and others, I'm certain."

"Has he given up work?"

"He's a retired civil servant."

"I thought he must be."

"Milo is single. Not overattracted to women, I get the impression, though he's perfectly sweet to us ladies, as men like that usually are. He lives alone, on one of those narrowboats on the canal. He calls it the *Mrs. Hudson*, after Holmes's housekeeper. A beautiful gleaming boat almost entirely covered in pot plants. We've had a couple of Bloodhound meetings on board. In fact, we had the last Christmas party there."

"He's there through the winter as well?" said Shirley-Ann in surprise.

"Oh, I think a narrowboat can be quite snug in the cold weather. It certainly was when I was aboard."

"I wouldn't care to live on a boat. You never know who's walking along the towpath, do you?"

"It takes all sorts, as they say. Did you find any like spirits among the others?" Polly probed, all too obviously.

"Jessica went to some trouble to welcome me."

Polly said stiffly, "I noticed that you went for a drink with her after the meeting."

"Just while the rain stopped, yes."

"She is quite an asset to the club," Polly admitted, but grudgingly. Her habitual warmth of spirit seemed suddenly to have cooled, and Shirley-Ann realized that this was what she must have been so agitated over. For some unknown reason it had been a mistake to be seen leaving with Jessica.

"She's up with all the latest books," Shirley-Ann remarked, trying to be neutral.

"Yes." Polly took a sip of her coffee, and the blue eyes watched over the rim. "And she can be helpful at taking the steam out of discussions when they get overheated. She has a sharp sense of humor, which I like. She's very bright, I'm sure of that."

Out with it, then, thought Shirley-Ann. How did she get up your nose?

Polly was saying, "She runs that art gallery in Northumberland Place."

"She told me. The Walsingham."

"I think she part-owns it."

"I got that impression."

"We all have a standing invitation to drop in for a cup and a chat." Polly was still testing the water.

"She did mention it."

"It's not for me to interfere," Polly went on. "It's no business of mine, but I think you should be careful. Jessica is deeper than she first appears."

"*Deeper*—what does that mean?"

"I'd rather not say any more than that." Her gaze shifted away, over Shirley-Ann's shoulder. "What's going on over there, do you suppose?"

Shirley-Ann turned. A policeman in uniform, rather senior from the look of his uniform, was standing with two other men in the passageway that leads to Broad Street. They were taking a lot of interest in the roof, or possibly an upper window of the building on the right.

"That's the Postal Museum," said Polly.

"Yes. When you say Jessica is 'deep,' do you mean she has secrets, or something?"

Polly's mind was no longer on Jessica. "I wonder if there's been a break-in. Some of those stamps are valuable. Have you ever been in?"

"Ages ago."

"What a shame, if someone has broken in. It's a lovely little museum, entirely staffed by volunteers, I believe."

"It might be nothing. They could be checking the security."

"Let's hope that's all it is." Polly looked at her watch. "I have enjoyed our chat. And you *will* come next week, won't you? It's so encouraging to have a new member, especially such a well-read new member."

"I'll be there if I possibly can."

"Wonderful. I'll pay for this. I insist, my dear. And I can't help it—I'm going to ask the policeman what's happened."

"A case for Inspector Maigret, perhaps," said Shirley-Ann, but the remark wasn't heard. Polly had dropped a five-pound note in the dish that came with the bill and was striding across the yard.

After their coffee together, Shirley-Ann liked Polly a little less than she had on first acquaintance.

CHAPTER EIGHT

A N AIR OF URGENCY WAS GUSTING THROUGH MANVERS
Street Police Station when Peter Diamond and Julie
Hargreaves returned from Saltford. Constables and
civilians carrying faxes, files, and clipboards hotfooted it
along the corridors. Phones were cheeping like cicadas. Diamond stopped a chief inspector and asked, "What's up?
Everyone's behaving as if King Kong dropped in."

"It's the ruddy media," he was told. "They won't leave us
alone."

"What media? The *Bath Chronicle*?"

"The nationals. Mainly the tabloids. Not to mention radio
and TV. They're driving John Wigfull spare."

"Why? What do they want?"

"A statement on the break-in. He's due to give one shortly,
but they won't wait."

"What break-in?"

"Where have you been all day? Someone did the Postal
Museum last night and pinched the world's oldest stamp."

"In Bath? I didn't know we had the world's oldest stamp."

The chief inspector managed a weary grin. "We don't anymore."

It emerged that the world's oldest stamp was not normally
kept in the Postal Museum, but had been loaned by the owner
(whose identity was a secret) for a special exhibition. It was

in the city of Bath on May 2, 1840, that the Postmistress mistakenly date-stamped an unknown number of letters bearing the new Penny Blacks four days before the service was due to start. An envelope bearing the famous stamp and date had survived for over a century and a half."

"What's the value?"

"Only two are known to exist. Covers, they call them when they mean the entire face of the envelope. One like it was sold in auction in 1991 to a Japanese collector for one million, three hundred and fifty thousand pounds. It's in the *Guinness Book of Records*. The biggest price ever paid for a postage stamp."

"Insured?"

"Their people are here already."

"What was the security?"

"They have video surveillance and strong locks on the doors. The stamp was on the upper floor in a special cabinet screwed to the wall. The thief got in through a window upstairs."

"Where was this?"

"You know that passage leading up the side of the building, from Broad Street to Shires Yard? He had cutting gear to break into the cabinet. The SOCOs are saying that he left by way of the window he forced. It was a sash window. He must have used a ladder."

"And nobody noticed?" Diamond said in disbelief.

"The theory is that he posed as a window cleaner and did it in broad daylight between seven and nine in the morning. As everyone knows who is out early, a small army of window cleaners is at work every day before the shops open, washing the windows. He could stroll up Broad Street with a ladder and a bucket, and no one would give him a second look. He'd have his tools in the bucket covered with a leather."

"Cool."

"John Wigfull doesn't think so. We're taking a lot of flak from the broadcast media, and the papers are going to have a field day tomorrow. The point is that we had a team guarding some painting in the Victoria Gallery, and no one seemed to know about the stamp."

As soon as they were alone, Diamond warned Julie that if asked, she should say she was working flat out on the Saltford bank murder. "You can't be spared, even for half a day, right? You've got all those statements from the staff to check, and it's opened up several new lines of inquiry."

"Has it?"

"Well, if you want to spend the day mopping John Wigfull's fevered brow . . ."

He felt in his pocket for the scrap of newspaper he had tucked away that morning. After reminding himself precisely what he had written, he went in search of Wigfull. The man of the hour wasn't difficult to find in one of the offices on the first floor. All the activity was focused there. Faxes and files were going in at a dizzying rate. The chief inspector was entrenched behind a large desk heaped with paper. His body language—the hunched look as he talked into a phone—said everything Diamond expected. One hand was curled around the back of his head. The big mustache was lopsided, as if it had partially collapsed, the brown eyes glazed and bloodshot. You had to feel sympathy.

A sergeant Diamond scarcely knew said unnecessarily, "He's terribly busy, sir. We're giving a press conference shortly."

"That's what this is about."

Wigfull put down the phone, and immediately it started beeping again. Diamond's hand was on it first, keeping it in place.

"Half a mo, John."

"I'm about to meet the press," said Wigfull.

"I know. Have you thought it through?"

"Thought what through?"

"The statement you're about to make."

"Certainly. I'm not wet behind the ears."

"May I read it?"

"It's being photocopied right now. You'll get one if you want it."

"What do you intend to say about Bumblebee?"

Wigfull looked into the distance like a camel unwilling to move. "I won't be mentioning Bumblebee. The Turner's got nothing to do with this. I've no doubt that we prevented a possible crime in the Victoria Gallery, but there's no connection with the loss of this stamp."

"I think you'll find there is, John, and I think the press boys will be onto it. They're not slow. You're going to face questions, so you might as well have something ready to say."

"About the Turner?" Wigfull was still uninterested.

"The message we had on the radio this morning." He fished it from his pocket again and read it to Wigfull.

> " 'J.M.W.T.
> Surrounded by security.
> Victoria, you challenge me.
> I shall shortly come to thee.' "

Wigfull stared at him without a glimmer of comprehension. "Well?"

"Isn't it clear to you?" said Diamond through the din made by the phone. "We were set up, John. The Turner was a distraction. The Victoria he was talking about wasn't the name of the gallery. It was the stamp. The Penny Black with Queen Victoria's head on it."

"Do you think so?" Wigfull said. His weary eyes held Diamond a moment, slipped away, and came back to him twice as large. "'Victoria, you challenge me.' My God. Why didn't I think of it?"

"There's nothing to be ashamed of," Diamond generously said. "It could have happened to any of us. So easy to get bogged down in one line of inquiry."

"When did you put two and two together?"

"A few minutes ago, when I heard about the break-in."

"The bastard's made a laughingstock of me. He told us what he was planning, and I didn't see it."

"Which is why you should be boxing clever when you meet the press. They will have cottoned onto this, John."

Wigfull raked his fingers across his scalp. "How would you handle it?"

"Tell them it's no ordinary break-in. It was well planned and boldly carried out. You're dealing with a smart aleck who takes pleasure in announcing his plans, but in cryptic form. Take them through the rhyme showing how devious it was. That 'Victoria' could have referred to half a dozen locations in Bath. Tell them this aleck is not so smart as all that, because he won't be able to sell the stamp. It would be like trying to unload the *Mona Lisa*."

"Good point," said Wigfull. "What does he hope to do with it—demand a ransom?"

"Probably. But I wouldn't open that can of worms with the press, even when they suggest it. If you'll take advice from someone who has dealt with those guys, don't be tempted to speculate on what might happen next. Deal with the facts as known. Tell them a full-scale investigation has been launched, and leave it at that."

"Peter, I appreciate this," said Wigfull.

"Forget it."

"No, I mean it."

"All right. Don't forget it until you've bought me a drink."

CHAPTER NINE

I N THE WINDOW OF THE WALSINGHAM GALLERY WERE TWO
large oils of clowns painted in such a way that the makeup
didn't entirely mask the features. The artist had sacrificed
some realism to reveal the character of the men and women in
performance, and it was skillfully done. It took you a moment to
see through the greasepaint, but once your eye adjusted to the effect, you could tell that one clown was grinning under the
painted smile and another was scowling; one appeared to be giving another, a woman, a predatory look; she was staring out,
aware of his interest, yet disdainful. The idea was not remarkable, but the artistry was. Shirley-Ann spent some time studying
the canvases before going in.

Instead of Jessica, a man popped up from behind an arrangement of blue and yellow irises on a desk at the rear of the gallery.
"Hi. Just looking around, or is there anything in particular you
wanted to see? He was dressed casually for the job, in a check
shirt and black jeans. His teeth were so regular that they must
have been fixed. An actor? Shirley-Ann didn't recognize him
from television, but the dark curls and brown eyes would have
suited him for a role as a heartbreaker in a soap.

"Actually, I just called in to see Jessica."

"Shopping," he told her. "She won't be long if you don't mind
waiting."

Something in his manner suggested he had a more lofty status than a mere minder of the gallery. Shirley-Ann wondered if this could be Barnaby, the husband. She told him she hadn't come about anything important. She would call back another time.

He assessed her with a long look. "You wouldn't be Shirley-Ann Miller, by any chance?"

She felt the blood rise and redden her cheeks. "How did you know?"

"Jess was talking about you. You just joined that coven she belongs to. The crime fiction people. What is it—the Baskervilles?"

"The Bloodhounds. I wouldn't call it a *coven*, but how did you recognize me?"

"She said you might call in sometime."

"Yes, but of all the people in Bath . . ." An uncomfortable thought had come to her. Had Jessica told him about the kinds of clothes she wore? Was it so obvious that she dressed out of charity shops?

"We don't get all the people in Bath dropping in and asking for her by name. I know most of the regular clients here." He stepped from behind the desk and toward her with right hand extended. "I'm known as A.J., and don't ask what it stands for, because I don't much care for the name I was given." His hand was cool, the grip firm. "I'll put the kettle on, unless you want to sample the cheap sherry she keeps."

"No, really," said Shirley-Ann, telling herself that he couldn't be Barnaby, the husband, unless Jessica used the name he didn't care for—which wouldn't be very loyal.

"Really what?" said A.J. "Really tea or really sherry or really you're in a frightful hurry?—because that patently isn't true if you dropped in for a chat with Jess. Sweet discourse makes short days and nights, so the saying goes, and I know of no one it fits better than Jess. My God, wouldn't she be flattered to hear that from me, always accusing her of being a motormouth?"

He was leaving her in no doubt that he knew Jessica extremely well. Personally, if Shirley-Ann had owned a gallery she wouldn't have left an overbearing man like this in charge.

"All right," she said. "Tea will be nice if you really think she won't be long."

"Take a look around," he said, as he stepped toward the alcove where the kettle must have been kept. "See what strikes you as worth the asking price. Between you and me, we have a new exhibition coming up later this week. You should come to the preview if you want to buy."

She didn't care at all for that male assumption that women would do as they were told, so she went straight to a tall-backed Rennie Mackintosh chair and tested it for comfort, still wondering what A.J.'s role was in the business, and in Jessica's life.

When he appeared again and saw her in the chair he said, "Careful, that's where you're supposed to sit to write the check." He handed her the tea. It came in a white porcelain cup and saucer, and there were two tea leaves floating, as if to let her know that he hadn't used a teabag. "She'll be back any second. She can smell tea brewing a mile away."

He was talking like a husband, but Jessica had definitely said she was married to someone called Barnaby. How could you get A.J. from that? Shirley-Ann tried some guesswork of her own. "You look like a painter."

"How come?" he said. "Spots on my jeans—or did I leave a brush behind my ear? Yes, I paint figures."

"The clowns in the window?"

"Christ, no. That isn't my style at all. I do nudes, but very Bath Spa, very tasteful, heavily shadowed over the naughty bits. She has three upstairs, if you're interested. They retail at between eight hundred and a thousand. Two years back I couldn't keep up with the demand, but everything went flat in the recession, including my nudes." He flashed the immaculate teeth. "Joke."

"So you combine painting with working in the gallery?"

"No. I don't work here. Just hold the fort for Jess on occasions. She's stuck with it all day, poor duck, so if I'm passing I look in and let her get some air. You're as hooked on crime as she is, I hear."

"Crime fiction," Shirley-Ann made clear.

"Jess buys books by the yard. You've got to find something if you're in here every day sitting on your butt. She doesn't get all that many callers. And about one in ten is seriously into art. Correction. One in twenty. Some people come in to ask the way to the nearest loo, for pity's sake. Or in the hope of making a killing with some faded print of *The Stag at Bay* that they picked up for a couple of quid in a car boot sale. Soul-destroying. But even that's better than no visitors at all. She can spend hours in here alone. Which is why she reads the Sara Paretskys and the Sue Graftons. The thick-eared action whiles away the time."

Shirley-Ann found herself galloping to the defense of two of her favorite writers. "Thick-eared? That's just what they aren't. They're intelligent. They take on issues."

"Like feminism." He barely concealed a sneer. "Or should I say postfeminism?"

"You can't have read them. They say more about modern society—and more convincingly—than most of the so-called serious novels."

He laughed. "I was winding you up. And I haven't read them. Being an artist, I'm into graphic novels, told in pictures—what you would call comics for adults."

"Thick-eared."

"With a vengeance. But the artwork can be brilliant."

"And do you enjoy winding people up, as you put it?"

"Enormously."

"Women in particular?"

His lips twitched out of the smile that was forming. "You're about to accuse me of sexism, or something worse. Women are just as good as men at piss-taking, you know. No, I treat 'em all alike. A sucker is a sucker is a sucker."

"Is that what you took me for?"

He grinned. "Just testing."

In spite of bridling at almost everything he said, she was beginning to enjoy the exchanges. She wouldn't confide in a man like that except under extreme torture, but she found the argument stimulating. Men of his sort should be put to work like bowling machines in women's assertiveness classes.

The sparring went no further because Jessica burst in carrying a Waitrose bag full of groceries. On seeing Shirley-Ann, she put her hand to her blond hair and pushed it back from her forehead, but there was no need. Even after the hassle of shopping she looked ready to step onto the catwalk in the pale blue suit she was wearing. "Well, this is *so* terrific!" she exclaimed.

"I just dropped in as you suggested," said Shirley-Ann. She had got up too quickly from the chair, teacup in hand, and slopped some in the saucer. She would never be poised like Jessica.

"I'm so pleased you did."

A.J. added without the hint of a smile, "And we just agreed that Mickey Spillane is the greatest crime writer in the world."

"We did not!" protested Shirley-Ann.

"Or was it Peter Cheyney? *Dames Don't Care.*"

Jessica said, "Give it a rest, A.J." Then, to Shirley-Ann, "He's full of crap. Do sit down."

"He's one of the New Men," said A.J. about himself. "He made the lady a superb cup of tea. Pot's still warm. Want one?"

"Warm is no good to me. Make a fresh pot." When they were alone, Jessica said to Shirley-Ann, "Sorry you had to find him in charge. He can be fun in small doses. I'll get rid of him, and then I can show you around in peace. He's extremely rude about all the work except his own."

"He kept me entertained. Does he really know anything about crime fiction?"

"A smattering. Just enough to irritate. You don't want to tell him too much about yourself. He's a dreadful tease, and he'll use anything he can discover."

"That doesn't surprise me at all."

When A.J. returned with the tea, Jessica thanked him for standing in for her and said she'd just seen a traffic warden starting to check the cars in Walcot Street.

"Did you make it up?" asked Shirley-Ann, after A.J. had dashed out.

She smiled. "He lives dangerously. Never buys a parking ticket. He'd do the same to me, only worse, much more bizarre. Probably tell me he saw a circus procession passing through and an elephant leaned against my car. And I'd fall for it, because the one time I disbelieve him you can be damned sure there *will* be a damned great jumbo sitting on my bonnet."

"He's an artist, he told me," Shirley-Ann said, keen to know more without probing too directly.

"Yes, that's how we got to know each other. His work sells quite well. Life studies, rather different from the usual thing. I'll show you presently."

"Of women?"

Jessica shrugged. "What would you expect? Male nudes don't sell unless they're by Michelangelo."

"Is that so?"

"Think about it. Would you like one in your sitting room, however well hung?"

In a more relaxed situation Shirley-Ann would have giggled. She wasn't sure if the image she received was intended, so a smile did for an answer. She let her eyes travel to the far end of the gallery. "It's bigger in here than I imagined."

Jessica showed her around. Her policy, she explained, was to specialize in the work of a select group of artists. By refusing to crowd the walls with everything that was offered, she was putting her judgment to the test. Early on, she had made a decision not to show abstracts, not because she disliked them, but because she found that the sorts of people who called at her gallery wanted something that gave them a way into the artist's vision. None of the work was slavishly representational. Each image from real life was enhanced by exciting and original use of color and design. All this was said with conviction. The people of Bath might be unadventurous in their taste, but Jessica wasn't knocking them.

They were large canvases, many priced in four figures, and

Shirley-Ann thought with amusement of the shock it would give Bert to see her being escorted around this gallery. Her devoted partner had it firmly in his mind that she only ever bought pictures from charity shops, and it was true. The pictures of elephants and dancers in the flat they shared in Russell Street had cost under a pound, every one. She'd had to brighten up the walls with something, and quickly. All they had when they moved in was a collection of framed James Bond book jackets dating from Bert's days as a student at Loughborough College. He was quite fixated on Bond.

Up a white spiral staircase were more paintings, including A.J.'s nudes, which weren't the crude or flashy things she had expected. The figures were painted with subtlety and draftsmanship, posed against strong light sources that cast much of the form into heavy shadow, letting the spectator's eye make sense of the areas exposed to the light.

"He's good," said Jessica. "I have to admit he's bloody good."

"Who are the models?" Shirley-Ann asked, and heard herself saying, too late to hold back, "Have you ever posed for him?" It was a tactless thing to have said, and she felt like slapping herself.

Jessica's large, shrewd eyes widened, but there was no obvious embarrassment. She answered coolly, "No. Why should I? They're professional models, I imagine."

They moved on to a view of a village church that Shirley-Ann was profoundly glad to recognize as one she knew. "Oh, Limpley Stoke! It is, isn't it?"

It was, and the moment passed.

Downstairs, they made fresh tea. The evening paper had been pushed through the door, and the headline was about a million-pound stamp theft in the city. It had pushed the story of the murdered bank manager off the front page.

"I don't approve of theft, but you've got to admire anyone bold enough to put a ladder against a window in broad daylight and climb up and nick the thing," said Jessica after briefly studying the report. "That's what happened, apparently. They're appealing for witnesses, of course, but they think people must have taken him for a window cleaner. The guys with the squeegees are out in force before the shops are open. Scores of them. I have mine done every morning. It's essential. You wouldn't believe the state they're in sometimes."

"The window cleaners?"

Jessica smiled. "The windows, lovey."

"I saw the police looking up at the Postal Museum window this morning," Shirley-Ann said. "I happened to be having coffee outside the French café, with Polly Wycherley, as a matter of fact." For the second time in a few minutes she wished she had guarded her tongue. The way Polly had spoken of Jessica should have made her more careful.

Jessica picked up on the remark at once. "You were with Polly?"

"Just for a coffee, yes."

"You knew her already, then, before the other evening?"

"No." She thought of saying that she met Polly in Shires Yard by chance, but she had never been a convincing liar. "She phoned me this morning when I was in the shower. She must be an early riser. I think she felt as chair of the Bloodhounds that she ought to follow up on the meeting and find out if I was coming again."

"Probably," said Jessica.

"We couldn't have known that a real mystery was unfolding in front of us."

The real mystery had ceased to interest Jessica. "Did she have any advice for the new member?"

"Oh, I think it was just a friendly gesture," said Shirley-Ann, resolved to stonewall.

"Polly is good at giving advice," remarked Jessica, and it didn't sound like a compliment.

"Well, I'm grateful for all the friendship. I feel as if I belong already. I'm certainly going to come again."

"Good—we can do with you," said Jessica more warmly. "It was getting polarized between the whodunit readers and the blood-and-guts lot. There's so much else we could talk about, but we hardly ever do."

"Apart from Umberto Eco."

Jessica smiled. "Apart from him. They're charming people, but they will insist on taking up positions, and it's only because they don't read widely enough. If Rupert were to try a Peter Dickinson for a change, with that fertile imagination thinking up the most amazing plots and settings—"

"Oh, yes!"

"—and still worked out as puzzles, with clues and a proper investigation, he'd be jolted out of the rut he's in. And I'd *love* to get Milo reading American thrillers. I know the way in for him. It's through the Fletch books."

"Gregory McDonald."

"Yes. He'd adore the humor, and he'd appreciate the logic of the plots and he'd soon be into Westlake and McBain and Block and ultimately Ellroy."

"There is a way in through women writers," Shirley-Ann pointed out.

"True." Jessica laughed. "True in theory. But you don't know Milo."

Shirley-Ann raised her eyebrows, and Jessica nodded.

Much more gossip about the Bloodhounds would certainly have emerged, but Shirley-Ann didn't want to appear overcurious. She turned the conversation back to the art and was rewarded with an invitation to a private view on Wednesday of the following week.

"I won't pretend it's anything amazing," Jessica explained. "Rearranging the deckchairs on the *Titanic,* A.J. calls it. The same people tend to come each time, but it does pull in a few dealers, and I sell enough to cover the cost of the buck's fizz and Twiglets. You'll see a couple of faces there you know. And don't, for God's sake, feel under any obligation to buy."

THE SECOND RIDDLE

THE LOCKED ROOM

CHAPTER TEN

WHEN JOHN WIGFULL EMERGED FROM HIS PRESS CON-
ference Diamond was in the main office reading
the poem—if that isn't too grandiose a description
of the four lines of verse that had misled everyone, including
himself.

"Was it grueling, John?" he asked, with a matey grin.

"I didn't expect an easy ride."

"You took my advice, I hope?"

"What was that?" said Wigfull in a hollow, preoccupied
tone. "Look, no offense, Peter, but I don't have time to talk.
There are urgent things to attend to."

"Like a strong coffee? The throat does get dry, answering
those damn fool questions."

Whatever the state of Wigfull's throat, his vocal cords had
no difficulty in projecting his growing impatience. "I'm heading a major inquiry. This is the world's most valuable stamp.
It's far more serious than your shooting in Saltford."

"Not in the eyes of the law, it isn't, and not to the bloke
who was killed. So you're calling for reinforcements, no
doubt?"

"I'll use every man and woman on the regional crime squad
if necessary." There was no doubting Wigfull's commitment.
His jaw jutted like Churchill's uttering the "blood, toil, tears
and sweat" speech.

"And what are your lines of inquiry?"

"For a start, I'm going to have that bloody poem analyzed by forensic."

"What for—to see if it scans?" Before Wigfull reacted to that, Diamond added, "Because if you hope to learn something from the copies that were sent to the media, you'd better think again. I've got one here." He held out the sheet of paper he had been studying, but Wigfull displayed no interest. "There was a time when it was possible to look at a piece of typing and say which typewriter was used, thanks to some tiny flaw in one of the characters. 'Pray examine this small irregularity in the letter *W*. It proves conclusively that the note was typed on Professor Moriarty's Smith-Corona.' Not these days, laddie. Moriarty puts it through a word processor and runs it off on a laser printer that gives a perfect finish, indistinguishable from a million others. Then he photocopies it. Your forensic friends aren't going to help you, John." A favorite theme of Diamond's, and worth repeating each time he got the chance.

Wigfull was not to be downed. "Wrong. With fluorescence under laser illumination they can get good fingerprints off paper these days."

"All the prints except the thief's."

"You can't say that."

"This guy is smart, John. He won't have left any prints. Have you checked the spelling?"

"The spelling?"

"Of the words in the note."

"Let me have another look." Wigfull snatched the scrap of paper from Diamond and stared at the words. "I can't see anything wrong with this."

"Nor I," said Diamond, after a pause. "Like I said, he's smart. We know the bugger can spell."

That "we" rang an alarm bell for Wigfull. He thrust his head forward combatively. "You and I had better get one thing straight, Peter. This one is mine. Just because I listened to you about the press conference it doesn't mean you can muscle in."

"Muscle in?" Diamond blandly echoed. "You know me better than that. I'm far too busy talking to bank clerks."

The grin faded as the week progressed. The bank clerks failed to revive it. Every one of them had a tale to tell of meanness, injustices, and slights inflicted by the former manager. If only the chief clerk, Routledge, hadn't confessed, the liturgy of complaints might have been worth listening to, because the bank was chock-full of potential suspects, and a number of customers with grudges would have come into the reckoning as well. Dispiriting for a keen detective, there was no question that Routledge had fired the fatal shot. Forensic confirmed his statement. By Friday, Diamond was so bored with the business that he told Julie Hargreaves to finish up at Saltford without him. He spent the day in the office attacking the stack of paper that was spilling off his in-tray and across the desk.

Late in the morning he took a phone call from Dorchester. John Croxley was formerly one of the murder squad at Bath, a pushy young inspector with an ego like a hot-air balloon. His naked ambition had grated on the nerves of everyone. He had transferred to Dorset CID in the period Diamond was away, a sideways move that had been greeted with relief in Avon and Somerset.

"Thought I'd give you a call, Mr. Diamond." The voice made a show of sounding casual. "I heard you were back. This isn't a busy moment, I hope?"

"Rushed off my feet—but carry on."

"Are you handling the Penny Black case, then?"

"Not at this minute. I'm on the phone to you, aren't I? Must keep it short, I'm afraid. How are things down there in Dorset? Statistics perking up no end since you arrived, I bet."

"To be perfectly honest, it's not entirely what I expected," Croxley confided. "I hadn't appreciated how much more rural this county is than Avon and Somerset."

"More what?"

"Rural. You know, countrified."

"You mean sheep-shagging?"

There was a pause. "I don't know about that. I'm not getting much work in the field of murder."

Diamond chuckled and said insensitively, "Plenty in the field of turnips, however."

"Not so much turnips as cattle, Mr. Diamond," Croxley said with total seriousness. His sense of humor had never blossomed. "My main job just now is noseprints."

"Is what?"

"Noseprints. It isn't widely known that every bovine noseprint is unique to the individual, like a fingerprint. You coat the animal's nose with printing ink and then press a sheet of paper against it."

"You wouldn't be having me on, John?"

"I wouldn't do that, Mr. Diamond. It's a scheme we've set up with the Dorset County Landowners' Association to combat the rustling of cattle. We've processed seven hundred cows already."

Diamond was containing himself with difficulty. "You get noseprints from cows? Go on, John."

"Well, that's all there is to it. They've recently put me in charge. I don't know why. It isn't as if I was brought up in the country. And I don't see much prospect in it."

"I don't know," said Diamond, tears of amusement sliding down his cheeks. "Things could be worse."

"Do you think so?"

"If it's their noses you deal with, you're out in front, aren't you?"

"I suppose so."

"Good thing you're not taking prints from the other end."

"I hadn't thought of that, Mr. Diamond."

"Think of it when you're feeling low, John. This is new technology, and you're the man who does it. Get your noseprints on the computer. You can set up—what is it they call it?—a database on all the cows in Dorset. You asked about prospects. You've got unlimited prospects, I would think. You could go on doing this for years."

"That's what I'm afraid of," said Croxley bleakly. "I was wondering if—with so much interest in the Penny Black business—you might be mounting a major inquiry, recruiting extra detectives."

"You'd be willing to give up your exciting new job?"

"If there was half a chance."

"No chance at all, I'm afraid. You know how it is with budgets as they are. I'd stick with the cows, if I were you. You could be the world's foremost authority on bovine noseprints."

When he put down the phone, he sat back and rocked with laughter for the first time in a week. He could hardly wait to tell Steph at the end of the day. But something else later that afternoon put it clean out of his mind.

On BBC Radio Bristol after the four o'clock news headlines, the presenter said, "Something different here. I've just been handed a note that my producer believes could link up with that cryptic verse we gave you last Monday morning. Remember? The one the police later said was almost certainly linked to the million-pound stamp theft from the Bath Postal Museum. The Penny Black, right? Well, this looks like another poetic effort from the cryptic cat burglar. It's printed on a sheet of A4 paper with no covering note. Came with the afternoon post, I gather. See what you make of this. Is it a hoax, or could it be a genuine clue? We'll be handing it pronto to the Old Bill, listeners, but you'll be able to say you heard it first on Radio Bristol. Are you ready with pen and paper?

> " 'Whither Victoria and with whom—
> The Grand Old Queen?
> Look for the lady in the locked room
> At seventeen.'

"That's all. We know who or what Victoria is this time, I think, but do we know of any locked rooms? And how does the number seventeen come into it? I'm sure we'll get some calls about this. If you have any brilliant suggestions before the end of the program, we'll be pleased to pass them on. I'll repeat the verse one more time."

The producer had diplomatically phoned the Bath police before the item was broadcast, so a radio was tuned in, and the entire control room heard it, including Diamond, whose sixth sense had told him something was afoot and got him from behind his desk at the critical time. The only notable absentee was John Wigfull, listening privately on a separate radio upstairs.

"This gets more and more like party games," a detective sergeant commented morosely.

"Is it genuine?" someone else asked.

"Who can say? It's got to be taken seriously after the first one."

"Yes, but why would they do this? Mr. Wigfull was expecting a ransom demand, not another riddle."

"Maybe they don't want a ransom. This could be some kind of publicity stunt, couldn't it? When is the university rag week?"

"Too early in the year for that. The students have only just gone back. If it is a stunt, then my money is on some smart-arse member of the glitterati."

"The what?"

"The rich and beautiful. The in-crowd. Hooray Henrys. Leading the Old Bill up the garden path is their idea of fun."

The debate was taken a stage further at a special meeting of senior staff convened by the Assistant Chief Constable. "Since we are bound to treat this development seriously," he said in preamble, "I decided to pool our wits and experience. If the riddle is anything like the first one, it may involve knowledge of Bath, and any one of you may have the piece of information that clarifies everything."

From the expressions around the oval table no one was confident of clarifying anything.

"John, this is your inquiry," the ACC said to Wigfull with a motioning of the upturned palm, "so why don't you give us your immediate thoughts?"

Wigfull cleared his throat. "Well, sir, we can reasonably assume that the Victoria referred to is the cover."

"The what?"

"The missing stamp, sir."

"Why not call a stamp a stamp?"

"Because it's attached to an envelope. There's a datemark. The whole thing is known as a cover. Like the first-day covers they sell in the post office each time a new set of stamps is issued."

"That sort of cover," said the ACC, as if he'd known all along. "Carry on."

Wigfull referred to his notes. "The first two lines:

> " *'Whither Victoria and with whom—*
> *The Grand Old Queen?'*

must surely be a coded way of telling us that he is referring to the cover. I think we should focus our interest on the third and fourth lines:

> " *'Look for the lady in the locked room*
> *At seventeen.'*

"I venture to ask three questions: Which lady? Which locked room? And which seventeen? The lady may, of course, be another reference to Victoria, the cover, but we should not exclude other possibilities. Does it link up with the last line, giving us a lady of seventeen? Do we know of any seventeen-year-old ladies in the present or the past who may be connected with the case in some way?"

Nobody spoke.

"The locked room may help to fix it," Wigfull went on. "If there was a local memory or story of some young woman kept locked up, for example. A prisoner. A mental patient. A nun, even. These are my immediate thoughts."

"Any response?" asked the ACC of the blank faces around the table.

Tom Ray said, "I was thinking along different lines, sir. The seventeen could be part of an address."

"That's rather good," the ACC commented, seeming to imply that not one of Wigfull's theories was even half good.

"Isaac Pitman, the inventor of shorthand, lived at number seventeen, the Royal Crescent. There's a plaque outside."

"What's he got to do with this?" Peter Diamond asked. "Did he have a seventeen-year-old sex slave?"

"I rather doubt it," said the ACC frigidly. "I happen to know a little about Pitman. He was a man of the highest principles. Like me he was a teetotaller, a vegetarian, and a nonsmoker."

There was an uneasy pause. Not even Diamond was going to press the matter of Isaac Pitman's sex life, or the ACC's.

"It was a long shot," admitted Ray.

Another theory was advanced by Keith Halliwell. "Is it possible that the seventeen refers to a time, like five P.M., or seventeen hundred hours?"

"If it does, we've missed it by ten minutes," said Diamond, glancing at the clock on the wall. "Personally I don't think this joker has given us enough to catch him. He wouldn't, would he? It's like that book *The Thirty-Nine Steps*. It's no good looking for the blessed steps. You know you're there when you find them. I mean, we could rabbit on all evening about seventeen this and that. Seventeen-horsepower cars; seventeen trees in a row; the seventeenth day of the month; or fifteen rugby players and two reserves. It gets you nowhere without more information."

"So your advice would be . . ."

"Ignore it. Continue with the other lines of inquiry."

"What lines?" murmured Ray.

Wigfull said, "We've been extremely thorough."

"With what result?"

"Investigations can't be rushed."

"I don't know," said Ray. "Peter Diamond nicks a bloke for murder two minutes after getting to the scene."

The ACC drew a deep breath, and said, "Gentlemen, let's confine this to discussion of the stamp theft. To ignore this new development would, I think, be negligent. Peter may be right in saying that the thief won't give much away, but if we can make any sense of the riddle, it may link up with other evidence."

"Was this character seen at all on Monday morning?" Diamond asked. "Did anybody spot the ladder against the window?"

"Unfortunately, no," Wigfull answered. "But we have six or seven descriptions of window cleaners near the scene reported as suspicious."

"Have you ever seen a window cleaner who *doesn't* look suspicious? What about forensic? Are they any help?"

"The thief seems to have used gloves. We've got an impressive list of fibers and hairs found in the room, but with so many people going through the museum by day, they could come from many sources. The display cabinet was forced with a rusty claw hammer. That's about it."

"And about the museum staff?"

"They're volunteers. Local stamp enthusiasts. They take turns to man the museum, at least two at a time. We've interviewed them all except two, who are away. Nobody seems to remember anyone casing the place in advance of the crime—but as several of them reasonably pointed out, how could you tell?"

Diamond let the meeting run its course without any more input from him. It was Bumblebee territory, and he didn't intend to get involved. They broke up shortly after six. "Have a good weekend, gentlemen," he said as he went out.

"Aren't you coming in?" Ray asked.

"No need. My murder is put to bed."

"So how will you spend the time?"

"House-training a new cat, if my wife can be believed."

CHAPTER ELEVEN

S HIRLEY-ANN WAS BETTER PREPARED WHEN SHE TURNED UP AT
St. Michael's for the next meeting of the Bloodhounds on
Monday evening. Rummaging one afternoon through a
carton of books in the Dorothy House shop she had pulled out
The Blessington Method, a dog-eared and rare Penguin of some
of Stanley Ellin's short stories. Having missed her turn the week
before, she was sure to be asked to speak about a book she could
recommend, and Ellin seemed an ideal, uncontroversial choice.
He was one of the American writers she admired most, particularly for his short fiction. She could hardly wait to discover how
many of the group were familiar with his work. If any of them
objected to short stories she would pluck up courage to remind
them that Poe, Conan Doyle and Chesterton had laid the foun-
dations of modern crime fiction with their short stories.

It must have been a lucky day, because she had also found
a thick-knit purple jumper as good as new in Dorothy House
for only a pound and she was wearing that tonight with a
black corduroy skirt from War on Want.

The evening was distinctly colder than the previous Monday, but dry. Down in the crypt the warmth from the central
heating wafted pleasantly over her face the moment she entered. Miss Chilmark, who seemed to make a point of getting
there early, said the place was like a furnace, and she was
going to speak to the caretaker. She marched past Shirley-Ann

with a determined look, but it turned out that she was only on her way to the cloakroom. If there was a complaint about the heating, it wouldn't get Shirley-Ann's support. Being so skinny—Bert called her slinky, which she rather liked—she could never get enough heat.

Jessica too was there already, snappily dressed in a charcoal-gray woollen dress. A wine-red scarf was draped with casual elegance across her shoulders and clipped with a huge silver buckle like a kilt fastening. "Glad you've come," she said, and seemed to mean it. "You're going to make such a difference."

Polly Wycherley waved a small, plump hand from across the room. She had already taken her place inside the circle and was removing things from her briefcase, determined to make amends for her lateness the previous week. "Who are we missing?"

"Only Milo," said Jessica.

"Rupert." Someone else spoke up. Chameleonlike, Sid in his fawn raincoat was standing against a stone wall. He had an uncanny ability to merge with the surroundings. "Rupert is always late."

An entire, unsolicited sentence from Sid. Perhaps he felt more comfortable with no other males present.

The door of the ladies' room opened, and Miss Chilmark came out reeking of some musky perfume. She was no longer complaining about the central heating. "I intend to make a stand on that dog tonight," she announced.

"Bareback riding?" murmured Jessica.

Miss Chilmark hadn't heard. "If it misbehaves, I shall tell Rupert I want it removed, and I expect the rest of you to support me."

A click from Jessica's tongue showed that she, for one, would not be included. "It only shook itself. Poor thing, it was wet. It's not as if it crapped on the carpet."

"You don't have to be vulgar. I was drenched. We had to interrupt the meeting. Don't you remember?"

"Well, it isn't raining tonight, Miss Chilmark."

"That's no guarantee of anything."

As if she hadn't heard a word about Rupert's dog, Polly remarked, "Milo isn't usually late."

"Hardly ever," said Miss Chilmark, scarcely aware that she had been diverted. She took her place opposite Polly. "Milo and I attach a lot of importance to good timekeeping. We are always the first to arrive."

"Perhaps he's ill," said Polly, fumbling in her case. "Once before when he was ill and couldn't come, he phoned me the evening before. I've got his number in my diary. I can phone him."

"Good idea," said Miss Chilmark. "I'll take over in the chair until you get back. Let's get under way before the dog arrives and ruins it."

"For heaven's sake," said Jessica. "It's ridiculous to phone the poor man. It's only five past seven."

After everyone was seated, there was a short debate about whether Polly would be justified in making the phone call. The consensus was that Milo was a grown-up and didn't have to be accounted for. Jessica gave Shirley-Ann a grateful look that said sanity had won the day, and shortly after, Milo came in, full of apologies. A lorry had broken down on Brassknocker Hill, and the traffic had been held up.

"Have we started, then?" said Miss Chilmark in a tone implying that she would have run the meeting more efficiently.

"I suppose we have," said Polly.

"Because I have a suggestion," Miss Chilmark went on. "I don't know who else has been following the reports of this stolen stamp."

"The Penny Black?" said Shirley-Ann. "Just across the street from here. Isn't it exciting?"

"That isn't the word I would choose," said Miss Chilmark, "particularly as it shows our city in such a bad light, but, yes, that is what I had in mind. I thought for a change it would be an interesting exercise to address ourselves to a real crime."

"We're readers, not detectives," Polly pointed out, quick to suspect that this might be a takeover. "We discuss fiction, not real crime."

"We talk about real crime most of the time, if you ask me," asserted Miss Chilmark. "Rupert is forever haranguing us about what happens on the streets. Well, now that something has happened on the streets that tests the intellect a little, let's see if our experience as readers is any help in solving it."

Jessica said cynically, "You mean set William of Baskerville onto the case?"

"Who's he?" Polly asked vaguely.

"The detective figure in *The Name of the Rose.*"

"Oh, yes." Polly looked annoyed with herself for having to be reminded.

Miss Chilmark said stiffly, "Mock me if you wish, but his methods stand the test of time."

Shirley-Ann wondered if this was the moment to mention—after the put-down she had got the previous week from Miss Chilmark—that she had checked the date of publication of *Il Nome della Rose,* and it was 1981, a full four years after the first of the Brother Cadfael series. But it didn't seem the right time for settling scores. She saved it up.

"Personally, I think you've made a marvelous suggestion," said Milo, galloping to the support of Miss Chilmark. Theirs was a strange alliance, the elderly gay and the starchy spinster. Apparently, all that they had in common was that they usually arrived before anyone else. "I'm fascinated to know if we can throw any light on the stamp theft. How about the rest of you?"

No one objected, not even Polly anymore, so Shirley-Ann, who was quite fired up, said, "It was extremely clever, if what the papers say is right, dressing up as a window cleaner and climbing through an upstairs window."

Jessica remarked, "Extremely obvious, I'd have said. What intrigues me is why he did it."

"Or she," put in Shirley-Ann, scoring on the rebound.

"Or she. It's the world's most valuable stamp. They're not going to sell it."

"People steal famous paintings all the time," Miss Chilmark pointed out. "They must have a reason."

"Well, there's the theory that a fanatical collector wants to own them. He doesn't do it to make a profit, just to gloat over what he possesses."

"Do such people exist?" asked Shirley-Ann. "Outside books, I mean."

"I'm sure they do. There are too many works of art that have just vanished over the years. And stamp collecting is a lonely occupation anyway. I don't have any difficulty picturing some middle-aged man with a personality defect poring over his collection."

"Or woman," Sid managed to say, and when everyone had got over the surprise there were smiles.

"Actually, very few women go in for collecting," said Jessica. "This acquisitive impulse is a masculine thing."

"Shoes?" Shirley-Ann reminded everyone.

"Hats, too," said Polly. "I have a cupboard simply stuffed with hats."

"I meant useless things like stamps and beermats."

"I don't think the person who stole it is a collector. I think they're going to demand a ransom," speculated Shirley-Ann. "That's what I'd do. Anyone who owns a stamp like that has oodles of money to spare. I'd ask for fifty thousand."

"How would you collect it?" Milo asked, stroking his beard as if the prospect really beckoned. "That's always the problem."

"Oh, I wouldn't handle the money at all. I'd let the owner know that it had to be transferred through his bank to a secret Swiss account."

"Do you have a secret Swiss account?" Polly asked Shirley-Ann in all seriousness.

"No, but with fifty grand as a deposit, I bet any bank would be only too happy to open one for me. I could afford to fly to Zurich and fill in the forms, or whatever."

"It can't be so simple," said Jessica.

"Can you think of anything better?"

Miss Chilmark interrupted the exchange. "Madam Chairman, this is getting us nowhere. When I suggested this as a topic, I had in mind the much more fascinating problem of the riddles—if that is the word—that were on the radio and in the papers, apparently composed by the person who stole the stamp. Couldn't we address ourselves to those?"

"By all means," said Polly, chastened. "Do you remember how they went?"

"I have them here." Miss Chilmark opened her crocodile-skin handbag and took out two press cuttings.

"There's not much point in discussing the first one," said Jessica. "That's been solved by events. What was it . . . 'J.M.W.T. . . .'

> " 'Surrounded by security.
> Victoria, you challenge me.
> I shall shortly come to thee,' "

Miss Chilmark read aloud.

"It's all been explained by the police," said Jessica. "They were tipped off that someone was planning to steal a Turner from the Victoria Gallery, so they doubled the security. But it was a bluff, and the real target was the stamp. Let's look at the latest riddle. That's much more of a challenge. Have you got it there?"

Miss Chilmark obliged:

> " 'Whither Victoria and with whom—
> The Grand Old Queen?
> Look for the lady in the locked room
> At seventeen.' "

"Is it by the person who wrote the first riddle?" said Milo. "That's the first thing to ask."

"It sounds similar to me," said Shirley-Ann.

"The styles do have a certain textual affinity," Miss Chilmark said with a donnish air. "There's a touch of the archaic in the word 'thee' in the first riddle that has an echo in the 'whither' in the second."

"Oh, come on. It's only some birdbrained idea of what poetry should sound like," said Jessica. "Straight out of *The Golden Treasury*."

"Nevertheless," insisted Miss Chilmark.

"You're probably right," Jessica was compelled to admit.

Miss Chilmark was keen to show that she had done her homework. "And of course there are allusions to other phrases. 'The Grand Old Queen' is reminiscent of the epithet by which the Prime Minister W. E. Gladstone was known, the Grand Old Man, often abbreviated to the G.O.M."

"Or the Grand Old Duke of York," said Polly seriously. She wasn't given to humorous remarks.

Miss Chilmark chose to ignore that. "Then 'Look for the lady' carries the idea of that card trick 'Find the Lady,' just as 'in the locked room' suggests another piece of trickery, the locked room mystery—that Milo happened to mention only last week. The undertone of hocus-pocus is inescapable."

"So what do you think it means?" asked Shirley-Ann.

If there was an answer, it wasn't communicated, because this was the moment when the door opened and the dog Marlowe padded in, headed straight for the circle of chairs, leaped onto the one beside Miss Chilmark and demonstrated affection for that horrified lady by lifting a large paw to her chest. In backing away, she tipped the chair backward. Rupert, who had come in behind his boisterous pet, was quick to react. He darted forward and caught the back of the chair before it hit the floor. An unseemly accident was averted. Nothing worse had resulted than a display of rather more of Miss Chilmark's legs than she or her companions desired. She was wearing pop-socks. As if to apologize for startling her, Marlowe jumped down and licked her lily-white left knee.

This was unfortunate. The dog had been much on Miss Chilmark's mind all week, there was no doubt of that. "Get it away from me!" she cried out hysterically. "It's going to bite me."

Clearly Rupert hadn't trained Marlowe to respond to voice commands, so he grabbed him by the scruff and hauled him to the other side of the circle. Marlowe gave a growl of protest. "He's frustrated now. He was only showing you affection," Rupert told Miss Chilmark.

Jessica suddenly said, "Does anyone have a paper bag?"

"What for?" said Polly.

"She's hyperventilating."

"Oh, what next?"

Miss Chilmark was taking deep, rapid breaths and going ominously pink. Her eyes had a glazed look.

Sid reached under his chair for a plastic carrier bag. He rummaged inside and took out a brown paper bag containing something that proved to be a secondhand novel by John Dickson Carr. After removing the book he handed the empty bag to Jessica, who placed the open end over Miss Chilmark's mouth and nose.

"She'll suffocate," said Polly.

"No," said Jessica calmly. "It forces her to rebreathe her own air. It should bring the acid-alkali balance of the blood back to normal and relieve the symptoms. Take the dog out of her sight, Rupert. You know it upsets her."

The usually ungovernable Rupert responded to the unmistakable note of authority and led Marlowe to the door without a murmur on his part or a whimper on Marlowe's.

The others watched in fascination as the bag expanded and contracted against Miss Chilmark's face, making her appear uncannily like a tropical frog. After a short time the remedy produced an improvement in the breathing. Jessica spoke some calming words, mainly to reassure Miss Chilmark that the dog was no longer in the room. The bag was removed from her face. Polly offered to drive her home.

Miss Chilmark said in a small voice, "I'd like to stay if you're quite sure the dog isn't coming back. I'm not entirely clear what happened."

It was decided that Miss Chilmark would benefit from a cup of coffee, so the break was taken early.

Shirley-Ann told Jessica she was awfully clever knowing how to deal with the hyperventilation.

"Not at all. I had an aunt who was prone to it. She always had a spare paper bag with her."

"Do you think Miss Chilmark is well enough to stay?"

Jessica smiled. "She wouldn't dream of leaving. She's won her point, hasn't she? The dog has been outlawed. Now she wants to enjoy her triumph."

This interpretation struck Shirley-Ann first of all as callous, later as discerning.

Presently Rupert returned, looking forlorn. "I left Marlowe with some old chums in the Saracen's Head," he informed everyone, and added pointedly, "He'll fit in anywhere if he's allowed to."

They resumed the meeting, and when Shirley-Ann offered to speak about Stanley Ellin's short stories she was warmly received. The group were better informed about Ellin than Shirley-Ann expected. Rupert and Jessica had each read the famous and gruesome story *The Specialty of the House,* and Polly, never to be underestimated, said she had copies of *The Eighth Circle* and *Stronghold* on her shelves at home. Fortunately no one had read *The Blessington Method*.

"What is the Blessington Method?" Jessica asked.

"That's what someone in the story asks. I'd better not say."

"Is it a long story? Why don't you read it to us? There's time, I'm sure. We've often had things read out, but never a whole story."

Fortunately Shirley-Ann rather enjoyed reading aloud. At school she'd won the Miss Cranwell Prize for Bible Reading two years in a row. So the Bloodhounds learned the sinister secret of the Blessington Method as practiced by the Society for Gerontology.

"You read it beautifully, but it's not to my taste at all," said Polly when Shirley-Ann had finished. "I found it chilling."

Jessica said, "His stories are chilling. That's the whole point."

"I know, dear. I *have* read some of his novels. This one struck home rather more forcibly. I'm not so far from being an elderly relative myself."

"It's not only about elderly people," said Jessica. "The principle behind it could be applied to any other potential misfits—the mentally ill, the unemployed, sexual deviants, racial minorities."

Rupert fairly sizzled with approval. "Have I discovered an ally at last? You're absolutely right, of course. Crime writers have a duty to bring the complacent middle classes face to face with the festering sores in our society."

"I didn't say that."

He gave one of his gummy laughs. "I said it for you, ducky."

Jessica was incensed. She pointed a finger at him. "Ducky, I am not—you patronizing old fart. And I don't need you as a mouthpiece. I'll say what I want myself."

Rupert turned to Milo and said, "Hark at her."

Someone needed quickly to defuse the tension. Milo glanced across at Polly. "Is it time, I wonder, for my contribution on the locked room mystery? I brought my copy of *The Hollow Man*."

"What a splendid suggestion," said Polly.

"And then we'll all sing 'Jesus Wants Me for a Sunbeam,' " said Rupert.

"What on earth makes you say that?" asked Polly.

"Darling, you've missed the point. If you're going to run this like a Sunday school, we might as well sing hymns."

"Don't you patronize me either," said Polly, taking her cue from Jessica.

"I wouldn't dare, ma'am, after what you did to my dog. I couldn't bear to be banished to the Saracen's Head for the rest of the evening."

Polly conceded a smile. "Milo, why don't you begin? We've heard more than enough from Rupert."

Milo took a deep breath that threatened a lengthy dissertation. Some of the smiles around the circle froze. He began: "A crime is committed in a sealed, locked room. Nobody except the victim is found there when the door is unlocked. A mystery par excellence. None applied more energy and brainpower to it than John Dickson Carr."

Shirley-Ann noticed that Sid nodded in support, and she recalled that he was one of the three people present who had claimed to have read *The Hollow Man*. Remarkably, his eyes were fixed on Milo, and his hands were rotating the flat cap on his knees. She had not seen him so animated before.

Milo was saying, "Some of you have criticized the classic detective novel for being unrealistic. At our last meeting I heard the word *preposterous*."

"From me. I'll repeat it this week if you like," said Jessica.

"No need. Improbability, John Dickson Carr boldly tells us in *The Hollow Man*, is not to be despised. It isn't a fatal flaw. On the contrary, it is the chief glory of the detective story— and that is as true of the books you people espouse as of those I prefer to read. We are drawn irresistibly to the improbable. Does anyone deny it? Rupert's mean streets and Jessica's lady sleuths are never more engaging than when some crime is committed in bizarre, unaccountable circumstances. And the supreme situation, the purest challenge to probability any writer has devised is the locked room puzzle."

Rupert couldn't resist saying, "Absolute piffle."

Milo glared at him. "You're going to tell us that no locked room murder ever really happened, no doubt. You'd be wrong. Before *The Hollow Man* was published, a Chinese laundryman was found murdered in New York in a locked room, and there have been other cases since. But I won't be sidetracked. My words may not impress you, but I fancy that Dickson Carr's might."

He brandished his copy of *The Hollow Man* like an evangelist preacher and Shirley-Ann secretly thought back to Rupert's remark about the Sunday school.

"Chapter seventeen is entitled 'The Locked-Room Lecture.' Ideally, fellow Bloodhounds, I should have liked to read it in the kind of setting Dickson Carr describes, after dinner, around the glow of a table lamp, with the wine bottles empty and coffee on the table and snowflakes drifting past the windows. But I suppose a church crypt is not a bad alternative."

With his audience well primed for the treat in store, Milo opened the book and glanced first at the Contents page. He turned to the right chapter. Then he blinked, frowned, and said, "How odd. I don't remember using this as a bookmark." He picked an envelope from between the pages and glanced at it.

He went silent. The envelope was yellow with age, the address in fine copperplate so faded that it was barely legible. In the top right corner was a single postage stamp with the head of Queen Victoria on a black background and the words ONE PENNY along the lower border. The stamp was overprinted with a cancellation mark saying PAID. Just below and to the right was the postmark, remarkably even and clear:

BATH
MY 2
1840

CHAPTER TWELVE

"IT'S IMPOSSIBLE," SAID MILO, BLUSHING DEEPLY. HE STARED at the flimsy envelope lying across the open book. "Impossible."

Miss Chilmark, seated on his left, had her hand pressed to her mouth. She swayed away from Milo as if he were contagious. A second bout of hyperventilation could not be ruled out.

On Milo's other side, Jessica took a long look and then raised her eyebrows across the circle at the others seated opposite.

"What is it?" Polly asked. "What have you got there, Milo?"

Rupert, having leaned across Jessica to see for himself, said, "Hey ho. What a turnup!"

"Somebody tell me," said Polly, becoming petulant.

"It would appear to be the missing Penny Black," said Rupert. "Milo, my old fruit, I salute you. I wouldn't have dreamed that you of all people would turn out to be the most wanted man in Bath."

"But I didn't steal it," Milo blurted out. "I'm no thief."

"You're among friends." Rupert went on as if he hadn't heard. "If we're honest, most of us have a sneaking admiration for you. This was brilliantly worked out. You don't need to say any more. Just shut the book, and we'll all behave as if nothing happened."

Milo's hands were shaking. He fumbled with the book and practically knocked the envelope to the floor.

"Careful!" said Jessica. "It's worth a fortune."

"I didn't take it," Milo insisted. "I don't know anything about this."

"You can be frank with us," said Jessica. "Rupert's right. We'll stand by you if you promise to give it back and say no more about it. We can keep a secret. That's a fair offer, isn't it?" She appealed to the rest of the circle.

"But I've done nothing wrong," Milo shrilled. "This is the first time I've ever laid eyes on the thing. Really."

"How did it get into your book?" asked Shirley-Ann.

"I haven't the faintest idea."

"None of *us* could have slipped it between the pages," said Polly, and then undermined the statement by adding, "Could we?"

"It's been here on my lap all the time," said Milo. "I'm not accusing any of you, but someone planted it on me, and I'd like to know how."

"What about when Marlowe came in and upset Miss Chilmark?" Shirley-Ann suggested. "In the confusion—"

"No," Milo interrupted her. "I kept hold of the book. I didn't leave my chair. It must have been done before I got here, but I can't fathom how. Someone must have broken into my boat. Oh dear, this is so distressing."

Shirley-Ann recalled being told that Milo lived on a narrowboat on the canal. "Have you had any visitors lately? Anyone you left alone for a few minutes?"

"Not for weeks."

"Do you lock the boat when you're not there?"

"Of course. I have a damned great padlock. I carry the key on my key ring." He produced it from his pocket. "This one. You see? I bought it from Foxton's. You get a guarantee that no other lock with a similar key has been sold from the same shop—and they're the only people who sell them in the west of England." He sighed heavily. "What am I going to do?"

"Go to the police," said Polly.

"They're going to give me a bad time, aren't they? They're not going to believe this."

Nobody said so, but Milo's reading of events was probably right. His camp manner wasn't likely to help him at the police station.

Shirley-Ann said, "Couldn't you just send it back to the Postal Museum in an envelope?"

"That's what Rupert and I said in effect," said Jessica. "The trouble is, there are six of us who know about this. He's going to have to rely on us all keeping the secret. Who's to say that any one of us won't let the cat out of the bag in some unguarded moment? Then he'd be in far worse trouble."

Polly said, "I don't really agree that we should stay silent. I think Milo ought to go to the police directly."

"So do I," chimed in Miss Chilmark. "Let the truth come out, whatever it is. What do the rest of you think? What about you?" she said to Shirley-Ann.

"I think the decision is up to Milo. I don't mind staying quiet if he doesn't want to get involved."

"And you?" demanded Miss Chilmark, swinging around to face Sid.

Sid's shoulders were hunched as usual. He said, without looking up from the floor, "I can stay quiet."

"No one will argue with that," said Rupert. "Milo, my old cobber, the house is divided. Four of us are willing to turn a blind eye, and two want to hand you over to the rozzers."

"That isn't right," Polly protested. "Milo tells us he knows nothing about this, and I'm willing to believe him. He has nothing to fear from the police. The sooner he reports this and gives them the chance to catch the real thief, the better."

"My sentiments exactly," said Miss Chilmark.

Milo gave a nod. "You're right, of course. I'd better hand this in as soon as possible."

"Do you want anyone to go with you?" Polly asked. "We can all back up your story. We're solidly behind you, Milo."

Milo thanked her and said he thought he would rather go alone. He placed the precious envelope tightly between the pages prior to closing the book. "The amazing thing is that it was here, like a bookmark, at the very chapter I was going to read out."

"The one about the locked room lecture?" said Jessica.

"Yes."

"Did you have a bookmark here?"

"No need. I knew it was chapter seventeen."

"But you'd opened the book to look at it?"

"Sometime during the week, yes. I suppose when the thief opened it, the pages fell open at the chapter I'd been studying. But why me? Why do a thing like this to me, of all people?"

There was no response from anyone. If any of the Bloodhounds knew the answer, or had a private theory, this wasn't the moment to air it. Polly suggested closing the meeting early—it was still only 8:45—and there was no dissent. Milo put on his overcoat and fur hat and was the first to leave.

CHAPTER THIRTEEN

SHIRLEY-ANN COULD HARDLY WAIT TO TELL BERT, HER partner, about the dramatic moment when the Penny Black was found. She gave him the update as soon as she got back to their flat in Russell Street. Bert was a difficult man to impress, a modern embodiment of the stony indifference displayed by the English archers at the Battle of Agincourt. Admirable, but frustrating when you were the French army at the charge, so to speak, with lances raised and banners unfurled. He listened in silence, hardly raising an eyebrow until Shirley-Ann had finished. Then came the comment: "I suppose we'll have the police around here asking questions next."

Bert had this unerring ability to raise alarming images in Shirley-Ann's brain. She pictured two burly officers in uniform sitting in the living room. She, straight from the kitchen, caught wearing that vulgar PVC apron with its lifesize image of an overdeveloped female torso in basque and suspenders. No good saying her regular apron was in the wash and this one belonged to Bert, a silly prize won in the rugby club raffle. She visualized the policemen eyeing suspiciously her shelves of books stacked with crime fiction and perhaps even finding on the bottom shelf among the atlases and art books the Stanley Gibbons Junior Stamp Album she had kept since childhood. "Interested in philately, are we?"

Shirley-Ann's brain was in such turmoil that she wouldn't be ready to sleep until much later. She didn't expect to hear much more from Bert until he'd finished his supper. He always ate a big meal with a glass of red wine at the end of the day, and tonight it was a full-size Marks and Spencer steak and kidney pie, heated in the microwave. He survived all day at the Sports and Leisure Center on dried fruit, pulses, and apple juice. It seemed to suit his metabolism. He had the physique of an athlete, so hunky, Shirley-Ann sometimes told him, that he could have doubled for Arnie Schwarzenegger, which was a slight exaggeration. He jogged in the mornings, and of course his work kept him in shape and burned up plenty of calories.

She wanted Bert's advice. He had a very clear-sighted view of things. She waited until he had cleared his plate and was finishing with a banana.

"Bert."

"Mm?"

"Do you really think the police will want to talk to me?"

"It's obvious. You're a witness. You could be a suspect as well."

"Oh, be serious. I didn't have anything to do with it."

"They don't know that. If—what's his name, the gay bloke?"

"Milo."

"If Milo can't explain how he got hold of the stamp, questions are going to be asked, aren't they?"

She nervously fingered a strand of her hair. "I suppose you're right."

"Don't know why you got mixed up with this lot."

"That's down to you."

He frowned. "Me?"

"Because you're always at the Sports Center in the evenings. You can't expect me to stay here on my own. It was in that 'What's On in Bath' pamphlet you brought home. I found it under Clubs and Societies, remember?"

"So how are you going to handle it?" Bert asked, positive

and forward-looking. Attractive qualities in a man, but not always easy to match.

"You mean if they come asking questions?"

"There's no 'if' about it."

"I'll tell the truth, I suppose. Mind you, I don't want to get Milo into more trouble than he's in already."

"You can't turn your back. You might as well go to the police and tell them what happened—before they come to you." Bert's urge to get things done was why a career in sport was so ideal for him. He called it "sports management," but Shirley-Ann suspected it had more to do with demonstrating step-ups than sitting behind a desk.

"I don't want to do that," said Shirley-Ann. "I don't want to shop Milo. I don't even know for sure if he went to the police after the meeting ended. He said he was going, but you never know."

"Shop him?" Bert repeated. "You're talking like a criminal yourself."

"Give over, Bert. I'm not going to the police, and that's final."

Bert softened a little. He relented to the extent of offering her a segment of orange. He put on his worldly-wise look, the sort of expression he wore when showing some novice how to hold a table tennis bat. "You've got to admit that they sound an odd bunch. This Rupert—he's the character with the dog, right?"

She nodded. "*Character* is the word for Rupert. He dresses like a stage Frenchman. Well, a rather gone-to-seed stage Frenchman. Black beret, striped jersey, and jeans. And he has this terribly, terribly well-bred English accent. Have I told you this already?"

"Some of it," Bert said.

"Listening to him, you'd think you were safe as houses, but he seems to cause havoc wherever he goes. He got the Bloodhounds banned from the Francis Hotel."

"Why?"

"I don't know the details. He can be pretty outspoken, and it's a very carrying voice. I'm not sure if he knows the effect it has."

"Better keep your distance, then. What about the women in the group? Are they more reliable?"

"There's Polly Wycherley. She's our chairman. A little white-haired lady with a fixed smile like you get across the jam and marmalade stall at the Women's Institute sale. She set up the group, and she holds it together. I think it's very important to her self-esteem to keep it going."

"Reliable?"

"I'd say yes like a shot except that Jessica—she's the one who runs the art gallery—seems not to trust her entirely."

"Any idea why?"

"There's some friction between those two. Polly was quite miffed because I stayed for a drink with Jessica in the Moon and Sixpence last week. And Jessica wasn't too pleased when I mentioned having coffee at Le Parisien with Polly. So there's a slight question mark. But I like them both in their different ways. Jessica is bright and liberated. Fun to be with."

"There's another woman in the group, isn't there?"

Shirley-Ann smiled. "Miss Chilmark wouldn't care to be described as a woman. A lady, if you please. 'There have been Chilmarks in the West Country for over seven hundred years.' She can't abide Rupert. Or Polly. Or any of us, except possibly Milo. She'd like to be chairman."

"So what's your opinion?" Bert asked. "Do you think Milo pinched the stamp?"

"I'd be amazed if he did. He's an intelligent man, or so I thought."

"But this wasn't a stupid crime," Bert pointed out. "The whole thing was set up as a kind of challenge, remember. There was that rhyme about Victoria that was on the radio and in the papers."

She nodded. "It was a jolly clever bluff. Everyone was fooled by it, including the police."

"So you reckon there's a good brain behind this?"

She nodded. "The way it was set up was really artful. Brilliant, in fact. That rhyme fooled everyone. The stupid bit was tonight—if Milo is the thief—revealing it to everybody."

"Unless he's still several moves ahead of the rest of you."

Her eyes widened. Bert was second to none at spotting devious goings-on. There was a lot of jockeying for position in sports management.

"So what's he up to, do you suppose?" She leaned across the table with the point of her chin resting on her upturned thumb. Her lips were slightly open. She half hoped Bert would say "Who cares about Milo?" and lean closer.

Instead he asked, "Does he know anything about stamps?"

Her chin came to rest less seductively in her cupped hand. "I've no idea. No one has mentioned it. He seems more hooked on Sherlock Holmes than anything else."

Bert rotated his finger thoughtfully around the rim of the empty wine glass. "Do you think he fancies himself as Holmes?"

Shirley-Ann giggled a little. "I suppose he might. He does wear a deerstalker. But I don't see why it should make him want to steal the Penny Black. Holmes didn't commit crimes; he solved them."

He expanded on his theory. "If he wanted to show off a bit, demonstrate his skill at solving a crime, he could pretend to find the stamp by Holmes's methods."

"But he didn't, did he? It turned up in the pages of a book."

"A stupid mistake. It proves he isn't in the same league as Holmes," said Bert. "He must have tucked it in there for safety and forgotten that he was using the same book to read from."

She pondered for a moment. "That sounds quite possible. What was he aiming to do with the stamp?"

"He'd have pretended to find it somewhere nobody else

would think of, and he'd have got his fifteen minutes of fame as the modern Sherlock who outwitted the police. The whole episode wouldn't have done anybody any harm provided that the stamp turned up again in perfect condition."

"That's rather neat. I do hope you're right," she said. "I don't like to think of Milo as a thief."

"I didn't say he wasn't one," said Bert in a change of tone. "They don't all wear flat caps and carry bags with SWAG written on them."

"Haha."

"He could have demanded a ransom for it. Fifty grand, or he burns it."

"He's a retired civil servant, for heaven's sake."

"Maybe he's been waiting all his life to do something really exciting."

"Silly!"

Bert said huffily, "If you don't think much of my opinions, why ask me?"

Now she'd offended him. He was so touchy about anything remotely suggesting he was stupid, which he patently was not. She supposed he had to endure a lot of thoughtless remarks at work from users of the Leisure Center who thought he was just a musclebound bloke in a tracksuit.

They cleared the table and watched television for an hour, but Shirley-Ann couldn't have told you what the program was.

CHAPTER FOURTEEN

PETER DIAMOND WAS STILL UP AFTER MIDNIGHT WATCHING television, picking holes in the plot of an old film, *To Catch a Thief*. Stephanie had quit after the first commercial break. "Far be it from me to drag you away from Grace Kelly," she told him. "See it to the end. I'm tired."

She was amused to see that the new kitten stayed on the arm of his chair, ready to pounce on his hand if he moved. It still had no name. Peter had this weird theory that the kitten would let them know what it wanted to be called. She was content to let the little tabby do its own job of winning approval. On the first evening, after the predictable flare-up when he'd spotted the cat-tray, her bruiser of a husband, the tyrant of Manvers Street, had stayed up most of the night with the kitten in case it cried. Big softie.

Then the phone rang.

She was still sitting up in bed reading when he came into the bedroom to hand over the kitten. "I'm going to have to go out, love. That was Wigfull."

Her eyes widened. "He isn't your boss, is he? What does he want at this time of night?"

"He's found a body."

"Personally?"

"So he says. Murder is my pigeon, not his."

"Where is it?"

"On a canal boat."

"In Bath?"

"Limpley Stoke. That boatyard near the Aqueduct. I've got to go."

"It's wickedly cold tonight. There's a frost."

"I'll take it carefully down Brassknocker," he promised.

"I wasn't thinking of your driving. I meant I'm going to freeze in this bed without you."

He smiled. "You'll have warmed up nicely by the time I get in."

"Thanks—I'll really look forward to that. You'll be as cold as Finnegan's feet on the day they buried him."

By daylight Brassknocker Hill offers a series of glorious, gasp-inducing views of the Limpley Stoke Valley. By night the descent from Claverton Down is even more dramatic, for you plunge into a vast, black void with just a scattering of lights. He would have driven cautiously anyway, without the frost warning. At the bottom he turned right at the Viaduct pub, joined the A36 and immediately left it by the traffic lights.

The entrance to the Dundas boatyard is an unprepossessing pull-in over uneven ground a few yards along the Bradford Road. The gate was open, and a few frost-coated cars were parked inside. He bumped over a couple of potholes and stopped beside an empty police car. Nobody was about. There was some kind of notice at the far end of the parking area. He groped in his glove compartment for a torch. The notice informed him: YOUR CAR IS AT RISK FROM THIEVES.

There was only one way to go: up a slope toward some temporary-looking buildings that turned out to be the boatyard offices. They stood beside a stretch of the old Somerset Coal Canal that was used for mooring. His torch picked out a small iron bridge and beyond it a row of narrowboats and other small craft.

Along the towpath he discovered that the moorings extended much farther than he had first appreciated, using both sides of the canal. Fifty or sixty boats must have been tied up there. He flicked the torch over some names painted in the florid lettering that is the canal boat style: *Henrietta, Occam's Razor, Charleen.* They were moored for the winter, he guessed, locked up, curtains drawn, with everything portable removed from the decks. If cars were at risk from thieves, then so were boats.

Presently voices carried to him. A torchbeam speared the darkness and dazzled him. He stepped out toward John Wigfull, two uniformed officers, and a bearded man in a deerstalker hat. They were beside a red narrowboat called the *Mrs. Hudson.* As if to proclaim that it was also a houseboat, some twenty conifers in pots stood along the roof, and there was a television aerial. The interior was lit, but nothing could be seen; the venetian blinds were closed at all the windows.

"This is Mr. Motion," Wigfull said, with a nod at the bearded man. "He owns the boat."

"Nice boat," said Diamond to Motion. "And you say there's a corpse inside?"

Wigfull said, "We found it together."

"*You* found it?" Diamond could have added that Wigfull was supposed to be fully stretched investigating a stamp theft, but there was no need. The point was made in the way he stressed the word *You.*

"Peter, can we take this from the beginning? We've got to wait for the SOCOs, so you might as well hear what happened. Mr. Motion walked into Manvers Street this evening and informed us that the missing Penny Black had come into his possession."

"So you've found it." Diamond took a longer look at Motion in his deerstalker, but without shining a torch into his face it was difficult to assess the man in these conditions. "A body *and* the stamp?"

Wigfull continued, "It turned up in a book. He doesn't know how it got there. He happened to be reading from this book at a meeting. There's a club called the Bloodhounds that meets on Mondays—"

"Hold on a minute. The what?"

"Bloodhounds."

"We're a group of local people with a mutual interest in crime fiction," Motion explained in a tone that expressed some irritation with Wigfull. Clearly they'd been over this a number of times already.

Wigfull said, "They bring their books to the meeting and read bits. When Mr. Motion opened his, the cover was inside—and when I say cover, I'm using the stamp collectors' term. I mean the envelope with the Penny Black. It was between the pages at precisely the section Mr. Motion had chosen to read from. Have I summarized the facts correctly, Mr. Motion?"

"Yes," said Motion wearily.

"He opened the book and made the discovery in the presence of six other witnesses. When he realized what it was, he came directly to the station and reported it. That was at five to nine this evening. I was called in and interviewed him from nine thirty onward."

"For almost three hours," said Motion.

"This wasn't a missing budgerigar you brought in, sir," said Wigfull, displaying some impatience of his own. "It's the world's most valuable stamp." He switched back to Diamond. "Mr. Motion insists that the book never left his hands from the time he started out for his meeting."

"Literally?" said Diamond.

Motion gave a nod.

"I see that you're wearing an overcoat, sir. Did you wear it for the meeting?"

"Obviously not," said Motion.

"You removed it, then, and still held on to the book? Not impossible, but not easy."

"You're splitting hairs, aren't you? I put it on a chair for a moment, but it didn't leave my possession."

"So we shouldn't take everything you say as the literal truth. Carry on, John."

Wigfull said, "We've been over this several times."

"You mean you covered the question of the overcoat."

"I established that nobody at the club had an opportunity to place the cover inside the book," Wigfull said, sidestepping the overcoat question. "It was likely that it was in the book before he started out—in which case, the perpetrator must have boarded this boat, got inside and found the book, and planted the cover between the pages. Mr. Motion insists that the boat is always locked. He uses a padlock with a key that is unique."

"Unique? Most padlocks are sold with two keys," said Diamond. Wigfull's complacent manner was bringing out the pedant in him.

"There were two originally," Motion explained. "One fell into the canal at least a year ago. I only have the one."

"Couldn't someone buy a padlock with a similar key?"

"No. Not in England. It's German-made. A strong lock, and expensive. From that locksmith in George Street. Well, you can see for yourself."

Diamond shone his torch on the steel padlock, now unlocked and hooked over an iron staple fixed to the top of the door. When the door was closed, the staple would slot into a hinged metal strap attached to the sliding hatch at the back end of the roof. It looked a secure arrangement. He wouldn't touch anything until the Scene of Crime Officers arrived. Certainly the padlock was heavy-duty. "Do you attach this at all times?" he asked Motion.

"Except when I'm aboard. Then I can close everything and bolt it from inside."

"And do you?"

"Do I what?"

"Always take the trouble to bolt yourself in?"

"Of course I do. I want my home to feel as secure as you no doubt wish yours to be." Motion didn't jib at crossing swords with Diamond. He had the confidence of someone well practiced with words.

Wigfull took up the narrative again. "Naturally, after questioning Mr. Motion about the stamp I decided to accompany him here and see if his story held up. When we got here, the boat was padlocked, just as he claimed. But when he opened it, we found the body inside, lying on the floor of the lounge."

"Before your very eyes."

"What?"

"Just like magic."

Wigfull said huffily, "I didn't find it particularly enchanting."

"But you can't think how it was done."

"Can you? Mr. Motion swears that nobody was aboard when he left for his meeting."

"What about the door at the front end?" asked Diamond.

"Prow," said Wigfull.

"Bolted from the inside," said Motion.

"The windows?" Diamond shone his torch along the side of the boat. There were five in view. "Fair enough," he said, for it was obvious that no one could have climbed through the narrow vents at the top. "No other means of access? Hatches?"

"There's a hatch to the engine, but that wouldn't let you into the cabin."

"You've got some explaining to do, sir."

"*I* have?" said Motion. "I'm more mystified than you are."

"The funny thing is," said Wigfull, "the place in the book where the missing stamp was found is the start of a chapter with the title 'The Locked-Room Lecture.'"

"Is that funny?" said Diamond.

"You can't deny it's a strange coincidence. What we've got here is a locked room puzzle. How did the body get into the boat when it was locked?"

"Right now, I'm more interested in the body. Do we know who it is?"

"He's face down."

"So it's male?"

"I examined him briefly to see if he was still alive. There was blood beside his head. He'd gone. No pulse. I don't know if you can see anything between the blinds." Wigfull crouched at the nearest window, but the slats on the venetian blinds were tightly closed.

"Do you have any idea who this man might be, sir?" Diamond asked Motion.

"None. I wasn't allowed to go in. I unlocked and reached for the light switch and saw the figure lying on the floor ahead of me and said 'Oh my God!' or something similar, and then this gentleman took over. That's all I can tell you."

The drone of car engines entering the boatyard stopped the conversation. Two bobbing sets of headlights came down from the road and advanced along the towpath: the Scenes of Crime team in the Land Rovers. In no time they were climbing into white overalls and stretching barrier tapes across the towpath, regardless that no one was likely to come along at this hour.

"If you'd open the blinds, we can take a look at the scene without disturbing you," Diamond suggested, but it was getting on for twenty minutes before this request was acted upon. The SOCOs had their procedures and stuck to them.

Eventually the senior man informed Diamond, "Victim is a male, white, aged about forty-five. Light brown raincoat over a blue sports jacket, black trousers, white shirt and black tie. There's a cap beside him, brown. The only injury I can see is the head wound."

"And the weapon?"

"Couldn't tell you. Nothing obvious in there."

Diamond turned to Milo Motion. "Know anyone of that description?"

"No."

"You live alone here?"

"Haven't I made that clear?"

"Not to me." He hesitated. "I'm bound to ask this, sir. Do you have a companion?"

"Absolutely not." Spoken with umbrage.

"They've lifted the blinds now. Would you look at this man and tell me if you recognize him?"

"He's face down."

"From his clothes and general appearance. We can't move him until the doctor has looked at him."

Motion bent closer to one of the windows. "He looks a little like . . . But that's impossible."

"Like who, sir?"

"Like a man called Sid. But he's one of the Bloodhounds. He does have a raincoat like that. No, it couldn't possibly be Sid. He was at the meeting with me until it ended. Besides, what would Sid be doing on my boat?"

CHAPTER FIFTEEN

NEXT MORNING IN THE BRIEFING ROOM AT MANVERS Street, Diamond assembled the Murder Squad. It didn't matter that half of them were officially seconded to Operation Bumblebee; Wigfull's people were ordered to attend. Murder took precedence over everything. Even so, the stamp's recovery had given the Bumblebees some encouragement.

Diamond soon put a stopper on that. "You lot may be feeling chipper this morning, but I got sod-all sleep last night. If there's anything to be pleased about, I'd like to know what."

A young inspector recently transferred from Radstock rashly told him what.

"That's the good news, is it?" said Diamond.

"Well, it sounds like good news to me, sir."

"Good news, my arse. You don't know who nicked it yet. Can't take any credit. It was handed in. Jack the lad made us look like the plods we are. What kind of good news is that?"

"It's bad news, sir," the inspector said in a sharp about-turn.

"Wrong again, squire. That isn't the bad news. The bad news is that somebody was killed last night. And there seems to be a link between the murder and the theft." He addressed the entire room. "The victim was a man of forty-six called Sid Towers, a night watchman. Towers was last seen alive in the center of Bath at eight forty-five last night. The body was discovered by Mr. Wigfull, here, and the man who handed in the stamp, name of Milo Motion. Got that? Milo Motion. Time: about one A.M. this morning. Location: on a narrowboat moored at the Dundas boatyard, across the road from the Viaduct pub. Victim was cracked over the head with some heavy object like a spanner. It hasn't been found yet. The divers are already at the scene in case it was thrown into the water, but I doubt it. This killer is smart—and that is an understatement. Milo Motion, who lives aboard the boat, locked up at a quarter to seven to attend a meeting in Bath, and when he got back with John Wigfull at his side the padlock was still in place."

"With the victim inside the cabin," Wigfull himself put in.

"I'd better tell you about the Bloodhounds. Wipe the smile off your face, Keith. These are crucial facts I'm giving you. Milo Motion belongs to a club—a literary society, he calls it—known as the Bloodhounds. They meet in the crypt of St. Michael's—that big church by the Podium—every Monday to discuss detective stories."

He broke off the narrative to point at someone making a sly aside to his neighbor. "Will you shut up and listen to this? Sid Towers, the murdered man, was a member of this Bloodhound club and was present at the meeting. And a strange thing happened. Milo Motion, the owner of the boat, had agreed to read a chapter from a book he'd brought with him. A book of his own, right? This chapter was on the subject of locked room mysteries, which I gather have a devoted following among people who read whodunits. He opened the book at the place he wanted and—what do you know?—there was the missing Penny Black lying between the pages like a bookmark. Everyone was shocked, not least Mr. Motion. The meeting ended early, and Motion came straight to us and spent the rest of the evening being put through the grinder.

"All told, it wasn't Milo Motion's day, getting lumbered with a stolen stamp and a murdered corpse. He insists that his boat was locked all evening, and he was the only person in possession of a key. Yet when he unlocked, the body was found there. So do we charge Motion with murder? Do we, heck! He has a better alibi than the Pope. I told you Towers was alive at eight forty-five. At five to nine, Motion was meeting the desk sergeant downstairs. He couldn't have traveled to the boatyard and back in ten minutes. And the rest of the time he was with John Wigfull. What we have, my friends, is a locked boat mystery."

One of Wigfull's team said, "He could have hired someone."

"Motion could?"

"Couldn't he?"

"To do a killing on his own boat?" said Diamond on a shrill note of disbelief.

"You said we're dealing with someone smart, or better than smart. Maybe this is the ultimate in bluffing."

"I don't see it, but I'm willing to listen if there's more to this theory."

There was not. Julie Hargreaves filled the silence that followed by saying, "Shall we discuss the stamp theft first?" She had worked with Diamond often enough not to be cowed by his black moods.

John Wigfull said, "Actually, I was about to propose the same thing."

"Do you want to take over?" Diamond offered. He spoke mildly, and it might have been sincerely meant. It was impossible to tell.

Wigfull didn't answer.

"This is your baby," Diamond pointed out.

Wigfull was practically squirming in his chair. The stamp theft *was* his baby, only there was no way he could dandle it on his knee with any pride.

Julie cut the tension by saying, "Sir, can we establish first that Milo Motion is a fall guy and not a thief? Whoever did the Postal Museum job—which was cleverly carried out, remember—he took some risks courting publicity with those verses—whoever did it was unlikely to hand the stamp in meekly, as this man Motion did. It would be a surrender, and a pathetic one at that."

"Go on."

"Is that a fair point?" said Julie, unwilling to be hustled. "I'd like to know if anyone disagrees."

Diamond looked to his left. "John?"

"It sounds reasonable to me," Wigfull was forced to commit himself. "After several hours with Motion, I can't see him as a master thief. He's bright, certainly. A loner. Eccentric, shall we say?"

"If you mean homosexual," murmured Diamond, "why don't you say so?"

"Because I don't know," Wigfull snapped back. "I didn't ask. His sexual preferences don't come into it. If you're asking me to make a guess, I'd say he probably is gay, but that's a superficial impression."

"Say it, John," said Halliwell. "The man's a jam duff."

"What does that make you?" said Diamond. "A paperweight?"

Wigfull was striving to make a serious point. "I don't think Motion has the bottle to carry out a theft, let alone bluff his way out of it."

"Are you sure there isn't a partner?" Diamond pressed him.

"He doesn't live with anyone, if that's what you mean. I just said he's a loner. To come back to your question, Julie, yes, he's been set up, in my opinion. We're looking for someone else."

Julie said, "Then we ought to look at motives. Why steal the stamp if you intend to give it back? The other day we were expecting a ransom demand. It didn't come."

Keith Halliwell said, "The stamp was just a pawn in a far more serious game."

"You're linking it to the murder?" said Julie.

"Of course. You sacrifice a pawn to achieve a better position."

"What better position?" asked Diamond.

"It ensured that Motion would go to the police and be questioned for some hours. His boat was unoccupied. Time enough for the killer to murder Towers and get away."

"Except that we don't know how he got into a locked boat or what brought Towers there."

"The locked room mystery," said one of Wigfull's team. "Isn't it remarkable that the Bloodhounds meet to discuss locked room mysteries and now we have one of our own?"

"Two," said Diamond, and now he began to function more constructively. "There's the mystery of the stamp and the mystery of the murder. It may be that Keith is right, and the stamp theft was a tactical move in a more serious game. We'd better keep an open mind. Since the stamp came up first, let's confine ourselves to that for a moment. Milo Motion can't explain how the Penny Black got between the pages of his book, which incidentally was *The Hollow Man,* by John Dickson Carr—if that means anything at all to a crowd of bozos who never read anything except the *Sun.* He kept it on a shelf on his boat with his other books. He had no visitors during the past week. On the evening of the meeting, he removed the book from the shelf and took it to the Bloodhounds. It didn't leave his possession at all. He's very clear about that. So what are we left with? The stamp was already between the pages when he took *The Hollow Man* from the bookshelf. John and I have seen the boat. It isn't very long. About sixty-five feet. Motion says he bolts it from the inside whenever he's aboard and padlocks it from the outside when he isn't. If the thief planted the stamp, he found a way to beat the locks and bolts. The cabin area of that boat is a perfect locked room. No hatches. No way in by the windows, which just have a narrow vent at the top. There's a door at either end. One end is bolted from the inside. Chubb security bolts at top and bottom. We've seen them. The other is locked from outside with this strong, close-shackle padlock, and there's only one key—on a ring in Motion's pocket."

Keith Halliwell suggested, "Could the thief have unscrewed the fittings on the door?"

"The padbar and staple, you mean?" said Diamond. "Nice try. We looked at it ourselves. The screws are rusty, so any recent interference would show. There isn't a scratch."

"The hinges?" someone else put in.

"They aren't accessible from outside—and they haven't been tampered with."

Halliwell said, "Someone must have a duplicate key, whatever Mr. Motion says."

"We've checked with the locksmith. It isn't possible. It's a feature of these locks, which are German-made, that each one is unique. There *were* two keys, but he dropped his spare one in the canal over a year ago. I simply don't believe that some passing bandit could have fished it out and known which padlock it fitted."

Halliwell was a stubborn cuss. "If he put his keys down somewhere, someone could have done the old Plasticine trick and got an impression."

"If," said Diamond. "But he insists that they are always in the pocket of the trousers he is wearing."

"There's the flaw. Can we believe him?"

"I'd say yes."

"There's got to be some explanation."

"You might be interested in what Dickson Carr had to say on the subject." Diamond felt into his jacket pocket and with a flourish produced a paperback of *The Hollow Man*. "Chapter seventeen is 'The Locked-Room Lecture,' the one Milo Motion planned to read to the Bloodhounds. The author states among other things that the explanation of a locked room problem is invariably disappointing."

"'So simple when it is explained,'" murmured Wigfull.

"What?"

"A quote from a Sherlock Holmes story."

"This is John Dickson Carr," Diamond said brusquely. "I was going on to say that in this lecture he classifies most of the methods used in locked room mysteries. I won't bore you with them all. He dismisses secret panels, secret passages, and so on as trick stuff, beneath contempt. He's pretty scathing about murders that are committed without the murderer actually entering the room, by gases, mechanical devices, and so on. And about suicide, when the gun disappears up the chimney on the end of a piece of elastic."

The gun on elastic earned some chuckles.

"As a variation it can be whisked out of a window. Then there are bullets made of ice that melt without a trace. There are poisonous snakes, impersonations, disguises, tricks with time. But the section of most interest to us is the one on ways of tampering with door locks. As Dickson Carr sums it up, there are three categories. First, the murderer can use bits of string and metal to turn a key which is still in a lock, but on the wrong side of the door. This doesn't apply to our problem. Secondly, he can remove the door hinges, as someone suggested, but in our case it didn't happen. Thirdly, he tampers with the bolt, using string or metal. One of our sets of doors, you'll recollect, was bolted from inside. However, the bolts aren't the primitive things Dickson Carr was describing in 1935. They're finger-bolts, set into the wood, invisible from the outside, and I defy anyone to open them with string, plastic, or anything else. If the killer isn't Milo Motion—and it can't be, for reasons I've stated—then he or she must have found a way of unfastening the padlock."

"Which is impossible," said Wigfull. "This is a sophisticated padlock with only one key, which remained in Mr. Motion's possession throughout the time I was questioning him."

"Are you certain it was locked when you arrived at the boat with Mr. Motion?" Julie Hargreaves asked.

Wigfull nodded. "I watched him closely. I had my torchbeam pointed at the lock. I saw him take the key from his pocket and use it. There was a click as he turned the key, and the shackle of the padlock sprang open. I haven't the slightest doubt that I saw the padlock being unlocked."

"Do we have a time for the murder?" Fred Baker, one of Diamond's more senior detectives, asked.

"You know what pathologists are like about times of death," said Diamond. "All he would say—if I can call the phrase to mind—was that the external symptoms were not in-consistent with a time of death up to four hours prior to when he examined the body. We know the poor sod was alive four hours before."

"And what was the cause?"

"Give me a break, Fred. We haven't had the postmortem yet. It was pretty obvious that he'd received a heavy blow on the head, but if I tell you he died of brain damage you can be damned sure the postmortem will show he choked on a fish-bone."

After a short pause, Keith Halliwell asked, "What do we know about the victim? Was there any bad blood between him and Motion?"

"Apparently not. Motion claims they were on cordial terms. He says Towers was an introvert, excessively shy. Hardly ever joined in the discussions at the Bloodhounds. Wouldn't even look you in the eye unless he was forced to. He worked as a night watchman in a furniture warehouse. Monday was his night off."

"Any family?"

"No. He lived alone in a top-floor flat in Oak Street, off the Lower Bristol Road, under the railway viaduct."

"Did he drive?"

"Good point. How did he get to the boatyard? He owned an old Skoda. And before anyone asks, yes, it was one of the cars parked near the entrance. We can safely assume that Sid Towers drove there after the Bloodhounds' meeting broke up. On the passenger seat we found a plastic bag containing a sec-ondhand copy of—you guessed—a John Dickson Carr novel."

"The Hollow Man?"

"No. *The Three Coffins*. I haven't read it yet."

"You'll be lucky to get the time, sir," Baker was bold enough to comment.

"I will, if you lot get your fingers out. The first thing is to find out about what happened last night at the Bloodhounds. Apart from Motion and the victim, there were five others in attendance: four women and one man. I'll give you the names presently. I want them interviewed this morning before the news of the murder breaks. If you're assigned to one of them, play it cautiously. You're on the case of the Penny Black as far as they're concerned. They know they witnessed something bloody unusual. They'll be expecting you, so get them to talk about the moment when Motion opened his book and found the stamp. Try and get a picture of what else happened at the meeting—whether anything was said by the victim or anyone else that could have provoked violence later. See if Sid Towers confided in anyone before he drove to the boatyard. I'm damned sure this murder has its origin in the Bloodhounds, so I want to know what drives these people, their hang-ups, their ambitions, the tensions between them, what they eat for breakfast, and what keeps them awake at night." He turned to Wigfull. "John, have I left anything out?"

Wigfull cleared his throat. "I don't want anyone forgetting that we're also investigating the stamp theft," he said huffily. "This is more than just a pretext for getting the facts about the murder. It's a serious crime that may or may not be connected with what happened to Towers. Be alert. Insist that you get a full account of the events leading up to the discovery of the Penny Black cover, and what happened after."

"Got that? The Penny Black is Mr. Wigfull's baby, and the murder is mine. And if one of you messes up, you answer to me," said Diamond. "Now Inspector Hargreaves will read out the teams."

He was content to let others carry out the interviews. An act of mercy to the witnesses, given the mood he was in. Instead, he decided to walk the short distance across Churchill Bridge and up the Lower Bristol Road as far as Oak Street to look at Sid Towers's flat. He asked Julie to come with him. On the way he thanked her for her contribution to the briefing. "I was too heavy, even by my standards," he admitted. "You got the thing back to what it should be. I don't know what came over me. Lack of sleep, I suppose."

"You're not at your best conducting meetings," she was bold enough to tell him.

"Was I an ogre, Julie?"

"Can I be frank?"

"You generally are."

"You were appalling."

"That bad?"

"The way you jumped on that new man. He was only trying to answer one of your questions. He didn't know that the form is to stay quiet until you've had your say."

"He will in future, won't he?"

"And I know there's a history between you and John Wigfull, but you didn't have to hammer him in front of his team. They know what he's like without you pointing it out."

"I'm not running the Women's Institute."

"A pity. They'd sort you out in no time."

He laughed. "You're probably right, Julie. My wife was a Brown Owl, and she keeps me in order."

She said, "Since I've gone out on a limb already, I might as well say it. You'd get more input from the team if you weren't so domineering. They don't like to speak out."

"Are they scared of me?" he asked, genuinely surprised.

"I don't think you have any idea how stroppy you sound."

He stared over the bridge along the gray ribbon of water. "If you want the truth, Julie, none of them is as scared as I am. Remember, I've been off for a couple of years. I don't know everybody anymore. I call a meeting, and it's a minefield. I can give instructions. I can interview a suspect. Put me in front of a crowd of faces wanting to see how I function as top dog, and I won't say I panic, but my insides don't like it."

"Well, it didn't show this morning."

The traffic halted conversation as they stepped toward the mills and warehouses, long since converted into the engineering and construction businesses that line this stretch of the Lower Bristol Road. Diamond knew the area from the days when he lived on Wellsway. On a fine day, or when his car was giving trouble, he would come this way into the city, down the steps from Wells Road and under the railway viaduct, passing the arches where the winos and derelicts spent the night. It amused him to think that some of these same arches once housed a police station. There was also once a mortuary for the storage of corpses dragged from the Avon.

Most of the Lower Bristol Road was an eyesore that some city planner would want to flatten before long, but there was still a dignity to the mills with their wooden hoist-covers projecting above the street, just clear of the container lorries that rumbled past. This was Bath's oldest surviving industrial landscape, and it was pleasing that the buildings were in use, even if the quays behind them no longer functioned.

To their right was the Bayer Building, a tall red-brick structure more ornate than the others, with arched windows and Bath stone trimmings. Seeing an opportunity to strike a lighter mood, Diamond said, "Bet you can't tell me what this was built for."

Julie gave it a look. "Something to do with engineering?"

"In a sense, yes."

"Plumbing?"

"Stays."

"I beg your pardon?"

"Corsets. Charles Bayer was the corset king. Our great-grandmothers had a lot to thank him for."

"Questionable," said Julie. "Some of them suffered agonies."

"Ah, but he also invented a little item that no woman should be without."

"What's that?"

"The safety pin."

Directly opposite the Bayer Building was the street where Sid Towers had lived until so recently. Presumably it had once housed the corsetworkers. Directly below the viaduct—it actually ran under one of the arches—and so close to the main artery to Bristol, Oak Street was not a place many would have chosen to reside in, except from necessity.

The houses were on one side only; a scrap merchant had the other side, with his business concentrated in the arches. The sound of metal-cutting shrilled above the noise of juggernauts from the end of the street. Several houses appeared to be empty. One or two presented a trim front, but the majority had surrendered. They were two-story terraced dwellings in local stone stained black at the top by coal dust. Remarkably, considering how small they were, several had been converted into flats.

They had to go under the arch to find Sid's flat, past some children throwing sticks for a dog that looked as if it should have been muzzled.

"This is the number I was given," Diamond said. There was nothing so helpful as a set of marked bell pushes.

"You did bring the key?" Julie queried.

He produced it from his pocket and opened the front door. "He lived upstairs, I gather."

The house they had let themselves into smelled of cat, and the probable offender bolted out of sight behind some rolls of lino at the far end of the hall. The stairs were bare and speckled with pink paint. But when they opened the door at the top, Towers's home turned out to be a barrack room ready for inspection. A narrow passage carpeted in red had four doors leading off. The first, the bedroom, was in immaculate order, the clothes put away, the duvet squared at each corner. The furniture may have been cheap and functional, but everything was dusted.

"The sort of place that depresses me the minute I enter it," grumbled Diamond. "No photographs, no pictures on the wall. Where's the evidence of the man who lived here? It could be a bloody hotel." He opened a wardrobe door and looked at the jackets hanging there and the shirts folded and stacked as if in a shop.

Julie said, "Almost as if he knew he was about to die."

"Not even a copy of yesterday's paper by the bed."

"If he buys one, you can bet it was tidied away before he left the house," said Julie.

"I get a sense of a stunted life when I see a place like this."

"An organized life doesn't have to be stunted," Julie commented. "He put things away, that's all."

"No use to us."

They looked into the kitchen across the passage and still found nothing out of place. The contents of the fridge were meager, but neatly positioned. There was a microwave oven and an electric hob, each spotless.

"Is this obsessive, would you say?" Diamond asked.

The living room was slightly more promising. It had one wall lined to the ceiling with white bookshelves, the books mostly without wrappers, though some had transparent covers and evidently came from libraries. There was a small television set and an armchair facing it. A Victorian writing desk interested Diamond. He opened the front and was gratified to find various things stacked in the pigeonholes: a checkbook, some payslips, electricity invoices, an address book, a writing pad and envelopes, and some second-class postage stamps.

"He liked his John Dickson Carr," said Julie, standing in front of the books. "He's got at least forty here. The other writer he collected has a similar name in a way—Carter Dickson. I wonder if there's a connection."

"Does it matter?" said Diamond, leafing through the address book. It was full of blank pages. The man seemed to have no friends or family worth listing.

Julie removed a Carter Dickson from the shelf. "*The Reader Is Warned*. Good title." She opened it. "Written in 1939—before the war. So were the Dickson Carrs, weren't they? When was *The Hollow Man* published?"

"Years ago. In the thirties."

"Are these books valuable, do you think? Was he a collector?"

"What are you thinking—that some valuable first edition provided the motive? Hey, that's an idea."

Julie picked a couple more books at random and opened them. "One of these says 'Withdrawn from stock. Warminster Public Library.' The other was bought for seventy-five pence. I don't think a serious collector would give them shelf room. He bought these to read."

"At least we know something about the man," said Diamond.

"I was right," said Julie, having opened another book. "Listen to this from the introduction: 'Carr was so prolific that he kept a second publisher provided with a steady supply of crime novels under the pseudonym of Carter Dickson.' "

Diamond's thoughts had moved on. "It could be army training that makes a man so tidy. Or his schooling. Or prison. I wonder if he had any form. We'll run a check."

"He wouldn't have been taken on as a night watchman if he had a prison record."

"He wouldn't tell them, would he?"

"Don't they make inquiries?"

"Yes, but it wasn't MI5 he was joining. He was only guarding office furniture."

"Who did he work for?" Julie asked.

Diamond picked up the sheaf of payslips. "Our old friends Impregnable."

CHAPTER SIXTEEN

LEFT TO FINISH HER BREAKFAST ALONE, SHIRLEY-ANN TOOK a slice from the toaster and covered it thickly in peanut butter—a secret indulgence. She didn't start work until ten, and finished at four. Civilized hours in theory, but the conditions weren't always so comfortable as the hours, for she was employed handing leaflets to tourists in front of the Abbey. On a warm day in summer, it was pleasant enough. Part of the job was to reinforce the message in the leaflets by pointing out the benefits of a bus tour. She didn't mind talking to strangers. Most of them were easy to approach, regardless of whether they wanted the tour. But on wet days the work was canceled—and that meant no pay, because she was on hourly rates. The most frustrating days were the indifferent, showery ones that are all too common in the English climate. She never knew when Mrs. Battle, the supervisor, would materialize and tell her to go home. Soon it would be over for another season anyway. At end of the month she would go back to stacking the shelves in Sainsbury's—if there were still vacancies.

Bert often told her that she ought to look for a full-time job. Her stock answer was that she was waiting for him to open the private health club he was forever promising to start in Bath. Then she would wear a white suit and be the receptionist. Bert really did have this dream of going into partnership with one of the top hotels and equipping it with the latest gym facilities, a swimming pool, steam rooms, saunas, and sunbeds. The only problem was finance. Up to now, the bank hadn't been willing to float a loan.

This morning she left the flat slightly earlier than usual, and she was glad she did, because as she turned out of Russell Street a police car drove up. That they were coming to call on her was confirmed later, when she met Polly Wycherley. The astute Polly, who must have known where to find her, came up to her in the Abbey churchyard and asked if she could take a few minutes off work. From the tense way Polly spoke, it was a request that couldn't be turned down. They cut through Church Street to the Bath Bun, the tea shop in Lilliput Court, near Abbey Green.

The shop had a cosy, tucked-away feel, situated as it was in a sunken court off one of the less busy streets. Shirley-Ann often escaped there. The framed mirrors on the pink walls and the brown-and-fawn zigzag design on the carpet weren't to her taste, but not much natural light penetrated there, so something had to be done to brighten the interior.

No other customers were inside at this time, which meant that the corner table was available, the only one with padded chairs. On the wall to Shirley-Ann's left was a greenish print of the Rokeby Venus, the one showing the rear view of the naked goddess admiring herself in a mirror. Bert had once joked that they were the best buns in the shop. It wasn't the kind of humor likely to appeal to Polly. This morning her little mouth was pinched into something like a stitched wound.

"Have you heard about Sid?"

Shirley-Ann had not. She was deeply shocked when she was told. The news had been on local radio at eleven.

"It's worse," said Polly. "He was found on Milo's narrowboat."

"*Milo's?*"

"Last night, after our meeting."

"Oh, no, Polly!"

"But Milo couldn't possibly have anything to do with it," Polly pointed out. "He was at the police station telling them about the missing stamp." She felt in her handbag for a tissue and blew her nose. Her hands were trembling.

"Sid murdered?" whispered Shirley-Ann. "I can't take it in. He was such an . . . inoffensive bloke. Who would want to harm him?"

"I'm as puzzled as you are," said Polly. "And the police aren't giving anything away. Have you had them call on you?"

"No." Shirley-Ann didn't like to say at this stage that she'd seen them stop outside her flat.

Polly said, "They came to me soon after nine. They must have known, but they didn't let on. He was killed last night, you see. I thought it was just about the Penny Black, but obviously it wasn't." Her face, usually pink, was blotchy this morning.

"You don't mind if I ask?" said Shirley-Ann. "What did they want to know?"

"The police? Everything I could tell them about the meeting and the Bloodhounds. Even when I spoke of Sid they didn't give me a hint that he was dead." Polly fumbled with a button of her coat. "It was underhanded not to tell me. I said things I wouldn't have mentioned if I'd known he was dead, poor lamb."

"What things?"

"Oh—that he's so quiet you forget he's there a lot of the time. And worse. I think I said he was dead wood. It makes me feel mean-minded."

"I'm sure no one could accuse you of that," Shirley-Ann tried to console her.

"Why me? Why didn't they go to someone else?"

"I suppose because you're the chair." Shirley-Ann drew back, and the conversation ceased while their order was taken. Once the girl had returned to the kitchen, she said, "What was he doing on Milo's boat? Are they friends?"

Polly frowned slightly. "Not as far as I know."

"He must have had some reason for going there. How did he know which boat it is?"

"That's no mystery. We had our Christmas party on the boat. Sid was there. It's called the *Mrs. Hudson*. I remember telling you." Polly's pale eyes studied Shirley-Ann.

"So you did." She held Polly's steady gaze.

Polly eventually said, "Sid knew Milo wouldn't be aboard the boat. We all knew he was going directly to the police station, and they were sure to keep him there for ages asking questions."

Shirley-Ann asked, "Do you think Sid was up to something?"

"It certainly looks like it, going out to the boatyard at that time of the evening. And the whole point is that he wasn't alone. The person who attacked him was aboard the boat as well."

Shirley-Ann felt goose pimples rising on her skin. "The only people who knew Milo was going to the police were ourselves. That means one of the Bloodhounds must have murdered Sid."

Polly folded her arms. Her lips twitched as if she couldn't bring herself to say any more.

CHAPTER SEVENTEEN

BY MIDDAY THE INCIDENT ROOM FOR THE NARROWBOAT murder—as it was already known at Manvers Street— was receiving information faster than the two civilian computer operators could process it. Reports had been coming in since eleven from the detectives sent to interview members of the Bloodhounds; the Scenes of Crime team had sent in their preliminary findings; and a time had been fixed for the autopsy. "Pity," said Diamond when the message was handed to him. "Any time but tomorrow morning would have been fine for me. I may not be able to attend. How would you like to stand in for me, Julie? One of us ought to be there."

This may have sounded like a request, but it was an order, and Julie Hargreaves knew her boss's Byzantine reasoning well enough not to question it. The head of the murder squad didn't care to admit that he fainted at the sight of a dissecting knife, even though almost everyone guessed this was so. Over the years, he had resorted to all kinds of stratagems to miss postmortems.

Moving inexorably on, he asked her, "Did you run that check on Sid Towers? Any previous?"

"A clean sheet, if that really is his name."

"Pity. What was he doing in someone else's boat, then? What was he up to?"

Julie had no theory to offer. Instead, she said, "I had a word with his employers. The big white chief at Impregnable says Sid was one of their most reliable men."

"Night watchman, wasn't he?"

"They don't call it that these days."

He rolled his eyes upward. "Tell me then. What's the jargon? What should I have said? 'Small hours surveillance specialist'?"

She laughed. "Anyway, he was guarding office furniture."

"And as we know, desperate men will stop at nothing to nick a filing cabinet."

Julie went on staunchly supplying the facts. "He's been with Impregnable for four years. He liked working alone, which suited them, because most security guards prefer to work in teams, particularly at night."

"A loner."

"Chronically so, according to the personnel director, only it didn't interfere with his work. He was conscientious, a good timekeeper, very observant."

"We could have used him here." He digested the information for a moment. "Impregnable are a big organization, aren't they? All kinds of security work. I've seen their vans around the city."

"They do a certain amount with the banks and building societies," said Julie. "Sid had worked on the vans. They also install security systems."

Seeing John Wigfull approaching, Diamond cut the conversation. "Something new, John? Am I mistaken, or are the whiskers twitching?"

"I was thinking—" Wigfull began.

"Wish I had the time. What about?"

"That riddle. The second one. I believe I've worked out what part of it means."

"Which part is that? Wait a minute, John." He flapped his hand in the direction of some of his officers in noisy conversation. "Zip it up for a mo, will you? Chief Inspector Wigfull is trying to make himself heard."

"Well, it's the last two lines," said Wigfull. " 'Look for the lady in the locked room / At seventeen.' "

"Yes?"

"It struck me that 'seventeen' must refer to the chapter in the book, the John Dickson Carr book that Motion was about to read from. Chapter seventeen. 'The Locked-Room Lecture.' If the lady is Queen Victoria, then the riddle tells us to look for her in the locked room at seventeen, and that's precisely where the Penny Black cover was found."

"You think so?" Diamond didn't sound bowled over by the deduction.

"It makes sense," Wigfull insisted.

"Perfect sense," Diamond said. "But it's too late, isn't it? Too late for us to do anything about it. This clever dick who pinched the stamp wasn't really giving anything away in advance. How could we have known that the stamp was going to turn up in chapter seventeen of some obscure book written sixty years ago? We didn't stand a snowball's chance. Like the first rhyme we were given, it's easy enough to work out after the event. Did you get the first two lines? How did they go, exactly?"

Julie remembered them. " 'Whither Victoria and with whom—The Grand Old Queen?' "

Wigfull said with understandable pique, "It's obvious, isn't it? The last two lines were the puzzle."

"So you worked out who the Grand Old Queen is?" said Diamond.

"Victoria, obviously."

"Can't say I'm with you there, old boy," said Diamond. "For my money, it was a reference to Mr. Milo Motion."

Wigfull blinked and said, "The man's gay! You could be right."

"You have to be an insensitive brute like me to get the point," said Diamond.

Wigfull said, "You are right."

"But where does it get us?" Diamond developed his theme.

"All we can say is that the stamp theft was done according to plan. The way your Penny Black turned up last night was no mistake. It happened exactly as predicted. Milo Motion was earmarked as the fall guy."

Julie said, "But it does tell us that the thief knew Milo would take the book to the Bloodhounds meeting and open it at chapter seventeen?"

"Right!" said Wigfull. "We can count the suspects on one hand."

"Two," said Diamond. "And you may need your feet as well."

"I'm speaking of the Bloodhounds."

"There are six of them."

"Ah, but we can eliminate Motion," Wigfull pointed out. "That leaves five: Mrs. Wycherley, Miss Chilmark, Mrs. Shaw, Miss Miller, and the man, Rupert Darby."

"What about Sid Towers?"

"He's dead."

"He wasn't dead when the stamp was stolen," Diamond reminded him. "If it were me investigating the stamp theft, I'd keep Sid Towers in the frame, dead or not."

"Was the man capable of such a theft?"

"Certainly. He was easily overlooked, but not dim. He knew all about security. He'd have known how to suss out a building for a break-in."

"I can see that. But he doesn't strike me as the sort to compose riddles drawing attention to the crime."

"Why not? He was a reader of whodunits. Plenty of time to himself to think it through. Setting a puzzle for the police might have appealed to him."

Wigfull weighed the suggestion. "I suppose it's possible. But why was he killed?" He raised a finger like an umpire as he answered his own question. "Maybe the killer took offense at the way he chose to return the stamp. The obvious suspect would be Motion, but he's the one with the alibi."

"Now, John," Diamond said sharply. "The murder is my business. I don't want interference."

"You offered *me* some advice."

"Here's some more, then. You said you could count the suspects on one hand. You've just added Towers. You must also add anyone Motion spoke to—anyone who learned that he was taking the Dickson Carr book to that meeting."

"That's scraping the barrel, isn't it? From all I hear, he's another loner."

Diamond gave a shrug.

Wigfull was forced to concede. "Technically, I suppose you're right. Has anything helpful come up in the interviews?"

"Nothing startling. They're still being fed into the system, but I've heard from all the officers who carried them out. We caught up with everyone in the end, all the Bloodhounds, anyway. A couple of them weren't at home, and we nobbled them later."

"My number one suspect is the man."

"Why do you say that?"

A rare smile lit Wigfull's face. "I'm speaking of *my* case, the theft of the stamp. I can't see any of those women walking through the streets of Bath with a window cleaner's ladder and bucket."

"Sexist."

"Two of them are middle-aged."

"What matters to me is whether they could murder a man," said Diamond, "and a woman can crack a bloke over the head with a blunt instrument whether she's middle-aged or twenty. We had a case in Twerton before you joined the squad. Two old people, well over seventy, married fifty years, regularly coming to blows and ending up in casualty. In the end she clobbered him with a hammer because he threw away the *TV Times*. Killed him. I often think of that when I'm putting the papers in the bin."

After a sandwich lunch, Diamond interviewed Milo Motion for the third time.

"Caught up on your sleep yet?"

Milo was temporarily installed in a bed-and-breakfast house opposite the police station in Manvers Street. He had come in to ask when he could expect to return to his floating home. The black beard accentuated the challenging tilt of his chin. Bushy was the word for it, Diamond decided. A family of small mammals could have found a habitat in that abundant growth.

"You can go back before the afternoon is out; I give you my word," Diamond promised. "It may not be restored to its former glory yet, because they took the carpet and one or two other items for forensic tests."

"I simply want a change of clothes," said Milo. "I'm not proposing to sleep there after what happened."

"Are you comfortable in the B and B?"

"Tolerably."

"You don't have a friend who would put you up?"

He gave a prim click of the tongue. "No."

"Why don't you sit down?"

"Is it going to take as long as that?"

"A few things need clearing up," said Diamond equably.

"If it's about the bloody padlock again . . ." Milo started to say.

"No, it's the Bloodhounds, sir. You were one of the founders, you told me. You should know everyone quite well."

Guardedly, came the answer: "That doesn't necessarily follow. I see most of them once a week, on Mondays. That hardly entitles me to speak of them with any authority."

"But you've known Mrs. Wycherley since the beginning."

"True."

"And the other lady, Miss, em . . ."

"Chilmark?"

"Miss Chilmark. You've known her almost as long. You told us last night that there was some sort of incident involving Miss Chilmark. Something about a dog."

Milo sighed. "It seems a century ago. The dog belongs to Rupert Darby. He's bloody inconsiderate, is Rupert. Miss Chilmark doesn't care for the dog at all, and of course it always makes a beeline for her. If he left it at home, or kept it on the leash, we wouldn't have any trouble. Last night at the meeting Rupert came in late as usual, and Marlowe—that's the dog—"

"Did you say Marlowe?"

"Marlowe, yes. That's its name."

"Funny name for a dog."

"It's the name of Raymond Chandler's private eye. You remember *The Big Sleep*?"

"It's still a funny name for a dog."

"Rupert told us why. You must have heard that Chandler quote: 'down these mean streets a man must go who is not himself mean . . .' Well, that dog adores a mean street."

Diamond nodded. "Go on. Tell us what this dog did that was so obnoxious."

"It jumped up beside Miss Chilmark and threw her into a panic. She had some sort of attack of breathlessness that was only brought under control thanks to swift action by Jessica—Mrs. Shaw."

"What kind of action?"

"She called for a paper bag. Sid produced one. His book was wrapped in it. Jessica held it against Miss Chilmark's face, and the attack subsided. That's all it was."

"Sid had a book with him?"

"I just said so."

"Why would he have a book with him? He didn't read things out, did he?"

"No, he was far too shy. I imagine it was for private reading."

"Did you happen to notice the title?"

"Of course. I'm not uninterested in books myself. It was *The Three Coffins*, by John Dickson Carr. Sid was an admirer of Dickson Carr's work."

"Are you familiar with this book?"

"Extremely familiar, yes, but under the English title."

"Isn't *The Three Coffins* English?"

"I should have said British. *The Three Coffins* was the title the book was known by in America. Publishers sometimes decide in their wisdom that a book will sell better over there with a different title. It's a blasted nuisance to collectors."

"So what was the British title?"

"*The Hollow Man.*"

"Really? But that was the book you took to the meeting."

"Yes, indeed. The first English edition, published by Hamish Hamilton in 1935. Unfortunately, my copy is without a wrapper, or it might be worth a few pounds."

"Let's get this clear," said Diamond. "You and Sid Towers each took a copy of the same book to the meeting on Monday?"

"You make it sound suspicious," said Milo, "but it isn't at all. Far more suspicious things happened than that. The explanation is simple. At the previous meeting I announced to everyone that the next time we met, I would read the locked room chapter from *The Hollow Man.*"

Diamond mentally ticked one of the points he had wanted to check. Wigfull would be cockahoop. All the Bloodhounds who were present the previous week knew that Milo would bring his book to the meeting and open it at chapter seventeen. Any of them could have placed the stamp between the pages—any clever enough to find a way of doing it.

Milo was saying, "I presume Sid brought along his copy to follow the text. In his quiet way he was quite an authority on Dickson Carr."

"And so are you, apparently."

Milo preened the beard, pleased by the compliment. "I prefer to be thought of as a Sherlockian, but, yes, I have a sneaking admiration for much of Carr's work. He made the impossible crime his own specialty. Wrote seventy crime novels, which isn't at all bad considering he was notoriously fond of the bottle and also led a complicated love life. And of course he found time to write a fine biography of Conan Doyle. He was quite an Anglophile until the Labour government was elected after the war. He couldn't abide socialism, so he went back to the States and only returned after Churchill was returned to power."

"How does politics come into crime writing?"

"My dear superintendent, it's all about conservatism and affirming the social order, or was for almost a century."

"The class system."

Milo gave Diamond a sharp glance. "However vile the crime, the reader can rest assured that order is restored by the end. Only in comparatively recent times have left-wing crime writers discovered ways of subverting the status quo. You're not a socialist, are you?"

"I'm a policeman," said Diamond. "We're neutral."

Milo gave a hollow laugh. He was becoming confident.

Diamond said, "Getting back to the incident with the dog—"

"You're going to ask me once again if I let go of the book in all the confusion. The answer is the same. I had it on my knees or in my hand throughout. No one could have tampered with it. No one." Milo shook his head. "Nothing like this has happened to me in years. Once in my youth I met a close-up magician, and he did remarkable things that I still can't explain, like removing my watch without my being aware of it and having it turn up inside a box of chocolates. This business with the stamp is just as miraculous. I can only account for it as a brilliant conjuring trick. I can't guess the solution."

"And the murder of Sid Towers—is that magic?"

"The circumstances are."

"Trickery."

"Magic or trickery, it's beyond my understanding."

"That's a conclusion I'm not permitted to make," said Diamond. "I've got to catch the conjurer. Do you have any suspicions?"

"Of whom?"

"The other Bloodhounds."

"How can I?" said Milo. "They're charming people, all of them. Oh, Miss Chilmark has the reputation of being a sour-puss, but she's all right when you take a little trouble with her, butter her up, you know. And Jessica Shaw went out of her way to help poor old Sid fit in. She took him for a drink on more than one occasion. No, I'm afraid if you're looking for suspects, they're a very unlikely bunch. Not like a detective story at all. In this case, I can't think of anyone with a grudge against poor old Sid."

CHAPTER EIGHTEEN

L ATER THE SAME AFTERNOON, DIAMOND DROVE MILO MOTION to the Dundas boatyard to collect his change of clothes from the *Mrs. Hudson*. A thick-knit sweater was likely to be among them, because now that the sun was disappearing behind the willows on the far bank, there was an unmistakable threat of frost in that cloudless sky. The Scenes of Crime team had finished work and left. The only police activity—apart from one luckless constable rubbing his hands to keep his circulation going—was a pair of divers searching the canal bottom for the murder weapon, and they didn't seem too happy either. What they were doing in the shallow water couldn't be described as diving, more a matter of wading about and bending double. On a blue tarpaulin on the towpath they had assembled their finds—a horseshoe, two plastic milk crates, a bicycle pump, a birdcage, about twenty beer cans, and several pieces of stone— the result of three hours' scavenging for fifty yards either side of the narrowboat. Diamond told them to give up for the day. The chance was slim that a killer so artful as this would have disposed of the weapon in so obvious a place, but procedure had required the search to be made. He asked Milo to check for any object missing from the boat that might have been used to crack Sid Towers over the head.

Milo said he was unable to think of anything, but he would certainly look.

The constable had to open up for them, because the door at the stern had been fitted with a fresh lock. Milo's German-made padlock had been stripped down and examined at the forensic lab. Pressed by Diamond for their findings, the scientists had reported no flaw in the mechanism. No sign, even, of tampering. It was described as a high-security close-shackle padlock. The locking mechanism provided over six million key variations, bearing out the manufacturers' claim that each padlock they sold in Britain had a unique key pattern.

Diamond had been over the narrowboat and its security arrangements many times in his mind without deducing how the body had been placed there, so this extra inspection wasn't embarked upon with much confidence. The murder of Sid Towers was becoming his own locked room mystery, his Gordian knot. If Milo Motion had spoken the truth, the facts were indisputable:

1. Milo locked the boat when he left it.
2. The key never left his person.
3. The keys fitted that padlock and no other. There was no second key.
4. The only other point of entry to the cabin was the door at the fore end, and this was bolted from the inside.
5. The padlock was still in position when Milo returned to the boat with Wigfull. He had opened it with the key and discovered the corpse of Sid Towers in the cabin.

Each time he looked for a flaw in the logic, Diamond was forced back to that qualifier: *if Motion had spoken the truth*. The hardware, surely, was foolproof; the human assurances had to be tested further.

The two men dipped their heads to enter the cabin, now stripped of its carpet.

"I want you to think hard and long," Diamond told Milo. "Do you keep anything in here that might have been used as a weapon? Some ornament, perhaps, like a heavy beer mug or a paperweight?"

Milo thought for a moment and shook his head. "Books are about the heaviest things in here. You couldn't kill someone with a book, could you?"

"It would take something heavier than those," Diamond admitted, eyeing the shelves of detective stories. "A really big dictionary might do the job."

"Can't help. I manage without one."

"Lucky for you. Good speller, are you?" he asked companionably. Putting the man at his ease might encourage him to talk more freely about the evening of the murder.

"Correct spelling was part of the education when I grew up."

"Mine, too." Diamond switched to a confiding mode. "I was at grammar school, but I never fully mastered the spelling. Bit of a handicap, because they deducted marks in every subject, and it all went on a weekly report card. There was a ritual on Saturday mornings called 'slackers' parade'— a painful encounter with the deputy head—and I was a regular on it. Then one of the English masters taught me the trick of avoiding words like *necessary*. You can always write *needful* instead. Good advice. So the next time, that's what I did— and still finished up on the slackers' parade. Pity he didn't warn me *needful* has only one *l* at the end. Tell me, what's the attraction of detective stories?"

Milo blinked and frowned, derailed by the unexpected admission of frailty by the man he'd come to regard as the embodiment of authority.

"I've never understood what people see in them," Diamond went on. "True crime, yes, I can read with pleasure. Fiction I can't."

"I suppose it's the not knowing."

"The what?"

"The not knowing . . . until the end," Milo explained.

"Not knowing who did it?"

Milo relaxed slightly. "That's true of some books, certainly, but not all. There are other things the reader is keen to discover these days. I mean, some books tell you right off who the villain is. There's the fascination of not knowing whether he gets away with the crime, or whether the good chap survives. There's much more emphasis on character these days, but there's always an element of surprise in the best mysteries. You should attend one of our Bloodhound meetings."

"I may end up doing that. Would you mind stepping into the kitchen, or the galley, or whatever you call it?"

"You'd like a coffee?" said Milo.

"No, Mr. Motion." Abruptly he was the investigator again. "We're checking for a possible murder weapon. Remember?"

"Ah."

Nothing was missing from the galley that Milo could recall.

"You appreciate the importance," Diamond said to take the edge off his sharp remark. "The choice of weapon can tell us if the murder was planned or was just a response to something unexpected. Did the killer bring a weapon here with murder in mind, or was it just a matter of snatching up the first thing that came to hand?"

"I follow you," said Milo.

"But you can't help me?"

"On this matter, no."

"While we're here, let's go over the business of the padlock," Diamond continued. "I know you've been through it so many times you could say it in your sleep, but something else needs to be explained, doesn't it? The boat was totally secure, according to you, and yet a murder took place in here."

"Don't you think I'd have told you by now if I knew the answer?" Milo said with injured virtue. "It's utterly beyond my understanding. What is more, they got in twice. Someone must have broken in earlier to put the stamp inside my copy of John Dickson Carr."

"There's no evidence that anyone broke in." Diamond was

swift to correct him. "If they had, we might have an explanation. Not one of the doors or windows was interfered with. Nothing was broken."

"What happened then? They couldn't have had a key. Mine is the only one in existence."

"That isn't true, is it? There's the spare one you dropped in the canal."

"If you want to nitpick to that degree, yes."

"How long ago did you lose it?"

"Last year. I told you."

"Exactly when, Mr. Motion?"

Milo sighed. "Toward the end of the summer. It must have been September."

"Can you recall the circumstances? I daresay it caused you some annoyance."

"Well, it did. I lost my car keys at the same time."

"So we're talking about a bunch—on a ring?"

"Yes."

"Did you try to recover them?"

"It happened after dark," Milo explained, tugging at his beard as if the whole episode was painful to recall. "If you must know, I was the worse for drink. Pretty unusual for me. A night out at the Cross Guns."

"The pub at Avoncliff?"

"Yes. Do you know it? Gorgeous on a summer evening. I had the boat tied up at one of the moorings just above the pub, that stretch of the canal before the aqueduct. Treated myself to a meal and a few beers, and when I got back—"

"Alone?"

"Yes. I opened up and stumbled a bit pulling open the door. The damned keys slipped out of my hand and over the side. Bloody annoying, but I knew I had spares for all of them, so it could have been worse."

"Next morning, did you try and get them out?"

He shook his head. "Hopeless. They would have sunk into the mud."

"Did you mention this to anyone else?"

"I may have done to the people in the next boat. Can't remember, frankly."

"What about the Bloodhounds? Would you have mentioned it to them?"

"Certainly not. Why should I? It wasn't an incident I'm proud of."

"We've got to think of all the angles."

"All I can say is what I know to be the truth," Milo stressed in a more defensive tone. "You can see for yourself that when I'm aboard the boat, it's just about impossible for anyone else to come in here without my knowing. You can hear every step, and there's nowhere to hide. It's all open-plan. Anyway, the cupboards are far too small to hide anyone."

"What exactly are you driving at?"

"If the murderer found some way of stowing away while I was still here, and remained hidden when I locked up, it would be possible to unbolt the door at the far end—unbolt it from the inside—and admit the victim."

Diamond almost snapped his fingers in triumph. Then, as the flaw in the revelation occurred to him, he converted the gesture into scratching his right earlobe. "But when you and Wigfull entered the boat, it was bolted from the inside at that end and padlocked outside at the other. Unless the killer was still aboard, it couldn't have happened."

"There you go," said Milo with an air of resignation. "I can assure you, there wasn't anyone here except poor old Sid. I'm as confused as anyone by all this."

"And as you remarked just now, there's nowhere to hide. Everything folds against the walls. The only lockers are outside the cabin, back at the stern end." Diamond paused, watching Milo. "The crucial question is whether your memory is reliable when you say you locked the boat."

"Of course it is!" Milo said petulantly. "I remember rattling the damned padlock, testing it with my hand to be sure it was secure. And it was. Later, when I returned with your colleague, Mr. Wigfull, I unlocked with my own key and had the shock of my life when I saw what was inside. It's impossible, but it happened. I am at a total loss to account for it. You need Dr. Fell for this."

"Who's he?"

"Dickson Carr's detective."

"A detective in a book? Great."

"Someone of his caliber, at any rate."

"Thanks for the vote of confidence," said Diamond. "Well, I think we need someone smarter than Dr. Fell. I've been through that chapter on the locked room lecture, and it's no help. I ask you. You've studied it yourself. This is a puzzle that defies all Dr. Fell's explanations."

Milo nodded. "I have to agree with you."

"And the locked room is only part of the mystery. What was Sid's reason for coming here?"

"I haven't the foggiest," Milo answered with a shrug. "He wasn't in the habit of visiting me. Besides, he knew I wouldn't be here. I told everyone I was going straight to the police station to hand in the Penny Black. Do you think the murderer lured him to his death?"

Diamond didn't want to trade theories any longer. "Look, why don't you pick out the clothes you need? I'll take a stroll along the towpath and see you in ten minutes."

He needed more time for reflection. Milo, surely, was a reliable witness. This, after all, was the one member of the Bloodhounds who couldn't have murdered Towers. Yet there was still a doubt. Any lawyer will tell you that witnesses tend to present themselves and their actions in the most favorable light, sometimes obscuring serious flaws in their evidence. Suppose Milo hadn't after all locked the narrowboat before leaving for the meeting. Suppose through carelessness or overconfidence he had left the padlock hanging from the staple still unfastened. At first he may have decided not to mention it; no one wants to admit to negligence, particularly to the police. Later, as the investigation proceeded, he would find it increasingly embarrassing. An act of carelessness would grow into a deception. He might even have lied to cover it up.

Human frailty seemed a stronger bet than mechanical wizardry. Ingenious locked room puzzles were the province of detective story writers.

He went across to the divers. They had unpeeled their wet suits and were stacking their van. He had another job for them tomorrow, he told them, further along, by the Avoncliff Aqueduct. A bunch of keys. They didn't sound overjoyed. With a wink at the constable on duty, he stepped briskly along the towpath. This stretch of waterway now used for mooring was historically the route taken by the barges transporting coal from the Somerset mines. Much more narrow than the main canal, almost two centuries old and edged with ancient flagstones, it had its own character, though the aluminum lift-bridge where it joined the Kennet and Avon was clearly a modern replacement. He stood for a moment staring at this bridge, deciding how the lifting mechanism worked. Clearly it had to be raised for anything the size of a narrowboat to pass under. There were counterweights projecting from the fulcrum, but the walkway was bolted down on the opposite side. He hauled on it to make sure. At this late hour nothing was about to pass into the boatyard, so his curiosity had to be set aside. He turned and started back toward the solitary policeman.

The question of most interest to him now was the one Milo had raised only a few minutes ago: What could have induced Sid Towers to visit the *Mrs. Hudson*? It was strange behavior considering that Milo himself was not going to be present. Why visit a locked boat after dark? One possible explanation was that the murderer had suggested meeting him there. If it was a trap, what was the bait? Or was it a threat? Maybe Sid had been under some pressure to obey the summons.

Blackmail?

He stepped aboard the narrowboat and found Milo in the cabin filling carrier bags with clothes. "I'm about ready."

"Good. It's cold in here. I don't know how you put up with it."

"Well, I've got no heating on. Normally it can be really snug."

"I walked to the end of the canal," said Diamond. "As far as that lift-bridge. It *is* a lift-bridge?"

"Oh, yes. It has to be raised each time a boat goes out."

"How do you lift it, then? So far as I can tell, the thing is bolted down."

"It is. We unfasten it with a windlass. Everyone using the moorings has one. You get one from the office."

"Like a spanner, you mean?"

"Yes."

"That explains it, then. Let me help you with those." He picked up one of the bags. "Ready to leave?"

"Will the constable lock up?"

"We'll do it."

They emerged from the cabin. Diamond pressed the strap over the staple and closed the padlock over it. "Where do you keep the windlass? I wouldn't mind seeing what it looks like."

"It's in the locker on the right. I keep the tiller in there with it."

Diamond pulled up the lid of the locker and peered at the collection of tools. "I can see the tiller. Can't see anything like a windlass."

Milo bent over and shifted the contents about. "Well, that's a damned liberty. It's gone. Someone must have pinched it."

"Are you sure?"

"It's always here."

"What size and weight is this windlass?" Diamond asked.

Milo extended his hands about eight inches. "It's iron. Not a thing you'd put in your pocket and forget about."

"Heavy enough to crack a man over the head and kill him?"

"Good Lord. Is that possible?"

"Problems?" said Julie, seated at a desk near the door.

Diamond made a sound deep in his throat like a growl,

pushed a computer keyboard aside, and perched his rear on one of the desks in the incident room. The civilian staff had finished work for the day.

He sighed. "No worse than yesterday. I'm boxed in, Julie. I don't care for it."

"Because of the way the body was found?"

"The whole shooting match. The bloody riddles. The missing Penny Black. This ridiculous Bloodhounds club. It's straight out of a whodunit. I'm a career detective, not a poncy Frenchman with spats and a walking stick."

"Belgian."

"What?"

"Hercule Poirot is a Belgian."

"I don't care if he's from Outer Mongolia. He's a figment of some writer's imagination—that's the point. Everything up to now is detective story stuff from sixty years ago. It shouldn't be happening in the real world. I'm being asked to deal with a locked room murder, for Christ's sake. If I crack it—I mean *when* I crack it—what am I going to be faced with next? Invisible ink?"

Julie allowed a suitable pause. She'd worked with Diamond long enough to know that these occasional outpourings weren't entirely negative in effect. Then she remarked, "Do you really need to crack the locked room mystery?"

He folded his arms. "You'd better explain yourself."

"Well, the great temptation is to go at this head on, as they did in those detective stories, puzzling over the locked room until we hit on the solution. That's what we're meant to do. Why don't we approach it another way?"

"Tell me how."

"There's only a handful of people who could have committed the stamp theft. Agreed?"

"Certainly—but that's for John Wigfull to unravel."

Julie refused to be deflected. "I mean the Bloodhounds. They knew from the previous meeting that Milo would be bringing in his copy of *The Hollow Man*—an opportunity that the thief found irresistible. If Milo himself is not the thief, then it has to be the person who planted the stamp in his book."

Diamond nodded. This was pretty obvious stuff.

She continued. "Someone who must have been at the meeting the previous week when Milo promised to read from the chapter on locked room mysteries."

"Or who was tipped off about what was said."

"All right," Julie conceded. "But it's still a small group, right?"

"Right."

"And so is the list of murder suspects."

Diamond held up a finger. "Careful, now."

Julie got up and crossed the room to argue her case. "Because the killer got inside the *Mrs. Hudson*, just as the stamp thief did. Be fair, Mr. Diamond. It's got to be the same person. I refuse to believe that two people independently worked out a way of getting inside that cabin without disturbing the lock. Two different people, each smarter than you? No way."

"So?"

"So instead of all this brain-fag over the locked room, I suggest we get talking to the suspects. You and I, I mean. I know we have a batch of statements, but there's no substitute for getting face to face with people."

"Doorstepping." He smiled.

"No, I don't mean house-to-house inquiries. I'm talking about the suspects, and there aren't many of them."

"That's your advice?"

She hesitated, detecting the note of irony. "I'm trying to be helpful."

"And you are." This was sincerely meant. Listening to Julie had helped him take hold of a doubt that had been hovering just out of reach for some time. "Only I'm not yet convinced that you're right about the thief and the killer being one and the same. Think for a moment about Sid Towers. What if he were the man who stole the stamp?"

"Sid?"

He gave a nod.

"The murder victim?"

Diamond gave his snap assessment of Towers. "Unassuming, easily disregarded, yet not unintelligent. A reader of John Dickson Carr. Imagine the quiet satisfaction Sid would have derived from surprising the rest of the Bloodhounds—that opinionated lot who thought they knew all there is to know about detective stories. This is pure hypothesis, but let's suppose he stole the Penny Black simply to make a point, not with his power of speech which was so underdeveloped, but through the written word, with riddles and rhymes. 'I'm smarter than all of you put together,' he was saying in effect, 'whatever you think of me.' And what a marvelous notion to have the stamp turn up between the pages of Milo's book—thus demonstrating a locked room mystery unknown to Dr. Fell or anyone else. Do you see what I'm getting at, Julie?"

"Sid was the thief? But Sid was murdered."

Diamond sketched the scenario as he spoke, and it made a lot of sense, even to himself. "Murdered aboard the narrowboat. Sid went back there, knowing Milo would be occupied at the nick for some time to come. Maybe he intended to leave a note, another riddle, even. He let himself in by the same brilliant method he used on the previous occasion—whatever that may be—only this time he was followed in by someone else, who picked up a windlass and cracked him over the head."

"Who?"

"That's the question. Could be one of the Bloodhounds who followed him there. Could be someone else with a grudge against Sid. Could simply be some evil person who was on the towpath last night and decided to mug the occupant. In other words, anyone from your half-dozen suspects to the entire population of Avon and Somerset, plus any visitors passing through. That's why I'm cautious, Julie. But it's only a hypothesis. I may be totally mistaken."

CHAPTER NINETEEN

O PEN-TOP TOUR BUSES ARE A FEATURE OF BATH THAT MOST
residents accept with good grace in a city that wel-
comes tourists. The two companies in competition are
distinguished by their colors: Ryan's Citytour in red and white
and Badgerline's Bath Tour in green and cream. Citytours operate from Terrace Walk, near the Abbey. The Badgerline tours
leave every thirty minutes from the bus station and are named
after city worthies like Prince Bladud, King Edgar, Ralph
Allen, John Wood, and Dr. William Oliver. All the buses stop
at convenient points to allow ticketholders to get off and ex-
plore, continuing the tour on another bus if desired.

Miss Chilmark was one of the minority who disapproved of
the open-tops of whatever color. For one thing she had a
house on the route and was convinced that people on the
upper deck looked into bedrooms. And for another, as a person of refined literary taste, she found it deplorable that Jane
Austen's name was on the back of a bus. You may imagine the
shock she received when crossing Pierrepont Street at ten
thirty in the morning to hear her own name spoken, amplified,
from one of these despised vehicles.

"Miss Chilmark!"

It must have been audible right across Parade Gardens.

She froze and tried to take an interest in a shop window,
telling herself she couldn't have heard correctly.

"Miss Chilmark!" Louder still and unmistakable, like a summons to the Last Judgment.

Deeply alarmed, she turned her head enough to see a female figure speaking into a microphone on the upper deck of a Badgerline called Beau Nash. Twenty or more interested faces were staring down.

"Miss Chilmark, this is Shirley-Ann Miller, from the Bloodhounds. Could I talk to you?"

Miss Chilmark was in no position to stop her from talking, but she had enough spirit to answer, "What gives you the right . . . ?"

She wasn't heard. Shirley-Ann's amplified voice drowned hers. "Shall we say eleven, by the Abbey door? Please be there if you possibly can."

The bus started to move off. The commentary continued, "Sorry about that, ladies and gentlemen. Personal. I happened to spot someone I know and it is rather an emergency. If you look to your left now you will see the archway leading to Pierrepont Place. At Number One from 1764 to 1771 lived the Linley family, and Mrs. Linley once had a maidservant called Emma Lyon, later to become famous as Emma Hamilton. To your right across the street at Number Two is the house occupied for many years as a winter home by the Nelson family— yes, *that* Nelson. Unfortunately for romantics like me, the dates are wrong. It is most unlikely that Emma and Horatio met in Bath, but there is a romantic story about the dazzlingly lovely daughter of the Linleys, Elizabeth, who eloped . . ."

Miss Chilmark, her mind closed to the commentary, turned unsteadily along North Parade Passage, pink with the indignity. Not once in her life had she been hailed from the top of a bus. Generations of Chilmarks had lived with dignity and decorum in this city. She was mortified to have been singled out for such public humiliation. She needed a strong coffee and a Sally Lunn to take away the shock.

"Yes, I'm awfully sorry about that," Shirley-Ann told her when they met. "I didn't mean to alarm you. I'm not very used to the public address system. Usually my job is handing out the leaflets, but today they were short-staffed, so I stood in for someone. It's a chance you don't turn down. A marvelous opportunity for me and only the second time I've done it. When I spotted you, I forgot I was holding the mike and it was live. And I desperately wanted to speak to you. Look, shall we sit down? You look dreadfully pale." She was wondering what to do if Miss Chilmark had another attack of hyperventilation. She didn't have a paper bag with her.

They went over to sit on one of the benches in the Abbey churchyard. A busker facing them was playing the recorder to an orchestral backing from a portable cassette player, but it wasn't any bar to conversation. "I like giving the commentary, and I think I'm rather good at it," Shirley-Ann said, giving a commentary to Miss Chilmark. "I get a real buzz when I'm up there with the mike switched on and all those faces turned my way. They hear more from me than any other guide gives them. I must admit I depart from the script a bit. And today I was fairly bombarding them with information, more than I intended to say. I'm in a bit of a state myself, to be honest. We're all in a state, and no wonder."

"What do you want?" Miss Chilmark asked.

"Just a few words."

"A few!"

What Shirley-Ann wanted was the chance to talk over the developments since Monday evening. It was right against her nature to suffer in silence. She had a chronic need to share her anxieties with some other woman. She couldn't trouble Polly again so soon after meeting her in the Bath Bun, and she didn't like to call at Jessica's art gallery in case the man A.J. was there. Miss Chilmark wasn't an obvious choice for a tête-à-tête, but she was the only choice left. Spotting her from the bus had seemed like destiny intervening.

"You must have heard about poor Sid?"

Miss Chilmark gave a nod. She was wearing a small version of Robin Hood's hat with a feather, and the feather was vibrating, whether with rage or the breeze it was impossible to judge.

Shirley-Ann did what she could to make this seem like a shared concern. "I heard the news from Polly. She had the police round yesterday morning. Well, so did I later. I dare say you did. But Polly is terribly upset. She cares so much about the Bloodhounds. We're like her own family to her."

Miss Chilmark said acidly, "If that's her idea of a family, she must have had a deprived upbringing."

"Well, you must know what I'm trying to say. The police are bound to think of us as suspects. This was a locked room murder—the very topic we were about to discuss on Monday evening."

"Not at my suggestion," Miss Chilmark was quick to point out.

Shirley-Ann sighed. "It doesn't really matter who suggested it. We all knew that Milo was going to read from the book, and we're all under suspicion. Did the police visit you?"

Grudgingly, Miss Chilmark said, "They did call briefly."

"You drive, don't you?"

"I beg your pardon."

"You have a car of your own?"

"I do."

"Then it's perfectly possible for you to have driven to the boatyard after the meeting finished. You're a suspect." Shirley-Ann added with more tact, "We all have cars, so far as I know."

Outrage had spread ominously across the suspect Miss Chilmark's features, and the feather was positively flapping.

Shirley-Ann said, "The detective who came to interview me made the point that it was the crime of someone of high intelligence."

Miss Chilmark looked a mite less outraged. "Low cunning, more like. I know whom I suspect."

"Rupert?"

"Who else?"

"But why? Why would he want to kill Sid? They weren't enemies."

"How can you tell?" said Miss Chilmark, her eyes on the Abbey front. "Sid—Mr. Towers as I prefer to think of him— was a quiet man. Who can say what his private opinions were? He wasn't the sort to articulate them at one of our meetings."

"But Rupert isn't a man to bottle up his feelings—and I can't recall him saying an unkind word about Sid, ever."

"He's a degenerate."

"Rupert?"

"You only have to look at him. That face."

"Now that really is unfair."

"Evil."

"I don't think of him as evil. Rather hollow-cheeked, I grant you, and he could do with some more teeth. He's no oil painting, but I find it a very watchable face. Anyway, it would be terrible if people were judged on their looks."

"His are clearly the result of many years of bad living."

And yours, Shirley-Ann thought, of mean-mindedness. "Or neglect."

"Depravity. He's constantly in public houses, so far as I can make out. His choice of reading is indicative—all that violence he wallows in."

"Really, Miss Chilmark, I've read a lot of those books myself and I'm not depraved, I hope. Millions of people read them. You admire *The Name of the Rose*, but it doesn't mean you want to go into a monastery, I mean a nunnery—oh, I don't know what I do mean, except that the books people read are no guide to their behavior."

Miss Chilmark turned to Shirley-Ann, her broad face pitted with disfavor. "Let me remind you that Mr. Towers worked for a security firm. They're ex-policemen, a lot of them. They know the ne'er-do-wells in this city. If something came to his notice in the course of his duties, something particularly unpleasant regarding one of the Bloodhounds, and that person felt at risk of being exposed, you wouldn't have to look hard for a motive for murder."

Shirley-Ann had forgotten that Sid was a security guard. It was the first reasonable comment Miss Chilmark had made. "But that could apply to any of us. Any of us could have a skeleton in the cupboard."

"Speak for yourself," said Miss Chilmark.

"Even if I had, I wouldn't see murder as the solution," Shirley-Ann said thoughtfully. Mentally she was reviewing the other Bloodhounds, wondering what skeletons they might prefer to keep hidden. Jessica? Polly? She had been going to suggest a meeting, if only to compare notes on what the police had said. Now, she was less enthusiastic.

"Poor Mr. Towers didn't batter himself to death," said Miss Chilmark. "Someone wanted him dead."

"At the meeting last night," said Shirley-Ann, "do you remember anything that Sid said or did that might have caused someone else to kill him?"

"I was too distressed to notice."

"Before that. Before Rupert arrived."

"The only thing I can recall him saying was at the beginning, before we started. There were four of us present—Mr. Towers and the three lady members. Polly asked who was missing—as if she couldn't work it out for herself—and Mr. Towers spoke Rupert's name, adding that Rupert is always late. It was so unusual for Mr. Towers to say anything that I noticed it particularly."

"He said something later," said Shirley-Ann. "Now what was it? A quip of some sort. Just a couple of words. I know! Jessica was giving us her theory about the stealing of the Penny Black. She said it could easily be a collector. She could picture some middle-aged man with a personality defect gloating over his stamps, or something like that, and Sid said, 'Or woman,' and we all smiled about it. You do remember, don't you? After all, you were the one who suggested we discuss the stealing of the stamp."

"I can bring it to mind now, yes. But I don't see that it makes any difference. None of us took offense, the ladies, I mean."

"Do you think it was Sid who took offense? Do you think he took the remark personally, about the personality defect? He could have thought it was aimed at him."

"Conceivably. Who can say?"

Shirley-Ann trawled through her memory of the evening. "After that, you gave us your theories about the riddle, and Sid made no comment at all, did he?"

"I can't remember any."

"The next thing was that Rupert's dog appeared."

"Spare me that." Miss Chilmark looked away at the recorder player.

"I don't remember Sid saying anything while you were distressed, but when Jessica asked for a paper bag, he supplied one. He took it from his carrier bag. A book was wrapped in it. So it was thanks to Sid that she had the means to cope with your attack."

Miss Chilmark appeared to wish to dismiss the episode from her mind. At any rate, she said nothing.

Shirley-Ann picked up the thread again. "Soon after, I read the Stanley Ellin story, and then Milo opened his copy of *The Hollow Man*."

"Before that, he insulted Mrs. Wycherley."

"Who did?"

Miss Chilmark looked as if she had bitten into a sour apple. "Who do you think?"

"Rupert?"

"You remember, don't you? 'Jesus Wants Me for a Sunbeam'?"

"Oh." Shirley-Ann tried to stop herself smiling.

"It was meant to wound, and it did."

"Yes, but it didn't have anything to do with Sid."

"It demonstrated the depths the man will sink to."

"Rupert. But we were talking about Sid and the things he did and said that evening," said Shirley-Ann. "And now I've remembered something else. At the end of the evening, after Milo opened his book and found the Penny Black, we were talking about what Milo should do next. Some of us said there was no need for him to get involved. He could send the stamp back to the Postal Museum, and no one need say anything about it. Someone—I think it was Rupert—asked Sid for his opinion and he said, 'I can stay quiet.' You must remember because you were one of the people who said he had a duty to go to the police. You and Polly insisted. Everyone else was inclined to turn a blind eye."

"Don't talk to me in that accusing tone of voice," said Miss Chilmark. "It was the proper thing to do."

"If he hadn't done it, he would have gone straight back to the narrowboat. Very likely, Sid wouldn't have been murdered."

"That, if I may say so, is about the most stupid thing I have heard you say," commented Miss Chilmark. "It's pure speculation and quite pointless. No one can say with certainty what would have happened. Anyway, my recollection is that Milo made up his own mind. It didn't require advice from me or anyone else. He would have gone to the police regardless, and quite right." She stood up. "And now, if we have quite finished this futile exercise, I have some business to attend to. Good morning."

She headed off in the direction of Waitrose.

CHAPTER TWENTY

J ULIE HARGREAVES ROUTINELY CLEARED THE SURFACE OF her desk at the end of each day's work. She wasn't compulsive about tidiness, but the desk was quite modest in size, and she would transfer everything she could to the filing cabinet and the wire trays. For the pens, pencils, and clips, she had an arrangement of cylinders called a desk tidy. All she expected to find in front of her when she arrived for work next day was the mail, if any. So this Wednesday morning Peter Diamond, whose desk was a disgrace, was making mischief. He had heaped her space with objects in transparent plastic bags—Sid Towers's possessions, ready to be collected for forensic examination. An outraged howl was the least he expected.

She deflated him by saying mildly, "It's a little early for Christmas, isn't it?"

He said, "You're an optimist." He still hoped for an eruption.

But she moved the dialogue smoothly on to professional matters. "Surely he didn't carry all this in his pockets."

"It's all the loose stuff from his car as well."

"Anything of interest?" She picked up one of the bags and rattled the contents. "Keys."

"For the car, the doors to his flat and the warehouse where he worked."

"Nothing so helpful as the key to a certain padlock?"

"You're a superoptimist."

She handled a bulkier package. "This will be the book he had with him at the Bloodhounds' meeting. *The Three Coffins*."

Diamond frowned as a fresh thought popped into his brain. "Where's the brown paper bag we heard it was wrapped in?"

Julie shifted some of the objects.

"Should be here somewhere," said Diamond, joining in. "Every bloody item has its own plastic bag and label."

"I don't see it, do you? Here's a carrier bag." Julie picked up the packet and read the label. "'Waitrose carrier used to contain book, *The Three Coffins*.' No mention of a brown bag."

"Come to think of it, he wouldn't fancy using it for his precious book after Miss Chilmark had been hyperventilating into it. Probably binned it."

"I expect so," said Julie, continuing to examine the collection. Packaged and labeled like this, anyone's possessions would have looked pathetic. There was about thirty pence in small coins. A five-pound note. A handkerchief. A comb. Two ballpoints. Half a tube of Polo mints. "Does it matter?"

"The bag? Only if it's missing," said Diamond, beginning to question his own assumption. "*Would* he have thrown it away, seeing that it came in so useful? Suppose the old dear had another attack. They could have needed it a second time."

"Unless it got torn."

"Nothing was said about that. Who held the bag to Miss Chilmark's face?"

"The art gallery owner. Jessica Shaw. She knew what to do."

"Then I wouldn't mind betting she kept hold of the bag, at least until the meeting ended."

Julie gave him a long look. He had this way of pursuing to tedium points that seemed trivial. Once in a while this paid a dividend. Still, it was difficult to understand why the fate of a brown paper bag had any importance.

"And the meeting broke up in some disorder after the Penny Black was discovered," he continued, talking more to himself than Julie. "She may not have returned the bag to Sid. Well, she couldn't have, or it would be among these things."

"Unless Sid got rid of it later."

Diamond didn't think much of that suggestion. "She could have left it in the crypt, in which case some cleaner will have tidied it up."

"Or she may have taken it with her."

"Jessica? Stuffed it into her handbag, you mean?"

"Or a pocket."

He liked that better. "Right. We'll ask her now. We'll take a walk to that art gallery she manages."

"What do I do with all this?" she asked with her hand on the heap of plastic packets.

"Leave it there."

"Cluttering up my desk? No thanks."

"You're not a slave to tidiness, are you?"

"But there's money here."

"This is a police station, Julie. If you can't trust the police . . ." He spread his hands like the Pope and tried to look as benign.

She gave him a long look, and said, "It's not your money."

"Yours neither. Get your coat. We've more important things to do."

She looked at her watch. "Can't do it. Sorry."

"Why not."

"Actually, I've got an appointment."

His blood pressure rose several points. She had no business making appointments in police time. "What's that?"

"The postmortem on Sid Towers. You asked me to go—remember?"

"Ah." He'd dismissed it from his mind. "What time?"

"Noon, at the RUH."

"We can fit this other thing in first. I'll get you there on time, I guarantee."

"If you say so." Not for the first time in her dealings with Diamond, Julie showed restraint. She could easily have remarked that if he could drive her to the RUH, it was odd that he was prevented from attending the autopsy himself.

The Walsingham Gallery window was being dressed, and Jessica Shaw was directing, gesturing to a man on the other side of the glass exactly where a painting on an easel should stand. She was engrossed, and so was a small crowd of bystanders, making it difficult for anyone to reach the other end of the narrow, flagstoned passage of Northumberland Place. Jessica seemed to be well aware that this was street entertainment. In a cherry-red woollen dress and with a thick white cardigan draped around her shoulders, she was conspicuous among her audience in their drab padded jackets and windcheaters.

"Mrs. Jessica Shaw?"

She didn't even turn to answer Diamond's inquiry, but carried on giving instructions. "More to the right. The right, the right, the right."

"Police," said Diamond. "CID. This may be inconvenient, but are you Mrs. Shaw?"

"It is inconvenient, yes."

"And you are Mrs. Shaw?"

"I am. That's it, A.J.! Perfect!"

In a tone of formality amounting almost to a warning, he gave his rank and name and Julie's, too. "Could we talk to you inside, ma'am?"

"But I have talked," she said, still staring at her window arrangement. "I had a sergeant here yesterday and he wrote down everything I said."

"This is the follow-up."

She sighed and turned her face to him for the first time. "And I'm trying to get this ready for a private view this evening. I've got over a hundred people coming. What do you think of it so far?"

"The window? I like it. Not so keen on the picture. Meant to be Avebury, is it?"

"God help us," said Jessica Shaw. "What a brutal expression that is. *Meant* to be. We just have to be grateful the artist isn't here."

They went inside. A.J. was sent to fetch more pictures and unwrap them. "I hope this won't take long," Jessica said to Diamond. "It's interfering with my livelihood, all this third degree." She found them chairs at the rear of the shop. "You want coffee?"

"That's going to delay the questions even more," Diamond pointed out.

"Not if A.J. makes it. White with how many sugars? Two?"

She'd guessed correctly. "Thanks. You should be doing my job," Diamond remarked.

Eyeing his bulk, she commented, "It's not much of a deduction. And no sugar for you, right?" she said to Julie. She gave the order to A.J. as he shuffled past with a large wrapped painting, then she confided to Diamond, "A.J. is a brick. It's all voluntary. I don't pay him a cent. I only wish I could sell more of his work."

"His work?"

"He's an artist."

"Is that his stuff in the window?"

"Lord, no. I keep him upstairs."

"Lucky fellow," said Diamond, then wished he had guarded his tongue. The look he got was all he deserved. She didn't blush, or betray any embarrassment. She simply gave him a cold stare. "First question," he said quickly. "When did you join the Bloodhounds?"

"Last winter. I was one of the last to join, except for the new woman, Shirley-Ann. She's only been a couple of times."

"So was Sid Towers already a member when you joined?"

"Sid? Yes."

"Had you met him before?"

"No."

"Did you know any of them previously?"

"Only Polly Wycherley. I joined at her invitation. She came into the gallery a couple of times toward the end of last year and noticed what I was reading. We discovered we shared an interest in crime fiction, so she told me about the meetings in the crypt. I went along reluctantly. She's a great persuader, is Polly. Have you met her?"

"Not yet."

"She's cooled toward me for some reason. Probably something I said. People like you and me ought to think before we speak. But I don't go to please Polly anymore. I go to be entertained. The members are well informed, but I can tell you there are some pretty eccentric ones among them."

"Lost their Marples, you mean?"

She raised her eyebrows. "Did I hear right? Was that meant to be a pun?"

" *'Meant* to be.' What a brutal expression."

Now she laughed, and it was clear from the look she gave him that she was beginning to alter her assessment of this paunchy policeman. "Anyway, 'eccentric' was the word I used. The Bloodhounds aren't so dim. They're well read. I like scoring points off them when I can."

"The meetings can be lively, then?"

"Lively? Deadly, as it turns out."

Now Diamond smiled.

"Yes," Jessica went on. "There are personality clashes. Rupert gets people excited."

"Mr. Darby, you mean?"

"Do I? I only think of him as Rupert. He's harmless, in my opinion, though others will tell you different. A classic case of arrested development. He's locked into the nineteen fifties, when it was chic to hang around Soho smoking Gauloises and going to jazz clubs. You'll get on famously with him, by the look of you."

Diamond's hand curled protectively over the trilby on his knees. "There were incidents with Miss Chilmark, I'm told."

"Silly old duck, yes. She's a frightful snob. The Chilmarks once owned half the city, if she can be believed. She can't understand why we don't prostrate ourselves each time she appears. What really gets to her is that Rupert is manifestly several points above her in the social scale and doesn't give a toss about decorum."

"How is it manifest?"

"His accent. To borrow a phrase from Dylan Thomas, he talks as if he has the Elgin Marbles in his mouth."

"There was an incident on Monday, I heard."

"There's an incident on most Mondays. He insists on bringing his dog, and she gets herself into a state about it. She started to panic, and we calmed her down."

This account was all too perfunctory. Julie intervened to say, "You're understating it, aren't you?"

"In what way?"

"Wasn't she hyperventilating? And didn't you act quickly to stop it?"

"Just the old remedy of holding a paper bag to her mouth," said Jessica dismissively. "She soon responded."

Diamond wasn't going to let this crucial matter get by. "What happened to the bag?"

"What do you mean—what happened to it?"

"Afterward."

"I don't remember, unless . . ."

"Unless what?"

". . . I kept it."

"Did you?"

"I may have done. In fact, I believe I did, just in case she started up again. She insisted on staying for the rest of the meeting. Rupert removed the dog, but I didn't want to take any chances, so I kept the bag by me. Now what happened to it at the end?" She hesitated. "Is this important?"

"Possibly not, but I'd like to know."

"Sid produced it in the first place."

"I know," said Diamond.

"I don't have any memory of returning it to him."

"Would you have thrown it away?"

"Doubtful. Not after it came in so useful. I'm wondering now if I kept the thing. I didn't want it in view, right in front of Miss Chilmark. I may have stuffed it in my handbag."

"You would have found it later, then."

"Not me. I carry things for years before I turf them out. It's probably still in there. Want me to fetch my bag?"

"Presently," said Diamond. The questioning had settled to a tempo that he didn't want interrupted. Give her half a chance and she would go back to her window dressing. "Tell me about Sid."

"That won't take long," she said. "He was a member before I joined. Polly told me once that he came on the advice of his doctor. He was painfully shy, poor bloke. The doctor's idea was that he was a crime fiction buff, so he would be encouraged to chip in. He hardly ever did." She smiled. "It was so rare if he did that we all turned our heads and scared him rigid."

"Did anyone try making friends with him?"

"Polly fussed over him sometimes like the old hen she is. If anyone else had spoken more than a couple of words, I'm sure he would have run a mile."

"And I understand you spent some time with him in the Moon and Sixpence on more than one occasion."

She colored slightly. "Are you trying to trip me up, or something? You make it sound like infidelity. I felt sorry for the guy, that's all. I thought someone should try and draw him out a bit, for his own sake. The others simply ignored him."

"No one was hostile?"

She shook her head. "There was nothing you could dislike about Sid."

"Someone must have objected to him."

"I know," said Jessica.

The coffee arrived in bone china cups, A.J. bearing it in on a lacquered tray. Potential buyers of the art had to be cosseted. From the efficient way he handed the cups around, A.J. had performed the duty more than once. "If it doesn't seem frightfully rude," he said, "I'll take mine to the front of the shop and carry on with what I was doing."

Alert to the possibility that A.J. was something more in this setup than a volunteer window dresser, Diamond watched him with interest. The man had an air of confidence that belied the menial tasks he was performing here. There was poise in the way he moved, and a suggestion of anarchy, as if any second he might execute some Chaplinesque trick with the tray, and his dark curls and mobile brown eyes reinforced the idea, though he was actually quite tall. However, Jessica was content to treat him as a domestic in spite of the approving things she had said earlier. They both appeared at ease with each other.

Intriguing.

But there were things still to be asked. "On Monday after the meeting ended, what did you do?"

"Went home," Jessica answered.

"Immediately?"

"Yes."

"Where's home, Mrs. Shaw?"

"Widcombe Hill."

"You've got a good view from there, I dare say."

"A view of a chapel roof with the words PREPARE TO MEET THY GOD painted in big white letters across it, if that's what you call a good view." She laughed. "A nice message to see each morning when we pull back the bedroom curtains."

"If that's the Ebenezer, it must have been there when you moved in."

"Of course. Actually, it doesn't bother us. I was just amused when you mentioned the view."

"When you got home that evening, was Mr. Shaw there?"

She put down her cup of coffee. "This is becoming rather intrusive."

"I'm sorry. That's my job," said Diamond. "I need to know if anyone can vouch for the time you got in."

"So I'm a suspect?"

"We're doing our best to eliminate you."

"That's precisely the message I see from my bedroom window."

He laughed. This had become an interview to savor. It was all too rare to meet a witness so adept at verbal sparring. Jessica Shaw had a quick intelligence. He told her, "You haven't answered the question yet."

"Which one? Oh, was Barnaby at home? No, he was not. He didn't get back till late. Lions." She folded her arms, enjoying Diamond's puzzled reaction to the last word, making it plain that she wasn't intending to add anything.

"Live lions?" he asked after taking a sip of coffee.

"Very lively, so Barnaby tells me."

Diamond's thoughts were on the safari park at Longleat. Julie was quicker on the uptake.

"You mean the Lions who collect money for charities, like the Rotary?"

"Didn't I make it clear?" said Jessica, eyes twinkling.

"You said he got home late," said Diamond. "What's late?"

"Oh, God. I don't keep a stopwatch for him. After I was in bed. Toward midnight. You don't regard *him* as a suspect?"

"We're trying to fix some parameters, that's all," Diamond hedged.

She rolled her eyes. "Could you fix my wonky exhaust while you're at it?"

"So you have a car?" He wasn't so slow himself when an opening came.

"Of course I have a car. I'm running a business here. And in case you were about to ask, I didn't use it on Monday evening. I didn't need to. It's just a short walk to St. Michael's and back."

"Would you give me the make and number?"

She told him it was a new Peugeot 306. White. It seemed there was money in art, even in these straitened times. Or perhaps Barnaby Shaw was the provider.

"Your husband. Is he in business?"

"Houses." She paused, playing her game of letting the wrong assumption take root, only this time Diamond was more alert. He wasn't thrown when she held her thumb and forefinger about three inches apart. "This high. He makes miniature houses."

He smiled.

She said, "Gullible people buy them for exorbitant amounts. He does a police station with a blue lamp at fifty pounds, if you're interested."

Diamond was more interested in the way the pupils of Jessica Shaw's eyes reduced in size and the edge of her mouth turned down when her husband was mentioned. He said, "Maybe we should check your handbag now."

"What do you mean—*we*?" She got up and crossed the room to where a leather shoulder bag was hanging over a tall-backed chair. "I'm not having my personal objects pored over by policemen, thank you." She released the catch, felt inside and straightaway withdrew a folded brown paper bag. "This I have no further use for."

CHAPTER TWENTY-ONE

A MESSAGE WAS WAITING FOR DIAMOND WHEN HE RE-turned to Manvers Street after delivering Julie to the Royal United Hospital for the postmortem. Would he contact DCI Wigfull as a matter of urgency?

Generally he avoided the man. From experience, he was willing to bet that this was a gripe over areas of responsibility, but in a police station matters of urgency can't be side-stepped. He picked up the phone.

"Well, have you found your stamp thief?" he asked while Wigfull was still self-importantly giving his name.

"Is that DS Diamond?"

"Who else?"

"As a matter of fact, I have found him."

"And is he a dead man?"

Was it an intake of breath he heard, or the wind abandoning Wigfull's sails?

"You still there, John?" Diamond asked. "Was it Sid Towers?"

"What makes you think it might be?" Wigfull parried, the annoyance coming through clearly.

"Doesn't everything point to him?"

"I wouldn't have said so."

"So you nicked someone else, then?"

"I didn't say that."

"Aren't you going to say anything, John?"

"Has someone been talking to you?"

"No, I worked it out."

"Have you also worked out how he got into the locked room?" Wigfull asked more warily.

"No. Have you?"

A distinct note of self-congratulation crept in. "I believe so."

"You've cracked it? Nice work," Diamond, profoundly surprised, was gracious enough to say.

"That's why I asked you to get in touch," Wigfull said with more élan. "I'm here in my office with the Assistant Chief Constable, wrapping up my part of the case, so to speak. Why don't you join us?"

Mr. Musgrave was by common consent the most approachable of Avon and Somerset's three assistant chief constables. His florid countenance and portly shape attested to thousands of pints taken convivially with colleagues. A good listener, fair in his dealings and appreciative of jobs well done, Arnold Musgrave was the ideal man to have drop into the office at an auspicious moment.

When Diamond arrived, Wigfull was saying with the air of a man confident of a commendation at the very least, "I daresay you're familiar with the detective stories of John Dickson Carr, sir."

"I daresay I am." The ACC chanced his arm. "My failing is I read these things and don't recall who wrote them or what they were about." Spotting Diamond at the door, he gave a broad smile. "Peter! You're looking chipper."

"It's all show," said Diamond. "I'm up to my ears in problems. Unlike John Wigfull here."

"He's about to tell us how he solved the case of the stolen Penny Black."

"So I heard."

"Could ease a few of your problems, Peter."

"My fingers are crossed, sir."

Both looked expectantly toward Wigfull, who smirked, producing a confident upward twitch of the large mustache. "We were speaking of Dickson Carr," he said with a donnish air. "These detective writers of fifty years ago were expected to set puzzles for their readers, the sort of brainteaser you could do to while away a train journey as a change from the crossword, and Dickson Carr was one of the best of them. He still has a devoted following, I gather. His forte was the locked room puzzle."

"Then I must have read one of them at least," the ACC decided. "Mind, I couldn't give you a title for love nor money."

This didn't matter to Wigfull, into his flow now. "A strange experience for me, dealing with a case like this one, with the hallmarks of an old detective story—the cryptic rhymes, the ingenious theft, the locked room puzzle, and the closed circle of suspects. But I relished the challenge. Something out of the ordinary. Once I knew of the connection with this group of detective story readers, the Bloodhounds, who meet in the crypt of St. Michael's, I was able to concentrate my inquiries."

Mr. Musgrave nodded. "Piece of good fortune, John, having one of them come to you with the missing stamp."

Wigfull wasn't having that. "The thief didn't do me any favors. It was deliberate, sir. Part of the plot. The way I see it, he was poking fun at the police, trying to show us up as, er—"

"Bumbling idiots?"

"Er, less than efficient, anyway. He stole the stamp and then handed it back, as if to prove he'd been toying with us. It was sheer bloody arrogance, coming on top of the rhymes he broadcast to all and sundry."

"So you rose to the challenge?" said Mr. Musgrave. "Good man."

Diamond observed all this in a tactful silence. Mr. Musgrave's genial manner masked a sharp wit. He was leagues ahead of Wigfull.

"I realized it was no ordinary theft," said Wigfull.

"Well, you would," Mr. Musgrave amiably agreed.

"Exactly, sir. It *was* a theft, but it was also a stunt. And it could only have been planned by someone with inside information. The perpetrator had to know in advance that one of the Bloodhounds, Mr. Milo Motion, was going to bring his copy of *The Hollow Man* to the next meeting and read from it. They were due to discuss locked room mysteries, and Dickson Carr's book contains the famous chapter on the subject. That is to say, famous to people who still have an interest in such things." Wigfull gave a superior smile. He liked to project the image of a modern man, more excited by information superhighways than detective stories.

"The missing Penny Black cover was dramatically discovered at precisely that chapter in the book—just as Mr. Motion was about to read it aloud." Now Wigfull leaned forward, eyes gleaming. "In the classic tradition of the detective story, we had a closed circle of suspects and, even more intriguingly, a locked room puzzle of our own, because the book had been on the boat all week and the boat was kept locked. Naturally I interviewed Mr. Motion at length—to his credit, he came to us at once—and I satisfied myself that he was not the man we were looking for. What would have been the point—giving himself away? He was genuinely shocked, I'm certain, and at a loss to explain what had happened. He insisted that the boat was remarkably secure. Bolted inside at the prow and padlocked outside with this." Dramatically Wigfull produced a sturdy-looking padlock from his drawer and held it out for inspection like Houdini preparing to perform.

"Is that it?" asked the ACC. "The very one?"

"The very one, sir."

"May I see?"

Mr. Musgrave first felt the weight of the padlock in the palm of his hand and then turned it over. "Looks pretty solid. German-made?"

"Yes, sir. It's a heavy-duty padlock, all right. Bought from Foxton's, the best locksmith in the West Country. This is top-of-the-range equipment."

Mr. Musgrave turned to Diamond. "Care to examine it?"

"Thank you, sir, but I already have."

Wigfull took hold of the padlock again and gave a fair impression of a sales rep, pointing out its special features, stressing that each padlock sold was unlike any other. "They are supplied with two keys. Mr. Motion informed us that he accidentally dropped one of his in the canal some time ago. I have no reason to disbelieve him. So for all practical purposes, the remaining key is unique. Mr. Motion is adamant that it never left his possession. It was on the key ring that he carried in his pocket with his car keys. I have it here now. You see?" Wigfull produced a key about two centimeters long, inserted it into the slot, and turned it clockwise. The steel shackle sprang open. "You push the top down again, and it closes. Would you care to try it, sir?"

This whole presentation was so spirited that it would have been churlish to refuse. Obligingly Mr. Musgrave took the padlock and tried the mechanism.

"One key," reiterated Wigfull. "I myself watched Mr. Motion unlock the padlock on Monday night prior to discovering the body aboard the boat. I am perfectly satisfied that it was properly locked and that he opened it with this key from his pocket. Yet there was Sid Towers in the cabin, dead. The impossible crime."

At this point Diamond thought Wigfull was overegging the cake.

Mr. Musgrave said, "You must have considered the possibility that Motion left the boat earlier without securing the padlock?"

"Indeed, I did, sir. I questioned him closely. He insists that it was locked."

"What other explanation is there?"

"If you'll bear with me, I'm coming to that. He says he has

a clear memory of pressing the shackle home and rattling the padlock to make sure it was secure. After all, that boat is his home."

"You believe him?"

"I do, sir."

Diamond gave a nod. "He satisfied me, for what it's worth."

"All right," said Mr. Musgrave. "How was it done?"

Wigfull placed the padlock and key on his desk and pushed them aside as if they no longer mattered. "Most of my inquiries—and I dare say yours, Peter—have centered on the events of last Monday evening. Who had the opportunity and a reason to visit the narrowboat? But the point about the crime, the theft of the Penny Black, I mean, is that it happened the previous week. On the Thursday we had that erroneous tip-off from Bristol, and on the Friday the first of those rhyming riddles, and on the same morning the theft occurred." He raised a finger to give significance to his next statement. "The whole thing was planned ahead."

"Most crimes are, in my experience." Even Mr. Musgrave seemed to have decided that Wigfull's theatrical manner was starting to reek of ham.

"How right you are, sir, but I'm suggesting that this was intricately plotted. Dovetails, every part: the tip-off to Sergeant Plant; the riddles; the theft at the Postal Museum; and the planting of the stamp in Motion's book. It was a high-risk undertaking, and the planning was worthy of the SAS. And it worked like a dream. The thief always intended to return the stamp after making monkeys out of everybody—ourselves and the Bloodhounds."

"With some success."

"True. But let's concentrate on the locked room."

"Good idea."

"Chummy knew a week in advance—"

There were limits to Diamond's tolerance. "For Christ's

sake, John," he appealed to Wigfull. "Let's not call him 'Chummy.' We both agree Sid Towers is the man."

"Is he?" said Mr. Musgrave, showing more interest than he had for some minutes.

"He fits the frame, sir," said Diamond. "The silent man with a lot to prove to some of those motormouths in the Bloodhounds. Trained in security, so breaking into the Postal Museum wouldn't be such a problem. He'd know plenty about locks and bolts. An expert on Dickson Carr. And of course he was found in the boat. Either Towers or the killer must have found a way into that cabin, and the logic is that it was Towers and he was followed in there and killed. Agreed, John?"

Wigfull muttered his assent, peeved that Diamond had hijacked the narrative.

Mr. Musgrave said, "This is fine as far as it goes, but it's all circumstantial, isn't it?"

Keen as he was to lead the discussion again, Wigfull had no answer. He turned to Diamond.

"Everything I just mentioned is," Diamond admitted, and added, straight-faced, "unless Mr. Wigfull here has some evidence I'm not aware of."

Wigfull's eyes narrowed. The opportunity was there, and he still had nothing to say.

For Peter Diamond, the silence was as good as a fanfare. "In that case, I'd better show you mine," he announced. Resisting the flourish he might have made—there was no need—he took from his inside pocket the brown paper bag he had recovered from Jessica Shaw. He unfolded it. "This, gentlemen, was the bag Towers produced on Monday evening when Miss Chilmark was hyperventilating. I'm sure you heard about the incident. He handed the bag to Jessica Shaw, who knew what to do. She held it against Miss Chilmark's face and stopped the attack. Afterward, Mrs. Shaw kept the bag, in case of a recurrence. Miss Chilmark felt well enough to remain at the meeting, you see. In the confusion at the end,

Mrs. Shaw popped it into her handbag and forgot about it. I recovered it from her this afternoon."

"Is it important?" asked the ACC.

"The bag on its own is not, sir. But if you look at it . . ." Diamond smoothed the bag against the surface of Wigfull's desk and handed it to Mr. Musgrave.

"There's writing."

Wigfull got up and came around the desk to look. "May I see?"

"Doesn't make a lot of sense," said Mr. Musgrave.

There were three lists of words in rows, written in an untidy hand in black ballpoint:

JACK	LOTION	TOMB
FLAK	OCEAN	DOOM
KNACK	POTION	WHOM
MAC	NOTION	GLOOM
LACK	DEMOTION	BLOOM
SMACK	DEVOTION	
BACK		
CRACK		
SLACK		

"They rhyme," said Wigfull. "They're rhyming words."

"Take a little time over it," Diamond suggested, as if he were coaching a five-year-old in reading.

Mr. Musgrave said, "Looks to me as if he was working on a piece of verse."

"The very thing I was about to say, sir," said Wigfull.

"Do you think he was composing another riddle?" said Mr. Musgrave.

"Look at the middle row," Diamond gently nudged them on. "What else rhymes with 'lotion'?"

"These other words?" said Wigfull.

"Apart from those other words."

"Ha—you're ahead of us," said Mr. Musgrave. "Motion.

He wanted something to rhyme with Milo Motion. Good spotting, Peter. This does look like the notes for another cryptic riddle. So how about 'Jack'?"

"'Attack'? " suggested Wigfull, still thinking about hyperventilation, and in some danger of succumbing to it himself.

" 'Black,' " said Mr. Musgrave. "Penny Black."

Diamond gave a nod. "That's my best guess, sir."

"And 'tomb'?"

"Locked room," Diamond guessed again.

"I'll buy that. Ha. Neat. So Towers was jotting down words to make his next press release. This isn't absolute proof, of course, but I'm satisfied, Peter. You've linked him to the crime."

Wigfull straightened in his chair. "Why didn't you show it to me before?" he demanded in a high, aggrieved tone. "It's evidence."

He was answered first with a long look, and then: "I got it from Mrs. Shaw less than an hour ago."

"Then she was withholding evidence."

"A paper bag?"

"If it's written on . . ."

"She hadn't noticed. Anyway, she'd forgotten about it. It was still in her handbag."

"Are you sure she hadn't noticed the writing?"

"Even if she had, why should she have thought it important?"

"Crafty old sod," said Mr. Musgrave. But it was Sid Towers he was talking about, not Jessica Shaw. "What's the old saying? 'Who knows most, speaks least.' "

Some of the steam dispersed as they all thought about silent Sid, dismissed by most of the Bloodhounds as a nonentity. This, surely, was the proof that he had stolen the world's most valuable stamp and devised a locked room puzzle capable of baffling the best minds.

John Wigfull's mind excepted.

"You were going to tell us how it was done," Mr. Musgrave prompted him.

Wigfull had a mountain to climb after that revelation. You could almost sense the effort of lacing his boots again and pulling on the rucksack. "Yes, sir."

"You're not going to keep us in suspense, I hope."

"No, sir." Manfully, Wigfull started again. "The crime, as I was saying, was meticulously planned. Sid Towers must have been working on it for weeks, if not months. He needed to find a way of getting inside the narrowboat when Milo Motion wasn't present. He had an opportunity to see the *Mrs. Hudson* for himself the previous Christmas, when the Bloodhounds held their party there."

"Aboard the boat?" said Mr. Musgrave. "Good place for a party."

"I checked, and he was certainly there, in spite of being so shy. I picture him at the party unwilling to mix, moving about the boat, looking at things. It's probable, isn't it, that a professional security officer like Towers would take an interest in the locks and bolts? I reckon he noted the type of padlock at that early stage. No doubt he'd come across such locks before. Probably knew they were supplied by Foxton's. If not, it was easy to note the name of the manufacturer and find out who stocked them."

"What was the point?" Mr. Musgrave asked.

"An amazingly obvious one. No disrespect, sir. Most of these locked room puzzles are obvious when they're explained. I think he went to Foxton's and bought one of those German padlocks himself. He waited for his chance to make a substitution."

"Good. I'm with you."

"Exactly when he made the switch I can't be sure. May have been months ago, or as late as the meeting before last."

"Are you saying he changed over the padlocks at the Bloodhounds?"

"Not exactly, sir." With a startling sense of drama for such a prosaic man, Wigfull pictured the scene. "Motion takes off his coat and hangs it on one of the coathooks near the door. Towers chooses a suitable moment to go to the gents. On the way he dips into Motion's overcoat pocket and finds the bunch of keys. He removes Milo's padlock key from the ring and replaces it with one of his own that fits the new padlock. Returns the keys to the pocket."

"Now he can unlock the boat."

"Right, sir. He leaves before Motion and drives fast to the boatyard to make sure he gets down there first. With the old key he unlocks the original padlock and replaces it with the one he bought."

"And when Motion gets back to his boat he uses the key on his ring to let himself in."

"In the usual way," said Wigfull, "unaware that the switch has been made."

"Neat," said Mr. Musgrave. "I like it."

John Wigfull beamed. "And of course Sid Towers is now in possession of a spare key. He can visit the boat anytime he likes." He brought his hands together in a gesture of finality. Then in case it appeared he was applauding himself, he rubbed them vigorously as if using a drying machine in a public toilet.

"The locked room mystery solved," said Mr. Musgrave. "What do you say, Peter?"

Diamond digested what had been said and then gave a nod. "Full marks, John." He meant it sincerely. He was genuinely impressed. The explanation had no obvious flaw. "And the reason we didn't find the key on Towers's body is that the murderer must have taken it with him."

"Or her," Wigfull was quick to point out.

Mr. Musgrave said to Wigfull, "You'd already thought of that, I'm sure."

Wigfull smiled. He'd scaled his mountain and was on the summit posing for pictures.

Mr. Musgrave reached for the padlock again. "It doesn't

look as if it was bought recently," he said, turning it over in his hand.

Wigfull had an answer to that. "He'll have done what any forger of coins does—roughed it up a bit to take off the sheen. They stick them in a bag with other metal objects and shake them about. Sometimes they bury them. They soon look worn."

Diamond had never judged Wigfull as short in intelligence; it was the sense of humor that was lacking. This wasn't an occasion for sour grapes. The man had just made a crucial contribution to the case, to *his* case, as well as Wigfull's own. "Wish I'd thought of it," he admitted. "I didn't come near to working it out."

CHAPTER TWENTY-TWO

F OR JULIE'S BENEFIT, AS HE PUT IT, DIAMOND HAD BEEN over Wigfull's explanation of the locked boat mystery point by point, and they could find no flaw. The substituted padlock and key answered every problem.

Finally he said, "I'm thinking of handing the whole thing over to Wigfull."

Julie blinked and frowned. She had sacrificed her lunch hour attending the postmortem, an unsavory duty she shouldn't have been lumbered with, and now he hit her with this. "What do you mean? Let him take over the murder inquiry?"

"Locked rooms and cryptic rhymes. It isn't my scene, Julie. He's motoring through it. Firing on all cylinders while I'm . . . I'm stuck in the pits."

She stared across the office at the big man as he stood by the window watching the traffic in Manvers Street. "What does that make me—a worn tire?"

Diamond was not easy to work with, but his saving grace was a sense of humor. Such a remark would usually produce a smile, whatever the pressures he was under. This time he sighed. He had taken heavy punishment. Actually he wasn't indulging in self-pity; this was about confidence. At this minute he genuinely believed John Wigfull would make a better fist of the case than he could. The strongest comment Julie could find to add was, "If you do anything so dumb, I'll ask for a transfer."

He turned to look at her, eyes widening.

"We've put all that Dickson Carr stuff behind us," Julie insisted. "We're down to brute murder. Nothing unexpected came out of the postmortem. No unexplained injuries. He was bashed over the head a couple of times with some solid implement. That isn't exactly a master criminal at work."

This earned a glint of amusement.

She added, "And you said yourself that the locked room mystery isn't a mystery anymore."

"Thanks to Wigfull."

"All right, thanks to him. Is that important? What we're left with is a straightforward case of murder."

"About as straightforward as a plate of spaghetti."

Julie grinned and held out her hands in appeal. "Come on, you've got the tricky stuff out of the way. We know Sid Towers stole the Penny Black and wrote those rhymes. And incidentally, that was your persistence that gave us the proof, not John Wigfull's."

This tribute didn't register anything with Diamond.

Staunchly, Julie continued to put the case in its most promising perspective. "Sid thought up this brilliant plot and carried it out, and then he was killed. We've got to find the killer. Is it too much to believe that it was a casual murder?"

He said a flat "Yes."

"Then surely it must have been triggered by Sid's actions." She looked toward Diamond, inviting him to pick up the thread.

But he would not.

So she pressed on. "I'm suggesting that one of the Bloodhounds felt deeply angered or threatened by what happened at the meeting."

There was, at least, a response from Diamond, even if it was not helpful. "The stamp turning up in Milo's book?" he said in a hollow tone. "Where's the threat in that?"

Julie turned a shade more pink, not in reaction to Diamond's ill humor, but because a theory—a persuasive theory—was forming in her brain. "Let's not forget that the stamp is worth millions. Suppose Sid wasn't working alone. What if he had an accomplice?"

He gave her a look that was only a fraction less bleak.

She added, "And what if their plan was to demand a ransom for the stamp?"

"Then they fell out, you mean?"

"Exactly. It wasn't in the plan to return the stamp unless and until they got a thumping great payoff. But Sid wasn't the hard man he made himself out to be. He got nervous and decided to return the stamp. The accomplice would have been shocked and deeply angered when it turned up in the book as it did, without a penny changing hands. It's enough, isn't it, to provide a motive for murder?"

Diamond was less excited about the theory. "It would be, if you can believe Sid capable of teaming up with anyone. My judgment is that he was a loner. That flat of his, upstairs at the end of a cul-de-sac; the job, the night work, the shyness everyone mentions. I can't see a man like that confiding what he thinks of the bloody weather, so how does he get around to teaming up with a fellow criminal? Sorry, Julie. I don't buy it."

"Why was he killed, then? Can you think of a reason?"

If nothing else, her persistence finally nudged him out of that negative mood. His brown eyes held her for a moment, looked away, and then came back to her. "Could have been something he found out. I suppose if one of them—one of the Bloodhounds—had a dodgy past, a criminal record, say, a man in Sid's line of work might have got to hear about it. Have you checked their form?"

That evening, Bath's glitterati descended on the Walsingham Gallery in numbers. Jessica Shaw's private views were not usually so well patronized, but since the papers were full of the Narrowboat Murder and it was known that the victim had attended a Bloodhounds meeting the same evening and

Jessica was a member, the chance of some inside information was too good to miss. With luck, some of her fellow members would also be invited. There was even the thrilling possibility of rubbing shoulders with a murderer—for it was stated in the papers that everyone at Monday night's meeting in the crypt of St. Michael's had been interviewed by the police. So the buck's fizz flowed and the eyes darted eagerly about, looking not so much at the art as the other guests. As some wit pointed out, it would have assisted everyone if instead of using those little red stickers to mark paintings that were sold, Jessica had attached them to her Bloodhound friends.

The minute she arrived, Shirley-Ann heard an unmistakable voice declaring in syllables brought to perfection by generations of privilege that most of the art on display was absolute balls.

On tiptoe to see over the mass of expensively coiffed heads, she glimpsed a black beret and moved determinedly in that direction. Gratifyingly, Rupert recognized her at once. It didn't matter that he greeted her as "Sally-Ann"; the warmth was genuine. He introduced the people beside him in his own florid fashion.

"My dear, in my endless quest for culture I once located this unlikely duo in a watering hole in Bradford on Avon, of all places. Tonight I met them in the Saracen's, sinking one or two before the party. Stephen and Pat Volk. Stephen's a screenwriter and a crafty old fox, he won't mind me telling you. Remember that extraordinary hoax about psychic phenomena that went out on television one Halloween and petrified the nation? With Parkinson playing it straight as the presenter. What the devil was it called, Steve?"

"*Ghostwatch.*" The playwright, reassuringly substantial, broad of shoulder, scant of hair, and dressed entirely in black, with owlish glasses, seemed subdued by Rupert's eloquence, but who was not?

Almost by definition, the most brilliant hoaxers were going to be self-effacing, Shirley-Ann mused.

"'Heads must roll at the BBC!' Loved it," Rupert was

crowing. "And speaking of heads, this is Pat, who sculpts them. Marvelous, strong, archetypal heads in amazing colors. If you can force a way through this drunken mob, as you must, you'll see her work upstairs. I was on the point of telling her she's the only one of this lot I'd consider buying."

Pat Volk smiled wryly. Rupert might talk like a patron of the arts, but his scuffed leather jacket, patched jeans, and the black beret speckled with dandruff didn't inspire confidence. Shirley-Ann smiled back. It was about all anyone could do when Rupert was in full flow.

"Sally-Ann joined the Bloodhounds just as we all became suspects in a murder case," he continued, projecting loudly enough for all the room to hear. "She's incredibly well informed about detective stories. You could ask her anything at all and she'd know. Try her. Here's one at random. Name the poison Agatha Christie used most commonly in her books."

Shirley-Ann felt as if half the room had suspended conversation to hear the answer. "Cyanide?"

"I wouldn't know, my dear," said Rupert, displaying his gaps in a fiendish grin, "but I'm sure it's a splendidly efficient poison, quite impossible to trace in buck's fizz."

From somewhere to Shirley-Ann's left, a familiar voice spoke up. "Of course she's right. It occurs in fourteen of the books, twice as many as morphine, which comes second." Milo, back in circulation and seeming no worse for his skirmish with the police.

"Ah, perpetual Motion," said Rupert. "The man's unstoppable. Why don't you join us, Milo? Hit Sally-Ann with some really searching questions."

Shirley-Ann saw an opportunity and seized it. "If it doesn't seem frightfully rude, I forgot to pick up a catalogue." She turned her back and was away. Talking to strangers was preferable to that sort of embarrassment. How could she have been so misguided as to think Rupert was a safe haven?

She had not traveled far across the room when further progress was barred by a plate of canapés. Predictably, Jessica stood out from her guests in a gorgeous outfit, a shimmering black sequin jacket over a peacock-blue dress. "I was on my way to rescue you," she said. "That Rupert! Cyanide in the buck's fizz! Believe me, I won't be wasting good poison on him. I'll strangle him."

"At least he doesn't have the dog with him."

"I wouldn't count on it. Have one of these, and come and meet my husband."

The husband.

This was one encounter Shirley-Ann hadn't anticipated. She followed eagerly as Jessica crossed the room, greeting almost everyone by name, and finally turning to remark, "I won't inflict him on you for long. Anyway, he's supposed to be handling the sales. I don't know how much trade he's doing."

Jessica's way of introducing Barnaby, as he was called, was to wave the plate of canapés and speak their two names. Then she moved away. Barnaby, seated behind a table with an account book in front of him, was a tired-looking man of about forty-five with tinted brown hair and one of those dark blue suits with a broad white pinstripe that are worn by MPs on the far right of the Tory party. At his side, in charge of the cash-box, was A.J., of all people, and the two appeared relaxed with each other. She'd taken it as likely that A.J. was Jessica's secret lover. Maybe he was; if so, he was putting on a fine show of innocence, or Barnaby was astonishingly tolerant.

"Shirley-Ann and I met last week," A.J. informed Barnaby. "She set me straight on my leisure reading. No more graphic novels. I'm under orders to read the American female private eye from now on."

"I didn't say anything of the sort," Shirley-Ann protested.

Barnaby's eyes slipped away to another part of the room, absenting him from the conversation.

She drew him back in. "How's it going? Have you sold any?"

He nodded. "Three so far."

"Nothing of mine," said A.J., so egocentric that he was unaware whether anyone else really cared. "The only things that sell these days are insipid pen and ink drawings of the Royal Crescent."

"Three. Is that good?" Shirley-Ann asked Barnaby.

He gave a shrug.

A.J. answered for him. "The commission from three won't cover the cost of the party, but Barnaby doesn't mind. He isn't in this for the profit."

Barnaby became slightly more animated. "I'm not in it at all. It's Jessica's show, not mine."

"Your money, pal," said A.J.

The husband flapped his hand dismissively.

A.J. was determined to make his point. "I'm an old friend of these two, so I can say this. Without Barnaby there would have been no party tonight. The wretched artists of Bath would be deprived of all this. The whole point is that he isn't all that interested in art. He does it because he likes Jess to be happy. Isn't that terrific?"

Shirley-Ann said that it was. She hadn't detected a trace of sarcasm or irony in A.J.'s tribute. She was confused now. They truly were like old friends, and she was going to have to revise her theory about them. Her admiration for Jessica soared. It isn't unusual for a brilliant and beautiful woman to win the devotion of two men, but it takes exceptional talent to keep them on friendly terms with each other.

Someone from the press butted in, wanting to be introduced to one of the artists, allowing Shirley-Ann the opportunity to smile politely and move away. She took a glass of buck's fizz from a waitress and headed for the side of the room that wasn't being dominated by Rupert. Possibly she would find someone else she knew, though she doubted if it would be another of the Bloodhounds. Who was missing? Only Polly and Miss Chilmark. The frost between Jessica and Polly, though unexplained, was apparent. And Miss C., poor old duck, with her potential for apoplexy at the sight of Rupert, would be more of a liability than an asset.

She got into an amusing conversation with two sparky women who had gatecrashed. Neither knew anything about art. They were looking for two hunky men to invite them to a pub, or, better still, a restaurant, when the party was over. They weren't sure about Rupert. He was probably good for the invitation, they estimated, but not good for much else except brilliant conversation. And he didn't seem to have a friend. The girl talk might have continued for some time longer if Jessica hadn't appeared suddenly at Shirley-Ann's side. Her vivacious expression of minutes before was supplanted by a look of stark anger.

"Did you see it when you arrived?" she demanded of Shirley-Ann.

"Did I see what?"

"Outside, on the window. Come and look."

Jessica practically scythed a way through her guests to the door, with Shirley-Ann following apprehensively. Outside, in Northumberland Place, Barnaby and A.J. stood together examining the Walsingham Gallery window.

"What do you think?" demanded Jessica. "What scumbag could have done this to me?"

Shirley-Ann looked.

Someone had been busy with a spray can, writing a message in large, crude, white letters across the main window:

SHE DID FOR SID

There was a moment while Shirley-Ann absorbed the meaning of what was written. Then she said, "That's horrible." She was truly appalled and outraged on Jessica's behalf. "What kind of person does a thing like this?"

"A rat, not a person," said Jessica. "A stinking rat. To think that all my guests must have seen it when they arrived. And I, in all innocence, was greeting them inside. Barnaby, I'm nauseated."

"We'll clean it off," said A.J.

"I didn't notice it as I came in," said Shirley-Ann. "And nobody was talking about it. I think this must have been done after the party started."

"With the lighting as it is, you don't notice it from inside," said Barnaby, quick to chime in with the reassurance. "I couldn't tell you when it was done."

A.J. rubbed at one of the letters with his fingertip.

"Don't do that," said Jessica.

He said, "I'm just seeing if it's still wet."

"We don't want your fingerprints on it if we call the police."

"Is that what you want to do—call the police?" asked Barnaby. "Is that wise?"

"What do you mean—is it wise?"

"Jess, my dear, it's a rotten thing somebody has done, but it's hardly a serious matter in the eyes of the law."

"It's vile," said Jessica.

"Yes, it is, but you're not going to get much redress. In fact, it wouldn't surprise me if they took more interest in what's written here than in catching the bastard. It will bring you more grief than satisfaction. My advice is to rub the window clean and forget about this."

"Look," said A.J., "why don't you go back to your guests and leave this to me? I can clean it up before anyone else sees it."

She said through gritted teeth, "I want to know who did this. Someone must have seen."

"Not necessarily," said Barnaby. "It wouldn't take more than a few seconds with one of those cans. The writing is rough. It's obviously been done in haste."

Jessica turned to Shirley-Ann. "What's your opinion?"

A difficult one. "If it were me," she said after a moment's consideration, "I think I'd rather it was cleaned off now. It's going to ruin the party if you call the police. And it's bound to get in the papers."

Jessica sighed. "I can't win. All right. Rub it off."

CHAPTER TWENTY-THREE

J ULIE WAS KEEN FOR SOME HUMAN CONTACT AFTER HER LONG session with the Police National Computer. "Ready to demonstrate your sleuthing skills, Mr. Diamond? Let's match you against the PNC. Which one of the Bloodhounds has a police record?"

"Only one?"

"That's all."

"The fellow with the mean-streets dog. Rupert Darby."

She shrugged and smiled. "You could have saved me nearly two hours of eye strain. Two prison terms, of six months and eighteen months, for obtaining money by deception. Seven fines for drunkenness and one for indecency."

"When was this?" Diamond asked.

"The indecency?"

"No, the bird."

"In 1977 and 1983."

"Long time ago. What was the scam?"

"I don't know. The PNC doesn't go into the details."

"But you will, won't you, Julie? That's where the human brain scores over the computer."

"It isn't the brain," she said. "It's hard slog."

"Put a hard slogger on the job, then. Delegate, Julie. I do. And get the facts on the indecency, will you? That could mean anything from streaking at a test match to pissing in a shop doorway."

She didn't complain. She wouldn't have told Diamond, but she was encouraged that the murder inquiry was back on track.

Diamond was off on another tack. "Funny idea," he said, "calling a dog after a character in a book. We've got a cat—well, a kitten, really. Steph brought it home. Haven't thought of a name for it yet. I wouldn't call it Marlowe."

"That wouldn't do," Julie agreed. "Is it a tom?"

"Yes."

"You could call it Sherlock, or Wimsey, or Father Brown."

He pulled a face. "It'll let us know."

Sitting in bed, clutching a mug of cocoa, Shirley-Ann told Bert about the writing on the Walsingham Gallery window. And why shouldn't she? It wasn't as if she had been asked to keep the incident to herself, though she appreciated that the words had been cleaned off in the hope that no one else would find out. She always told Bert everything. It would have made her feel furtive not to have spoken to him.

"Who did it, then?" he asked, yawning. He was already horizontal, physically tired. So much of his day was spent doing sport that if the truth were told he wasn't much of a sport at night.

"Wrote the words on the window? I've no idea," said Shirley-Ann, with energy still to burn. Even the weekends were filled with football refereeing that tired Bert. "It could be anybody. Milo was at the party and so was Rupert, but I wouldn't read anything into that. It may have been done by someone who didn't come."

"Someone bitter about not being invited?"

"Well, yes."

"Who, for instance?"

"I didn't see Polly or Miss Chilmark there. I suppose either of them could have sneaked up and got busy with a spray can."

"Just out of spite?"

"I don't know them all that well, but I wouldn't put it past one of them. They're formidable ladies, those two. The only thing I doubt is whether they'd use that way to register a protest."

"It doesn't have to be one of the Bloodhounds," Bert pointed out.

"Do you think so?" Shirley-Ann said dubiously.

"It could be some artist with a grudge. Someone whose work wasn't included in the exhibition."

"I suppose that's possible," she admitted, disinclined as she was to look outside the Bloodhounds.

"Someone who knows about the Narrowboat Murder," said Bert. "The thing that was written *does* refer to the murder, doesn't it?"

"I'm sure it does."

"Plenty of people in Bath must have read the papers or seen something on TV. All the reports mentioned that the victim was at the Bloodhounds meeting earlier in the evening. Almost anyone could have linked Jessica to the murder."

"So?"

He said wearily, "So is there any point in trying to work it out?"

She was silent for a while. However, she remained sitting up, taking sips of the cocoa. Eventually she said, "Bert, do you think there's anything in it?"

Bert twitched. He had almost dozed off. "What?"

"I said, do you think there's anything in it? Is it possible that she did for Sid?"

"Who—Jessica?"

"Mm."

He said, "I'm pretty tired, you know."

"It isn't fair asking you," said Shirley-Ann, with more consideration. "You haven't met her, so how can you have an opinion?"

There was an ironic laugh from under the quilt. "You've told me enough about her. You never stop talking about that lot. If you want my opinion, yes, I think she's well capable of murder."

"You *do*? *Jessica*?"

"All she had to do was follow the bloke—what's his name?"

"Sid."

"Follow Sid after the meeting that night, catch him off guard, and crack him over the head with some heavy object. A woman could do that as well as a man if she crept up behind him."

"Why? Why would she do it?"

"Why would anyone do it? Nobody knows. All I'm saying is that she's as capable of clocking the bloke as anyone else. What age is she?"

"Around thirty, I'd guess."

"Well, I tell you this. Most of the women in my over-forties group tonight could lay a man out cold with a blow on the skull, no problem. I wouldn't like to tangle with some of them."

"But she liked Sid. She took him into the Moon and Sixpence a few times, she told me. She knew quite a bit about him, his job and everything. She said he had guts to come to the Bloodhounds. She admired him."

"That doesn't mean she's innocent. She had a high opinion of him, you're saying. She believed he was all right. That's exactly the sort of person who gets angry and homicidal when it turns out they were mistaken."

"I don't see Jessica like that at all, Bert. She isn't hot-headed."

"Ice-cool, is she?"

"She's well in control, anyway."

"Calculating?"

"Now you're twisting my words."

For a time, no more was said. Bert began to breathe more evenly, while Shirley-Ann weighed Jessica's capacity to kill. She finished her cocoa and put her Snow White mug on the bedside table. The clock showed it was past midnight. Bloody nuisance. Bert had really set her brain into overdrive, yet she needed her sleep in case she was offered another chance as tour guide in the morning. She spoke her thoughts aloud. "I suppose if she found out there was another side to him . . . if he wasn't the placid, unassuming bloke she took him for, and she caught him in the act of letting himself into Milo's boat—which meant that he, Sid, of all people, was the stamp thief—then she might have got mad with him, but I still don't see it. Not Jessica. She's too intelligent. She operates in far more subtle ways. No, the only way I see Jessica getting violent is if . . ." She caught her breath at the idea, at the same time bending her legs to her chest and clasping her hands around her knees. "That's it! They were in cahoots. They worked together. Are you listening, Bert? Jessica and Sid worked out this brilliant scheme to amaze the Bloodhounds. Sid was a security man, right? He knew how to beat the video cameras and special locks at the Postal Museum. And he had some way of getting into Milo's boat as well. I don't think he'd have done it by himself. It was Jessica who put him up to it. At those meetings at the Moon and Sixpence, they planned the Penny Black job. Sid's expertise and Jessica's intelligence—quite a combination. I reckon she made up those riddles. And together they devised a way of getting into Milo's narrowboat and placing the stamp in his copy of *The Hollow Man* so that it turned up at the meeting. Okay, what they did was dangerous and illegal, but they returned the stamp and they didn't expect anyone to work out how it was done. Only something went wrong. For some reason Sid decided to go back to the boat. Maybe he thought it was an opportunity to do some real burglary while Milo was talking to the police. Or he could have left some trace that he thought they were sure to find. Jessica was suspicious and followed him. She was furious. The perfect crime she'd planned was about to be undermined by Sid. She hit him over the head, locked him in, and left. That's it, Bert! . . . Bert, are you listening?"

She grabbed Bert's shoulder and gave him a shake. He had drifted into a shallow sleep and heard nothing. He said from a long way off, "Yes?"

"I said she did it, Bert. Jessica did for Sid."

"All right," muttered Bert apathetically.

"Only somebody worked it out and tried to make it public tonight. I wonder who."

"Who what?"

"Who sprayed the words over Jessica's gallery window."

"Someone with one of those aerosols, I expect," said Bert in an interval of clarity.

"Well, you don't have to tell me that," she said.

"Must have got some on their clothes," added Bert. "You can't use one of those things outdoors without some of the spray getting on your clothes." It was his last contribution that night.

She pondered that for a time. Then something stirred in her memory that would keep her awake another two hours. She pressed her hands to her face and said, "I thought it was dandruff. Well, would you ever?"

CHAPTER TWENTY-FOUR

S O COMPREHENSIVELY HAS BATH BEEN FACELIFTED IN THE last twenty years that it is quite a treat to discover streets that have escaped the restorers and stonewashers. One charmingly down-at-heel example is Hay Hill, north of the center, which is actually just a convenient shortcut from Lansdown Road to the Vineyards and the Paragon. A shortcut for pedestrians, that is to say, for no cars run through it. You know that Hay Hill will give some relief from Georgian formality as soon as you reach the betting office on the corner of Lansdown Road. A strip of worn paving descends between undistinguished eighteenth-century artisan houses. The dozen or so dwellings are irregular in style, height, and coloring, and the railings fronting most of them supply only a semblance of order. The rest of the ironwork on view—basement grills, inspection covers, lampposts, and drainpipes—is a hotchpotch. Few of the windows match in style; in fact, some have been bricked up. Here and there graffiti scar the walls, but it might be argued that the people who painted one of the buildings in layers of pink, yellow, and brown, like a monstrous cake, were guilty of vandalism before the marker pen writers got to work.

To Hay Hill, then, came Diamond and Julie Hargreaves the next morning to call on Rupert Darby. Rupert's house was the one with more flake and crumble than any other, and with weeds growing up the walls.

The bell push on the door may have been working; it was difficult to hear for the noise of traffic cruising down Lansdown Road. Anyway, there was no response. Diamond tried rattling the letter flap and instantly wished he hadn't. It was a plastic thing that fell off. A low, vibrating noise like a power drill driving into wood came from inside. As he bent to look through the gap there was an almighty thump against the door, and he found himself inches from the bared teeth of a large dog.

He stepped back and turned his attention to the window, which was coated in dust. A faded gingham curtain blocked any view of the interior. After some unproductive tapping on the glass—the main panel had a crack the width of the frame—he went back to the door, tried the handle, and discovered that it opened.

Julie warned, "I wouldn't if I were you."

But he had a confident way with dogs. Opening the door a fraction, he presented the back of his right hand for inspection. There was some sniffing, some contact with a moist nose, and then a reassuring warm lick. He increased the gap just enough for Marlowe's brown head to look out. With German shepherd in its genes, this beast wasn't going to roll over and have its chest scratched, but it had quit growling.

"Show him your hand, Julie."

This sounded like an order. He thought of adding, "Trust me," but he wasn't certain she would take encouragement from that.

She had two dogs of her own, and she knew enough to be cautious in a situation like this. After some hesitation she did as Diamond had done. There was no rending of flesh. By degrees Diamond opened the door fully, and Marlowe padded out to the pavement. The big dog didn't growl anymore, but neither did it make any concessions to friendship. It sniffed at their shoes, circled them, trotted to the house opposite, and sprayed the neighbors' wall. Diamond took this as approval. He stepped through the open door.

A first impression of the interior was that this place was more of a crash pad than a home. It smelled of stale beer and old socks and dog. The board floor was littered with clothes, books, papers, crockery, beer cans, and cardboard boxes. In the far corner was a mattress, and on it a body was lying covered by an army greatcoat.

Julie went to the window to admit more light. Dust peppered her hands when she tugged at the curtain. It hadn't been disturbed in months.

The body under the greatcoat spoke. A voice as mellifluous as Gielgud's, totally out of keeping with the surroundings, told them, "Please go away, whoever you are, and try again at some civilized hour."

Diamond said, "It's gone ten, Mr. Darby, and we're the police."

Marlowe heard his master's voice and lolloped in from the street. Picking up a tin plate between his teeth, the big dog carried it across the room, leaped on the mattress, and put in a claim for breakfast. There was a clang as the plate struck Rupert's head.

Rupert misinterpreted the knock. "I can report you for this," he said without stirring. "It's police brutality, and it's outrageous."

"It's your dog," Diamond told him. "It's asking for food."

"The hell with it. What's a dog for, if it doesn't keep the fuzz from marching into one's home?"

"Do you want us to feed it while you wash?"

"If you can find one of his cans. There might be some under the window." Rupert gave a moan and stretched. One of his feet, wearing a striped sock, appeared from under the greatcoat. He propped himself up on one elbow, rubbed his eyes, and said, "Is it the state of my head, or is one of you wearing a skirt?"

Diamond formally spoke their ranks and names. Expecting the usual snide remarks about female cops, Julie busied herself locating some tins of Pal under a beret and opening one for Marlowe.

Rupert was too sleepy for snide remarks. He needed all his concentration to stand up. His night attire (and no doubt the basis of his day attire also) was a T-shirt and boxer shorts. He tottered to an open doorway that must have led to whatever passed for a bathroom in this unedifying setup.

Diamond warned him, "We haven't got all day."

Rupert riposted over the sound of running water, "My day doesn't start till noon."

He emerged after a few minutes wrapped in a gray blanket and cradling a mug of coffee. "I'd offer you some, but I can't find a spare cup. You're welcome to look if you wish."

Diamond spoke for them both. "I don't think we want any. What we'd appreciate is a place to sit down."

Two chairs had to be cleared of the items heaped on them. Rupert found his beret and jammed it on his head. Apparently it was a vital accessory, though like everything else in this place it looked shabby, speckled with white particles that he didn't bother to brush off. He squatted on his mattress wrapped in the blanket, looking like an exotic species of toadstool.

"Convenient place you have here," Diamond said politely, since there was nothing polite he could say about the way it looked.

"You mean with the Lansdown Arms at one end and the Paragon Bar and Bistro at the other?" said Rupert, with a grin. "Yes, that was a consideration, I admit. Tell me what this is about."

"We're inquiring into the death of Sidney Towers."

His face lit up. "Thank God for that. I thought it was something I'd done."

"Isn't it?" said Diamond.

"Certainly not." The shrill note in his voice made it sound as if he were the last person you ought to suspect of anything.

"You're one of this group who call themselves Blood-hounds, right?"

"That's no crime, is it?" said Rupert, now ready to defend his reputation. "Well, the name may be a crime, I grant you. A gift for the gutter press. It wasn't my suggestion, officer. If I had my way, we'd call it the Crime Noir Club and attract a different class of member."

"When did you join?"

"At least three years ago. I think only Polly Wycherley and Milo were ahead of me. No, I tell a lie. The Grand Duchess was already in."

"You must mean Miss Chilmark."

He smiled. "She who must be indulged."

"And Sid?"

"Joined six months after me, though you would hardly have noticed. He made being inconspicuous into an art form."

"You don't sound all that enamored of the other members, Mr. Darby, yet you stuck with the club. Why?"

"Oh, it gets me out of my local for a couple of hours." Rupert gave his smile that resembled a country churchyard. "And I have a mission. I want to persuade those poor, blink-ered bastards to read some books that deal with the real crimes of our time and the misery and despair that they en-gender. You can't make converts overnight. They're fixated by ancient puzzle stories with maps in the front and snobbish characters suffering from xenophobia."

"What's that?"

Julie murmured, "Hatred of foreigners."

Rupert went on. "And they also talk endlessly about timetables." Without more preamble, he launched into an ex-traordinary monologue. " 'By your leave, my lord,' declared the inspector, with a deferential cough. 'There is only one possible killer. He left here at seven ten and got to the station by seven fourteen to catch the seven fifteen, but the seven fif-teen was delayed because of the fog, and the first train in was the seven seven, running twelve minutes later. On the seven fifteen, which actually arrived at seven thirty-two, he would have missed his connection at seven twenty-seven, but the seven seven got him to Crewe by seven twenty-five, and he caught the seven twenty-seven and was in Little Fartington precisely at eight.' " Rupert paused and grinned wickedly. " 'Or so he believed. Actually it was still only seven o'clock. He knew how to use a timetable, but *he didn't know about British Summer Time,* so the murderer has to be the German, Herr Von Krapp.' "

This earned some genuine laughter. "Did you make that up, or was it done from memory?" Diamond asked.

"I'm still pissed from last night," Rupert said, without answering the question. "My point is that these people know nothing of real crime."

"And you're well qualified to tutor them."

Diamond got a sharp look for that. "If you mean that I read books that give it to you straight," said Rupert, "with the smell of blood and the pain and the suffering, yes."

Tempting as it was to go into Rupert's criminal record, Diamond held off. At this stage he needed the man in good humor. "Tell me about the meeting last Monday," he said. "You were late, I believe."

"Very likely," said Rupert airily. "I'm not much of a time-keeper. When I got there, Marlowe—that's my dog"—Marlowe lifted his head from the plate of Pal and looked around—"Marlowe happened to go in ahead of me. He likes the meetings. As far as I can gather, the poor animal—who's just an overgrown puppy—well, look at him—unwittingly caused a panic by showing affection to that old bat, Miss Chilmark. I don't know why. She's never done a blessed thing to deserve a friendly lick from Marlowe or anyone else, for that matter. A more disagreeable old crone would be hard to find. When I got in, she was acting up, making a big production number out of it and having hysterics. It took a bag over her face to calm her down. Thank God for Jessica. Jessica Shaw."

"We know Mrs. Shaw," said Diamond.

"Capable woman. I didn't see the end of this performance. I had to take Marlowe next door to the Saracen's Head and settle him there with some drinking chums of mine. Of course he was no trouble at all. When I got back to the crypt, order was restored. Well, of course it was. Milady manufactured the whole melodrama so that she should have her way. You should have seen the triumphant look she gave me."

"And then?"

"Oh, the new woman read us a short story."

"The new woman?"

"Shirley-Ann Miller," said Julie.

"Is that her name?" said Rupert. "I never discovered. She joined a couple of weeks ago." He chuckled. "And regrets it now, no doubt. As I was saying, she read us something by Stanley Ellin, an American with a nice gift for the macabre. After that, I made some innocent remark that Polly took personally, silly old coot. They're such wimps, these people. What's wrong with some lively confrontation? Milo attempted to calm us down with his piece on the locked room puzzle. We all resigned ourselves to being bored out of our skulls for the rest of the evening—well, *I* did—and then, of course, he gobsmacked us all by opening his book and finding the bloody stamp."

"Good. I'd like to hear more about that," said Diamond. "Can you remember what was said?"

"Give me a break; I'm barely awake yet!" He took a sip of coffee. "As far as I recollect, Milo went crimson and kept saying what happened was impossible. I found it excruciatingly funny and said so. I remember trying to rib Milo about it, but he was far too shaken to take a joke. His first comment was that one of us must have planted the stamp on him somehow. Then he backtracked a bit. After all, whoever pinched it in the first place had committed a serious crime. Milo had to admit that he hadn't let the book leave his hands, not even when Miss Chilmark was throwing her tantrum. So without a clue as to how the thing was done, we got around to talking about what to do next. Polly—our top banana—said firmly that Milo should go straight to the police."

"Polly made this suggestion?"

"Yes."

"You're sure?"

"Yes, Polly. Does that remove her from your list of suspects? Have you met her?"

"Not yet," said Diamond.

"Watch her eyes when she smiles. They don't change at all. But Milo was reluctant to throw himself on the mercy of the Old Bill. He expected a workover from you people. Well, he's more fruit than vegetable, isn't he? I'm sure you treated him with the utmost consideration, but there was solidarity from some of us. I was willing to keep quiet, and said so. So was Jessica. As for the new woman, Sally . . . ?"

"Shirley-Ann."

"Thank you. I may be muddled about the name, but I've got her number all right: the sort of bright-eyed little body who wears a knitted hat and knows about homeopathy. She suggested he send the stamp back by post. Good thinking. He might have got away with that. The trouble was, as Jessica pointed out, we all had to agree to button our lips, and two of the company weren't willing to do that."

"Polly and who else?"

"Who do you think?"

"Miss Chilmark?" said Diamond.

"Right. The Grand Duchess."

"How about Sid? Did anyone ask him?"

"Yes. He said he could stay quiet." Rupert threw back his head and guffawed. "Sid offering to stay quiet! It was the funniest thing all evening. He should have taken a bow for that. None of them saw the joke except me. So there it was. Two in favor of blowing the whistle and four against. But of course, to work, the vote had to be unanimous. Milo isn't slow on the uptake. He could see that. He marched off to do his duty as a responsible member of the public."

"Leaving the rest of you to talk it over?"

Rupert shook his head. "There was no more talk, squire. The meeting broke up. I've no idea what time it was."

"Eight forty-five, I was told," said Diamond. "What did you do?"

"Went into the Saracen's to collect my dog."

"Who with?"

"No one. We all went our different ways. I may have had one drink. I wasn't there long. I rescued Marlowe and took him for a walk. The poor old tyke was bursting. Some people's idea of fun is tanking up my dog with Guinness."

"So where did he lift his leg?"

"That is rather personal, isn't it? Along the riverbank."

"And then did you come back here?"

"Yes. I needed to eat by then."

"Can anyone vouch for your movements?"

"I can."

"I mean an independent witness, Mr. Darby."

"No one I can think of. Look, you don't seriously suspect—"

"Have you got wheels?"

"What?"

"Wheels. A car."

"Now, come on," said Rupert, drawing the blanket closer around him.

"Have you?"

He sighed. "An ancient Lada that I keep in Beehive Yard by special arrangement with a drinking chum who has a business down there. I suppose you'd like to know if it's taxed and insured."

"No," said Diamond. "I'd like to know if you used it last Monday evening."

"Absolutely not, seeing that the tax ran out in August."

"Would that stop you?"

Rupert wasn't meant to respond, and didn't. Most of the

questions he couldn't have answered more directly, thanks to the conditioning of his education. He was a pushover, the type of suspect Diamond generally found easy to entrap—when there was anything inconsistent. There was the police record with this one, too. Yet he was a fellow who made you smile, even when he was on the defensive. His comments on the other Bloodhounds had brought them vividly to life. It would be almost a pity to put the boot in.

"Fair enough," said Diamond. "Let's talk about Sid Towers."

"There isn't much to say, is there?"

"Did you ever meet him in any other place than the crypt of St. Michael's?"

"You mean the pub afterward?"

"I mean anywhere at all."

Rupert closed his eyes in thought. "Aboard Milo's boat last Christmas. The Bloodhounds' party. Sid was there, trying to merge with the woodwork."

"Nowhere else?"

"Can't remember an occasion."

"Perhaps he was in touch some other way," suggested Diamond. "A letter?"

"The phone?" Julie contributed.

"What on earth about?" asked Rupert, his gaze moving suspiciously from Diamond to Julie. "He and I had practically nothing in common."

Diamond couldn't hold off any longer. He'd kept the goodwill flowing past the point when it was still productive. His voice took on a harder tone. "I have to think of every possibility, Mr. Darby. Let's face facts. Sid worked with a security firm. They keep files on people. I want to know if he got nasty with you. Demanded money in return for his silence over your prison record."

A muscle twitched in Rupert's cheek.

"You wouldn't want your literary friends to know you've done bird, would you?" Diamond pressed him. "Obtaining money by deception. Twice. And the other convictions aren't too edifying. How many fines is it for drunkenness? Indecency? What are you—a flasher? What would Miss Chilmark say about that if she found out?"

"She wouldn't say a word. She'd be hyperventilating again," said Rupert, buying time with an easy jibe. There was a pause while he adjusted mentally. Then: "If you want to know, it was a joke that misfired. I was up for the fifth time before Bath Magistrates on a drunk and disorderly charge and it was December twenty-third. After the beak fined me fifty quid I lowered my trousers and treated him to a view of my backside with the words MERRY CHRISTMAS stuck to it. It was a paper decoration off a Christmas cake. I was done for contempt of court and indecency. 'Pull up your trousers and face the bench, Mr. Darby. You may have thought that seasonal goodwill justifies some leniency over this disgusting exhibition, but the law is not to be mocked. You are fined one hundred pounds for the contempt, and a conviction for indecency will be entered on your record. Merry Christmas to you, too, and, let us hope, a sober New Year.' "

Diamond wasn't smiling. His disappointment was crushing; after Julie's work on the PNC he'd really thought he had a handle on Rupert Darby. The blackmail theory had just sunk like a punctured balloon. The man wasn't a sexual deviant. He was a clown. A couple of prison terms for fraudulent deals weren't going to worry an extrovert like this.

He turned to Julie and told her they were leaving.

They passed St. Michael's as they returned down Broad Street. Diamond decided to look into the crypt. "It's where the bloody thing started, Julie. And the way things are going, we'd better send up a prayer while we're there."

Inside, a playgroup had taken over for the morning. While three-year-olds were squabbling over wooden trains it was difficult to picture the Bloodhounds in session discussing locked room murders. The woman in charge was monopolized by a tearful girl who wouldn't budge from her lap, so Diamond sorted the problem of the boys and the trains. It was a wonder to Julie that his bulk and his gruff manner didn't frighten children. She'd seen plenty of adults in awe of him. The reason seemed to be that he didn't patronize kids; he listened to them solemnly and talked back to them with sincerity. He'd told her once that his wife, Stephanie, had miscarried several times. He'd said nothing else.

Now that harmony was restored, they looked at the layout of the crypt. There was a row of hooks near the door. The playgroup supervisor had her coat hanging there, and beside it, the children's tiny garments with gloves attached to elastic and dangling from the sleeves.

"This, presumably, is where Sid Towers switched Milo Motion's keys," said Diamond. "Fished the bunch out of his coat pocket, slipped the original off the key ring and replaced it with a key he'd bought from Foxton's. He could turn his back to the circle of chairs and make the switch without being seen. Simple."

"The quiet man. Everyone underestimated him," said Julie.

"Except wily John Wigfull."

She smiled. "That really irks, doesn't it?"

He nodded. "But I blame myself."

Back at Manvers Street, there was a message asking Diamond to contact PC Hogarth.

"Who's he?"

"I thought you knew, sir," said the woman who had taken the call. "He seemed to know you."

"Where was he calling from?"

"I'm afraid he didn't say."

"What was it about?"

"He wanted to speak to you personally."

"Well, that's a fat lot of use. He isn't one of my detectives, I can tell you that."

Julie hadn't heard of the man either.

It was another hour before PC Hogarth called in again. "He said he's down at Avoncliff, sir," said the woman from the wireless room.

"Avoncliff? Avoncliff?" A lightbulb switched on in his head. "Jesus Christ. The divers."

CHAPTER TWENTY-FIVE

WITHOUT LOOKING UP, JULIE WAS AWARE OF SOMEONE in a brown suit, carrying a tray. She was sure from the way he was moving steadily between the tables in the police canteen that he would come to hers. Her first impulse was to leave, but she still had most of her lunch in front of her. Although she rarely ate much at this time—today's meal was just a tuna salad and some yogurt—she knew some food was essential to get her through the afternoon.

"You don't mind?" John Wigfull said, as he pulled out a chair.

She minded, but she knew he wouldn't go away whatever she replied. A grin like broken glass was spread under that great broom of a mustache. He wasted no time over pleasantries. "I hear your boss goofed over the divers, poor blighters. What was that old catchphrase: 'Don't forget the diver'?"

"There was never any question of forgetting them." Julie found herself distorting the truth in defense of Diamond. "It was always going to be a long job."

"A soul-destroying job, I should think. Not even a proper diving assignment. It's only a few feet deep at the most. More like wading than diving. They weren't too thrilled, I was told."

"Really?"

"It's a bit much, being left that long."

"They were just getting on with the job, I expect," she said casually. "They didn't want one of us standing over them."

"You're very loyal, Julie. Always have been."

She forked some food into her mouth.

He didn't hand out compliments without wanting some return on them. The pumping started. "How's it going? Is he getting anywhere with the murder?"

She answered with as much conviction as she could muster. "We're following several leads."

Wigfull allowed that claim to wither and die in silence.

"Personally," he said finally, "I'd have handled it differently."

"Oh, yes?"

"I'd have given you more freedom to act. He doesn't delegate, does he?"

"If you don't mind, it's no business of mine to discuss Mr. Diamond's handling of the case," she was quick to tell him.

"Yes, but what's your part in the investigation? Sitting in front of the PNC. Don't deny it. I saw you yesterday. You should be out conducting interviews, not stuck in front of a ruddy screen by the hour. That's a sure way to get a headache."

She couldn't resist saying, "I thought you were all in favor of information technology, Mr. Wigfull."

He swayed to one side, as if riding a blow. He was still cockahoop over Diamond's lapse. "You can say that again, Julie, but I wouldn't put my best DI on the job. We employ civilians to operate the hardware. Whose form were you checking? One of the Bloodhounds?"

"It was just routine," she said, fencing as well as she could.

"Leaving no stone unturned, eh?"

"Well . . ."

He followed up quickly. "The divers will vouch for that, poor buggers. They must have run out of stones to turn over."

This amused him vastly. The whole table shook, and he spilled some of his coffee.

Julie remained impassive.

He went on to say, "He isn't a team man, is he? If you worked for me—"

"But I don't," Julie cut in, wanting to put a quick end to this.

"Anytime you'd care to . . ."

"Thanks," she said in a tone that made clear how unwelcome the prospect was.

Now the offer turned into a threat. "It could happen sooner than you think. I sorted the stamp theft, didn't I? Proved that Towers was the man and showed how he did it. That didn't go unnoticed. Someone's going to give me a crack at the murder soon. They want a result."

End of commercial. The talk turned to performance-related pay. Wigfull was one of the few at Manvers Street in favor of it. He had nothing to fear from appraisals, he said.

When she finished and was carrying her tray back to the collection point, Wigfull called after her.

She turned. "Yes?"

"Tell your boss."

"Tell him what?"

"What I said: 'Don't forget the diver.' "

That afternoon there was some rare autumn sunshine, and Shirley-Ann Miller took a slow stroll through Sydney Gardens and along the canal towpath. In the winter months this is a part of the city where you may walk for stretches without seeing anyone, yet once it was the fashionable place to be and be seen, a park you paid an entrance fee to visit, with a bandstand, grottoes, a labyrinth, and regular firework displays. It was all so cherished by the Georgians and Victorians that when the canal builders and railway engineers wanted to cut through, elaborate measures were insisted upon to disguise the construction. So there are tunnels, balustrades, and wrought iron bridges that are a credit to the planners, though rarely seen by modern visitors. Shirley-Ann was not the sort who looked for solitude, but after a morning doing her damnedest to hand out leaflets about the bus tour and getting not much response and a couple of vulgar suggestions, she wanted a break from people.

She had decided to walk as far as Top Lock, along the last, spectacular section of the canal before it joins the Avon. Here, after a wooded stretch, you suddenly look right and become aware that you are on an escarpment above most of the city except the church spires. That view always lifted Shirley-Ann's spirits. This lunchtime she would walk as far as the lockkeeper's cottage, a small gothic building of great charm restored by the Canal Trust—in no way as notable or noble as the sights she pointed out when she was giving her commentary on the bus, but pleasing to Shirley-Ann because she thought of it as a personal discovery. Today, however, she was distracted along the way by a discovery of a different kind. At Sydney Wharf Bridge, where George Street crosses the canal, the towpath switches sides. She climbed the cobbled slope on one side and passed over the bridge to rejoin the path by way of the descending steps by the Mercedes-Benz showroom. Her view of the towpath was hidden until she stepped onto it—which was why she was surprised by the man and woman coming towards her. She felt herself blush scarlet. The woman was Jessica Shaw.

Jessica, the murderer.

She did for Sid.

After the long, sleepless night when her mind had fizzed with the facts that pointed to Jessica's guilt, this was the last person on earth Shirley-Ann wished to meet.

Worse still, the man was A.J. Meeting Jessica at all was rotten luck; catching her out with her fancy man was a double blow from the fates. Of course she'd been sure in her mind that Jessica had something going with A.J., but up to now the liaison hadn't been paraded in front of her.

On the narrow towpath she couldn't avoid them without making it obvious.

They weren't actually arm in arm or holding hands, but so close to each other that they were practically in contact. Recognizing her, they broke off the earnest conversation they were having. Jessica said, probably in case A.J. hadn't spotted who it was, "Shirley-Ann, what a nice surprise."

A.J. half-lifted his hand in greeting and said, "Small world."

Shirley-Ann couldn't have felt more embarrassed if she had caught them in bed. She managed to say, "Isn't this a treat? The weather, I mean."

"Glorious." Jessica seemed unfazed. In a short, wine-red padded coat trimmed with black fur, and with black leggings and ankle boots, she looked more suitably kitted for the cat-walk than the towpath.

Since the weather hadn't yielded much in the way of conversation, Shirley-Ann remarked, "I passed some swans back there. A pair, with their family. At least five cygnets. Fairly grown-up, but really sweet."

"I expect we'll see them, then," said Jessica.

"They're worth looking out for, and the place is easy to spot. There's some pampas grass and a little wild area where they nest. They mate for life, don't they?" *Dear God,* she thought, *what am I saying?*

"I've no idea," said Jessica evenly.

"Nor me," said A.J.

Words, words in profusion, were Shirley-Ann's instinctive means of dealing with embarrassment. She had a horror of silences. She had to communicate something to get her over the mating-swans gaffe. "By the way, I did enjoy the preview last night. A party like that must have cost you an arm and a leg—all the buck's fizz and the refreshments. It seemed as if the whole of Bath had crowded in there. I hope you sold lots of pictures."

"We just about covered our costs," said Jessica. "An

evening like that isn't only about the money you take. It's a way of spreading the word."

"PR," said A.J.

Jessica added, "Most of them there last night have never bought a piece of work from the gallery and never will, but that isn't the point."

"I understand."

"It was a near-disaster, actually," she went on. "I'm still hopping mad about that vile thing that was written on the gallery window."

"We've dismissed that," said A.J. quickly. "We agreed to erase it from our minds, didn't we?" He was addressing Shirley-Ann now.

"Absolutely," she confirmed with all the conviction she could summon up, considering she had thought about little else since the party.

Jessica said, "I'd like to know who it was. I've got my suspicions."

"Let go, Jess," A.J. urged her, talking like a husband.

"If that's their game, they could try again."

"It was a prank," said A.J. "Someone with a warped sense of humor. You don't think anyone could seriously suspect you of murder? I mean, you had a lot of time for the bloke who was killed. He was a bit of a loner, you told me, lacking in confidence. You took him under your wing."

Took him under your wing and used him to pinch the Penny Black, thought Shirley-Ann cynically. Then clobbered the poor beggar because he stepped out of line and put the plot at risk. She was finding it a great test to keep her conclusions to herself.

"That isn't the point," said Jessica. "We all know I wouldn't have harmed Sid in a million years, but if this evil-minded bastard points the finger at me again, I'm going to the police."

"He won't," said A.J.

"How do you know it wasn't a woman?" Jessica demanded, and Shirley-Ann, with her weakness for speaking first and thinking afterward, almost told her why.

A.J. grinned, and said, "Fair point, but I'm sure it's a closed book now. Hadn't we better get back and open the gallery?"

They moved on.

Shirley-Ann's thoughts were in ferment again as she continued toward Top Lock. She didn't give a thought to the marvelous view or the cottage. She was puzzled over the relationship between those two. Was it the modern morality that had stopped them from showing any embarrassment at being seen in each other's company? True, she had seen them together before, in the gallery, but this was something else, surely, being met along a secluded towpath. It was evident to anyone that they knew each other extremely well, almost like brother and sister. Yes, that was *exactly* the feeling she got from them, an intimacy that didn't give rise to shame.

Up to now Shirley-Ann had always believed she could tell if a woman was concealing a relationship. She'd spotted the signs quite early in several of her married friends. This was baffling, because there was no suggestion of concealment. In A.J.'s company, Jessica behaved as if she had every right to spend major time alone with him.

And there was still a huge question in Shirley-Ann's mind. Where did Sid Towers fit into this ménage? To plot the theft of the Penny Black, there must have been meetings with Sid, long meetings to work on the details of an intricate plot. They must have cased the Postal Museum and talked over ways of gaining entry. They must have worked out their diversionary tactics, the riddles, and how to publicize them. There was the challenge—still a mystery to Shirley-Ann—of getting into Milo's locked boat. All of this must have been talked through by Sid and Jessica. Long sessions, debating ways of carrying out such an elaborate plot. How had Jessica achieved this without alerting A.J. or her husband? Or was either of them involved as well?

She walked on, unenlightened.

*　　*　　*

"He said what?"

Julie repeated the phrase for Diamond's benefit. " 'Don't forget the diver.' "

"Ah."

"His idea of a joke."

"It's one of those radio catchphrases, if I'm not mistaken. When I was a kid we listened to the radio a lot." He eased back in his chair, ready to reminisce, surprisingly untroubled by Wigfull's barbed message. "I enjoyed them. *Ray's a Laugh, Take it from Here, Educating Archie,* and, of course, *The Goons.* The characters had their set phrases. All they had to do was repeat them each week, and the audience would be rolling in the aisles. And applauding." He smiled. "Mind, 'Don't forget the diver' was before my time or Wigfull's."

"I should hope so," said Julie. "I looked it up. It goes back to the nineteen twenties."

"The *twenties*?"

"It seems there was a one-legged man who used to dive off the pier for pennies at New Brighton. It was his catchphrase in the first place. Then it was taken up by Tommy Handley during the war."

"That would be *ITMA*."

"Yes."

"I don't remember *ITMA* either," said Diamond. "Did John have any other gags to share with you?"

"That was the only one," said Julie. Truth to tell, she'd thought twice about passing that one on, but it was obvious that something had put her boss into a sunny mood. When she'd walked into his office he'd been humming "Yellow Submarine." "No, there was another joke," she said, "but it was unintended. He expects to take over the case."

He chuckled. "I've heard that one before, too."

"Once he did take over," she reminded him.

"Only after I resigned. It's not going to happen again." He opened the drawer in front of him, and took out a rusty object and let it fall on the desk with a metallic clunk. "Keys, Julie. A bunch of keys. The reason those divers got in touch was that they'd finished the job."

"Those are . . . ?"

"The keys Milo Motion dropped into the canal."

"Brilliant." She understood his singing now. "So now we know Milo was telling the truth about where he lost them."

"Yes. Only there's more to it than that." He took a padlock from the same desk drawer. "This is the one that was on the door of the *Mrs. Hudson* on the evening Sid Towers was found dead. Watch."

He picked up the bunch of keys and selected one, and a powdering of rust dropped on to the desk. He inserted the key into the lock and turned it. The shackle sprang open. Still holding the padlock, he watched for Julie to react.

She put her hand to her mouth.

"Say it," he said.

She was frowning. "You say that's the padlock that was on the boat?"

He nodded.

"And those are Milo's original keys?"

"Yes."

"Then it wasn't a substitution. According to John Wigfull's theory, Sid Towers fitted a new padlock to the boat, but that can't be so. This must be the original padlock. We've been working on a false assumption."

For a man who had been working on a false assumption, Diamond didn't look at all downhearted.

Julie said, "John Wigfull's theory about the locked room doesn't work after all."

"Right, Julie. He's up shit creek without a paddle."

A fresh thought struck her. "Aren't we also?"

"Yes," he said blithely. "And isn't it refreshing?"

CHAPTER TWENTY-SIX

"**A**REN'T YOU GOING TO TELL JOHN WIGFULL HE WAS wrong?" Julie asked.

"Not yet," Diamond told her. "What time is it?"

"Twenty to four, near enough."

"Jiminy Cricket!"

"Something you forgot?"

"Get your coat. We have an appointment at four with Miss Chilmark."

"An appointment? Sounds like the dentist."

"Miss C. is the sort of woman you don't visit without prior notice. I fixed it this morning."

"And you want me there?"

"In case she has an attack of the vapors."

"Oh, thanks," she said, flushing at the man's insensitivity to her rank and experience. "What do I bring—smelling salts and a paper bag?"

"Just a pair of handcuffs."

Julie's eyes opened wide. Her resentment was put on hold. "You don't seriously think she's the murderer?"

"I'm seriously asking you to have a set of cuffs with you."

The address, appropriately for someone of Miss Chilmark's reputation, was the Paragon, a terrace dating from the eighteenth century. Jane Austen stayed there when she first came to Bath. It was in the area they had visited that morning, actually quite close to Rupert's seedy abode in Hay Hill. Rather to Julie's surprise, Diamond proposed to walk there.

"Why not?" he said. "We won't be late if we step out."

"But if you're planning to bring her in . . ."

"You think the lady might object to walking half a mile in handcuffs?" He grinned at the picture it conveyed. "If necessary we'll radio in for transport. All right?"

Diamond was not a quick walker, so the timing was about right. They stepped up to a white painted door at two minutes past the hour. The gracious curve of the Palladian terrace stretched away in pleasing perspective. Traffic zoomed past unendingly, but the broad pavement with its triple-stepped curb kept the vehicles from encroaching too obviously on the Georgian formality.

After some delay the door was opened by a frail white-haired old lady in a lavender-colored suit.

Diamond was slightly thrown. This wasn't the kind of person he'd been led to expect. "Miss Chilmark?"

"I'm afraid you've come to the wrong door. She lives in the basement. Don't worry. It happens all the time." She extended a shaky hand toward the railings to their right.

Miss Chilmark in the basement? They leaned over the railings and peered down. True, it was in better order than basements generally are, whitewashed, clear of litter, and with a dwarf conifer in a pot by the door. They went down the stairs.

The bell was answered quickly by a sturdier woman, probably twenty years younger, who ushered them inside. The light was poor down there. Diamond's strongest impression of Miss Chilmark was of the heavy floral scent that wafted from her. In the cramped entrance he couldn't avoid passing so close that his eyes watered. She was in a black jacket over a garish multi-colored dress that rustled when she moved. She glittered at the ears, throat, and fingers.

"We came to the wrong door," Diamond explained, just to get the conversation started, but it was an unfortunate start.

"Oh," said Miss Chilmark in a long, low note of despair. "Did you tell her who you were?"

"No, ma'am. Simply asked for you and got directed down here."

This wasn't reassurance enough. "Where's the police car? I suppose she saw that."

He told her that they had come on foot, and got such an improved reaction that he wished he had started with it. They were led through a narrow hallway at some risk to the china plates clipped to the walls. Shown into what Miss Chilmark announced as her drawing room, they had a first impression of a dry atmosphere smelling like the inside of a biscuit tin. It was a place noticeably less colorful than its owner. Faded Indian carpets on a wood-block floor. Pale blue emulsioned walls with a number of gilt-framed portraits of po-faced Victorians and smug, tweed-suited figures from between the wars, judging by their clothes. Two ancient armchairs and a settee with blue-and-beige covers. A gas fire from the nineteen sixties with a mantelpiece over it, on which were six or seven books and some rock specimens acting as paperweights for letters. Above that a large print of a cathedral with a spire.

"You see, it isn't a basement at all from this side," Miss Chilmark was quick to point out, striding to the window to draw the chintz curtain farther aside. "I have the ground floor and the garden."

"This is because it's built on a slope?"

"Yes. That's Walcot Street at the bottom. The whole house belongs to me, only it's too much for a single lady, so I let out the other floors."

This might have been more credible if she had retained the floor above as well, with the front door access. She was not the kind of woman who willingly moved into a basement in her own house, even with the view of Walcot Street from the rear. The furnishings told a different, more convincing tale; that this was the last retreat of someone who had known more affluent times.

"Salisbury, isn't it?" Julie remarked, having stepped to the fireplace to admire the print.

"The tallest spire in England," Miss Chilmark said with some pride. "And built seven hundred years ago of Chilmark stone."

"You own a quarry?" said Diamond.

"The stone came from the village of Chilmark."

"You own a village?"

"Of course not." Lesson one: She had little sense of humor. "I thought everybody had heard of Chilmark stone. It's known as the architects' stone, because it's unmatched as a building material. Salisbury Cathedral, Chichester, Wilton House. I'm afraid my best sherry ran out when I had some visitors at the weekend, and my wine merchant hasn't delivered yet. Would you care for Earl Grey tea instead?"

He told her not to bother. "We're here to investigate a crime. You heard about the death of Sid Towers, no doubt."

"Dreadful," said Miss Chilmark. "Such an inoffensive man. Why do these things always happen to the nicest people?"

"Is that a fact?" Diamond said, tempted to challenge such a sweeping statement, but needing to move on. "You and he belonged to the same club, of course. The Bloodhounds."

"Yes."

"You're one of the senior members, right?"

"I joined a long time ago, so I suppose I'm entitled to be so described."

"Before Sid?"

"Yes. Why don't you sit down?"

Acting on the suggestion, he felt the shape of a spring press into his rump, confirming that the settee, like its owner, had seen better days. "We're finding it difficult to get a sense of what Sid Towers was like. Maybe you can help us, ma'am. Outside the Bloodhounds, did you know him at all?"

She reddened. "What on earth are you implying, Superintendent?"

"Is the answer 'No'?"

"Of course it is."

"I meant nothing defamatory. He worked in a security firm. What's the name? Impregnable. Have you had any dealings with Impregnable, Miss Chilmark?"

"I can't think why you imagine I should."

"Have you got an alarm system, for example?"

"On the house? Certainly not. One of those bells would be unthinkable on a listed building like this."

"Security inside? Sensors, fingerbolts, window locks?"

"I have excellent locks. I've no need for anything else."

"That's clear, then," said Diamond. "On the evening he died, last Monday, you went to a meeting of the Bloodhounds. I'd be grateful if you would tell me what you remember of that evening, and of Sid in particular."

She clicked her tongue. "It was all extremely distressing for me personally, I can tell you that."

"Before you tell me that, what happened at the very start? Were you the first to arrive that evening?"

"No, Polly—Mrs. Wycherley—was there before me, and so was poor Mr. Towers."

"Those two arrived first? I want you to think hard about this. When you got there, were they in conversation?"

"Mr. Towers never had anything amounting to a conversation with anyone."

"Where were they standing?"

"How do you mean?"

"It's clear, isn't it? Where was Mrs. Wycherley?"

"She wasn't standing at all. She was already seated inside the circle. We arrange the chairs in a circle."

"You do this yourselves?"

"Yes, whoever gets there first. I helped Mr. Motion the previous Monday, when we happened to be the first there. On this occasion he was a little late, held up by the traffic. He drives, you know, from Limpley Stoke, where the boat is."

"So Sid and Polly Wycherley must have got the room ready this week?"

"I presume so. I wasn't there early enough to see."

"Polly's the chairman, isn't she?"

"She does her best," said Miss Chilmark, examining the back of her hand.

"You sound as if you don't have complete confidence."

"Oh, I'm old-fashioned enough to expect a chairman to lead the discussion. On this occasion I took some initiative myself, and it was generally welcomed, I may say."

"How did that come about?"

"Well, at the start of the meeting—this was before the whole thing descended into chaos—I suggested that we apply our experience of detective stories to a discussion of the real crime that happened in our own city—the theft of that stamp from the Postal Museum."

Diamond glanced toward Julie and then back to Miss Chilmark. "Did you, now? What made you think of that?"

"As soon as I read the report in the *Chronicle* I knew it was right up our street. For once we had the chance to test our wits on a real unsolved crime."

"Can you remember what was said?"

"I have a very clear recollection, yes. First, we addressed the question of why it was done, stealing such a well-known stamp. Mrs. Shaw, the lady from the Walsingham Gallery, who isn't backward in putting across her opinions, gave us the theory that it was stolen at the behest of some fanatical collector. Miss Miller, who joined only the previous week, thought it was more likely that a ransom would be demanded. She even had a theory as to how the money could be collected through a secret bank account in Switzerland. Then they turned to me, and I moved the debate on to the far more intriguing question of the riddles that were sent by the thief."

"Ah, the riddles."

"I had copies with me. We quickly decided that it would be sensible to apply our minds to the latest one."

" 'Whither Victoria and with whom,' " chanted Julie.

"Yes."

"And did anyone throw any light on it?" asked Diamond.

A look of self-satisfaction passed fleetingly over Miss Chilmark's face. "I flatter myself that I did. As a graduate in English literature I was able to demonstrate that the two riddles had textual similarities that suggested they were composed by the same person—the archaisms such as the use of 'thee' in the one case and 'whither' in the other, for example."

"Very astute," said Diamond. "And what was your answer to the riddle?"

"Oh, we didn't get that far," said Miss Chilmark. "This was the point when that degenerate chose to appear, and chaos ensued."

"You're speaking of Rupert Darby now. This incident."

"Only the latest in a series of incidents," said Miss Chilmark, going pink at the memory. "He behaves deplorably. He has from the beginning. One looks to the Chair for discipline, or at least some effort to maintain order. She doesn't check him. One week, without so much as a word of warning, he arrived with the dog—a savage brute—and expected us to ignore it. A large, untrained, malodorous, terrifying dog. Mrs. Wycherley did nothing about it, in spite of my protests. Last week it came into the circle and shook its coat, drenching us all and ruining my clothes. This week it attacked me."

"Bit you?"

"I'm sure it meant to bite. They had to drag it off me. No wonder I had difficulty breathing."

Julie, who kept two large dogs of her own, couldn't stop herself saying, "If it meant to bite you, I'm sure it would have. They don't mess about."

Diamond said quickly, "So you think Mr. Darby brings the dog to cause you distress?"

"I'm certain of it."

"Some personal grudge?"

"I've given him no cause for one."

"He lives quite close, doesn't he, across the street in Hay Hill?"

Miss Chilmark drew herself up in the armchair. "What are you suggesting now?"

"I'm not suggesting anything, ma'am. I'm stating a fact. You're almost neighbors."

"The man lives in squalor," she said with distaste.

"You've visited him?"

"God forbid! I wouldn't need to. The state of the windows. The curtains. I try not to look when I am compelled to walk past."

"Considering the way you feel about this man, I'm surprised you haven't given up the Bloodhounds. It can't be any pleasure."

Her lips contracted into a tight, orange-colored knot. "Why should I allow him to hound me—literally hound me—out of an activity I've enjoyed for two years or more? Tell me that."

The defiance was admirable, the English gentlewoman at her finest. She was at one with the steely-featured ancestors whose portraits lined the walls.

"Forgive me, I'm still trying to understand the appeal of this club," said Diamond. "From all I've heard, you have very little in common except that you all read detective stories."

"Isn't that enough? People don't have to be like peas in a pod to function as a club. We speak of books we can recommend. Tastes differ, of course, and one doesn't have to agree with everything that is said, but discussion can be stimulating. Some of them will never break out of Agatha Christie and Dorothy Sayers. You can see that. Personally I favor a more demanding writer. I don't suppose you are familiar with Eco."

Diamond had heard of the so-called ecowarriors, who occupied the trees at Swainswick when the bypass was under construction, and he doubted if they would have Miss Chilmark's seal of approval, so he said, "No, ma'am, I can't say it's familiar."

"He. Eco is the name of an author."

Julie looked equally unwilling to commit herself.

"Umberto Eco," Miss Chilmark said, rolling the *r* and

chanting her syllables like a native Italian, "the greatest of modern writers. To describe him as a crime writer would be to belittle the man, regardless that *The Name of the Rose* is, beyond question, the finest detective story ever written."

"I saw it," said Julie. "With Sean Connery."

Witheringly Miss Chilmark said, "I wasn't speaking of the film."

"It was good," said Julie.

"I doubt it. How could any film live up to the achievement of such an intricate and intelligent book?"

Julie retorted evenly, "So what is your opinion of *Foucault's Pendulum*?"

It was a delicious moment, the more enjoyable for being so unexpected. It didn't matter that Diamond had no idea who Foucault was or why his pendulum was of interest. The question hit Miss Chilmark like a cannonball.

She became inarticulate. "I, em, I can't say that I, em, that is to say, got on with it too well."

Before she could repair her defenses, Diamond said, "Do you drive?"

"You mean a car?"

"Well, I don't see you on a motorbike."

"I own a small car, yes. A Montego."

"Where do you keep it?"

"I rent a garage in Lansdown Mews."

"The color?"

"Blue. Dark blue. Why do you ask?"

"Registration?"

She gave the number. An F registration: quite a seasoned car.

"Did you use it on the Monday evening after the meeting?"

"Of course not. It's only a short walk from here to St. Michael's. Besides, I was far too shaken by my experience with the dog to take the wheel of a car."

"So what happened? Did you walk home?"

"Yes."

"Didn't anyone offer to drive you?"

"I can't remember. If they had, I wouldn't have accepted. You see, I was well enough by then to make my own way back here."

Miss Chilmark's fitness interested Diamond. During the interview he had been assessing her physique. Though probably around sixty, she was a sturdy woman, not incapable, he judged, of cracking a man over the head with a heavy implement.

"And after you got home, did you go out again?"

"No. Why should I?"

"Was anyone here that evening? A visitor?"

The look she gave him removed any doubt that if roused she was capable of violence. "How dare you?"

Diamond smiled faintly. "Miss Chilmark, I wasn't suggesting anything risqué; I was trying to find whether you had an alibi for the time when the murder took place."

"Surely you don't believe . . ." Shocked, her voice trailed off.

"But it turns out you don't have one," said Diamond. "Shame." He heaved himself up from the settee and crossed the room to examine one of the portraits, of a mustachioed man in a gray suit with a cravat, one thumb tucked into a waistcoat pocket to give a good view of a gold watch chain. His young wife stood at his side in a long blue dress. She was holding an ostrich-feather fan. Three small boys were grouped in front, one of them in a sailor suit looking up adoringly at his father. "Family?"

Miss Chilmark's mind was on other things. There was a pause before she responded. "Er, yes. My grandparents, with Papa and my uncles Esmond and Herbert."

"Handsome family."

"Grandpapa was mayor of Bath before the First World War."

"Really? Did they live in this house at the time?"

"Yes."

"It passes down through the family?" He swung around from the painting and looked at her. "You did say it belongs to you still?"

She made a murmur of assent and nodded.

"Of course, if we had any doubt we could check who pays the Council Tax," Diamond dropped in casually to the dialogue.

There was an uncomfortable silence.

He then added, "Or we could ask the old lady upstairs."

"You can't do that!" said Miss Chilmark in a panic. "Well." She cleared her throat. "Technically, the house isn't in my possession any longer. Living here, as I have all my life, I still tend to think of myself as the owner." She had just been caught out, but she was doing her damnedest to gloss it over.

"Technically?" repeated Diamond. "You sold the place?"

"On the firm understanding that I may remain here for life."

"And how long ago was this transaction?"

Miss Chilmark rested her hands on her thighs and pushed out her chest in an attempt to reassert herself. "I don't see that this is a matter for the police."

"It is if you mislead us," said Diamond. "We expect truthful statements, Miss Chilmark. If we don't get them, we ask why."

"A misunderstanding."

"I don't think so, ma'am. When did you sell?"

"In January 1993."

"A painful decision, I'm sure."

"One's circumstances alter," said Miss Chilmark philosophically.

"You had some hefty expenses to meet?"

"Do I have to go into this? It isn't easy for a single lady to exist on a private income in these expensive times. My savings were depleted through inflation and some bad investment advice, so I took stock of my position, my future, and decided it was wise to realize the asset of the house. I have no family to pass it on to. I can now face my declining years with reasonable confidence."

They left soon after. Outside in the street, Julie said, "You pressed her hard about her circumstances."

"And I haven't finished," said Diamond. "She's gone through a mint of money. I'm not convinced about the bad investments—unless it's something like a gambling habit. We need to do some digging, Julie. You see, if she sold the house—what?—a couple of years ago, she must have made a bomb. You wouldn't buy an entire house in the Paragon for much under four hundred grand—even with a sitting tenant in the basement. What's happened to the money?"

"Banked, I expect," said Julie.

"There wasn't much sign of spending, was there? That basement could do with some redecoration. Furniture ought to be replaced—that settee, anyway. She runs a five-year-old car. Is this a woman who came into several hundred grand?"

"People do live meanly sometimes."

"The jewelry—all that sparkly stuff—wasn't genuine, was it?"

"It looked like imitation to me," Julie admitted.

"I want you to make some discreet inquiries," he told her. "Go through the local papers for 1993. Find out which estate agent handled the sale. Go and sweet-talk them. Get the price if you can, the bank she used and the name of the new owner, presumably the old lady we first met. Once we know the bank . . . Can you handle this?"

"Without breaking the Data Protection Laws?"

"I didn't mention them, did I?"

"But you'd like to see a bank statement if I can rustle one up?"

"I would."

"If you say it's necessary, I'll do my best."

He turned to look her in the face. "What's this 'if you say it's necessary'? Do I sense a whiff of insurrection?"

She shook her head. "It's just that I still have a pair of

handcuffs in my coat pocket. You asked me to bring them, but they weren't needed."

"Only thanks to you, Julie."

"Oh?"

"The cuffs were there to shock the old bat. Break down her defenses. You did that in a much more subtle way, with your knowledge of Chinese literature."

"Chinese?"

"Foo So."

She laughed. *"Foucault's Pendulum.* That isn't Chinese. It's a book by Umberto Eco, the writer she was talking about."

"I don't care. It was brilliant, Julie. It shook her rigid. Shook me, too. How on earth did you know about that?"

She said, "I don't think I'll tell you."

"Come on."

"You'll be disappointed. It was pretty obvious, really."

"No!" he said, thinking back, picturing the room. "It wasn't one of those books on the mantelpiece?"

"There you go. Am I still brilliant, or have you changed your opinion?"

He didn't answer. They were interrupted by the beeping of Julie's personal radio. She took it out. "DI Hargreaves."

"Do you have Superintendent Diamond with you, ma'am? Over," the voice from Manvers Street asked.

"Yes, I do."

"Would you tell him he's wanted urgently here? A message has just been received. We think it could be another of those riddles."

THE THIRD RIDDLE

SUSPENSE

CHAPTER TWENTY-SEVEN

THE ASSISTANT CHIEF CONSTABLE, ARNOLD MUSGRAVE, sat behind his desk with his hands covering his eyes as if they were sore. Across the room, from armchairs in opposite corners, John Wigfull and Peter Diamond watched in the uncomfortable knowledge that everything they had patiently and plausibly stitched together had just been unraveled.

Mr. Musgrave took a deep, troubled breath and dragged his fingers slowly down his fat features. Finally he propped his chin on his clenched fists. "To sum up, then," he said, his voice edged with reproach, "we're back with the locked room mystery we started with. Your neat theory about the narrowboat has been blown to smithereens, John."

"So we're led to believe, sir," Wigfull said with a sideward glare at Diamond.

"Sometimes I wonder if you two are singing from the same hymn sheet." Mr. Musgrave dressed him down sharply. "You can't argue with the facts. Nobody changed the padlock. It was the same one Milo Motion bought originally. The key picked up by the divers at Avoncliff fitted it perfectly. Right?"

"Right, sir," admitted Wigfull.

"Worse than that, the thief is still at large." Mr. Musgrave turned the spit relentlessly. "This new riddle turns up this afternoon, proving you were wrong about Sid Towers. He can't have been the evil genius who thinks up these damned rhymes and stole the Penny Black."

"I thought we all had a stake in that theory, sir," the maligned Wigfull couldn't stop himself from stating. "If you remember, last time we met, DS Diamond produced the paper bag with those lists of rhyming words scrawled on it. That seemed to clinch the case against Towers."

Mr. Musgrave took a breath, as if to exercise self-control under extraordinary provocation. "I don't say you're alone in your delusions, John. If this latest riddle is genuine—and I believe it is—we've all cocked up."

"Would you mind repeating the verse, sir?" Diamond asked before his own shortcomings were opened to scrutiny.

The ACC picked a slip of paper off the desk and read the words in a monotone that underlined his distaste:

> "'To end the suspense, as yours truly did,
> Discover the way to Sydney from Sid.'"

There was a pause before Diamond said, "To *Sydney*?"

"It's the way this blighter works," said Wigfull. "It's gibberish. He doesn't want us making sense of the thing until after the event."

"That isn't my understanding of gibberish," Diamond said. "The other riddles did make sense."

"Yes, but only when we had all the information. There's no way we could have worked out from that first riddle that the Postal Museum was about to be done over."

"We do have a better chance now," said Diamond. "We know how two of the riddles worked out. We have some insight into the man's thinking."

"Or woman's," said Mr. Musgrave. "Let's not make any sexist assumptions. But you're right about that, Peter. Just because we didn't crack the other riddles, it doesn't mean we give up on this one. I'm as baffled as you are about this reference to Sydney. Does anyone in this case have an Australian connection?"

Diamond glanced toward Wigfull. "It hasn't come up."

"What about the first line: 'To end the suspense, as yours truly did'?"

Wigfull, touchingly eager for some credit, now took a more positive line: "That 'yours truly' is worth noting—the sort of old-fashioned expression that was used before, with words like 'thee' and 'whither.' Not quite so dated as those, I have to say, but it fits the style of the earlier pieces."

Mr. Musgrave said, "I don't think there's any question that this comes from the same source. The typeface is the same, and I'm pretty sure the paper is as well."

"How was it delivered, sir?" Diamond asked.

"The same as before—all the local media got it first."

"Another thing, sir," said Wigfull, trying to be more positive. "This time the whole tone of the message is more direct, as if the writer *wants* us to get the solution. 'To end the suspense' . . . It's almost as if he or she has a need to be unmasked. Look at it from their point of view. They commit a masterly crime and put out these clever rhymes, and get no recognition. In the end, the desire for glory gets the better of them."

"That's an optimistic view." Mr. Musgrave turned to Diamond. "What do you think of that?"

"I hope John is right. God knows, we need a breakthrough."

"All right. What about this second line: 'Discover the way to Sydney from Sid.' We know who Sid was. Who the devil is Sydney if it's not Sydney, New South Wales?"

"We have some Sydneys in Bath," suggested Diamond. "Sydney Place, Sydney Road, Sydney Gardens, Sydney Buildings, Sydney Wharf."

"Sydney Mews," put in Wigfull.

"This is better," said Mr. Musgrave. "Any connections with the Bloodhounds?"

"None that I know," said Diamond.

"Not one of them lives in any of those streets?"

"No, sir."

"Nothing there of interest, then. What about Sydney Gardens?"

"Well, you have the museum there," said Wigfull, and as soon as the words were out he gripped the arms of his chair. "Oh Lord, do you think they're planning another theft?"

Diamond, not often to be found imbibing culture in his spare time, needed to be reminded which museum this was. The Holburne of Menstrie, a converted hotel in the park at the end of Great Pulteney Street, possesses collections of silver and ceramics that rank among the best in Europe, as well as paintings by Guardi, Zoffany, Turner, and Gainsborough.

"Better tip off the security people in case," said Mr. Musgrave. "Do it now." He picked up his phone and held it out to Wigfull. When the call had been made, he said, "Let's shelve the riddle for a moment. Where exactly are we with the murder inquiry, Peter?"

"Still interviewing, sir." This sounded lame, and Diamond knew it.

"The Bloodhounds?"

"Yes. They've all given statements to the murder squad. I'm doing the follow-up with DI Hargreaves. Talked to Mr. Motion, of course, Mrs. Shaw, Mr. Darby, and Miss Chilmark. There are two to go—Miss Miller and Mrs. Wycherley."

"Any angles?"

"No one can be eliminated yet, sir, except Milo Motion, who was here being interviewed when the murder took place. It was physically impossible for him to have got back to the boatyard and murdered Towers before he clocked in downstairs. Otherwise, not one of the Bloodhounds has an alibi worth mentioning. So far as I can make out, every one of them had the use of a vehicle, so they could have got out to the boatyard."

"Do you seriously think a woman could have done this?"

"Cracked Sid over the head? No problem."

"Miss Chilmark?"

"She may be getting on a bit, sir, but she's still a sturdy woman."

"What about the motive?"

"For Miss Chilmark? Something emerged that made me wonder. Julie Hargreaves is working on it now."

"What's that?"

"She seems to have got through a mint of money in recent years. She sold the house in ninety-three. Ought to be in the lap of luxury now, but she isn't. I want to find out why."

"Blackmail?"

Diamond spread his hands. "Her reputation is very important to her."

"Did anything useful emerge from the other interviews? Mrs. Shaw?"

"Very little. It's more a matter of what she didn't tell than what she did. I knew from another source, from Milo, in fact, that she made definite attempts to be friendly with Sid. Out of sympathy, possibly. I'd be very surprised if any of it was meant as a come-on. She took him to the pub on more than one occasion after the Bloodhounds finished. When we talked, she told me about Polly Wycherley fussing over him, but she volunteered nothing about the drinks she had with him herself. I brought that up, and then she was forced to admit to it."

"You think she was holding back?"

"Before I mentioned it, she was saying that if anyone else had spoken more than a couple of words to Sid, he would have run a mile."

"But she did?"

"Yes."

"And did *he*?"

"Run a mile? I've no idea."

"Does Mrs. Shaw have anything to hide?"

"Not that I've noticed. She's on pretty close terms with the fellow called A.J. who helps in the gallery. There could be something in that, but I don't get a sense that they're having an affair. I couldn't raise a blush from her, anyway."

"Is that the way you work?" said the ACC. "You seem to be staking a lot on Sid as a blackmailer."

"What other motive is there, sir? He wasn't shafting anyone's wife."

"Let's have the rundown on Rupert Darby, then."

"Talk about blackmail. On the face of it, Rupert was a plum ripe for picking. A prison record that Towers could easily have checked on."

"Through his links with Impregnable, you mean?"

"Yes, sir. Only Rupert doesn't turn a hair when you talk about his form. He could hardly wait to tell me the story of his conviction for indecency—for mooning at a magistrate. He gave his impression of the beak pronouncing sentence, quoting every word. Spot on, and amusing, too. The man glories in his image as an old lag. He likes to shock."

"Not a victim, then?"

"I don't see it."

Mr. Musgrave vibrated his lips as if he suddenly felt a draft. "If you discount Darby as a suspect, you're left with the women."

"I don't make sexist assumptions, sir."

This wasn't well received. The ACC drew back in his chair and pointed his finger. "Don't make assumptions of any sort, Peter, least of all about me. Better get through those interviews PDQ. We've got the media on our backs. You're going to nail this joker fast."

CHAPTER TWENTY-EIGHT

ANNOYED WITH HIMSELF FOR HAVING PROVOKED SUCH AN outburst from the ACC, who was normally the most agreeable of the high-ups, Diamond returned to the second floor resolved to channel his discontent into the pursuit of the killer. This case was a brute, but there was no point in taking it out on the people upstairs.

He found Julie in the incident room holding a phone to her ear. She rolled her eyes upward.

"Who is it?" he asked.

She mouthed the words, "The bank."

Miss Chilmark's bank. Julie must have made progress to get this far. While he'd been baiting the top brass, she had been beavering away on the things that mattered. Thank God for Julie. She had made this sort of exercise, ferreting for information, her specialty. She kept tabs on the networking between local government, business, and trade. She always knew someone to approach.

"Any joy?"

She shook her head and continued to listen to the phone while fiddling with a pencil, standing it on one end and then sliding finger and thumb down its length, and reversing it. At last she thanked her informant and put down the receiver. She gave Diamond a smile, not of satisfaction, but resignation. "Confidentiality. They won't tell me anything without authority. I did get a few things clear from an estate agent—and not the one Miss Chilmark dealt with. In this town the agents all know each other's business. The house was sold to a Mrs. Nugent-Thomas in January 1993, just as Miss Chilmark stated."

"For how much?"

"Three hundred and thirty thousand, with a clause inserted to allow her to remain a tenant for life."

"And what did she do with the proceeds?"

"That's what I was trying to discover."

"Who from?"

"A bank cashier. I thought she was sure to be good for some inside info. I used to babysit for her. It was worth trying. Doesn't matter. Plan B should get us there, even if it's a more roundabout route."

He shook his head. He hadn't the patience for Plan B, whatever that was. He'd been a front-row forward in his time. "Get the number again, and ask for the manager."

Julie gave him a do-you-think-this-is-wise look and pressed the redial button.

"Ringing?"

She nodded.

"Tell the switchboard you have a personal call for the manager from, er, Douglas, Isle of Man. Give my name but not the rank." Front-row forwards weren't picked for their subtlety, but occasionally they used the dummy pass.

Julie's eyes widened. She knew her boss well enough not to hesitate. After getting through and repeating his instruction precisely, she handed the phone across.

Diamond's face underwent a change. Suddenly he was a picture of affability, pink and smiling as if his day so far had been spent feeding pigeons in Abbey Green. "Who am I speaking to? . . . Right. This is Peter Diamond, Douglas, Isle of Man branch. How are you, old boy? Must be all of ten years since we last spoke. At staff college, wasn't it? Look, this is probably nothing, but one can't be too careful. We've got a young fellow here wanting to open an account with a single check drawn on a personal account at your branch. There's more than a slight question mark about the check. Do you happen to have a Miss Hilda Chilmark as a customer? . . . Good. That's the name of the account holder. I daresay you have a terminal in front of you. It might be worth pressing a couple of keys. . . . Already? You're quicker than I am with the damned thing. First it's a question of whether the balance covers the amount. Even if it does, I have my doubts whether your customer filled this in as it now appears. . . . Actually, three thousand two hundred pounds, but it looks to my cashier as if the words 'Three thousand' might be an addition, squeezed in front, you know, and so, to my beady eye, is the number three where the digits go. . . . The name of the drawer? John Brown, if you can believe that. . . . Ah! I'm glad you agree. . . . Well, I'd be grateful if you would. . . ." He smiled at Julie.

She murmured, "I didn't think you were capable of this."

He put his hand over the mouthpiece. "You didn't hear any of this, Julie." In a moment, the manager was back in contact. Diamond now put on a caring expression, listened and then said, "Well, this does sound like a try-on. Most of her current balance, you say? . . . It looks as if we may be onto something rather unpleasant. You won't mind me asking. Have there been any other four-figure debits on the account recently? . . . Indeed! . . . But by the lady herself at your branch? One can't argue with that. Between you and me, I wish I lived in such style. This does look like a one-off. Look, I'd better get back to this chappie right away. Rest assured that we'll stop it at this end and get a proper investigation under way directly. Doubtless you'll be hearing from Head Office shortly. . . . Not at all. It's our job to keep a lookout. Thanks." He put down the phone and told Julie, "She's been drawing a thousand a week in cash for at least a year. What are the odds on blackmail?"

Julie's thinking hadn't got past the thousand a week. "That's a stack of money to get through."

"Every week. You couldn't do it."

"Couldn't I?" she said. "Give me the chance."

"Let's keep our minds on the job, shall we?"

She smiled. "What next, then? Back to Miss Chilmark?"

"Not tonight. I want to interview Shirley-Ann Miller."

She didn't often query a decision, but this one seemed hard to justify. "Do we need to bother? I mean, if Miss Chilmark was being blackmailed . . ."

"We don't know if she was."

"You brought it up, Mr. Diamond," she reminded him. "It may not be true, but it's worth putting to her, surely?"

"This morning you were prodding me into visiting all the suspects."

"Yes, but nothing was happening then. Now we're inundated. You must have heard about this new riddle sent to the press this afternoon."

"I was informed by the Assistant Chief Constable," he said with an air of martyrdom. "When did you hear about this?"

"Only a short while ago. It's all over the front page of the *Chronicle*. The desk sergeant had a copy."

"Into print already? And what do you make of it?" he asked.

Julie shook her head. "Sounds very like the other riddles to me, except that they were about the Penny Black. Could be some publicity seeker, I suppose. I mean, I thought we'd agreed that Sid wrote the others. We have the writing on the paper bag as evidence. True, it was just a list of rhyming words and not lines of verse, but I thought that was pretty conclusive."

"So did I until an hour ago," said Diamond. "All we've got is conflicting evidence, Julie. An impossible murder in a locked room, a dead man who continues to taunt us with riddles, and a woman who lives in a basement and gets through a grand a week. You were right about the other suspects. We want the whole picture. Get your coat."

They'd done enough walking for one day, Diamond decided; this time, they inched toward Russell Street in the evening line of traffic. He used the time constructively, justifying the decision to visit Shirley-Ann Miller. At this stage of the investigation she was the least likely suspect, he cheerfully conceded, but she was potentially the most valuable witness. As a newcomer to the Bloodhounds, she must have observed each of the members acutely, getting those first impressions, alert to the dynamics of the group, the antagonisms and suspicions, linkups and alliances that undoubtedly existed. In the two meetings she had attended, she may well have seen the crucial events that led to the murder. By all accounts she was not reticent. Her recollections ought to be worth having.

It was after five when they rang the bell at the Russell Street flat. An appetizing smell wafted from the interior the moment Shirley-Ann Miller opened the door. Her PVC apron was quite a knockout, the lifesize image of a torso and thighs clad in a black basque and suspenders and worn in the appropriate position. Unfortunately Shirley-Ann's large round spectacles and pale features under the helmet of dark hair didn't square too well with the rest of the effect.

"Obviously not a convenient time to call," Diamond mentioned apologetically after introducing himself and Julie.

"Oh my God!" Shirley-Ann looked down at the apron and tried to cover it with her hands. "I forgot I had this on. What on earth must you be thinking? It isn't mine, actually." She reached for the bow at the back, tugged off the apron, and bundled it onto a chair before escorting her guests to the back of the house.

"I meant your cooking," Diamond explained. "Don't let it burn."

"It's all right. It's only a beef casserole I took from the

freezer. I can give it as long as I like." She showed them into an open-plan area where the aroma was well-nigh irresistible. This was a once-gracious, high-ceilinged Georgian reception room now ruined by a divider, a central shelf unit that failed to mask a kitchen sink, refrigerator, and dishwasher. On the near side of the unit was a carpeted living area with armchairs, television, and low tables cluttered with newspapers, books, junk mail, and crockery.

"Do sit down. Just park everything on the floor. You'll have to take me as you find me. With both of us working, Bert and me, it's difficult to keep up with the housework."

"Bert being . . ."

"My partner. That's the whole point, really, that we're partners. When two of you share a place, it's two homes squeezed into one. Neither of you wants to throw anything away in case the relationship comes to an end, so you end up with two of everything. It's only been six months. Tea?"

Julie had tuned in to the quick tempo of Shirley-Ann's speech, and she spoke for them both. "Please."

The rate of words actually increased, at no cost to the beautiful articulation. "Bert does his best to keep the place in order. He's much more orderly than I am, but he isn't here as much, so my untidy habits win the day. You don't need to tell me what this is about," she said, crossing to the kitchen area to fill the kettle. "I expected you before this. Well, I've talked to one of your sergeants already, and he told me to expect another interview. Not that I can help very much. I don't believe I spoke a single word to the poor man who was killed, and that's pretty unusual for me."

"You joined this group, the Bloodhounds, quite recently."

"I've only been twice. Quite an experience, both times. Had no idea what I was letting myself in for."

"What prompted you to go along?"

"Force of circumstance, really. Bert is out most evenings at the Sports and Leisure Center, where he works. That's when it's used most, so he has to be there. It's all very well having a gorgeous hunk for a lover, but you pay a price. I do a lot of reading in the evenings, only there are limits. When I heard about the Bloodhounds, it sounded right up my street."

"How did you hear?"

"From one of those little booklets listing what's on in Bath. Bert brought one home from the Center, knowing how I wallow in detective stories and thrillers. He's never moved on from James Bond, which he knows like some people know their Bible, I may say. They're not for women, those books. Bert doesn't like anything else, so our conversations about reading are rather limited. Anyway, I went along to the meeting, and they were glad I joined, I think. They could do with some new members. I was told quite a number have left since it was set up. You have to be a real enthusiast." She picked some mugs off the floor and took them to the kitchen sink to wash.

"Did you know any of the others before you joined?" Diamond asked. He had found a rocking chair and cleared it of golfing magazines. Julie, too, had made herself a space and was seated in a deep armchair.

"No. They were all new faces to me. But they went out of their way to be friendly. Some of them did, anyway. Jessica— that's Jessica Shaw, who owns that art gallery in Northumberland Place—took me for a drink at the end of the first meeting, and I also had an invitation to the preview at her gallery this week. Then Polly Wycherley—she's the chair, and one of the founder-members—invited me for a coffee at Le Parisien a day or two later. I've had coffee twice with Polly. I think she takes her duties seriously."

"What do you mean?"

"The second time was the morning after poor Sid Towers was killed. Polly came up to me when I was at work. I was only handing out leaflets about the bus tour, so it was easy to take a few minutes off. It was the first I'd heard about what happened. Polly had been interviewed by some of your people that very morning, and she was worried because she'd made some ghastly, insensitive remark about Sid before they told her the bad news."

"What remark was that?"

"I don't remember. No, wait, I do. She told them he was dead wood, meaning he didn't contribute very much to the Bloodhounds."

"Unfortunate."

"Yes. She was mortified."

"Did she have anything else to say?"

"Let me think. She was very shaken. Well, it was obvious to both of us that one of the Bloodhounds must have murdered Sid."

"How did you come to that conclusion?"

Shirley-Ann switched off the kettle and warmed a fancy teapot shaped like the face of Sherlock Holmes, with a deerstalker lid. "We knew Sid drove to Limpley Stoke after our meeting and into that boatyard where Milo had his houseboat. The policeman who gave Polly the news told her Sid's car was found down there. Didn't know what he was up to. Whatever it was, he must have thought there wasn't much chance of being disturbed, with Milo having gone to the police station and sure to be there some time, to explain about the stamp. Obviously he was wrong. Someone else went to the boat as well. And it had to be one of the Bloodhounds, because we were the only people who knew Milo wouldn't be home."

"Polly had worked this out?"

"She didn't actually put it into words. I did."

"You're a bit of a sleuth yourself, then," said Diamond, watching her pop two teabags into Holmes's head.

"I'm sure Polly was of the same opinion," said Shirley-Ann. "She's very astute, and she was in a fine old state about the murder."

"Why do you think she confided in you?"

She blushed. "I don't know. Perhaps she thought I was so new in the club that I was the only one who couldn't possibly have a motive for murdering Sid—which is true when you think about it. Everyone else had known him some time."

"Fair enough. They'd been coming for years, some of them. Mr. Motion, Mrs. Wycherley." Casually, Diamond tossed in Miss Chilmark's name, as one of the long-standing members. "Quite a formidable lady, from all I've heard."

"I thought so at first," said Shirley-Ann. "She presents a strong front—seven hundred years of Chilmarks, and that sort of patronizing nonsense that people of her sort sometimes use to justify their pretensions. I think she's brittle, though. She panics easily."

"The episode with the dog?"

"Rupert's dog, yes."

"You're sure that was genuine?"

She frowned. "Do you mean, Was she acting? I didn't think so. She worked herself up in anticipation, but that's different. We had a bit of a scene the previous week, when Marlowe— that's the dog—shook himself dry and made some of us wet in the process. She'd obviously fretted all week over that. At the beginning of the next meeting, before Rupert arrived, she was asking the rest of us to support her in excluding the dog. When the crisis came, it was real, I'm sure."

"The hyperventilation?"

"Yes."

"Rupert was the thorn in her flesh?"

"Absolutely."

"Did you happen to notice how she behaved toward the other men?"

Shirley-Ann's eyebrows lifted a fraction at the question.

Diamond couched it another way. "A maiden lady, rather brittle, to use your expression. Is she nervous of men?"

"If she is, it doesn't show. She gets on well with Milo, helps him to put out the chairs when they arrive early."

"And Sid Towers? She wasn't in awe of him?"

"I don't think so. Like the rest of them, she behaved as if

he wasn't there most of the time—which is probably the kindest way to treat a painfully shy man."

Diamond moved the questioning on. "I'd value your opinion, Miss Miller. You know that Sid was murdered later that evening, and you observed everything that happened at the meeting. Did you form any theories?"

"About who did it? No."

"No suspicions, even?"

"Well . . ." She poured the boiling water into the teapot, busying herself with the task. "Not at the time."

"You've got your suspicions now?" Diamond pressed her.

She was trying to hold back, which clearly went against nature for Shirley-Ann. "Oh, nothing I'd call a suspicion."

"What would you call it, then—an inspired guess? Woman's intuition?"

This dart hit its target, but failed to achieve the desired result. It brought out the militant in Shirley-Ann. "Would you like the tea in a mug, or all over your head?"

At this point Julie had an intuition of her own: to wade in, but on Shirley-Ann's side. "I wouldn't even ask," she told her. "He's like this all the time. You wouldn't believe the things I've heard him say to women. God knows you wouldn't hint at something you know unless it was properly thought through and based on common sense. Intuition, be blowed!"

From the expression on Diamond's face, he might as well have had the teapot upended over his bald patch. Luckily he was lost for words, and it was the effusive Shirley-Ann who supplied them.

"You're spot on. I *do* know something. I wasn't going to mention it."

"But you will, to make a stand for women," said Julie, dangerously close to overdoing this.

Shirley-Ann, fired up, proceeded to tell them about the words she'd seen sprayed on the window of the Walsingham Gallery and cleaned off by Jessica's husband, Barnaby. "And those are facts," she said finally. "To hell with intuition."

Julie's onslaught had wrongfooted Diamond, but he was grateful for the result. "'*She did for Sid*'—those were the words?"

"Yes."

"You saw them yourself?"

Now that she had an ally, Shirley-Ann was becoming assertive. "Didn't I just say so? Jessica practically dragged me into the street to look."

"Who else was there?"

"Her husband, Barnaby, and A.J., the artist."

"We've met A.J.," said Julie. "He seems to be around a lot of the time."

"You can say that again," said Shirley-Ann, all discretion abandoned. Her sisterly bond with Julie was bringing spectacular results. "I'm surprised the husband puts up with it."

"With what?" said Diamond.

"Oh, I've met them out, walking along the towpath at Bathwick like a married couple."

"Arm in arm?"

"I didn't say a courting couple."

"Side by side, then?"

She nodded. "That suggests a much more permanent relationship, to my jaundiced eye."

"I see. But you say the husband was present when the writing on the gallery window was discovered?"

"That's what's so amazing. He and A.J. were together all evening, looking after the picture sales. They don't act like rivals. In fact, they seemed to be getting on rather well."

"And whose decision was it to rub out the writing?"

"Barnaby's. Jessica was all for calling the police, but he advised her that if she did, it was quite likely the words would be taken seriously."

"It was entirely Barnaby's decision?"

"Well, not entirely. Jessica turned to me and asked what I thought, and I had to say it would ruin the party if they called the police. Sugar?" She handed a mug of tea to Diamond.

"So it didn't get reported."

"Not until now. They're going to be furious with me for speaking out."

Withholding information was apparently of trifling importance. Diamond let that pass for the present.

She continued, "I've been agonizing over this ever since it happened. At the time I thought it didn't matter if it wasn't reported. It seemed so obviously dotty, the suggestion that Jessica would have harmed Sid. She really liked the poor man; felt sorry for him, anyway. She's told me that herself."

"And have you changed your opinion?"

"Actually, I have." She gave them the theory she'd worked out in bed the previous night, the conspiracy between Jessica and Sid that had gone wrong and resulted in Jessica murdering Sid. "What do you think? Is it feasible?"

Diamond was too wily to say. "What interests me right now is who shares your suspicion, who put the message on the window."

"I can tell you," Shirley-Ann said, and then clapped her hand over her mouth.

"You saw it happen?"

"No." The flow of words stopped abruptly.

"But you know who was responsible, do you?"

She didn't answer.

Instead of a rebuke, she received the unexpected warmth of Diamond at his most charming. "You've been very candid with us, Miss Miller, and I appreciate that. We'd never make progress at all without the help of honest people like you. If you know the identity of this person—" He stopped at the sound of someone entering the flat.

Shirley-Ann said, "This has got to be Bert. He nips home before the evening session."

Diamond got up from the rocking chair as the door opened.

Shirley-Ann said, "Hi, darling, you're early. Don't be alarmed. This lady and gentleman are from the police."

Diamond supplied their names.

For one worrying moment it appeared as if Bert was stripping for a fight. Without a word he unzipped the top half of his black tracksuit. He wasn't particularly tall, yet the muscle formation around his neck and shoulders—he was wearing a pale blue singlet—spoke for many sessions with weights. In fact he didn't become aggressive. Shedding the tracksuit top was his way of asserting that this was his territory, his home. He tossed it over a chair back and asked mildly if the kettle was still hot.

Julie happened to be nearest the teapot and offered to pour him some, only to be told by Shirley-Ann, "Thanks, but Bert has his own herb tea."

"From an 007 pot, I daresay," Diamond commented.

Bert shot him a surprised look.

Shirley-Ann said, "I was telling them what a wiz you are on James Bond."

"Don't exaggerate," said Bert. He had a high-pitched voice for such a hunk of manhood.

Shirley-Ann went close to him and gripped his solid upper arm. "Oh, come on. If I had to have someone answering questions on *Mastermind* to save my life, I'd pick you." Turning to Julie, she remarked, "There's a wise head on these chunky shoulders."

Bert basked briefly in the compliment. Then he reminded her, "That isn't what they came to talk about."

She said to him, "We've had our talk." Turning back to Diamond, she explained, "Bert's very law-abiding. He told me I should have reported what happened, and I've told you everything."

Diamond wasn't interested in Bert's probity or Shirley-Ann's lack of it. Bert's arrival had put a stop to a promising conversation. "Not everything, ma'am. You didn't finish. You were on the point of telling us who wrote those words on the Walsingham Gallery window."

Hearing it put so bluntly caused Shirley-Ann to bite her lip and say, "Was I?"

Julie gave a confirming nod.

Shirley-Ann deferred to Bert, spreading her hands as if uncertain whether she should go on.

He said, "You can only describe what you saw. They can put two and two together, the same as we did."

She nodded, cleared her throat and said to Diamond, "I hate to get anyone into trouble, but I did happen to notice someone that evening with tiny spots of white on him, like snow or something."

"Who?"

"Rupert. Rupert Darby. It was on that beret he wears all the time. The spots showed up against the dark material. At the time I thought it must be dandruff. It was lightly speckled, mainly toward the front. I remembered much later."

"We were in bed," Bert confirmed.

She added, "That was when it dawned on me that it could be something other than dandruff."

"Paint from a spray, you mean?"

"Well, yes." She nervously fingered some strands of her dark hair. "I could be mistaken. Probably there's some innocent explanation."

"Did it look like paint from an aerosol?"

"I think so."

"You must be reasonably sure. Were the spots even in size?"

"Yes, and very small. Look, even if Rupert did write the words, it must have been meant in fun. He'd had a few drinks already with some people he met in the Saracen's Head. He was probably tipsy."

"Was he sprayed on his clothes, or hands, at all?"

"I didn't notice." She thought a moment. "There may have been some on his shoulders, I think, which put the idea of dandruff into my mind."

"Who else have you told about this?"

"Only Bert."

"You haven't spoken to Rupert?"

The idea horrified her. "He's the last person I'd speak to. I scarcely know him, anyway. He gets my name wrong. Look, if you speak to him about it, you won't bring me into it, will you?"

"Was Rupert at the party in the gallery?"

"Yes, he was already there when I arrived, with the people I mentioned."

"Did you catch their name, by any chance?"

"Yes, it was unusual. Faulk, or Volk, or something like that. She was a sculptor and had some work in the exhibition. He was a television writer."

"He'd met them in the Saracen's?"

"So he said."

"And when do you think the words were sprayed onto the window?"

"I've no idea. I didn't notice them as I came in, but I didn't look specially. I just went to the door, as you do. With all the spotlights on inside, and the people, you tended to look straight *through* the window, not at it."

"Since the party, have you spoken to anyone at all, any of the Bloodhounds, that is?"

"Only Jessica and A.J. this morning on the towpath. I told you about that." She was becoming twitchy, making little nervous movements, probably regretting what she had told.

"You met them this morning?" Bert said. "Was that wise?"

"They just happened to be there, love. It wasn't planned. I couldn't avoid saying something."

Diamond took over again. "You didn't tell us what was said. Was the incident discussed?"

"I'm not sure." Swiftly, Shirley-Ann corrected herself. "I mean, yes, it was. Oh, I do feel dreadful about this now. A.J. said we were going to erase it from our minds, and I sort of agreed. He said it must have been done by someone with a warped sense of humor. Jessica was still furious about it and said she wouldn't have harmed Sid in a million years. She said if the bastard—I'm using her words now—if the bastard pointed the finger at her again, she was going straight to the police."

"You've done her a good turn, then," Diamond summed up. "Saved her the trouble." He smiled.

Shirley-Ann didn't smile back.

"You didn't tell her about the spots on Rupert's beret?"

"Good Lord, no!"

"And you won't be mentioning what you saw to anyone else? Not Polly, not Milo, not Rupert, not anyone?" Having secured a nod from Shirley-Ann, he turned to Bert. "Nor you, sir. I'd like us all to be clear about that."

CHAPTER TWENTY-NINE

O UTSIDE THE ASSEMBLY ROOMS, WHERE THEY HAD parked, Diamond asked Julie, "What did you make of that?"

"The story about the beret?"

"Yes."

"It's got to be true, hasn't it? And we can check. Even if Rupert has noticed by now, and been busy with the white spirit, some microscopic paint spots are going to remain. Forensic will find them. Simple."

"Simple?"

"Well?"

"First, catch your beret." He stood by the car, jingling the keys, coming to a decision. "Look, Hay Hill can't be more than three minutes away. We can cut through by the toyshop, and it's just at the end of Alfred Street. We'll leave the car here."

Halfway down the passage called Saville Row, he paused to study the menu in the window of La Lanterna, in the amber glow of the streetlamp that gives the place its name. His gastric juices were threatening mutiny since being exposed to the aroma of Shirley-Ann's casserole. For a man of his appetite, it had been too long since lunch. "I don't want to spend the rest of the evening over this damned beret. It may be just a distraction."

"Would you rather leave it to me?" Julie offered.

"No, I want to see the man, as well as his beret." He suppressed the thought of food and started walking again. "To tell you the truth, Julie, I'm mightily intrigued. This kind of schoolboy stuff, writing slogans on windows, doesn't fit my impression of Rupert at all."

"Too sneaky, you mean?"

"You've got it. He gives it straight from the shoulder, whatever his other failings may be. If he had his suspicions about Jessica, he'd tell her, wouldn't he?"

Julie agreed with a murmur. "Unless he's the killer himself."

He didn't respond to that. He walked on in silence past antique shops that had iron shutters over their windows.

"Deflecting suspicion," Julie explained.

"I get the point."

"If he felt we were closing in, he might do something like this in desperation."

After another long and awkward pause, he said, "You know, it's a curious thing: Although Rupert is the one disreputable character in the Bloodhounds, the jailbird, the barfly, the cause of all the upsets, I haven't seriously cast him as the killer up to now. Maybe it's time I did."

In the evening gloom, Hay Hill looked and felt even less enchanting than it had on their previous visit. A strong breeze was gusting between the houses, disturbing dead leaves, paper scraps, and a discarded beer can that rattled against the railings before dropping into someone's basement. No lights were at Rupert's windows. The only response was from Marlowe the dog, barking at them through the space where the letter flap had been.

They decided to ask at the local. The landlord at the Lansdown Arms thought they might find Rupert in the Paragon Bar at this stage of the day. The waitress in the Paragon said he'd had a skinful at lunchtime, and he was probably out to the world until later. He usually came in sometime after seven. Sabotaged by appetizing whiffs of seafood cooking, Diamond was willing to wait there for Rupert. He persuaded Julie into discovering if the Paragon's "Meal in Itself"—of French fish soup with croutons, cheese, and grain bread—was a fair description. In Julie's case, it was.

Julie asked him how the kitten was settling in.

"Too well," said Diamond. "He really likes the football on TV. I'm trying to watch, and he's up against the screen patting it with his paw. He can't understand why the little men won't let him have the ball."

She smiled. "Has he got a name yet?"

"Most of the names I've called him aren't complimentary. He nicks things and stashes them away: keys, combs, pens, watches, a toothbrush. I found a stack of little objects in one of my shoes. You go to put them on in the morning, and your toes hit an obstruction."

"A genuine cat burglar?" said Julie. "You ought to call him Raffles."

"Raffles!" His eyes lit up. "He might approve of that."

Customers crowded in. Most of Bath seemed to know the tiny bar. Rupert had not appeared yet. To justify keeping the table (there were only three in this tiny room), Diamond ordered himself an extra dish of crêpes with trout, broccoli, and cheese filling. But eventually, about seven forty-five, they paid their bill and left.

More knocking at the house in Hay Hill succeeded only in goading Marlowe into hurling himself against the door.

They returned to the car and drove up Bathwick Hill to Claverton, a mile east of the city, to interview the only suspect they had not met.

Polly Wycherley lived alone in a semi named Styles in a quiet road behind the university. A few pink rose blooms were enduring October staunchly in the small front garden.

A halogen floodlight came on as they walked up the path. "Better defended than I am," commented Julie.

"She may not have two large dogs."

Diamond glanced up and noted the burglar alarm high on the front of the house.

But no dogs. They heard slippered footsteps respond to the doorbell, then bolts being drawn. The door opened as far as the safety chain permitted, and a suspicious-sounding voice asked who it was. Diamond gave their names and presented his ID at the narrow opening.

From inside came the sound of the chain being unfastened. "Before you open up," Diamond said, "are you Mrs. Wycherley, ma'am?"

She confirmed that she was.

"That's all right, then," he said, and added, with a wink at Julie, "we can't be too careful."

Polly Wycherley didn't take it as the waggish remark it was meant to be. Opening the door fully, she said, "That's a fact. You hear of such horrific things these days. You can't even feel safe in your own home."

And no wonder, Diamond thought when he stepped into the hall. The walls were hung with objects that suggested anything but safety: a Zulu shield and crossed assegais; a leopardskin; a war drum; and what looked like a witch doctor's mask. It was quite a relief to pass into the living room, filled mainly with bookshelves, each volume protected by a transparent wrapper that Polly must have fitted herself. The relief was short-lived when he caught sight of some of the titles: *Kiss Me Deadly*, *The Beast Must Die*, *Blood Money*, and *The Body in the Billiard Room*. On one of the shelves was a box opened to display a set of dueling pistols. Here was your sweet silver-haired lady, bolting her door against the horrific world outside before settling down with a grisly murder, surrounded by her collection of weapons. Mind, a sense of order prevailed. But on the whole he preferred the clutter at Shirley-Ann's.

"I know practically nothing about books," he said, to get things started, speaking from an uncomfortable Hepplewhite-style sofa with wooden arms and back, "but this looks to be a fine collection, Mrs. Wycherley. You obviously take care of it, too."

"You mean my plastic covers? They protect the dust jackets," she explained as if that were self-evident.

"But isn't that unfair to dust jackets?"

"Why?"

"They don't want protecting. They want to get on with their proper job."

She saw the logic in that and laughed. "They lose their value if the jackets are damaged."

"So this is an investment?"

"It's more than that," she said. "I couldn't put into words the excitement to be had from finding a good first edition."

"In its jacket?"

"The jackets are indispensable."

"But the book you read is the same whether it's a clean copy like these or some dog-eared old paperback from a charity shop."

"I have hundreds of those," she said. "I keep my reading copies in a spare room upstairs."

"You don't read these?"

"No."

"What have you got upstairs? Just crime?"

She smiled. "My dear superintendent, there's nothing unusual in that. People have always enjoyed a good mystery, from prime ministers to ordinary folk like me. I didn't have so much time for reading when my husband was alive. We traveled a lot. But in the last twelve years I've become quite addicted."

Diamond had no need to steer the conversation. Polly moved smoothly on to the prescribed route.

"That was how I came to found the Bloodhounds. You go to a function and meet other enthusiasts and find you have a lot in common. We've had six very enjoyable years. This dreadful tragedy is going to put an end to it, I fear. I've already canceled the next meeting. Just imagine! We'd all be staring at each other wondering who was capable of a real murder. You couldn't possibly talk about books. Let me get you a nice cup of tea."

"No, thanks—"

"Then perhaps Inspector Hargreaves . . . ?"

"Nor me," said Julie. "We just had something."

"But a cup of tea always goes down well. Or coffee? I'm due for one about now."

Diamond said firmly, "You don't mind if we talk about the evening Mr. Towers was killed?"

"I do have decaffeinated, if you prefer," Polly offered, unwilling to be denied. It was almost a point of principle to provide hospitality. Perhaps she wanted time in the kitchen to marshal her thoughts.

"You were one of the first at the meeting, I understand."

She gave a nod. "To make up for the previous week, when I was late. Stupidly, I dropped my car keys down a drain in New Bond Street. I got them back, but I hate being late for anything, so I made a special effort this time. I do wish I could get you something. A drink?"

"No, thanks. You drove down to the meeting?"

"I always do. I could take the minibus, I suppose, but it does involve some walking, quite late in the evening, and you can't . . ."

". . . be too careful."

She smiled. "I was the first to arrive. Sid came soon after."

"Did you notice his behavior? Did he seem nervous?"

"No more than usual. In fact, rather less. He actually said things a couple of times during the meeting."

"Do you remember what?"

She fingered a button of her cardigan. "I can try." After a pause, she said, "Yes, at the beginning, someone wondered who was missing, and Sid mentioned Rupert, and added that Rupert was always late—which is true."

"Anything else?"

Polly dredged her memory. "We were talking about the missing stamp. Miss Chilmark had suggested we might be able to throw some light on the mystery. Someone—Jessica, I'm sure—came up with the theory that some fanatical collector may have taken it. She suggested he might be a middle-aged man with a personality defect, and Sid interrupted to say that it might equally have been a woman."

"Sid said as much as that?"

"No, he just interrupted with the words 'Or woman,' but that was essentially the point, and quite fair. I don't think he spoke again until nearly the end of the meeting. However, he did produce a paper bag at an opportune moment. I expect you've heard about Miss Chilmark's attack?"

Diamond nodded. "But let's stay with Sid. You said he spoke at the end?"

"I mean after the discovery of the stamp. There was a difference of opinion as to whether Milo should go directly to the police. He was in two minds, you see. He felt he might come under suspicion and—please don't take offense at this—several of them clearly believed he might be treated roughly. In fact, only two of us, Miss Chilmark and I, were for Milo going to the police. Sid was asked, and what he said was that he could stay quiet—which nobody doubted."

This was the first Diamond had heard of a split of opinion at the end. "If the majority favored staying quiet, how was it that Milo came in to report the matter?"

She smiled, and Rupert's comment came back to Diamond: "Look at her eyes when she smiles." She said in a self-congratulatory way, "Good sense prevailed. Milo listened to us and saw that he had a public duty. The others may have been willing to turn a blind eye—"

"But you weren't?"

"It didn't come to that. Nobody made any threats. Milo reached his own decision."

Diamond understood now. Democracy wouldn't have

worked. Polly and Miss Chilmark had felt they had a public duty. Milo had been left with no option.

"Getting back to Sid," he said, "the more I hear about him, the more I think he wasn't the doormat that his quiet behavior suggested."

"That's a fact," Polly said firmly. "Sid may have been reticent, but he was no fool. He knew as much as any of us about detective stories, with the possible exception of Milo. John Dickson Carr was his special interest."

"I've seen the books in his flat."

This drew an interested "Oh?" from Polly. "I always imagined he must have a collection."

"They wouldn't be of use to you," he told her. "Most of them had no jackets, and those that did were withdrawn from libraries. Do you collect Dickson Carr, ma'am?"

She waved vaguely across the room. "I have a few of the collectable ones. He was very prolific."

"A writer of crafty plots, I gather. I can see why the locked room stories appealed to Sid, considering his line of work."

"As a security officer? Actually I doubt if he came across that sort of thing working for Impregnable. It doesn't often happen in real life, does it?"

Diamond let that pass. He had a sense that Polly was doing her best to manipulate the interview now that she was over the surprise of their visit. The image she presented, of the homely woman in twinset, tweed skirt, and slippers, with her soft curls, teapot, and sweet smile, had slipped once or twice already. He remembered the reservations about her that he'd got from Jessica Shaw and Miss Chilmark. "I understand Sid joined the Bloodhounds on the advice of his doctor."

"Dr. Newburn, yes. My doctor, too. A lovely person. Dead now, unhappily." The saccharine smile appeared again. "Of natural causes. Dr. Newburn got in touch with me and asked if I thought it would work. He knew of my involvement. Sid was recovering from a breakdown. I said I couldn't promise anything, but he was welcome to come along, and I'd make sure he wasn't put under more stress. My conscience is clear in that regard, anyway."

Spoken serenely, ignoring the logic that Sid's introduction to the Bloodhounds had led to his death.

"This breakdown. What was the cause?"

"I couldn't tell you. He did let drop the fact that his house had once been burgled. A horrible thing to happen to anybody. Would that lead to a breakdown, do you suppose?"

"Your guess is as good as mine, ma'am." After a suitable pause he said, in the tone of someone testing a theory, "I'd appreciate your reaction to a thought I had. We know that Sid enjoyed a locked room puzzle. I'm wondering whether the reason he drove to the boatyard was simple curiosity, to work out for himself what must have happened. What you had was a Dickson Carr setup. Milo did make this clear?"

"Indeed, yes. He showed us the key to the padlock and said where he'd bought it and how impossible it was for anyone to have a spare key."

"Quite a challenge for a man like Sid, a student of the locked room puzzle. Trained in security, too. The question is: Did he go down to Limpley Stoke to have a quiet look around the narrowboat and see for himself?"

"You could well be right," said Polly.

"Then either he surprised the murderer or the murderer followed him there and surprised him. That's the logic of it, isn't it? Either way, Sid got the worst of it."

"Poor Sid," said Polly. She got up and went to a sideboard and took out a box of chocolates. Her need to be seen as hospitable was almost pathological. "All soft centers," she said as she offered them.

Diamond shook his head, and Julie took her cue from him. "But don't let us stop *you*, ma'am," Diamond said. He was still weighing up this woman, trying to picture her wielding a windlass at the unsuspecting Sid. Was it plausible? She was sixty, at least, short and overweight, with a tendency to wheeze when she breathed, yet if she had caught him from behind, say, or bending forward, one blow could have done the job. A couple of blows were what the pathologist had reported.

The motive was harder to pin down. What about opportunity, then?

"Just for the record, Mrs. Wycherley, would you mind telling me where you were between the hours of nine and midnight on that evening, the evening Sid Towers was killed? I have to ask everybody."

She took the question placidly enough. "Here, for most of the time. I drove back here directly after the meeting. It's in the statement I made to the sergeant who called."

"Directly?"

"Well, I spoke to one of the others for a short time. Who was it? Miss Chilmark, I think. I thanked her for supporting me. We agreed it was the proper course of conduct. She's a difficult person, I have to say, but on this occasion I was glad to have her on my side against the Young Turks in our club."

"Were you the last to leave the crypt?"

"I generally am. I like to close the door myself. Miss Chilmark was just ahead of me. Don't misunderstand me. We probably didn't talk for more than a couple of minutes after the others had gone."

Julie came in with a useful question. "Did you notice who left first?"

"After Milo, do you mean? He was the first out."

"Yes."

"Sid. But he always is quick to make his getaway. I mean *was*. God bless him. He was in dread of anyone getting into a conversation with him. I think some time ago Jessica Shaw practically dragged him by the coattails to one of the local pubs. She caught him once more, but he was wary after that."

"Who left after Sid?" Diamond asked.

"You *are* asking some questions. It must have been our new member, Shirley-Ann, followed by Jessica or Rupert; I'm not sure who. Then Miss Chilmark and I. We were all out within five minutes and going our different ways."

"And you drove straight here?"

"I thought that was clear, Superintendent."

They established next that no one could vouch for Polly's presence in the house on the night of the crime. She had watched *News at Ten* and an old Stewart Granger film, but that was no alibi.

At Diamond's request, Polly then dictated a list of all the Bloodhounds since the club had begun in 1989. Her memory appeared to be functioning brilliantly. "Tom Parry-Morgan, Milo, myself, Annie Allen, Gilbert Jones, Marilyn Slade-Baker, Alan Jellicoe, the Pearce sisters, Colonel Twigg, the Bentins from Oklahoma . . ." She completed it without pause until she got to Rupert's name, and Diamond asked how this charming but wayward man had come to join.

"Quite by chance," Polly recalled. "We used to meet in the Francis Hotel. A corner of the Roman Bar. We were more informal then. Rupert happened to come in for a drink and overheard our discussion and joined in. He's like that,' loves an argument. He gets very animated after a few drinks. We were asked to take our meetings to another venue after one evening when he was particularly noisy. That's how we moved to the crypt."

"What did Rupert think of that?"

"Well, he couldn't say much, could he? He was the cause of our ban. The crypt isn't licensed, but it's next door to the Saracen's Head, which suits him well, I fancy. He's a mischief maker at times, but brilliant in his way, and I thought it was in all our interests to keep him as a member."

They got up to leave. Diamond thanked Polly for seeing them at such a late hour.

She said, "I hope I've been of some help, but I doubt it. I can't think how this ghastly thing happened."

"It's becoming clearer to me, ma'am," he told her. "And, yes, you have been helpful. The Bloodhounds have been meeting for six years. That's mainly down to you. I mean, you put a lot into it. I've heard this from several sources. For you, it's more than just a way to pass a Monday evening."

She said modestly, "It isn't any hardship."

"Ah, but you do make a point of encouraging them. A phone call here and there. The odd cup of coffee."

"I enjoy it."

"Keeping up with the other members, I mean. Did you get to know Sid away from the meetings?"

She returned his gaze with cold eyes. "Not at all."

"Never met him outside the crypt?"

"He was unapproachable."

"Of course." At the front door, he paused. "I noticed you have a burglar alarm fitted on the front of your house."

"Yes, I do."

"Very sensible. You have it serviced on a regular basis, I'm sure."

"Of course. They send a man every six months."

"That's all right, then." He put on his trilby, stepped away from the house and turned to look up at the box fitted under the eaves. "It's too dark to see. Out of interest, Mrs. Wycherley, does it happen to be one of the Impregnable alarms?"

"No," she said, with just a hint of mockery, "it's a Chubb."

Down at the central police station, John Wigfull was lingering in the incident room. The civilian clerks had long since finished. One sergeant was trying to look busy in front of a screen.

"Working late, John?" Diamond commented.

Gratified to be found still on duty, Wigfull actually smiled. "Needs must. I'm just back from the Holburne Museum, making sure the night squad are on their toes."

"Expecting some action tonight?"

"That's the pattern. There isn't much delay after the riddle is sent. The Penny Black was taken the night after, and it turned up on the day the second riddle was received."

"Good thinking. So it's a strong presence down at the museum?"

"Six men."

"Strategically posted?"

"It's not an easy building, but I think six should be enough."

"To end the suspense?"

Wigfull frowned uncertainly.

"I'm quoting the riddle, John. 'To end the suspense, as yours truly did . . .' "

"Ah."

". . . 'Discover the way to Sydney from Sid.' And that's what you've done. Six good men posted in Sydney Gardens should end the suspense sooner than Johnny expects."

"I'd like to think so," said Wigfull.

"So are you off home?"

He shook his head. "I'll stick around, I think. Stay in touch with the lads down there."

"A chance for some quiet reflection, eh?" Diamond said. "You're still pondering over the locked room mystery, I daresay. Any fresh theories?"

Wigfull's mustache moved strangely, and Diamond thought he might be grinding his teeth. He had no theories he wanted to share.

When invited for a coffee in the canteen, he declined.

"So whodunit, Julie?"

They had the canteen entirely to themselves, apart from the woman who had served them, and she was reading a Barbara Cartland in the kitchen. This was to be the last coffee of the day. Diamond had an apricot pie to go with his. By the time he got home, Steph would have eaten.

Julie couldn't give an answer, and was wise enough not to guess.

"We've seen them all now," Diamond reminded her chirpily. "Heard all their stories."

"And got more questions than answers," she said.

"Clues, then. Let's examine the clues."

"Rupert's beret?"

This wasn't high on his own list, and he explained why. "I'm keeping an open mind on that one. If we *ever* get hold of the damned thing—and I mean to have one more try tonight—and if we find it spotted with paint, what does it tell us—only that Rupert may have written an unkind message on a gallery window."

Julie was unwilling to dismiss the beret. "It means we ought to question him again for sure, in case he really found out something about Jessica."

He made no response, preferring a bite of the pie. "Another clue?"

"The paper bag, if you prefer," she said.

"It isn't what I prefer," he said, "it's what we have to deal with." Both of them were tired, and it was showing.

Julie said, "Since we're talking whodunits, I think the bag is a red herring. I mean the writing on the bag. We thought it proved that Sid composed the riddles. We were obviously mistaken."

"You mean if this third riddle is authentic?"

"Yes."

"Very likely is, Julie. Similar type, similar paper, similar distribution."

"So what are we to make of the writing on it? They *are* lists of rhyming words."

"True."

"And they seem to refer to what was going on. You pointed out yourself that one of the lists rhymes with the word 'motion,' and another with 'black,' presumably for Penny Black."

"And 'room'—for locked room."

"What was Sid up to, then, if he wasn't working on a new riddle?"

"You're making an assumption there, Julie, that I can't automatically accept."

"What's that?" She screwed up her face, trying to work it out. Not easy, after more than thirteen hours on duty. "You're questioning whether Sid made those lists?"

He finished the pie and wiped the edges of his mouth. "Think of that paper bag as evidence we pass on to the CPS. What do they want from us? Continuity of evidence. Remember your promotion exams. First, they want to know where it originated."

"A secondhand bookshop."

"By no means certain."

"They nearly always use brown paper bags."

"So do plenty of other shops."

"It did contain a book."

"All right. Who owned the book?"

"Sid."

"Yes, but where was it from? We can't say. Maybe not from a shop at all. Maybe from another collector, someone else in the Bloodhounds, someone who jotted lists on a paper bag."

"And gave it to Sid by accident?"

"Or design."

"That's really devious."

"This murder is, Julie. I'm not saying this is what happened. As well as examining the start of this chain, you have to look at the end. What happened to the bag after it left Sid's possession?"

"It was jammed against Miss Chilmark's face."

"But who by?"

"Jessica Shaw."

"And then?"

"It ended up in Jessica's handbag. Oh!" She put her hand to her mouth. "She could have written the lists."

He said nothing, letting this take root.

Julie moved to the next stage in the logic. "But she handed us the bag. If she'd used it herself to make lists, she'd never have done that. She isn't daft. She would have destroyed it."

"Unless she wanted us to see the lists."

Julie frowned. "And assume they must have been written by Sid. Why?"

"To shift suspicion."

Her eyes widened amazingly for one so tired. "I hadn't seen it like that at all."

"It's only one end of the chain, remember."

"Can we get a handwriting expert on to this?"

"I sent the bag away with a sample of Sid's writing," he said, "but I'm not optimistic. Graphologists like joined-up writing. This wasn't. And—before you ask—none of the words was misspelled. No point in running a little test for our suspects."

She said, "It does bring us to another clue."

"What's that?"

"The writing on the gallery window. 'She did for Sid.' Someone—probably Rupert—believes Jessica is the killer."

"Or wants us to believe she is." He was finding this session helpful. He moved on to the most elusive of all the elements in this case: the motive. Succinctly, he laid out the options for Julie to consider. The best bet was that Sid had been a blackmailer. At Impregnable he had unusual opportunities to pick up tidbits of information about people's private affairs. He had access to confidential files and he worked with ex-policemen with inside knowledge of the indiscretions of some of the most outwardly respectable residents of Bath. Certainly there were questions about Miss Chilmark's regular withdrawals of large sums from the bank. Jessica, too, might be vulnerable to blackmail if she was having an affair with A.J. Rupert had a past, but he was quite open about it. Of the others, Polly seemed well defended in every sense, and Shirley-Ann was surely too new on the scene to have fallen a victim.

There were two big problems with the blackmail theory, he admitted to Julie. Firstly, there was no evidence that Sid had received money in any appreciable amounts. He lived in that depressing flat in the shadow of the viaduct in Oak Street and worked unsocial hours as a night watchman. Surely a blackmailer's lifestyle would have shown some improvement? And the second problem was the manner of Sid's death. Why would a blackmail victim choose to put an end to the extortion in such an elaborate fashion, in a locked cabin on a boat?

So he outlined his alternative theory, the one he had touched on while interviewing Polly. This postulated that the killing had not been planned. It was sparked by the Penny Black turning up in the astonishing way it did. Sid—the Dickson Carr fanatic—was so excited, so intrigued, by a real-life locked room puzzle that he went to the boat to examine it for himself. There he met the person responsible. Sid was killed because of what he discovered, not who he was.

"What was the murderer doing there?" Julie asked.

Diamond gripped the edge of the table as a thought struck him. His eyes shone. "Julie, that's the whole point. Brilliant! You haven't told me whodunit, but you've given me the solution to the locked room mystery."

It was after ten that evening when he returned to Hay Hill, this time alone, Julie having been released from duty as a reward for her brilliance.

Rupert's house still had no light inside. The dog barked furiously.

The waitress in the Paragon Bar and Bistro told him Rupert must have gone somewhere else for a change. She hadn't seen him all evening. Neither had the landlord at his other local, the Lansdown Arms.

He looked at the clock and decided there was time to try the Saracen's Head, a mere five minutes away, down the hill in Broad Street. The Saracen was still doing good business toward closing time, but there wasn't a beret to be seen. Diamond was given some abuse by a well-tanked customer for giving a shout out of turn. A glare put a stop to that, and got the barman's attention as well. After a quick consultation among the bar staff, one of them pointed to a table in one of the partitioned sections. Here, it seemed, Rupert occasionally held court, telling tall stories about his encounters with the great and the not-so-good, surrounded by a delighted crowd of regulars. These were the people who looked after Marlowe the night that unruly animal was banished from the Bloodhounds' meeting.

It emerged that Rupert had indeed called in for a beer much earlier, about seven. One glass of bitter. He had been dressed as usual in beret, black leather, and blue cords. Less usually, he hadn't brought Marlowe because, he had explained, he had been invited for drinks at another pub, and dogs weren't welcome in some houses. He had left after five minutes. Nobody knew any more about this arrangement.

There are one hundred and forty public houses in and around Bath.

Diamond treated himself to a brandy before going home.

CHAPTER THIRTY

FOR JOHN WIGFULL THERE WAS NO SLEEP THAT NIGHT. About midnight he parked his car opposite the entrance to the Bath Spa Hotel and walked briskly through Sydney Gardens to the Holburne Museum. A less conscientious officer might have parked closer to the building, in Sydney Road, say, just around the corner. Wigfull was determined to give nobody a clue as to his presence, and that included his own men. When the side door of the museum opened and the sergeant looked out, Wigfull put his finger to his lips and went silently in.

The Holburne is not an easy building to make secure. It looks like a cross between an English country house and a Greek temple. Built toward the end of the eighteenth century as a hotel with a classical facade of a pediment and four columns mounted above three arches, the original structure has undergone several alterations in its two-hundred-year existence, notably the addition of an extra storey and balustraded walls at each side. The front is open to the road. Where once there were railings,.there remains only a low wall facing Great Pulteney Street. Two watchman's boxes have a purely decorative function now. At the rear, a combination of drainpipes and footholds between the stone blocks would be as good as a ladder to an intruder. Fortunately, the alarm system is modern and efficient, and there are floodlights at the front and security lights right around the building.

The six policemen posted strategically inside and on the roof were in radio contact, and Wigfull made sure that they were alert. As well as calling them a number of times on their personal radios, he took the extra precaution of visiting them half-hourly. He made no friends that night, but nobody slept on duty.

By 6:30 next morning, nothing suspicious had occurred. Disappointed at having failed to trap the villain, but relieved that the museum was intact, Wigfull stood on the roof eating chocolate and watching the first glimmer of dawn over Bathampton Down. It was safe, he decided, to return home for a few hours' rest. Leaving instructions to the senior man to keep up the vigil until the relief team arrived at 8 A.M., he took the short cut through Sydney Gardens toward his car. A light frost had blanched the lawns.

Cold as it felt outdoors, this was a charming place to be at this early hour. In years past, Sydney Gardens had been a mecca for Bathonians. It had brass bands, a bowling green, a maze, grottoes, and firework displays. Two emperors, Napoleon III and Haile Selassie, had walked these paths. So had Jane Austen, Emma Hamilton, and Lord Macaulay. This morning John Wigfull, Chief Inspector, justifiably content after a night's policing, had the entire place to himself.

Except for one dog.

He spotted it in the distance coming over the narrower of the two railway bridges, a large black poodle, trotting with that air of purpose special to dogs. Instead of staying on the path, the poodle started across the broad sweep of lawn toward the laurel bushes on the far side. Wigfull, almost as purposeful, continued his brisk walk, thinking of other things. Ahead, he knew, was the railway cutting. All that could be seen of it was a massive stone retaining wall, and he wondered why a number of park benches were positioned opposite, as if users of the park might wish to turn their backs on the lawns and trees and stare at blocks of grimy stone. In 1841 Brunel had been permitted to navigate his Great Western Railway through the gardens, provided that the trains would not spoil the vista, so the track was laid in a deep gully impossible to see from the benches. Brunel had fulfilled the contract handsomely. The bridges for pedestrians were a pleasure to use, elegant and unobtrusive. Wigfull would need to cross the railway and the canal a short way on to reach his car. He didn't get that far, because his attention was caught again by the dog.

That it was a poodle had been clear from the moment he had seen it, for it was clipped. Large standard poodles are not often seen these days. This was a fine specimen and probably should not have been off the leash. The owner had not appeared. In his days as a beat officer, Wigfull might have gone to investigate, but this morning he had more important things on his mind than a stray poodle.

The poodle had other ideas. Halfway across the lawn, it switched direction and came lolloping toward Wigfull. Only then did he notice something odd. He was no expert on poodle clipping, but he had always thought they were supposed to have pointed muzzles, whatever outcrops of hair were permitted around the top of the head and the mane.

This one had a beard. Or side-whiskers growing below the jawline like some Prussian aristocrat of a century ago. A strange extravagance, and not symmetrical. There was definitely more of it on the right of the jaw than the left.

Wigfull stopped to look.

He had been mistaken. He wasn't looking at a beard, but something the dog was carrying between its teeth. Something as dark as the rest of the coat.

"Here, boy!"

He stopped and held out his hand.

The dog approached to within a few yards before changing its mind and racing away.

But in that short time, Wigfull saw clearly what the dog had in its mouth: a black beret.

"Oy! Come back!"

The beret could have belonged to anyone, been discarded

by anyone. But there are not many owners of berets in Bath.
He knew of one of them. He decided he had better go in pursuit.

There is no chance of outrunning a dog, but they don't usually dash at top speed for long. This one stopped after thirty
yards or so and looked back, wagging its pom-pom tail.

Wigfull called some encouraging words. The dog dropped
the beret and barked. It was ready for a game.

"Come on, then!"

It didn't come. It ran off again—not without picking up the
beret.

Wigfull wondered if this was worth the trouble. His shoes
were going to be ruined. He looked about him to see if the
poodle's owner was anywhere in sight. No such luck.

Away to his left, on the far side of the lawn, was a Roman
temple, or, rather, a twentieth-century reconstruction, an up-
market rain shelter. The poodle was heading toward it fast. If
he could only trap it in there . . .

He covered the distance quickly. The dog had gone inside
and was crouching under the stone seat that extended around
the three enclosed sides. The beret was still in its mouth.

Wigfull was wary of going too close. If the poodle felt cor-
nered, it might get aggressive. Up to now, it had seemed playful, but this was a new situation.

He ventured just inside the temple and tried clicking his
tongue in a friendly way. The dog gave a low growl.

"It's all right, old fellow," Wigfull said reassuringly. "I'm
just a friend. Are you going to give me a present? I'd like
that."

The dog growled again. In the gloom of the temple its eyes
had a reddish glint that Wigfull didn't care for.

Then he remembered the bar of chocolate he had in his
pocket to sustain him through the night. There were still several pieces left. Did poodles eat chocolate?

"How about this, then?" He held a piece out. "Just the job,
eh?"

The dog was definitely interested. It raised its head and sniffed. Only it didn't move from under the seat.

"Come and get it, then."

No chance, the poodle seemed to say.

In case he was more of a threat standing up, Wigfull crossed to the side opposite the dog and sat down, still holding out the chocolate in his open palm and speaking encouragingly.

There was a break in the deadlock. The dog let the beret slip from its jaws and took a couple of deep sniffs. Then it got up, leaving the beret, and crossed to where Wigfull was sitting, put its nose to the chocolate, decided it was edible and took it.

He noticed it was wearing a collar with a name tag, but he didn't dare put his hand under its neck. He found two more pieces of chocolate. The first he fed to the dog, and the second he planned to throw through the temple pillars onto the path outside. The dog would run after it, and Wigfull would retrieve the beret.

But it didn't happen like that. A voice from nowhere, echoing around the stone walls, impressive as an oracle, spoke the words "What are you feeding that dog?"

Wigfull jerked his hand away and looked guiltily to his right.

A man carrying a spade like a weapon stepped from behind a pillar. He was dressed in a scuffed leather jacket, black jeans, and gumboots. He looked dangerous.

"Only chocolate," said Wigfull.

"You've no business feeding him anything," said the man with the spade. "What's your game?"

Wigfull explained that he was a detective, a chief inspector, and he was trying to remove the beret from the dog, because it might be evidence in a case he was involved in. It sounded unconvincing, even to him, and on this, of all mornings, he wasn't carrying his identity card. He'd changed into a padded jacket for the night and left the ID in his suit at home.

The poodle growled at Wigfull.

The man said, "Bloody liar."

Wigfull pointed across the temple at the beret, still lying on the floor.

The man said, "Chief inspector, my arse. You were feeding him something. You weren't after the beret. You hadn't even bothered to pick it up. You were after my dog. He's a thoroughbred poodle, is Inky, and you well know it."

"He's yours?" said Wigfull.

"Why else would he be running loose in the park? I'm the deputy head gardener here."

The dispute continued for some time before Wigfull convinced the gardener that he was, indeed, one of the top men at Manvers Street and not a dog snatcher. Finally, they went their different ways, Wigfull with the beret in his pocket, and the gardener leading Inky to a council van.

Annoyed with himself, Wigfull walked on toward the far end of the gardens and crossed the railway and the canal, thinking of things he should have said. He was so preoccupied that he failed to notice something far more sinister than a poodle with a beret.

CHAPTER THIRTY-ONE

ABOUT TWENTY TO SEVEN THE SAME MORNING, A JOGGER on his regular route along the towpath, approaching the point where the canal passed under Cleveland House and Sydney Road before entering Sydney Gardens, caught sight through the tunnel of the first of the two wrought iron bridges. He always looked forward to this point of the run. Aside from the boost of knowing that he was two-thirds of the way home, there was the sheer pleasure in the spectacle of the white-painted bridge framed by the arch of the tunnel.

Except that this morning something was different.

When you are jogging for exercise, you don't stop to get a better view of things along the way. As he approached the tunnel, the jogger thought he could make out an object suspended beneath the arch of the bridge, but he couldn't tell what it was. It isn't possible to run through the tunnel, so he climbed up to Sydney Road to enter the Gardens, cross by the iron bridge, and take the little gate down to rejoin the towpath. When he got closer he saw that he was not mistaken. Something was hanging from the bridge, and it was a body.

This section of canal is one of Bath's secrets, as charming as anything in the city, almost two centuries old, yet constructed with visual appeal, with sweetly curved passing places, and glimpses under the arches of several bridges, their reflections patterning the water.

By eight, the reflections included an inflatable dinghy, police, park officials, a doctor, and two ambulancemen. The entire area was cordoned off. The body was photographed in situ and seen by the police surgeon before police performed the tricky operation of cutting it down and lowering it into the dinghy. The dead man was dressed in a black leather jacket, striped shirt, navy blue corduroy trousers, and black shoes. He was thin, about six feet tall, and looked about forty-five. His neck was obviously broken, confirming a considerable drop. This, the surgeon pointed out, must have been an efficient hanging. Most suicide victims use a chair or a ladder and rarely break their necks, and in consequence die slowly.

The pockets of the leather jacket were found to contain a five-pound note, some loose change, a set of keys on a ring, and a padlock. An alert constable pointed out that the padlock was of the same make as the German one featured in the locked room case currently being investigated by the murder squad. The incident room was informed at once.

Peter Diamond had no breakfast that morning. He drove the short distance from his home in Weston to the Royal United Hospital in time to see the body brought into the mortuary. He was allowed to unzip the body bag and confirm that the dead man was Rupert Darby. And the noose was still around his neck. The rope had been cut higher up.

A real sense of loss affected the big detective on seeing Rupert's gaunt face, the bluish lips parted, revealing the gaps between a few nicotine-stained teeth. In that one short meeting the previous morning he had enjoyed talking to Rupert, quickly getting attuned to his irreverent wit and warming to his vitality. What remained of the man was wholly pathetic.

He would have liked to examine the arms and torso for possible bruising, but that was the pathologist's prerogative. To remove the clothes prematurely would be a major breach of procedure.

After viewing the corpse, Diamond went home briefly.

Steph offered to cook his usual bacon and eggs, but he didn't fancy anything except a black coffee. He told her he expected another long day.

John Wigfull arrived an hour later than usual, with heavy shadows around his eyes, and was startled to find so much activity in the incident room. For a few nerve-racking minutes, he wondered if in the short time he had been away, the thief had got into the museum.

Diamond told him about Rupert Darby.

In turn, Wigfull told Diamond about the beret he had found. He didn't go into the problems Inky the poodle had given him, merely stating that he had picked up the beret soon after six thirty. "I'm bound to say I wondered about it when I saw it," he added.

"Where was it?" Diamond asked.

"Em, I picked it up in that temple thing near the railway bridge. Do you know where I mean?" He produced the beret from his pocket. "By the look of this, some animal has chewed it about a bit. A dog, I'd say. Do you think it was Rupert's?"

"Sure of it." Diamond flattened the beret on a table. "You can see where the paint spray got to it."

Wigfull hadn't heard about the paint, or the graffiti on the Walsingham Gallery window. He had to be told. He studied the tiny paint spots that covered about a third of the beret and said humbly that if he'd realized how crucial a piece of evidence this was, he'd have treated it more carefully.

Diamond had not deliberately withheld information, he made clear; he'd only heard about it late the previous afternoon. There had not been an opportunity.

Wigfull, floundering in his own deceit, made no objection. Instead, he said, "He must have taken off the beret to fit the noose over his head. Probably left it on the bridge, and a dog picked it up."

"His own dog, I expect," said Diamond, reasonably enough.

"I shouldn't count on it," said Wigfull, going red. "I did happen to see a large poodle running loose in the gardens—quite near the temple, actually."

"Could have been the poodle, then."

"Doesn't really matter, does it?" said Wigfull, trying to emphasize the larger considerations. "The crucial thing is that we found it and confirmed what you heard about the paint marks. Pretty damning. This writing on the gallery window was a desperate attempt by Rupert to throw suspicion on someone else, wouldn't you say?"

"Looks that way," Diamond said.

"And when it didn't succeed, when you followed up yesterday, asking for him in all his usual haunts, he heard we were onto him and topped himself."

Diamond wasn't having that. He hadn't hounded Rupert to his death. "You're wrong there, John. This hanging wasn't something he thought of yesterday evening. It couldn't have been."

This drew a frown from Wigfull.

Patiently and without condescension, Diamond explained. "It was in the third riddle:

> " 'To end the suspense, as yours truly did,
> Discover the way to Sydney from Sid.' "

Wigfull's long, silent look showed that he dearly wanted to know what Diamond was getting at.

"The riddle predicted this hanging," Diamond went on. "'To end the suspense': That's what happened this morning. Rupert was suspended from the bridge. When he was cut down, we ended the suspense. It was a play on words, John, a gruesome double meaning. So it was all planned. 'Discover the way to Sydney' is what we did, except that we guessed wrong and picked the bloody museum instead of the bridge.

If we'd thought more about every sodding word in the riddle, we might have anticipated this."

"Might not."

Really, Diamond had to agree. The lines had tantalized, as the previous riddles had. To have penetrated their true meaning would have required the brilliance of one of those fictional sleuths the Bloodhounds revered. He knew his limitations.

Wigfull took a more positive line. "At least you have your murderer, and I have my locked room thief," he pointed out. "All we have to do now is work out how it was done."

"You're assuming Rupert Darby is your man?"

"Aren't you?" said Wigfull, blushing scarlet.

Diamond said, "If you really want to know, John, I think you couldn't be more wrong. I know how it was done, but I'm damned if I know who did it."

"You're talking about the locked room mystery? You think you've cracked it?" said Wigfull on a shrill note of disbelief.

Diamond had cracked it all right. He was certain now, after thinking it through, going over it many times in his mind since getting the flash of inspiration the evening before. As he'd told Julie at the time, the breakthrough had come with her question: "What was the murderer doing there?"

Between them, on a table, labeled and bagged, were the contents of the dead man's pockets. Diamond pointed to the polythene bag containing the padlock. "Take a look. Is it, or is it not, indistinguishable from the padlock on the narrowboat?"

Wigfull turned it over several times. "It's the same make, certainly. But we've been through this before, my theory about a substitute padlock. You know we have. I thought I had the answer until you showed it was impossible. This padlock can't have been used. Milo's was on the door when we opened it that night, and he had only the one key. You proved that yourself when your divers found his old bunch of keys in the canal and the damned thing fitted. This doesn't prove anything unless the keys happen to be identical, and we were told by the locksmith that such a thing couldn't happen."

"Just in case, let's put that to the test," said Diamond. He went to a drawer and took out Milo's padlock and the key that fitted it. "Pass me the other bag, would you—the one containing Rupert's keys?"

"Do you think you ought to be handling them?" said Wigfull.

"The keys, please."

Wigfull shook the bag and dropped the key ring on the table top. He wasn't going to risk leaving *his* prints on them.

All work was suspended in the incident room. Everyone in there—detectives, filing clerks, computer operators—gathered around the two senior men. Julie Hargreaves was there, and Keith Halliwell, on tenterhooks to hear the explanation.

There were four keys on the ring: one of the Yale type that looked like a front-door key; a plastic-topped one that was probably for a car; and two small narrow ones, identical in shape. Diamond slotted one of the latter into Milo's padlock and tried unsuccessfully to turn it. To leave no one in any doubt, he tried the other, still with no result.

Wigfull said smugly, "You see. It doesn't match. Let's compare it with Milo's key. I'm willing to bet the whole shape is different."

He was right. When placed together, the two keys were clearly cut for different locks.

Diamond was not discouraged. Far from it. "Right. This is the way it was done. It's going to make you groan, it's so simple. This is Milo's padlock, right? And this is the key that fits it, the one key available at the time. Milo had possession of the key, so Milo was the only person who could open the padlock at any time. Everyone agreed?"

There were some cautious murmurs. Nobody really wanted to be shown up as gullible.

"Now imagine Milo going to his locked boat anytime you

like. He uses his key to open the padlock. Now what does he do?"

Halliwell said, "Removes the key and replaces it in his pocket."

Diamond wagged a stubby finger in confirmation. "Right. The keys go back into his pocket. What about the padlock?"

"He doesn't put that in his pocket," said one of the computer operators. "It's too bulky."

"So what does he do?"

"Leaves it hanging on the staple."

"Correct. Locked or unlocked?"

A moment's hesitation. Then, from Wigfull: "Unlocked, presumably. No point in locking it while he's at home. If he wants privacy, he can use the fingerbolts on the inside of the door."

Diamond gave a nod and referred the matter to everyone else by spreading his hands. "Reasonable? Now, let's take this on a bit. Milo is aboard his boat, sitting in the cabin watching TV or cooking. The door is bolted from the inside. The padlock is hanging from the staple outside the door with the shackle—this arched bit at the top—unfastened. Anyone could lift the padlock off. Are you with me still?"

There were nods and murmurs all around.

"Now along comes our villain with a similar padlock—different key, of course—unhooks Milo's padlock and substitutes his own. Done in a moment without Milo being aware of it. He goes away and waits for his opportunity."

There were definite sounds of understanding.

"You're onto it, aren't you?" said Diamond. "Milo decides to go out. And what does he do to lock his door? Simply closes it, lifts off the padlock—the new padlock, believing it to be his own—and slots the hasp over the staple. Puts the padlock in position and presses it home. He doesn't need to use his key. They lock automatically, as anyone who has used a padlock knows."

They were not only up with his explanation now; they were ahead. The murmurs were of appreciation.

"But of course," Diamond said, "the padlock he's just attached to his boat belongs to the villain, who can now unlock it at will. So the villain lets himself in, does his dirty work, and leaves. And when he leaves, he fixes Milo's padlock on the door and presses it closed. Milo comes back later, unlocks as usual, and can't fathom how someone could have got inside his cabin."

Julie said, "Nor could anyone else until this moment."

Halliwell said, "You've cracked it."

Even Wigfull was nodding.

A couple of people applauded, and almost everyone joined in.

Diamond flushed with embarrassment and reminded them that there was work to be done. His stock had never been higher at the Bath nick.

Later, at the bridge in Sydney Gardens, he examined the scene of the hanging. The approaches were still cordoned off. The Scenes of Crime officers had come and gone. Part of the rope was still attached to the iron parapet.

"If you wanted to end it all," Diamond said to Julie, who was with him, "there are worse ways than this. You sit on the railing here with one end around your neck and the other attached to the bridge and jump down. Mercifully quick."

"Is that what happened?" Julie said. Something in his tone had suggested otherwise.

"He certainly broke his neck."

She nodded. "Only I notice you haven't used the word *suicide* once."

"Because I'm not sure," he said.

"Murder by hanging would be pretty unusual, wouldn't it?"

"Very."

"Have you ever come across one?"

"Never. The victim is going to struggle, isn't he? I reckon

you'd need a couple of people to carry it out. It's not as if his arms and legs were pinioned, as they are in a judicial hanging. Unless he were very feeble for some reason, or so pissed out of his mind that he didn't know what was happening—"

"That might be true in this case," she said.

"He was out early last evening," Diamond confirmed. "I did establish that he had a quick pint in the Saracen's Head about seven and went off to meet someone else."

"Did he say who?"

"No. But it was at some other pub, which was why he didn't have the dog with him. He told them in the Saracen's that you couldn't count on every pub accepting animals."

"So it *was* a boozy evening," said Julie. "Do we know what time he died?"

He shrugged. "They can never tell you with any precision. Between midnight—when Wigfull came through here—and six thirty in the morning."

Julie tried to picture the scene. "If he was drunk by then— I mean so helpless that someone could hang him—this would be a long way to bring him. Can you get a car along these paths?"

Diamond's immediate response showed that he'd given the problem some thought already. "Yes, you can drive straight in from Sydney Place. There's no gate."

"Difficult to prove," Julie remarked.

"Impossible."

"I meant the possibility of murder."

"You never know what the postmortem may show up," he said. "I've asked Jack Merlin to do it."

Merlin was the top forensic pathologist in the west of England. He would have to drive seventy miles, from Reading. He and Diamond knew each other of old, but he would have needed some convincing that a routine suicide by hanging was worth the journey.

"You do believe there's something suspicious," Julie probed.

He made some indeterminate sound and pulled a face. "Nothing very solid."

To draw him out, she said, "There wasn't any suicide note. If he did this from a sense of guilt, you'd think he would want to confess."

Again, he gave a shrug. "It's early days to worry about a note. Could be at his house, or in the post. The thing that makes me pause for thought is the padlock being found in his pocket. If you were going on a bender with a friend, would you carry a damned great padlock with you? What would be the point? It's not as if he was going to try the locked room trick on Milo's boat again. No point in that, surely? The only reason I can think of is to link him with the killing of Sid Towers. That *may* have been Rupert's way of telling us he was guilty. But as you just pointed out, he could have done that better in a written confession."

"And if we're talking murder," said Julie, "the padlock in his pocket is a lot easier to plant than a fake confession. It still frames him."

Diamond turned and looked along the strip of blue-green water toward the second iron bridge. "Another murder on the canal? I wonder, Julie. I wonder."

The first task after entering the house in Hay Hill that afternoon was to open a tin of dog food and pour some water into a bowl. Marlowe was ravenous.

Julie saw to it. "Poor thing—he's been alone here since seven last night. I'm going to take him for a walk. You don't mind?"

"If it doesn't take long."

He opened some windows.

The second task was to find the suicide note, if one existed. He looked in the obvious places, over the fireplace and by the bed. On the kitchen table. Beside the ancient typewriter in the back room.

No joy.

He found some cash, about thirty pounds, in an old box file, along with an out-of-date passport, letters from the local Job Center and the Social Security office, unfilled tax declaration forms, doctors' certificates, and beer mats with some names and addresses scribbled on them that meant nothing to Diamond. Nothing so helpful as a diary. A testament to a chaotic existence. He was learning nothing new about Rupert.

While his thoughts were still full of the dead man, he felt a sudden pressure against his leg. "Jesus!"

Marlowe was back from his walk and wanting more food.

Julie followed the dog in. "He's a super old thing really," she said. "Just wants some training. I'm sure he'd pick it up."

"You'd better open another tin before he has my leg," said Diamond, less enchanted.

"Found anything useful?" she asked.

He shook his head.

"So we wait for the postmortem?"

"Well, I did ask the police surgeon to take a blood sample. There may be some news on the alcohol content. We'd better be getting back to the nick, anyway."

"What about the dog?"

Diamond's mind was on other things.

Julie said, "We can't leave him here and forget about him. What's going to happen to him?"

He yawned and said as if such details were beneath him, "The Dogs' and Cats' Home at Claverton, I reckon."

Julie's blue eyes moistened at the thought. "We can't just stick him in a home."

"My cat, Raffles, came from there."

"He's not a young dog, you can see that. No one would want to take him on."

"There's no alternative."

"There is. He can come home with me. I'll have him."

His eyes widened. "You've got two dogs already, haven't you?"

"So I'm used to it."

He felt compelled to ask, "What's your husband going to say?"

"Charlie? I'll talk him into it."

"But if you've got the dog with you already . . ."

She smiled. "Exactly. When he sees Marlowe, he won't turn him away."

He didn't pursue it. Julie's domestic arrangements were her own business. They drove back to Manvers Street with Marlowe seated contentedly on the backseat, spreading gusts of his doggy breath around the car.

CHAPTER THIRTY-TWO

BACK AT MANVERS STREET, THERE WAS A MESSAGE WAITING from the police surgeon: Rupert's blood alcohol level had been high, at 100mg/100ml, but not excessively high. Diamond screwed it up and tossed it into the bin. "I'd have expected double that figure if he was legless."

Julie pointed out that 100mg was above the legal limit for a driver, and Diamond said offhandedly that this wasn't about pinching a dead man for drunk driving.

She was treading on eggs, but she wasn't going to let him get away with a cheap jibe. "It's worth remembering when the blood sample was taken, about eight this morning. We don't know when he had his last drink, but the alcohol must have been metabolizing for some time. It would have been a higher reading if we'd got the blood earlier."

He rolled his eyes at her use of the word *metabolizing* and said, "Too bad we didn't, then. You must be right, I suppose. I'm a dead loss at science. You've got to make allowances, Julie."

She surprised him by saying, "You, too, Mr. Diamond."

"What?"

"You've got to make allowances."

"What for?"

"For the metabolic factor."

"Ah." He grinned faintly.

Still unhappy with the result, however, he arranged for a driver to collect the sample and take it at once to the Home Office forensic laboratory at Chepstow. They would check for other substances; it was not inconceivable that one of Rupert's drinks had been spiked. But of course a test for drugs would take time. He hated delays.

His mood didn't improve when he looked into the incident room. The impetus seemed to have gone out of the inquiry, as if everyone there was just cruising now. The general idea was that Rupert's hanging had confirmed him as the murderer, even though no confession had yet come to light. Diamond, they felt, was just being bloody-minded now, and he added more fuel by ordering an immediate search for witnesses and yet another check of all the suspects and the people they lived with, this time to establish their movements since seven the previous evening—an exercise guaranteed to create more resentment and hostility.

He said he would take his share of the flak by checking on Jessica Shaw and the men in her life. Halliwell and a detective constable were sent to the Paragon to interview Miss Chilmark. Julie went off to the Badgerline offices to find where Shirley-Ann Miller was this morning, and after that to the Sports and Leisure Center to check on Bert. DS Hughes and DC Twigg were dispatched to Claverton to call on Polly Wycherley. And, just for the record, as Diamond put it, DS Mitchell went out to the boatyard to talk to Milo Motion.

Instead of going directly to the Walsingham Gallery, Diamond started at the Locksbrook Trading Estate, west of the city, where Jessica's husband rented a unit for his ceramics business. It was high time to meet that patron of the arts, Mr. Barnaby Shaw.

Asked to wait in the showroom, he felt like Gulliver in Lilliput, surrounded by what must have been the entire range of miniature buildings in Barnaby's stock: houses by the hundred, stately homes, churches, pubs, and castles. Finely made as they were, to a man as incorrigibly clumsy as Diamond, such exquisite little pieces represented a thousand potential hazards. He stood uneasily in the only space of any size that he could find, trying to stay clear of the slowly revolving display stands. It was a mercy when Barnaby's assistant called him into the managerial suite.

Having negotiated the showroom without mishap, the big man tripped on an Afghan rug and lurched forward, grabbing Barnaby's welcoming hand and practically dragging him to the floor. Bits of china around the room rattled, but nothing was broken.

"Never look where I'm going," he admitted. "When I was a kid, my knees were permanently covered in scabs."

The p.a. escorted him to an armchair.

Barnaby looked more shaken than his guest. Trim in a gray suit, with a maroon shirt and toning tie and pocket handkerchief, he wasn't dressed for wrestling. Diamond watched the way he scooted back around his desk; he looked used to staying out of trouble.

They discussed the miniatures politely. Barnaby had started making matchstick models thirty years ago and progressed by stages to ceramics. He sometimes did commissions for people who wanted their homes immortalized, but it came rather expensive. Diamond said honestly that he considered it a waste of money, adding tactfully that he was always breaking things.

Barnaby submitted easily to the questioning.

"Yes, I was here until late yesterday evening catching up on the orders. It gets very busy in the run-up to Christmas."

"Christmas already?" Diamond said in mock horror. "Anyone with you?"

"Last night, you mean?"

"Yes."

"Not after six, when the staff left."

"So what time did you get home, Mr. Shaw?"

"Must have been well after midnight. About one thirty, I'd

say." He was fluent in his replies, unaware (presumably) of Rupert's death, giving the impression of a small businessman pressed to the limit, but cheerful. But he obviously found time to dress well, even if the three-piece suit seemed a little wasted on the trading estate.

"Did you speak to anyone at all in that time?"

"Certainly—on the phone."

"But you weren't seen by anyone?"

"No."

"When you got in, was your wife in bed?"

"I presume she was."

"You don't know?"

"We sleep in separate rooms."

That fitted, Diamond thought. He was hard pressed to think what Jessica Shaw found attractive in this dull, overworked man, unless it was the money he made from his titchy houses. No, to be fair, he was dapper. And he took the trouble to tint his hair.

"Do you happen to know how Mrs. Shaw spent the evening?"

"You'll have to ask her. I haven't seen her since early yesterday. She was still asleep when I left this morning." He put his hand to his mouth as a thought struck him. "Look, nothing's happened to Jess, has it?"

"Not to my knowledge."

"Someone else? A.J.?"

"I was going to ask you about him, Mr. Shaw. A close friend of the family, obviously."

"Well . . . yes," said Barnaby, as if he needed to ponder the matter before confirming it. "He's extremely helpful."

"In what way, sir?"

"With the gallery."

"You mean setting up the exhibitions, and so forth?"

"Financially, also. He has a large stake in the business."

This was new information—though Diamond tried to make

it seem familiar. "Well, he would want to see it succeed—as one of the exhibitors, I mean."

"I doubt if Jess could keep it going without his help," Barnaby placidly agreed. "I certainly couldn't fund it out of my profits. I chip in when I can, but the overheads are terrific. You wouldn't believe the business rate in the city. The heating bills, the publicity. A.J. takes care of all that."

So A.J. was the patron of the arts. "Out of his sales?"

"Lord, no. He doesn't sell much at all. He's a proficient artist, but not commercial. He has a private income."

"And did he help with the party the other evening—the, em, preview?"

"He was a great help, yes."

"I meant financially. Did he pay for the booze?"

"No. Actually, that was my gift to Jessica. I chip in when I can. It's easier to fund a one-off event like that than meet the regular bills, as A.J. so generously does."

Barnaby's own generosity of spirit was increasingly puzzling to Diamond, trained to look for the jealousies and rivalries in relationships. This wanted probing further. "He does this out of friendship, does he?"

"Essentially, yes," Barnaby confirmed. "He has a stake, in a sense, because he hopes to sell his paintings, and probably he could insist on a one-man show if he wanted. However, he's content to be treated as any other artist wishing to exhibit."

"That is altruistic." Diamond took a deep breath and dived in. "I don't wish to be offensive, Mr. Shaw, but haven't you ever wondered about his motives?"

"I don't understand you."

"Your wife's an attractive woman."

"Oh, I see," said Barnaby coolly. "You're suggesting a liaison of some kind?"

"In your shoes, I would have given it more than a passing thought."

"But you're not—and you don't know Jess."

"I've met her."

"What I mean, Superintendent, is that she can be trusted absolutely. I understand why you mention the matter. She's a modern, intelligent woman, but she has an old-fashioned notion of fidelity. I won't pretend that she and I are locked into a passionate marriage. I just know that Jessica would never be unfaithful."

"That must be a great consolation."

"When she spends so much time in the company of another man, you mean?" said Barnaby. "I know exactly what you're getting at. I've no doubt that she and A.J. are close. Intellectually, they may be flirting outrageously. Physically, no."

"Would you mind enlarging on that?" asked Diamond.

"On what?"

"Flirting intellectually."

Barnaby Shaw smiled. "If you haven't indulged, it's hard to explain. Let's put it this way. The attraction two people feel for each other is channeled in certain ways. If there is sexual energy, it may find an outlet through other means. Music, perhaps. Or food."

"Lunchtime walks?"

Barnaby gave him a sharper look. "I'm not explaining myself very well, am I? Intelligent people—and the two we're discussing are very bright indeed—may indulge in a kind of ritual, finding some means of amusement, some game, that diverts their energy and is fulfilling."

"That's enough?"

"It would be enough for Jessica."

Such sophisticated goings-on were outside Diamond's experience. He wasn't sure that he was convinced by the rationale. It was not impossible that Barnaby was trying to convince himself.

"I'd like to ask you about the graffiti that appeared on the gallery window on the evening of the party," he said.

For the first time, Barnaby was rattled. "Who told you about that?"

"It came to my attention."

"The young woman with the glasses and the fringe? Miss Miller?"

"I think it's fairly common knowledge, Mr. Shaw. There were plenty of people at the party."

"Yes, but they didn't all see the writing. In fact, nobody remarked on it until we noticed it ourselves. It wasn't very obvious with all the lights on in the gallery. One tended to look through the windows, not at them."

"I see. And did your wife have any idea who was responsible?"

"No idea whatsoever, but she was pretty upset about it."

"Which was why you decided to wipe it off without reporting it?"

"Left to herself, Jess would have called the police."

"Why didn't she?"

"Because we persuaded her that it wasn't a serious matter. It was better to ignore it."

"You say 'we.' Who was involved in this decision?"

"A.J. and I and Miss Miller."

"So Shirley-Ann joined in, did she?"

"Jessica brought her out of the party to look at the writing. I think she was the first one of the Bloodhounds she could grab. There were others there, but—"

"Which others?"

"Milo Motion and that character with the beret. Rupert."

"Anyone else from the Bloodhounds?"

"No, the two women, Miss Chilmark and Mrs. Wycherley, aren't on the gallery mailing list."

"Why is that?"

"You'd have to ask Jessica."

Diamond resolved to do that. Before leaving Barnaby, he had one more question of significance. "You saw the message on the gallery window. Has it crossed your mind, just fleetingly, that it might be true?"

"That Jessica did for Sid?" Barnaby was candid. "I gave it

some thought later, yes. But I honestly couldn't think of any reason why she would do such an immature thing. My wife is an unusually clever woman."

In the car he took a call from Keith Halliwell, reporting that Miss Chilmark wasn't at home. The old lady upstairs in the Paragon house had said that she might have gone away. She'd seen her the previous evening getting into a taxi—a black cab—and carrying a small suitcase.

"*Miss Chilmark did a runner?*" Diamond piped in amazement.

"It seems so."

He told Halliwell to start checking with taxi firms and heard the faint sigh of despair.

He drove to Orange Grove, left the car in front of the Empire Hotel, and walked the short distance up the High Street to Northumberland Place. A.J., unflustered, welcomed him to the gallery and offered him a coffee. Jessica, he told Diamond, should not be long. She was with a dealer upstairs. "If your business can wait a few minutes, Superintendent, I'm sure she'll be immensely grateful. It isn't often she gets a chance to do business with the big boys from London."

"I'll start with you, then."

"With me? I shouldn't think I can help much."

"You can save Mrs. Shaw from some tedious questions about things that happened last week."

"Is that all?" A.J. was reassured. The smile was reinstated. "Fire away, then. I thought this must be about the frightful business this morning in Sydney Gardens."

"You heard about it?"

"From Shirley-Ann Miller a short time ago. Of course, we know nothing firsthand."

"She was quickly onto it," said Diamond, slightly deflated.

"The jungle telegraph works well in Bath. I think she works in public relations, doesn't she?"

"Tourism."

"Well, she's pretty hot at public relations as well. Did you say you'd like a coffee?"

"No, thanks."

He was shown to the tall-backed Rennie Mackintosh chair. After making up his mind that it really was a chair, though unsuited to his physique, he tried his weight on it, perched awkwardly, and then got up saying, "I'm happy to stand. You knew Rupert Darby, sir?"

"A slight acquaintance only," said A.J. "Jessica invited him to the preview we had here. Rather a carrying voice, which can be an asset at a party, because everyone else then raises the volume, and it all sounds wildly successful."

"You hadn't met him before that?"

"No. I'd seen him around in Bath. Easy to recognize from Jessica's description. The beret, the voice, the dog."

"Was the dog at the party?"

"No, I'm speaking of seeing him in the street. You want to know about the party. He and I didn't exchange more than a few passing words as he came in. He isn't the sort who waits to be introduced to people. He was in there straightaway. I wouldn't have thought he was the suicidal type."

Diamond gave a shrug. His thoughts were no longer on Rupert's personality. At this minute A.J. interested him more. He might have stepped out of a holiday brochure with his welcome-to-paradise smile and designer shirt and jeans. Barnaby had spoken of a private income, and some of it must have gone on the teeth, which were as even as computer keys. Was this young buck likely to be content with "intellectual flirting"?

"I understand you have a large stake in the gallery, Mr. er . . . ?"

"A.J. will do."

Diamond was shaking his head. "Not any longer, sir. I'm gathering evidence, you see. I have to insist on full names."

A.J. frowned. "Does it really matter? The *A* is for Ambrose. I cringe each time I have to own up to it."

"And the *J*?"

"Jason. Hardly much better."

"That isn't your surname, is it?"

"No. That's"—he cast his eyes upward—"Smith. Ambrose Jason Smith. Now can we talk about something more important, for pity's sake?"

This business over the name had quite upset A.J. All the more incentive for Diamond.

"Are you a local man . . . Mr. Smith?"

A glare. "No. Born in Devon, but the next twenty years I spent in and around Winchester. I went to school there."

"The public school?"

"Yes. If you want the whole sordid truth, I was not a credit to them. Got expelled eventually. Went to art college and then had a few poverty-stricken years in Paris."

"And now you're stricken no longer?"

"That is correct."

Diamond waited.

A.J. explained, "The family forgave me."

"To come back to my question, you have a large stake in the gallery. Is that so?"

"I help out with the overheads. I'm also a regular exhibitor. I wish you would tell me what this has to do with the police."

"You're a close friend of Mrs. Shaw's."

"That's a sinister-sounding phrase. She's a married woman, Superintendent. If you're implying what I think you are, you'd better have a care what you say."

"Some words were sprayed on the gallery window on the night of the preview party."

A.J.'s reaction was less dramatic than Barnaby's. He was still well in control. His brown eyes looked into Diamond's and then toward the window. "How did you hear about that?"

"The words, I was informed, were 'She did for Sid.' "

"So?"

"You were one of the people who decided to remove them without reporting the matter."

"To put it in context," said A.J., adopting a lofty tone, "it was obviously a piece of misplaced fun. We were having a party. People have a few drinks and do daft things. We thought it was in bad taste and wiped the window clean. If that's a crime, you'd better arrest us all."

From above came the sound of footsteps. Jessica was about to descend with her dealer.

"Another question," said Diamond. "Where were you last night from seven onward?"

"God, you really are taking this seriously. In the bar at the Royal Crescent Hotel and afterward at the Clos du Roy Restaurant, where I dined alone. But if you wish to make inquiries, a dozen bar staff and waiters can vouch for me."

"And after you'd eaten?"

"I went home and watched television. Would you like me to tell you what the program was?"

Jessica's black-stockinged legs and blue strappy shoes appeared at the top of the spiral stairs. She led down a small silver-haired man in a black overcoat and a bow tie. Quick to sense that the deal she'd been doing upstairs might be undermined if she introduced a policeman, she said smoothly, "My dear Mr. Diamond, how good of you to call again. This is quite a morning. If you'll forgive me for a moment, Mr. Peake has come specially from London, and he has another gallery to see. I'll just point him in the right direction, and then we'll do business, I promise."

Diamond nodded, allowing the subterfuge to pass, before starting up with A.J. again. "You live in Bath?"

"Queen Square."

"Nice and central."

"Yes."

"Is there anyone . . . ?"

"I am a bachelor."

"Did you go out at all last night?"

"I went home to sleep, Superintendent, and sleep is what I did."

Back came Jessica. "Wonderful. He wants seven, including that big one of yours, A.J. We've got to celebrate. Is there any bubbly left over from the party?"

"Before you do—" Diamond began.

"You're to join us," said Jessica. "It isn't every day we do three grands' worth of business."

"Sorry, but you're joining me," said Diamond, "and there's no bubbly on offer. We might run to coffee in a plastic cup, but that's the best I can promise."

"I don't think I understand."

"I'm taking you in, Mrs. Shaw. For questioning."

CHAPTER THIRTY-THREE

O UT OF CONSIDERATION FOR HIS PASSENGER, HE DROVE
to the back of the central police station, and they entered through a side door. Even so, several heads
swiveled when he escorted Jessica, teetering high-heeled
along the corridor in the pale blue Armani suit she'd put on
for the London art dealer.

In Diamond's office the phone was flashing like a burglar
alarm. He pulled out a chair for Jessica and asked if she
wanted that coffee tasting of plastic. She requested water.

He read the written messages left on his desk. Julie Hargreaves had spoken to Shirley-Ann Miller and confirmed that
she had a good alibi for the previous night. Halliwell had
traced Miss Chilmark to Lucknam Park, the country house
turned hotel at Colerne, and was on his way there; lucky bastard, he wouldn't be drinking out of plastic cups. And Jack
Merlin, the pathologist, couldn't, after all, get to Bath next
day; the postmortem on Rupert Darby would have to be post-
poned unless someone else took over.

After collecting tea for himself, Diamond sat opposite Jessica, observing her, deciding on his strategy. She was drum-
ming her fingers on the desk. There didn't seem much
advantage in gentle sparring.

"Mrs. Shaw, why did you write those lists of words on the
paper bag?"

The finely shadowed eyes narrowed, but there was nothing else to register the body blow this was meant to be. This lady wasn't simply going to roll over and tell all.

"The bag you used to treat Miss Chilmark's hyperventilation. I have it here." He opened his desk and took it out, enclosed in a transparent cover. "They happen to rhyme, these words. 'Jack, flak, knack, mac' . . . It looks like working notes for a poet—or at least a writer of verse. In this case, they rhyme with 'black.' There's a second column rhyming with 'motion' and a third with 'room.' I could be wrong, but those are words that feature in the case under investigation: Penny Black, Milo Motion, and Locked Room. Working notes?"

Jessica's only response was the merest movement of the padded shoulders.

"You did write them yourself, didn't you?" he pressed her. "Sid Towers had nothing to do with it."

Not even a flicker this time.

"It can't have been Sid because of the fresh riddle in verse that was published yesterday. Sid is dead. He couldn't have been our poet." He watched her minutely. This wasn't achieving anything. "I'll be frank," he said. "Until this morning I still wasn't certain. You know what happened this morning?"

No answer.

"Mrs. Shaw?"

A sigh. "Yes, I heard what happened."

"Another death," he said. "Rupert Darby's death."

She said calmly, "You're not telling me anything I don't know."

Encouraged that there was two-way traffic now, he said, "Let's go back to the riddle for a moment:

> " 'To end the suspense, as yours truly did,
> Discover the way to Sydney from Sid.'

"In style, it was not dissimilar from the other two. It was on similar paper, in an identical typeface, and distributed in the same way to the local media. That wasn't some publicity seeker messing about, Mrs. Shaw. 'To end the suspense' . . . It was written in the knowledge that a man would shortly be found hanging from a bridge in Sydney Gardens. Isn't that plain?"

"If you say so."

"You must have read the riddle in the paper."

"Yes."

"Did you write it?—that's the question."

"I did not."

"Did you write the others?"

"No."

He paused, letting the gravity of her situation take root. He studied the paper bag as if he hadn't seen it before. Then he looked up and started again, but less abrasively. "Until yesterday afternoon, I was taken in by these lists. Thought they were written by Sid. Had to be."

She held his gaze with her dark brown eyes.

He said, "If Sid wrote them, it was natural to assume that he was our poet, the composer of the riddles, the joker who stole the Penny Black and magicked his way into a locked boat. They looked like working notes, the first notes for a riddle that never appeared, because Sid was killed before he completed it." He spread his hands. "I boobed. We all make mistakes. But what am I left with?"

He took his time. Passed his hand around the back of his neck and massaged it. "What I'm left with, Mrs. Shaw, is the alternative. You wrote the lists." Another pause. "Do you follow my thinking? The bag was Sid's. He handed it to you. You handed it to me. True?"

She sighed—a reluctant admission. Yet the logic of what he had said was inescapable.

"We call that continuity of evidence, Mrs. Shaw. That's why it's clear that if Sid didn't write the lists, you did." He leaned forward, hunched over his desk, watching her. "Makes you my prime suspect." An exaggeration, but he had to find some way of getting through. "I'm trying to give you every chance. This isn't a formal interview. If there's an explanation, now's your opportunity."

She looked down at her fingernails, not persuaded, it seemed.

He said, "The postmortem hasn't been done on Rupert yet, so this may be premature, but I expect it to confirm that he met his death by foul play."

She caught her breath—the first unguarded response. "He hanged himself."

"He was found hanging."

"I don't follow you."

"I think you do. We took a blood sample. The man was well tanked up, some way over the limit, probably incapable of rigging up a noose."

She said, "This is in the realm of speculation." Fair comment, too.

He found himself analyzing his performance so far. This isn't the approved interviewing technique, he told himself. It isn't an interview at all yet. I'm laying out all my cards while she sits there denying everything.

He picked up his cup and did damage to the inside of his mouth. Tea from the machine was always too hot or tepid. "Could I have a sip of that water? I'll get you some fresh."

She pushed the beaker across the desk.

He said, "It may be speculation now, but we'll know soon enough. The postmortem will show if there was a struggle. You can't string a man from a bridge without handling him roughly."

Jessica drew herself up in the chair and said scornfully, "You're not seriously suggesting that I did this to Rupert?"

"You probably couldn't have done it alone," he conceded.

"Why should I do it at all?"

"That's no mystery," he said. "We recovered his beret, and it has traces of sprayed paint."

Another sharp intake of breath. The wall of indifference was crumbling.

He told her, "I know all about the graffiti sprayed on the gallery window. Mean."

She started to say, "How—"

"I've discussed it with your husband and your friend A.J."

"They told you?"

He moved relentlessly on. "Rupert was at the party with paint on his beret."

She said, "Are you sure of this?"

"I can show you the beret if you like. The real point is that it gave you, and possibly someone else, a clear motive for silencing Rupert. He would have exposed you."

"I didn't know it was Rupert."

He got up, walked to the window and looked out.

She repeated, with more fervor, "I didn't know it was Rupert."

He let a few seconds pass. Then, without turning from the window: "Do you still deny writing the riddles?"

"Of course I deny it," she said passionately. "I didn't write them. I didn't kill anyone."

"But you wrote those lists of words on the paper bag."

"It doesn't mean I'm a killer."

He said, "But you wrote the lists. You will admit that much?" By now, he reckoned, she ought to be ready to admit to the lesser crime.

She showed she had spirit. "Is this going to take much longer?—because I have things to do. I assume I can walk out whenever I wish. I'm not under arrest, or anything?"

He said in sincerity, "Mrs. Shaw, I brought you here so that we could talk in private, away from the gallery. I'm giving you the opportunity to explain your actions."

Coolly, she asked, "What actions? I've done nothing illegal."

"At the very least, fabricating evidence."

"How can you say that?"

"Look, if you didn't write the lists as notes for a riddle, you wrote them for another purpose. You were taking a considerable risk, of course, but it was—what's the term bridge players use?—a finesse. The winning of a trick by subtle means, playing a low card. And you played it with a skill anyone would admire. You didn't volunteer the bag. You waited for me to ask if it was still in your possession. And when you handed it across, you didn't draw my attention to the lists. You let me find them myself and conclude that Sid wrote them. You conned me and my team. Why? Why mislead the police? You must have had something to hide."

She shook her head.

"Someone to shield, then?"

The color rose to her face.

He said mildly, "A.J.?"

A jerk went through her like an electric shock.

CHAPTER THIRTY-FOUR

LUCKNAM PARK, AN EIGHTEENTH-CENTURY MANSION AT Colerne, northeast of Bath, and latterly converted into a four-star conference hotel, might not have been the obvious choice for a bolthole, but it was Miss Chilmark's. No backstreet hideout for milady, thought Diamond with amusement, as it became obvious that the drive through the grounds would add another half-mile to the six he had just completed.

On arrival, he was welcomed like a paying guest and given a phone message. It was from Julie. Would he call her urgently? He didn't recognize the number.

He found himself talking to a switchboard operator at the Sports and Leisure Center who told him Inspector Hargreaves was waiting for his call.

"Mr. Diamond?" The note of relief in Julie's voice was gratifying and disturbing at the same time. "I'm so glad I've caught you."

"Trouble?"

"It's about Marlowe."

"Who?"

"Marlowe. The dog. Rupert Darby's dog. I took him on. Remember?"

He said in amazement, "You're calling me about the dog? What's it been up to now?"

"Nothing. He's done nothing wrong."

"Well?"

"I'm here at the Sports Center to interview Bert Jones, Shirley-Ann Miller's partner."

"I know that, Julie."

"Yes, but before going in, I thought I'd better give the dog a chance of a walk, if you know what I mean. I walked him around the edge of the car park at Manvers Street, but he didn't seem to get the idea, so I thought I'd give him another opportunity here."

"Of lifting his leg, you mean? Do we have to go into all this, Julie?"

"Yes, Mr. Diamond, we do," she said earnestly, "because as we were walking about, I happened to look closely at his coat. Marlowe has this dark brown hair, as you know, but I noticed that one area of it seems to be going white."

"He's an old dog, you mean? You'd rather not take him on at this time of life?"

"Please listen, Mr. Diamond. The white bit is only on his left side. It isn't natural. When I looked at it closely, I saw it was lots of little points of white. It's paint from an aerosol spray."

He was stunned into a brief silence. He'd been reluctant to give his full attention to Julie's fussing over the dog, and now this was hard to take in. "Are you sure?"

"Certain. I scraped some of the specks off with my fingernail."

"Julie, Rupert didn't have the dog with him at the gallery party."

"That's the whole point. Do you see what it means? If the dog was sprayed with the aerosol, it must have been done at some other time."

He was ahead of her now. "Right. It means we can't be certain when the paint got on the beret."

"Exactly. We've been assuming it was done when the gallery window was sprayed. We can't anymore."

He was silent for a moment, pondering the significance.

The evidence of the beret, linking Rupert to the graffiti, was undermined. The spray had been used elsewhere, and Rupert's dog had got a burst of paint. Rupert could have been trying out the aerosol, practicing.

Diamond was humble enough to say, "You've had time to think about this, Julie. What do you make of it?"

She started to say, "I'm as confused as . . ." Stopping in midsentence, she began again. "There may be a way of finding out whether there was spray on the beret before Rupert got to the gallery that evening. If you remember, he was supposed to have arrived with some people he met at the Saracen's Head."

"Right, and if they happened to have noticed . . . What the devil was their name? Shirley-Ann gave it to us."

"Volk. They're from Bradford on Avon."

"I'll get someone onto it. Have you finished with Bert Jones yet?"

"I haven't even started. I wanted to catch you first."

"You did the right thing, Julie." Before putting down the phone, he added, "Sorry I was short with you. Thought you wanted advice about the bloody dog. How is Marlowe, by the way?"

"He's not a bloody dog, Mr. Diamond. He's great. I'm just keeping my fingers crossed that Roger accepts him."

"Your husband?"

"No, Roger is one of my other dogs. He's rather unpredictable."

"So is Marlowe, by all accounts."

He made a call to Manvers Street and dispatched a car to Bradford on Avon. After replacing the phone, he stared blankly around the elegant entrance hall with its enormous fireplace and portraits; after the brain-stretching session on the paint spray, a conscious effort was required to remind himself why he was here.

Keith Halliwell was with Miss Chilmark in a spacious guest room overlooking the croquet lawn. Clearly in a state of some embarrassment, if not distress, the lady didn't even look up from the chintz armchair where she was seated. Her appearance had undergone a change that Diamond couldn't immediately define, until he realized he was meeting her without makeup. The green eye shadow and orange lipstick and foundation had created a different woman from the one he was presently seeing. Of the two images, he thought he preferred this paler, more vulnerable version.

He took note of a plate of canapés and a half-empty glass of what looked like whiskey on the occasional table in front of her. He also noted the glint of a second whiskey glass on the floor and partially obscured by a fringe around the base of the armchair Halliwell must have been using, and was informed, "I sent for something to calm her down, sir. A drop of Scotch is supposed to be good for the nerves."

"And was it good for yours?"

Halliwell gave a twitchy grin.

Diamond turned to the matter at hand. "You gave us a fright, Miss Chilmark, disappearing like that."

She said nothing.

"How long have you been here?"

Halliwell said, "Since yesterday, sir."

"Control yourself, Keith. I'd rather hear it from Miss Chilmark. You remember who I am, Miss Chilmark? I visited you in the Paragon. Nice place. Nice address. I'm surprised you left it." He lowered himself into another armchair opposite her. The furniture here was built for people of his size. He usually had to back into chairs like a carthorse easing between the shafts. "I was getting worried about you. Two of the Bloodhounds are dead. Did you hear about Rupert Darby?"

She nodded, still without looking down.

"Caught it on TV West, did you?" Diamond pressed on, with a jerk of the head toward the appropriate section in the wall unit. "They filmed me standing on the bridge over the canal where it happened. Sydney Gardens. Do you know the place? You must do."

Another nod.

"Can't expect you to waste much sympathy on Rupert Darby," he said. "He was no friend of yours, was he?"

She looked up, which was some encouragement, even if her broad, colorless face was registering nothing.

"I said he was no friend of yours. You don't have to stand on ceremony with me, ma'am. It's good riddance as far as you're concerned, isn't it? He made your life a misery."

She found her voice. "You've no right to put words into my mouth, Superintendent."

"In the absence of any words from you, ma'am, I was having to speak for both of us. I said Darby made your life a misery. Isn't that so?"

She gave him a distrustful look. "What are you suggesting?"

He said on a quieter note, "Simply helping you to get started, ma'am. There are things to be explained, aren't there?"

She shifted in the chair, nervously rubbing her hands. She sighed.

Generally, Diamond preserved a formal neutrality when interviewing. It seemed unlikely that this old dowager with her tendency to hysteria would evoke any sympathy at all from him, yet curiously she did. Her life was narrow, her values based on little else but status and snobbery. Everything she espoused had been undermined. Here she was, ashamed, discredited, being questioned by the police. To restore any self-respect was probably beyond her.

She closed her eyes at first, as if it made speaking less painful. "I'm not at my best. I don't know what to say about him—Rupert Darby. Since I heard about his death, I've been trying to understand him, if not forgive him. At the time of the various incidents at the meetings, I was incensed by his behavior. I felt sure he really set out to persecute me. Now that, em—"

"Now that he's dead?"

"Yes. I'm less certain. I can't be sure. Possibly what happened with the dog was due mainly to negligence on his part."

"Failing to control the dog, you mean."

"Yes. He couldn't really have known that it would run straight to me and leap on me. So I'm trying, I'm beginning, I'm *wanting* . . . to take a more charitable view of what happened. Do you understand?"

By Miss Chilmark's lights, this was a turnaround on a par with Count Dracula turning out to be the tooth fairy. Was it Rupert's passing that had prompted it? Diamond wondered. Or had a much larger crisis put the incidents into a new perspective?

She said, "I had no idea he was suicidal."

Diamond told her, "I wouldn't worry about Rupert if I were you." He changed his posture. Instead of leaning forward, demonstrating concern, he rested his back against the chair. "It wasn't anything to do with Rupert that brought you here, was it, ma'am?"

A little shudder went through her. "No, it was another matter." Then, silence.

"You may not feel you want to speak about it," Diamond spoke the obvious, "but if you do, I think it may become easier to live with. Locking it in is not the best way."

She said with a penetrating stare, "You know, don't you?"

"A certain amount, ma'am, enough to understand how difficult this is for you. But it can't go on, can it? The cost—"

"How did you find out?"

Swiftly he changed tack. He didn't want her knowing he'd tricked her bank. "I was going to say the cost in stress is more than you can bear."

The evasion was transparent. Miss Chilmark closed up again. "Anyway, I don't see that my private affairs have anything to do with the police."

The story had to be coaxed from her. He wished he had Julie with him instead of Halliwell standing there like the recording angel. "Keith, I may be getting a call downstairs. Do you mind?"

Halliwell had the sense to leave.

Diamond smiled faintly, wanting to convey encouragement. "See it from my point of view, Miss Chilmark. Darby died last night. You went missing. I'm bound to be concerned. I accept that the two events weren't connected, but I have to ask your reasons. I believe someone has been taking advantage of you. Threatening you, perhaps. Am I right?"

She gave a convulsive movement, a sob like a hiccup. From her sleeve she produced a paper tissue and put it to her face, and sobbed several times more.

Diamond waited uneasily.

Finally Miss Chilmark looked at him intently through a film of tears. "If I tell you, will you promise not to pursue it?"

Without knowing what she was about to say, how could he give such an undertaking? He answered, "If it doesn't bear on the matters I'm investigating, I wouldn't wish to get involved." A "promise" worthy of Machiavelli, but she scarcely seemed to be listening, she was so distressed.

In a voice threatening any second to dissolve into weeping, she began to tell her story. "It goes back to when my parents were killed in an accident, a car crash in France, in 1961. A head-on smash with a lorry near Rouen. It was dreadful. They were in their early fifties, both of them. I was twenty-six, their only child, very naive. I'd been given an extremely sheltered upbringing. You may imagine the shock, and the problems, the responsibilities, I had thrust upon me. I was at a loss, quite unable to cope."

"Anyone in your shoes . . ." Diamond murmured.

She went on, "There was all the complexity of the inquest and of getting them home. I knew Mummy and Daddy would have wished to be brought home and buried here. As often happens in a crisis, someone came to my rescue, a solicitor who worked with Daddy. Did I say Daddy was the senior partner in Chilmark, Portland, and Smales? This young man—I'd rather not give his name—shouldered the whole thing. I was nominally the executrix, but he arranged everything for me. Went to France and brought them back. Saw to the funerals, the wills, the shares. Advised me on how to invest my legacy, which was considerable. I couldn't have got through without him. And he was only a name to me before. I don't believe Daddy had ever mentioned him—but then he never spoke much about his work. And I have to say that his behavior to me in all this time—vulnerable as I was—was impeccable. He was the perfect gentleman."

She reached for the whiskey. "Do you mind? I must. My voice."

"Take your time." He suspected it was not so much the voice as the gentleman under discussion who made the long sip of whiskey a necessity.

Miss Chilmark continued in a low, confidential tone, "The next thing that happened was a mystery to me at the time, and not at all unpleasant. I received a Valentine, the only proper one I've ever received. Oh, people sent silly, jokey things at school, but this was beautiful, like a Victorian card, with lace edging and a silk ribbon. There was a lovely verse inside, but no clue to the sender. Nothing. I was deeply curious, of course. I would lie awake wondering who sent it, hardly daring to hope it might have been the young man who had done so much to solve my legal problems. Then about six weeks after, he phoned me with the good news that the probate had come through. At last I could invest the money, write checks, and so on. Not that I had any great plans, but it was a kind of landmark. I suppose I looked on it as the end of my parents' tragedy. I could look forward now, and think of my own life."

"Were you working at this time?" Diamond asked.

"In employment? No. Daddy didn't want me working. He belonged to that generation that thought women of good class should not go into employment. I worked hard in the house and garden, but not for a wage.

"I was telling you about the probate. My kind solicitor said we ought to celebrate with a meal out the same evening. I didn't know what to say. I knew enough about the profession to be sure that my father would never have suggested such a thing to a client, but he was another generation. Part of me wanted to accept. He'd been so kind throughout, and now that the legal part was over . . . Well, to cut the story short, I went out to dinner with him the same evening at the Hole in the Wall, which at that time had a reputation unrivaled in Bath. He was a charming companion. He wasn't terribly good-looking, or anything, but he had an unusually attractive voice, like an actor's. He bought champagne, and toward the end of the meal he told me the Valentine had come from him. Of course I was overwhelmed by the whole thing. I had no experience of men. I think the champagne affected me, too.

"After the meal, he walked me back to the Paragon. It was raining, and he had an umbrella, and he asked me to take his arm while he held it over both our heads. I was extremely happy. As we approached the house, he said he hated mixing business with pleasure, but he had a couple more papers for me to sign. I half knew it was just an excuse for him to come inside, but I wanted the excuse. I don't condone my behavior."

"It's all in the past," said Diamond.

She lowered her eyes. "You won't need telling what happened. I was a willing participant, and I have to say that he was considerate. Gentle and understanding. People's attitudes to such things have undergone a revolution since then, but by the standards of that time, we were wicked. That evening I didn't care. He didn't stay for more than an hour, I suppose. If I'm honest, I was relieved he didn't spend the night with me. I don't think I was ready to sleep with a man, literally sleep with him, I mean. He left before midnight, and I sank into my bed and slept until quite late next morning, when I woke and felt like a scarlet woman. These days the only thing that makes a young woman feel guilty seems to be eating a bar of chocolate."

He gave an encouraging smile. To make a remark even faintly resembling a joke, she must have been feeling calmer.

"That evening wasn't the only occasion," Miss Chilmark went on. "He came to the house at other times in the weeks that followed. He was usually there on some pretext. A letter about my bank arrangements, or something. I have to say that I invited him as often as he suggested coming. We would go to my bedroom, and . . . he never stayed long. We didn't really go out together, and I suppose that made me suspicious that there was a reason why he didn't want to be seen with me in public. I didn't really want to admit it to myself, I wanted so much to keep him. Then the inevitable happened. I discovered that I was pregnant."

So honest was the recollection that Diamond's image of the solid middle-aged woman opposite had been supplanted by a mental picture of the desperately vulnerable twenty-six-year-old she had been. He remembered those times, and the moral climate and the pains and blunders of young love.

"Of course it was a shock, a tremendous shock, but in a way I'd been hoping something like this would happen. He'd always been vague about our future together. This was going to force us to a decision. I saw it as my chance to bring him to the registry office, if not the altar."

She shook her head, sighing deeply. "When I told him, his whole manner toward me changed. He told me to get rid of it. Those were his actual words. 'It'—as if the child inside me was an object. I was horrified. I said something about getting married, and he told me quite brutally—as if I should have realized already—that he was already happily married with two children of his own. As I say, I'd guessed it really, but refused to admit it to myself. I was his mistress. He regarded my pregnancy as my mistake, a hazard that you have to face. We'd taken no precautions. I don't know if you can understand this, but I would have felt that birth control in any form would have made me into a loose woman."

"So you had the child?"

She nodded. "Alone. He refused to have anything more to do with me. His attitude was that if I wasn't willing to go to an abortionist, it was my bad fortune. So I made my own arrangements. I confided in a cousin, a woman who lived in Exmouth and worked in a private nursing home. We'd spent holidays there sometimes, and I'd got to know her quite well. She was the only person I could think of asking. I said I wanted to have the baby, but I wouldn't be able to keep it. I couldn't face the shame of bringing up a fatherless child. So my cousin Emma told me she knew of women who were desperate to adopt and had been turned down for some obscure reason by the adoption agencies. If I was really willing to give up the child within a short time of the birth, she could arrange it. So that's what happened. When I got toward the end of the pregnancy—when it was getting obvious, I mean—I went away to Exmouth. The child was born. I suckled him for a week or two, and then Emma took him away. He was registered as someone else's child, you see. It was highly illegal, but he was legitimized. Part of the understanding was that I should not be told the identity of the couple who were given him. I came back to Bath and resumed my life. I've never had another serious relationship."

"Did you name him?"

"No. It was thought to be better if the adoptive mother gave him a name."

"And you were not to have any more to do with them?"

"That was the understanding."

"Hard, I'm sure."

"Very—but I understood the thinking behind it. Over the years I've had times when I've wept a little, and times when I've wondered just what my son was like, but I kept my side of the bargain. I made no attempt to trace him. Fortunately I couldn't, not even knowing his name."

She paused. She had shredded the paper tissue in her lap. She picked up one piece and dabbed the corner of her eye.

Diamond prompted her. "You said you kept your side of the

bargain, as if someone else did not. Did the father—your lover, I mean—did he know of these arrangements?"

"No. He had nothing more to do with me."

"So it was someone else."

She nodded. "About two years ago, I received a letter from someone who clearly knew a great deal about what had happened. He mentioned the date of birth, the place and the name of my cousin Emma, who died in 1990. He asked to meet me at a stated time by the west door of the Abbey. It wasn't exactly a threatening letter, yet there was so much in it that only I could have known. So I decided to go along."

"A blackmailer?"

"No."

"But you paid money. You've been making regular payments." She had been frank, and so would he.

"He's not a blackmailer. He's my son."

"Your *son*?"

"I couldn't refuse him, could I?"

"Are you certain?"

"Absolutely."

"How do you know?"

"A mother's instinct. Whatever one thinks of him—and I know he has taken advantage—that first meeting outside the Abbey was a revelation. He wanted to know what his own mother was like as much as I longed to see him. It was genuine, I swear to you. We went for a coffee together and for a long time simply looked at each other. An opportunity I never expected to have. A miracle. We weren't breaking faith with anyone, because he'd long since left his adoptive family."

"What's his name?"

She shook her head. Her expression tightened. "I'm not going to say and you can't make me. What has happened between us is strictly private. It isn't illegal. I'm allowed to support my own child, for heaven's sake."

Diamond sighed. "When did he tell you he needed money? Right at the start?"

"It was obvious. He's thirty-two. He should be making his way in the world, but these are dreadful times for his generation. He was sent to a good school. It ought to help, but he's been unable to get regular work. I had more than enough money, so I gave him some. He was living in Radstock, with no prospect of employment, so I persuaded him to come here—to Bath, I mean. There are more opportunities here."

"What does he do, then?"

Miss Chilmark clicked her tongue. "You won't get it out of me that way. Can't you be satisfied with what I've told you already?"

Diamond tried some gentle persuasion. "Look at your situation. In a couple of years you've gone through most of your fortune for this man. You sold your family home to stay in credit with the bank. You must have realized you were running through the money—or, rather, he was. You came here because you can't bring yourself to tell him it's the end of the line for this particular gravy train. You ran away. Are you going to be able to pay the hotel bill?"

She covered her eyes.

He asked, "Do you have any idea where all the money has gone?"

No answer.

He said, "If what he's been doing is legal, we can't touch him." More tenderly, he said, "I'm going to arrange for Inspector Halliwell to drive you back to your home. You can't run away from your son. You haven't the funds. You've got to tell him you're almost skint. Or I have. I'm willing to talk to him. I think I know who he is, you see." He paused. "Would his name be Ambrose Jason Smith?"

Miss Chilmark gave a cry as if of pain and thrust her face more deeply into her hands. She wept uncontrollably now, for her son, and her mistakes and the cruelty of fate.

CHAPTER THIRTY-FIVE

KEITH HALLIWELL WAS IN HIS CAR HAVING A NAP WHEN A heavy tread across the gravel alerted him. He woke instantly, like a dog expecting a walk.

"Any joy, Mr. Diamond?"

"*Joy* isn't the word I'd use," said Diamond. "Anyway, she's packing her case up there. Going home. I've offered you as chauffeur."

"Right, sir. And a message came through from Sergeant Filkins. That Bradford on Avon enquiry. He spoke to the people. The, em . . . ?"

"The Volks."

"Yes. And it's quite definite that Rupert Darby's beret was marked with paint before the art gallery party. They say he actually complained about it when they met him at the Saracen's Head."

Diamond's interest quickened. "Rupert mentioned it himself, did he?"

"Apparently there was an incident at the Lansdown Arms, his local. He went in with his dog early in the evening, his usual time, for a quick drink. On the way out, some merchant banker was playing about with what Rupert took to be a tin of hairspray."

"Merchant banker?"

"Rhyming slang, sir. Rupert's expression."

After a moment's thought, Diamond responded with a distinct note of affection, "I can hear him saying it in his plummy accent, too."

"Some of it got on his beret. Later he found it was paint."

A low rumbling like a growl came from deep in Diamond's throat. "I wish we'd known this earlier. What about this character with the spray? Is there a description?"

Halliwell shook his head. "Rupert had nothing to say about him."

"Well, it tells us one interesting thing: Rupert didn't recognize the bugger."

"Is that useful?"

"It is if we're dealing in murder here. It eliminates just about all our suspects."

"You think Rupert was murdered, sir?"

"I can't rule it out."

"Shoved over the bridge and hanged?" Halliwell sounded skeptical. "That wouldn't be easy, would it? It would take some strength to get the noose around his neck and heave him over the railing."

"Two people could do it."

"No question . . . but where are we going to find *two*?"

Diamond turned and looked up at the window of the room he'd just left. "Be patient with the old girl, Keith. She's had some shocks."

"I'll treat her like my own mother, sir."

"I wouldn't go that far."

"What's next for you, Mr. Diamond?"

"A little culture." He ambled across to his own car and started up.

For once he didn't curse when he saw the usual queue for the roadworks beginning to form on the London Road approaching Bath. He was in a more positive frame of mind. A pretty demanding investigation was coming to its climax. Mysteries that had seemed impenetrable had been solved by—what?—steady detective work, or brilliance? Either way, he had now disentangled the problems of the locked room puzzle, the riddles, the paper bag, and Miss Chilmark's secret payments. There remained only the unmasking of the killer.

Or killers.

This was when the likes of John Wigfull would run to their computers and start keying in information in the expectation that a mighty buzz from the megabytes would produce a perfect offender profile. "Your murderer is a writer of verse in possession of a ladder and window-cleaning materials and a car or other means of transport, with access to a computer and printer, possessing also a twisted sense of humor, a better than average knowledge of philately, detective stories, padlocks, and the topography of Bath. Now arrest the bastard, you dim plods."

The solution to this one, Diamond had long ago decided, wasn't going to come out of a computer. It required deductions on a more sophisticated level, an understanding of the strange workings of the human mind, fathoming why such a bizarre series of crimes and murders had been necessary or desirable. The sequence of events had almost certainly started with some weirdo wanting to score points, whether from frustration, a grudge, or just a wish to impress someone else. The Bloodhounds had been picked as the patsies. Then the thing had erupted into violence, into murder. Was the first murder always part of the plan, or an unwished-for consequence? And was the second, the killing of Rupert—if murder it was— made necessary by something Rupert knew, or was it cynically carried out to derail the investigation? The latter, surely. It seemed inescapable that the staging of the "suicide" was an attempt to frame Rupert as the conscience-stricken killer of Sid Towers. In other words, to draw a line under the case.

And it hadn't worked.

Ten minutes later, he walked into the Walsingham Gallery, only to be told by a young woman with cropped blond hair that it was Jessica's day off. He was also informed with just a hint of a smile that A.J. wasn't expected in today either.

"Any idea where I can find them? It's important." He showed his ID card.

"You could try the house. You can phone from here if you like."

With maddening inevitability, an answerphone message came down the line from Jessica's.

He turned to the blond woman. "Do you have a number for A.J.?"

She shook her head. "They could be out for a walk. They walk by the canal sometimes."

"It's a bloody long canal."

He tried Barnaby Shaw's business number with a little more success. Barnaby thought Jessica had spoken about going to the framer's. An artist had delivered a picture with a chipped frame, and she wanted a new one for it.

"Which framer?"

"The Meltone Gallery, in Powlett Road."

"Can you find me the number?"

There, the trail went cold. Mel, of Meltone, hadn't seen either of them all day.

It was Keith Halliwell, back at Bath Central, who got the inquiry back on course. Spotting Diamond as he stomped in, the frustration writ large, he reported that Miss Chilmark was now installed at the Paragon again. "She blubbed a bit, but I did my best with her, and she cheered up no end when she got back. There was a nice note from someone saying he'd call later. I went out and got her a box of Mr. Kipling's."

"Jesus Christ."

Halliwell went white. "Did I do wrong?"

"Did this note say what time?"

"I don't know. Teatime, I suppose. That's why she wanted the cakes. What is it now?"

It was ten to four. Diamond actually ran out of the building to his car. He drove white-knuckled, at the limit of his nerve, bucking two sets of traffic lights on the way to the Paragon. Leaving the car to create the mother and father of all tailbacks in the homeward traffic, he dashed across the pavement and down the basement steps.

A.J. had not yet arrived. The disappointment showed when Miss Chilmark opened the door. She had changed into one of her high-necked oriental dresses and restored the makeup in lashings. She would be in thrall to that extortionist for as long as he cared to trouble her.

Diamond told her he would wait inside.

She protested, "But I'm expecting a visitor."

He said, "That's who I want to see." Then he banished her to the kitchen at the back.

Ten minutes went by, Diamond just to the left of the door, trying to be invisible through the frosted glass while squeezed behind the foliage of a tall benjamina.

About four twenty, someone descended the steps to the basement in a businesslike way. The doorbell rang. Diamond stepped out and flung open the door. The uniformed police constable standing there started to say "Is that your car parked out . . . ?" Then he practically choked as he recognized Diamond.

Miss Chilmark came eagerly from the kitchen, saw the policeman, and said hysterically, "Oh, my God, what's happened?"

"This officer has come to tea—that's what's happened," Diamond told her through gritted teeth, tugging the man inside and slamming the door. "Give him his Mr. Kipling, and I'll see to him later."

A short time after came the visitor Miss Chilmark was expecting. Upon seeing Diamond, A.J. did a double take, turned about, and bolted up the stairs, but Diamond's large right arm groped through the iron railing, grabbed a leg, and pulled the man off balance. He fell heavily and gashed his hand on the edge of the bottom step.

"Looks like you're nicked."

The emergency was not over. Before relieving the traffic chaos outside, Diamond called Bath Central and had a message radioed to all units. He wanted Jessica Shaw brought in. She might be heading away from Bath in a new white Peugeot 306. He gave the registration.

Back at Manvers Street, A.J. was waiting in an interview room, stroking the fresh Band-Aid on his hand. He had recovered his composure enough to tell Diamond, "I don't know what the fuck this is about. You're going to pay for this."

"Save it." Diamond ignored him, and fiddled with something on the desk. His cackhandedness defeated him. "Someone's got to get this bloody contraption working for me." He walked out again.

A further twenty minutes passed before he came back with a sergeant, who attended to the tape recorder. "You'll have to wait, squire," Diamond now informed A.J. "They're bringing in Mrs. Shaw. Like I thought, she was heading out of town in the car." He grinned. "Luckily, there's still one hell of a snarl-up on the London Road."

He went down to the canteen for sausages, eggs, and chips. It was half a lifetime since he'd eaten. Casting around for a vacant table, he glimpsed a large mustache topped by a pair of tired, red-lidded eyes. Eyes that made contact. John Wigfull gestured to him to come over. Difficult to ignore. Promising himself that he would soon escape, he carried his tray across.

Wigfull actually came to life and pulled out a chair. "You've cracked it, I hear. Pulled in Mrs. Shaw and her boyfriend."

"I really need this," said Diamond. "Haven't eaten since breakfast, and that was cold toast and marmalade."

"Letting them stew, are you? Want some brown sauce?" Wigfull glanced around for some, but Diamond didn't seem to care. He had already started eating. "It did cross my mind more than once that two people had to be involved." Wigfull was clearly expecting a rundown on the case. "And when

Darby was strung from the bridge, it really had to be them working together."

Diamond spoke between mouthfuls. "Wise after the event, John?"

"No. I don't mind admitting I was confused up to that point. But the hanging clinched it, to my mind. Just about impossible for one person to hang a man. You'd have to be exceptionally strong—or the victim feeble. And this plot was always too complex to have been masterminded by one individual. They're an odd pair, those two. Too clever by half. Milking the old lady's bank account, weren't they?"

A nod from Diamond. "That's how the art gallery kept going."

"And the smart new Peugeot she was driving?"

"I expect so."

"Surprising, really, that the husband didn't object."

"To the gallery being funded like that? He didn't mind." Against his inclination, Diamond found himself being drawn into a dissection of the case. "To Barnaby, A.J. was just a third-rate artist with a private income. If he wanted to throw money at Jessica, fair enough."

"I meant the relationship," Wigfull explained. "Why didn't he object to A.J. screwing his wife?"

"Because it wasn't happening. This is the whole point. They aren't lovers. Barnaby convinced me of that. Intellectual flirting, he calls it."

"Get away," said Wigfull.

"Straight up. Their relationship is nonsexual. They got their kicks in other ways. The courtship display stops short of the act itself. These two are games players. That's their turn-on. It's like a grown-up version of truth, kiss, or dare, ultimately leading to destruction. The crimes arose out of A.J.'s need to impress her. He's given her most of the money he creamed off from Miss Chilmark, but that wasn't enough. He planned a spectacular stunt."

"Stealing the Penny Black and having it turn up at the

Bloodhounds' meeting? That was spectacular, no question. It proved he was smarter than any of them. The riddles. The business with the padlocks. Bloody clever."

"Yes, but it went wrong," said Diamond. "He didn't reckon with Sid. Here was a bloke who was a Dickson Carr buff with an interest in locked room puzzles, so naturally he was fascinated by what had happened. He drove out to look at the narrowboat and came along the towpath while A.J. was in the act of replacing the padlock. I think A.J. heard him coming and hid inside the cabin, grabbing a windlass for a weapon. Everything had worked brilliantly up to then. He'd almost got away with a perfect crime. He was angry and scared at the same time, and he panicked. He cracked Sid over the head, probably meaning to knock him out, no more, but it killed him. You can never tell with skulls until you give them a bash." He forked up some more chips. "And everything after that was done to cover up."

Wigfull had been over that scene a thousand times in his mind and never pictured it so vividly before. He tried to sound casual. "So when did Jessica come into it?"

"After Sid was killed. She suspected A.J. was responsible, and she didn't want us to find out. With luck, he'd get away with it. There was a chance that everyone would assume Sid had stolen the stamp and staged the locked room trick."

"And we did," said Wigfull.

"Well, it fitted the facts. After all, he was the Dickson Carr expert, and he had plenty to prove to that lot who thought him thick because he didn't ever have much to say for himself. This theory was an ideal cover for A.J. It meant anyone at all—not just someone in the know—could have been on the towpath that night and attacked Sid. Tidy. It let A.J. off the hook. And then the writing on the paper bag seemed to confirm that Sid had written the riddles."

"Jessica did that."

"Yes. She admitted it to me. She was covering up for A.J. To be fair, I don't think he'd told her anything. She's not slow, that woman. She worked out that he'd done it. Later it all began to unravel, of course. So Plan B was devised to frame Rupert and fake his suicide."

"They were both in on that?"

"By this time, yes. This killing was not accidental. It was planned in cold blood. They staged the graffiti incident, making sure Rupert was well sprayed first. It was simple to surprise him coming out of his local. A.J. must have done that. Rupert hadn't met him."

"Fair enough," said Wigfull, "but what about the message— 'She did for Sid'? Why on earth would they draw attention to their own guilt?"

"First, it wasn't true. She didn't do for Sid. A.J. did. Second, if anything went wrong, who would suspect that they wrote up the message themselves?"

"And they got Rupert tanked up the next night and hanged him?"

"After writing another riddle supposedly by Rupert, predicting his suicide. Case closed. End of story."

"So they hoped," Wigfull said, and sighed. "You're good, Peter. I've got to admit you're better than I am."

"Yes," said Diamond abstractedly, glancing at the clock. He'd practically finished the snack. A portion or two of treacle pudding would go down a treat. Very soon he would start the first interview. He was hoping Wigfull would take the hint and leave. A couple of minutes alone would be nice. With any luck, Julie would be back from the Sports and Leisure Center by now. She ought to be in on the interviews.

But Wigfull still had something on his mind. "What about this character, A.J.? Is he really Miss Chilmark's long-lost son?"

"She seems to think so," Diamond said, making it clear that his mind was on other things.

"If he isn't, and it's all a con, he ought to be done for that as well as murder."

"Maybe."

"Well?"

Diamond said irritably, "Well what?"

"Is he the son, or isn't he?"

"Most probably not. It's a side issue."

"Could he have conned Miss Chilmark?"

"Easily. It was part of the arrangement when the child was given away that she wasn't told the name of the parents or the child. Anyone of approximately the right age could have knocked on her door and claimed to be the son if—and it's a big 'if'—they knew the story."

"Why does he call himself A.J.?"

"Doesn't like the name he was given. Ambrose Jason Smith. It is quite a mouthful. At one time . . ." His voice trailed away. He really didn't want to prolong this.

"Yes?" said Wigfull. "At one time, what?"

"Oh, I had another theory about A.J."

"You've got to tell me now you've started," said Wigfull. "It won't take a minute, will it?"

Diamond sighed and felt into the inside pocket of his jacket. He had several pieces of paper there. He started sorting through them as he talked. "I asked Polly Wycherley to write down the names of everyone who had ever been a Bloodhound, thinking, you see, that there might be some former member with a grudge against Sid. Here it is."

"No one called Ambrose Jason Smith, I'll bet," said Wigfull.

"No, but there was a name—this one—Alan Jellicoe, that made me pause."

"The initials?"

"Yes," said Diamond. "Coincidence, I expect."

Wigfull was more suspicious. "I wouldn't count on it. Don't you think this is worth following up? After all, he could have made up the A. J. Smith identity just to con Miss Chilmark."

Diamond didn't want to push this. Wigfull had a point. It ought to be checked, but if there was anything to it, the truth would come out. There were hours of interviews stretching ahead. Call him Smith or Jellicoe, he was still sitting in an interview room waiting to be charged.

"If I were you," Wigfull went on, "I'd ask Mrs. Wycherley to come down here and have a look at him. Has she seen him lately?"

"No, she wasn't invited to the gallery party. She and Jessica don't get on too well."

"All the more reason to check."

Diamond yawned. "You're a persistent bugger, John. All right, I'll arrange it. Alan Jellicoe. It is a little out of the ordinary." His eye scanned the list again. Something else was stirring in his brain. Tom Parry-Jones, Milo Motion, Polly Wycherley, Annie Allen, Gilbert Jones, Marilyn Slade-Baker . . .

"There's another coincidence for you."

"Someone you know?"

"Put it this way," said Diamond. "I know someone called Bert Jones." He handed the list to Wigfull to read.

"This says Gilbert. You don't shorten Gilbert to Bert, do you?"

"Some people might. It's the name of Shirley-Ann Miller's partner." He looked up at the canteen clock. "Julie was going in to interview that bastard over two hours ago. I've heard sweet Fanny Adams since."

He was on his feet and out of the canteen before Wigfull had time to draw breath.

Chapter Thirty-six

THE SPORTS AND LEISURE CENTER, BUILT IN CONCRETE and reconstituted stone in 1972, is a structure more functional than decorative, a prime example of what has been called the packing-case style. By day, it manages to be unobtrusive, sited on the Recreation Ground away from Bath's grander architecture. At six thirty this October evening it was a garish yellow monolith, caught in the artificial light.

They found Julie's car at 5:25 P.M. at the far end of the car park. Rupert's dog, Marlowe, on the backseat, had set up a fit of barking and yelping that considerably helped the search.

Instantly this was upgraded to an emergency. Every available officer was called in. By 5:45, over forty mustered in the floodlit area in front of the main entrance off North Parade.

Diamond addressed them through a loudhailer. There were two missing persons, he impassively announced. DI Hargreaves, a female officer, was known to many of the search party. She was five foot eight, with short blond hair, and was dressed in a light brown leather jacket over a black sweater and black leggings. She was possibly being detained by Gilbert—better known as Bert—Jones, aged about thirty, five foot nine, with a bodybuilder's physique, dark hair, and brown eyes. He was an employee of the Sports and Leisure Center, probably dressed in a dark blue tracksuit. Jones was not known to be armed, but was under suspicion of violent crimes and should be treated with extreme caution.

Diamond explained that in a few minutes the fire alarm would be sounded to evacuate the building. Users of the Center were to be directed by uniformed officers toward the main doors, where a watch would be kept for the suspect. If he was not found, a full search of the building would then take place, starting with the ground floor and moving up. Senior staff from the Center would give assistance. Particular attention was to be paid to enclosed spaces, changing rooms, saunas, storerooms, and cupboards.

Assistant Chief Constable Musgrave materialized at Diamond's side and said, "I hope you've got this right, Peter. We're going to take some stick if not."

Diamond had the foresight to turn off the loudhailer before saying tersely, "She hasn't radioed in. The car is still here in the car park. What else do you expect me to do, sir?"

"But can this really be our man?"

The blare of the alarm put a timely stop to the exchange. Diamond stepped toward the main doors to keep a watch on people as they streamed out of the building. The task was fraught with difficulty: He was the only police officer capable of recognizing Bert Jones, and he was having to rely on the help of three of the Center staff who worked with the man.

The response to the alarm was quick, almost too quick. Early evening was a peak time at the Center. The foyer filled quickly, and a bottleneck formed at the one exit Diamond allowed to be used. Reasonably enough, he wanted a sight of everyone leaving the building. Inside, uniformed police were doing their best to control the exodus and calm nerves, but there were still people complaining. It could easily tip over into panic.

And if there wasn't trouble within, there were problems developing outside. The public assembling on the forecourt were dressed in a variety of skimpy sports kits. On a cool October evening, middle-aged women in leotards were not going to stand in the open for long. There were shivering kids from the swimming pool without even a towel to dry themselves; someone on the staff was sent for a stack of towels to hand around.

Upward of two hundred people had passed the checkpoint before the real flow stopped, and only a few more stragglers were seen emerging. The alarm was silenced and the search party went in. A few officers remained to deal with the public. Keith Halliwell suggested letting the people back inside the foyer, but Diamond was totally absorbed in the search, increasingly sure that serious harm had come to Julie.

Halliwell tried again. "I think we should let them back in, Mr. Diamond, I really do."

Diamond thrust the loudhailer into his hands. "Do it, then."

He kept track of the operation with a personal radio. A few who had believed the alarm to be false were being winkled out, and so were others who had insisted on returning to the changing rooms before leaving. There were protests from some of the women caught half dressed by young policemen; they were unconvinced by the logic that the rooms were supposed to be unoccupied.

The search of the ground floor did not take long. Much of the space is taken up by the main sports hall, a vast place like an aircraft hanger, divided only by netting, where badminton, aerobics, and netball can take place simultaneously. The swimming pool and the indoor bowls hall were equally simple to check.

The searchers moved upstairs, into a warren of corridors and offices, viewing galleries and smaller rooms for table tennis, weight training, and aerobics. This took longer. A party of rebels was located in the bar and restaurant, called the Winning Post, and some angry exchanges were brought to a stop only by an angrier instruction from Diamond over the radio link. He had other priorities than getting involved with a crowd of bolshie drinkers.

Soon after 6:30 P.M., the word came through that every part of the building had been searched.

"She's got to be here somewhere," Diamond insisted to Mr. Musgrave. "Her car is still outside. She knew the dog was in there. She wouldn't have left it that long. Either she's hurt, or she's being kept against her will."

"Was the car park checked?" Mr. Musgrave asked. "It goes right under the building, you know."

"Of course."

"Yes, but is Jones's car still here? Do we know what he drives?"

It was a useful suggestion, and Diamond acted on it at once. One of the Sports Center people said Jones drove an old white Cortina. A check with the Police National Computer confirmed this and supplied a registration number. A search was started.

With some reluctance, Diamond acceded to Mr. Musgrave's suggestion that the public be allowed to return to their activities. "If the car is missing," said the ACC, "we can safely assume he's abducted Julie and driven her away. Then we're into a full-scale emergency."

"Aren't we already?" muttered Diamond, striding off to look at cars.

Within a few minutes, Jones's white Cortina was found in the section reserved for staff. Diamond walked around it, looking through the windows. Then he had the boot forced open—a stomach-churning moment, but it turned out to be empty except for some sports clothes. He had the engine immobilized.

"In that case," he said, "there's only one place the bastard can be. I want torches and ladders. And I want twenty men and at least three authorized shots for this. Keith, get the floodlighting turned on at the rugby ground."

The Center had a vast flat roof with several levels. It was decided to start from the side nearest the road. Ladders were not after all required, because there was access by way of the restaurant balcony on the top floor. About twenty of the searchers lined up on the roof and began a slow sweep of that level under Diamond's personal supervision, with the marksmen positioned to target any figure making a break. It wasn't so open an area as Diamond expected; a number of ventilation shafts were capable of providing cover for a fugitive.

On any investigation he experienced moments of numbing despair; he couldn't change his nature. But this was infinitely worse. It wasn't mere depression; it was hell. He despised himself. It wouldn't take much more to persuade him to jump off this bloody roof. He'd made a whopping misjudgment, totally failing to see the danger in sending Julie to interview Jones. The neatness of the case against A.J. and Jessica had blinded him to other suspects. Up here, on this godforsaken roof, Peter Diamond was getting his payoff. He had a reputation for decisiveness. When the decision led to a disaster . . . if, as he had to expect, Julie was found dead . . . then only one decision would be left to him.

His thoughts went back to his last conversation with Julie, over the phone, when she'd been trying to alert him to her discovery of the paint spots on the dog, and he'd made the idiot assumption that she was reconsidering keeping the dog. Trivial, but it shamed him now. He'd never valued Julie sufficiently. She was ace, a clear thinker. He knew it, so why hadn't he listened first time?

The line moved steadily across the roof, toward the edge that overlooked the Recreation Ground. There was a brisk wind up here, making it difficult to be heard. He was directing the operation with a torch, waving it in a circular motion to bring the line forward and holding it still above his head when he needed to stop them. They seemed to have got the idea.

Quite suddenly, the whole area ahead was illuminated. Keith Halliwell had acted on his order and the floodlighting on the rugby ground, where Bath RFC played its matches, was switched on. The Sports Center was sited next to the ground, and the lighting, on masts, was close enough to make a real difference.

At the same time, Diamond thought he heard a shout from a woman. There were women in the police line, and he couldn't be sure if one of them had reacted to the lights. He held the torch high and asked for silence by a sweeping motion with his free hand.

The wind increased in strength.

He could hear nothing more. He waved the line forward again.

Almost immediately there was another cry. It *was* a woman's voice, no question, and it seemed to be saying "Here!"

No one was in sight ahead, where the sound seemed to have come from. They had passed the last of the ventilation shafts.

He signaled another halt and asked the man nearest to him if he'd heard the voice. He said he thought he had, but he couldn't understand where from. Diamond considered ordering everyone to do an about-turn; clearly there was no one ahead of them, so maybe it was some acoustic effect.

Then he heard it again, and this time it was a cry for help.

He took some quick steps forward, and understood. The roof of the Sports Center came to an end, but beyond it, at a lower level, was the new stand of the rugby club, the Teacher's Stand, built only a season or two ago. Its superstructure of seventeen white cones, like the tops of so many medieval jousting tents, was silhouetted against the floodlighting.

"She's down there," he said. "That's where she's got to be."

The gunmen had moved forward and taken positions on the edge of the roof. He hissed an order to them to get out of sight.

There was a way down to the back edge of the stand roof. The buildings were virtually linked. Making the descent was awkward for a man his size, but he was first there. Three of the party followed him.

He gestured to the others to stand still.

He called her name.

Nothing.

"Julie, this is me—Diamond."

A clear voice, shrill and urgent, answered, "Here!"

She was alive! He still couldn't see her, but the voice was unmistakable. It seemed to have come from in front of the cones. There was a chunk of equipment projecting above the level of the roof.

He took a few steps to his right, then ducked down fast.

Two figures were lying flat, almost obscured by a satellite dish. If Jones, powerful man that he was, had Julie by the throat, he could snap her neck. This couldn't be rushed. And it was no use relying on the guns.

Diamond crept forward, commando style, flat to his stomach. He beckoned the others on.

Then Julie spoke again. "For God's sake hurry up, Mr. Diamond. I've made the arrest. All I want is someone to take him away."

Sheepishly, he stood up. Once more he'd underestimated her. Julie had Bert Jones in an armlock, her leg braced and keeping him immobile in a very effective hold.

A couple of constables handcuffed Jones and got him upright.

Diamond put out a hand to help Julie up, and she hesitated. He asked if she was all right, and she said she'd injured an ankle, and hadn't wanted to take any risks, so she hadn't attempted to bring Jones down herself. They'd been lying there for over an hour.

"I don't know how you managed it," Diamond said without thinking that his surprised tone might give offense. "He's a fitness expert."

"I've done my training, same as you or anyone else," Julie said. "I know how to restrain a man."

"A bodybuilder?"

"My instructor said you grab his arm before he grabs yours."

"Did he, indeed!"

"Did *she*."

"Right," he said in a dazed way. "Right, Julie."

They used Diamond's car to drive back to Manvers Street. Marlowe traveled with them, giving an occasional whimper; he'd spent too long cooped up in the other car.

Julie explained what had happened when she had gone to interview Bert Jones in his office on the first floor. "He didn't seem troubled that I was there—not at first, anyway. I asked him about his movements the previous evening, and he said he'd been working late at the Center on some paperwork, ordering equipment. It sounded reasonable. I asked if anyone else could confirm what time he left, and he said it was after midnight and he'd been alone in the building. He often worked late. He had an arrangement with the security staff to let himself out. Then I asked if he used the computer to order his equipment, and immediately I could tell he didn't like the question. It wasn't unreasonable; the screen was sitting on his desk between us. He came over all aggressive, asking what the hell it mattered whether he'd been using the computer or sitting with his feet on the desk. I tried to explain what I was getting at with my question."

"You'd better explain to me," said Diamond.

"Some computers log the time and date when they're in use. We could have looked it up and seen on the screen that he clocked off at midnight, and that would have provided proof of his statement. Just as good as a witness. He said this computer didn't have a function like that. It was obvious there was something he wanted to hide, so I probed a little more. I asked to see duplicates of the order forms he'd been preparing. He tried to stall me. I insisted it was important. I had him worried, even if I wasn't sure why."

"You were on to him," said Diamond. "I reckon the riddles

were printed on the Sports Center equipment. We could have compared the typefaces."

"Well, he certainly took it seriously," said Julie. "He got up and went to the door, saying he had to go somewhere to look for these forms. I was getting suspicious and said I'd go with him. In the corridor outside, he suddenly started running. He bolted up a fire escape to the roof, and I followed. There was one hell of a chase up there, and it ended on the rugby club stand."

"With one of the best tackles all season."

"Maybe," she said with a smile, "but I twisted my ankle doing it, and . . ."

"The trainer was a long time coming on."

"You said it, Mr. Diamond."

After the ordeal on the roof, Julie was more than entitled to go off duty, but she insisted on being present when Bert Jones was interviewed. There was much that she still wanted to know.

Jones sat with arms folded in the interview room, his facial expression saying "I'll see you in hell first." Diamond impassively went through the preliminaries of a recorded interview. He had seen this kind of posturing so often before from suspects.

"Let's start with your name. Most people know you as Bert, but it's Gilbert Jones, isn't it?"

A nod.

"You signed up for the Bloodhounds—four years ago, was it?—as Gilbert."

Another nod.

"Why?"

Jones frowned and said sullenly, "Why what?"

"Why Gilbert? Why not Bert?"

No response.

"It's not such a dumb question," Diamond told him. "I want to understand your motive in all this. You're smart. You know enough about people's perceptions to see that the likes of Mrs. Wycherley and Mr. Motion would be more impressed with a Gilbert than a mere Bert. Right?"

"If you say so."

"No. I'm asking you."

Jones hesitated. "All right, some places I'm known as Bert, some Gilbert. That isn't a crime, is it?"

"Right. You work in—what do you call it?—sports administration. Some people think a man who goes around in a tracksuit and trainers all day can't have a serious thought in his head. Just a jock. Just a Bert, anyway. Put on a jacket and tie and call yourself Gilbert, and they'd see you in a different light. The truth is that you're quite an intellectual. You read a lot. James Bond, isn't it?"

Reddening suddenly, Jones thrust a finger across the table at Diamond. "Don't talk down to me."

"That's what I'm saying," Diamond cheerfully pointed out. "You're entitled to respect. You had to get a qualification for the job you do, right?"

"Three years' training and a diploma," said Jones.

"Where did you do it?"

"Loughborough."

"The best—and bloody hard work."

Jones eyed the big detective, uncertain now whether his achievements were being mocked.

Diamond stared back. He was convinced that the source of this man's behavior was a grudge, a deep conviction that the world undervalued him. "Headwork," he stressed. "I don't say there isn't a physical element—of course there is—but there's a damn sight more bookwork and study than any outsider appreciates, right?"

No response except a twitch of the mouth that seemed to signal assent.

"You're an expert on Ian Fleming's work. An authority," Diamond said without a flicker of condescension. "You went along to the Bloodhounds as Gilbert Jones, ready to talk about

Fleming, and something went seriously wrong, because you only lasted a couple of weeks. I have a suspicion why. I've met these people, full of self-importance. Something was said about you, or your background, or the books you read, that turned you right off the Bloodhounds and left you feeling bitter. It doesn't matter what."

Jones was spurred into saying, "It matters to me."

"What was it, then? What did they say?"

His face creased at the mention of it. This was an open wound. And it was still hurting. "They called them blood-and-thunder thrillers. Ignorant bastards. They as good as told me I was wasting my time and theirs by talking about them. What do they know about it? Far better people than them appreciate Fleming—President Kennedy, Kingsley Amis. I still shake when I think about it. Those books changed the face of the spy story. The research was terrific. The attention to detail. Just because something is a worldwide success, it doesn't mean it's pulp. Agatha Christie sells in millions, but the Bloodhounds were willing to talk about her."

"Was that really what this was about—Fleming's reputation?" Diamond asked. "Or was it yours that was being rubbished?"

A muscle twitched in Jones's neck. "They knew nothing about me. I didn't tell them what my job is."

"It was even more of a slapdown, then. They judged you personally, by your voice, your manner . . ."

"It wasn't a slapdown. They chose to ignore me once they knew I admired Fleming and no one else."

"So you quit after three weeks?"

"Should have quit after one."

"And then forgot the whole thing until an opportunity came to get revenge?"

Jones wouldn't accept that. "No. I didn't forget."

Of course he hadn't forgotten. The wound had festered for years. "Then you met Shirley-Ann Miller, who moved in with you. Like you, she's a reader of crime stories."

"She reads everything."

"So you had James Bond in common. She decided to join the Bloodhounds."

"Off her own bat," Jones was keen to make clear. "I didn't put her up to it."

"You didn't?" Diamond glanced at Julie; the lie hadn't escaped her. Shirley-Ann had told them herself that Bert brought home a brochure from the Leisure Center and pointed out the existence of the Bloodhounds, knowing how much she enjoyed detective stories. It was a side issue, and Diamond chose not to pursue it. Even if Shirley-Ann had been used, she wasn't an accessory in these crimes.

"She doesn't know a thing. She has no idea I once went to some of their meetings."

Probably true. "You sat back and waited to hear what she said about these know-it-alls who snubbed you. It was the opportunity you wanted. You decided to have some fun with them."

"Fun?" said Jones, as if it were a foreign word.

"Show them up."

"Right." He preferred that. His actions weren't motivated by humor. He'd been deadly serious.

Diamond underlined the point. "You wanted to show up their tiny minds." This was emphatically the right way to handle Jones. The man craved admiration.

"I saw my chance, and I took it. Specially when she told me the same old gang were still running it. The gay bloke with the ridiculous beard and that old witch, Polly. Shirley-Ann likes telling me things. She sometimes says she could talk for Great Britain. I don't mind. I was riveted. I was given a very accurate account of that first meeting she attended."

"When they agreed to discuss the locked room puzzle?"

"Yes."

"And you decided to act—hit them with a real locked room puzzle, to prove that a James Bond reader was smart enough to frame the lot of them with one of their favorite plots."

"Something like that," agreed Jones, though the irony of what he had done seemed to escape him. This had never at any time been a mere intellectual exercise. It was the revenge of a deeply embittered man.

"You thought up a way of stealing the Penny Black early one morning when the window cleaners were out in force. Your partner wouldn't suspect anything, because you go jogging in the mornings anyway. This time, you took a ladder and a bucket. You must have visited the museum before then and found the weak link in the security. So you put your ladder to the window, let yourself in, and came out with the stamp. Is that a fair summary?"

Jones said, "I didn't take it for personal gain."

"We're agreed on that," said Diamond amiably. "This was all about proving a point, not making a profit. By this time, you were ready to garnish the plot with the first riddle. You composed it on your computer at work and ran it off on the printer in the evening when no one was about. Correct?"

Jones gave a nod. He was willing, even eager, to claim responsibility for the clever stuff with the stamp and the riddles. Would he be as ready to admit to murder?

"What made you choose Milo as the fall guy, I wonder? Why was he singled out as the one who would be off-loaded with the stolen stamp? Was it something he said at those meetings you attended that caused such offense?"

"He said they were written for people with sick minds."

"That *is* over the top," agreed Diamond, regardless that Jones himself had a mind that was sick *and* over the top. "Practically everyone has read Bond. I have. What did he mean?"

Julie murmured, "The violence."

Diamond said, "It's all very tame by today's standards, isn't it?"

"I doubt if Milo Motion has read anything written in the last thirty years," said Jones.

"So you took your revenge on Milo?"

"Yes, and you don't know how it was done."

"Don't I?" said Diamond, his own ego challenged. "Don't I?"

"Let's hear it, then," Jones sneered.

He heard it from Diamond, point for point. The extra padlock from Foxton's. The switch while Milo was aboard the boat, enabling Jones to unlock it later.

The deflating of Gilbert Jones was satisfying to behold. "All right, you worked it out," he eventually conceded, "but not one of them could."

"I'm sure you're right. Your planning can't be faulted. It would have been a perfect crime if Sid Towers hadn't got curious and driven out to the boatyard just as you were replacing the original padlock."

Jones didn't deny it. He said, "I didn't mean to kill him. I mean, I hit him from behind, but I only wanted to make my getaway. He hadn't seen me. If he'd survived, you would have been none the wiser."

"And Rupert?" said Diamond, leaping ahead. "Why was he killed? He hadn't insulted your brainpower. He wasn't even a member when you joined the Bloodhounds."

This was the crux of it. Sid's death may not have been planned, but Rupert's was. Stringing a man from a bridge isn't accidental.

Jones was silent for some time. Then he shook his head. "You've got to see it my way. You were closing in. I was worried. It was only a matter of time before you got round to me unless I did something dramatic to put you off. I'd be up for manslaughter at the very least. Maybe murder. I needed someone to take the heat off me. First I thought of Jessica Shaw. She's clever. Clever enough to have written the riddles. And she was holding a party at the art gallery. I decided a message on the window would get some attention. If nothing else, it would create a distraction."

"And buy time?"

"Well, yes. But I needed someone else to be blamed for writing up the graffiti. Rupert Darby."

"Why Rupert? He hadn't even crossed your path."

"That's exactly the point," said Jones with the pitiless logic that had sentenced Rupert to death. "He was a stranger to me."

"You marked him with the paint spray," said Diamond. "You'd never met him, but he was easy to recognize with the beret."

"And it struck me then that Darby was a better choice than Jessica. And if he committed suicide, or appeared to—"

"You mean, if you were to murder him."

Jones didn't balk at the mention of murder. It was secondary to his plan. His locked room crime was the proof of his brilliance in the face of the Bloodhounds, the police, his workmates, all the people who had ever slighted him. It had to remain undetected, regardless of the consequences. The killing of two hapless men had been incidental. What mattered was that he succeeded. Murderers of his kind are rare, but they exist; they lose all sense of proportion and nothing is allowed to thwart them.

"It would look like he'd killed Sid Towers and decided to do away with himself. Especially if I wrote another riddle."

"Which you did. You've got some talent there," said Diamond. "Pity you didn't leave it at poetry."

Jones shrugged.

Diamond said, "Killing a man you hardly knew at all."

"But the riddle had to work out," Jones said, his blue eyes widening in a way that revealed his unbalance. "It had to work out."

Adding a confession of his own, Diamond said, "When I first saw the body hanging from the bridge, I was sure it was the work of two people. I overlooked your strength training. Even so, it couldn't have been easy."

"He was in no state to struggle."

"Drugged?"

"I did add something to his seventh vodka."

"In which pub?"

"Don't ask. It was some night," said Jones. "He told me himself it was one of the best benders of his life."

"And then what? You drove him to Sydney Gardens . . ."

"He couldn't stand straight by this time. I stuffed the padlock in his pocket."

"The one you used to get into the narrowboat?"

"Yes. And I found his key ring in his pocket with his house key and attached the padlock keys to it. He had no idea what I was doing. Then I dragged him out of the car to the bridge, fixed the rope to the railings, slipped the noose over his head, and heaved him over." There was a chilling sense of satisfaction in the way it had been done.

"In the end it was down to muscle power, your perfect crime," said Diamond.

"It's the way you use it," said Jones.

"We know all about that," Diamond told him. "How's your arm feeling now? Capable of signing a statement?"

Nothing would be gained from protesting at the callous way two likable men had lost their lives. Gilbert Jones was irredeemable.

At home in Weston, in his armchair in front of the TV, with Raffles chewing his shoelaces, Diamond asked Stephanie what she was reading.

"It's that book you brought home the other day," she said, "*The Hollow Man*."

"I meant to read it," he said. "I only looked at one chapter in the end."

"Will you get around to it?"

"I shouldn't think so. Detective stories aren't my thing at all. I've got no patience with them. Nothing like the real thing."

"The bank murder, you mean?"

He gave her a sharp look. "That was another story."

Please turn the page for a bonus chapter
from Peter Lovesey's newest novel,

UPON A DARK NIGHT

Available in hardcover
from
THE MYSTERIOUS PRESS

It has been said . . . that there are few situations in life that cannot be honourably settled, and without loss of time, either by suicide, a bag of gold, or by thrusting a despised antagonist over the edge of a precipice upon a dark night.

From *Kai Lung's Golden Hours*, by Ernest Bramah (Grant Richards, 1922)

1

A young woman opened her eyes.

The view was blank, a white-out, a snowfall that covered everything. She shivered, more from fright than cold. Strangely she didn't feel cold.

Troubled, she strained to see better, wondering if she could be mistaken about the snow. Was she looking out on an altogether different scene, like a mass of vapour, the effect you get from inside an aircraft climbing through dense cloud? She had no way of judging; there was just this blank, white mass. No point of reference and no perspective.

She didn't know what to think.

The only movement was within her eyes, the floaters that drift fuzzily across the field of vision.

While she was struggling over the problem she became aware of something even more disturbing. The blank in her view was matched by a blank inside her brain. Whatever had once been there had gone. She didn't know who she was, or where this was happening, or why.

Her loss of identity was total. She could recall nothing. To be deprived of a lifetime of experiences, left with no sense of self, is devastating. She didn't even know which sex she belonged to.

It called for self-discovery of the most basic sort. Tentatively she explored her body with her hand, traced the swell of her breast and then moved down.

So, she told herself, at least I know I'm in that half of the human race.

A voice, close up, startled her. "Hey up."

"What's that?" said another. Both voices were female.

"Sleeping Beauty just opened her eyes. She's coming round, I think."

"You reckon?"

"Have a look. What do you think?"

"She looks well out to me."

"Her eyes were definitely open. We'd better call someone."

"I wouldn't bother yet."

"They're closed now, I grant you."

"What did I tell you?"

She had closed them because she was dazzled by the whiteness. Not, after all, the whiteness of snow. Nor of cloud. The snatch of conversation made that clear. Impressions were coming in fast. The sound quality of the voices suggested this was not happening in the open. She was warm, so she had to be indoors. She had been staring up at a ceiling. Lying on her back, on something soft, like a mattress. In a bed, then? With people watching her? She made an effort to open her eyes again, but her lids felt too heavy. She drifted back into limbo, her brain too muzzy to grapple anymore with what had just been said.

2

Some time later there was pressure against her right eye, lifting the lid.

With it came a man's voice, loud and close: "She's well out. I'll come back." He released the eye.

She dozed. For how long, it was impossible to estimate, because in no time at all, it seemed, the man's thumb forced her eye open again. And now the white expanse in front of her had turned black.

"What's your name?"

She didn't answer. Couldn't use her voice.

"Can you hear me? What's your name?"

She was conscious of an invasive smell close to her face, making the eyes water.

She opened her other eye. They were holding a bottle to her nose and it smelt like ammonia. She tried to ask, "Where am I?" but the words wouldn't come.

He removed the thumb from her eye. The face peering into hers was black. Definitely black. It wasn't only the contrast of the white background. He was so close she could feel his breath on her eyelashes, yet she couldn't see him in any detail. "Try again," he urged her. "What's your name?"

When she didn't answer she heard him remark, "If this was a man, we would have found something in his pockets, a wallet, or credit cards, keys. You women will insist on carrying everything in a bag and when the wretched bag goes missing there's nothing to identify you except the clothes you're wearing."

Sexist, she thought. I'll handbag you if I get the chance.

"How are you doing, young lady? Ready to talk yet?"

She moved her lips uselessly. But even if she had found her voice, there was nothing she could tell the man. She

3

wanted to ask questions, not answer them. Who was she? She had no clue. She could barely move. Couldn't even turn on her side. Pain, sharp, sudden pain, stopped her from changing position.

"Relax," said the man. "It's easier if you relax."

Easy for you to say so, she thought.

He lifted the sheet and held her hand. Bloody liberty, she thought, but she was powerless. "You were brought in last night," he told her. "You're being looked after, but your people must be wondering where you are. What's your name?"

She succeeded in mouthing the words, "Don't know."

"Don't know your own name?"

"Can't think."

"Amnesia," he told the women attendants. "It shouldn't last long." He turned back to her. "Don't fret. No need to worry. We'll find out who you are soon enough. Are you in much pain? We can give you something if it's really bad, but your head will clear quicker if we don't."

She moved her head to indicate that the pain was bearable.

He replaced her hand under the bedding and moved away.

She closed her eyes. Staying conscious so long had exhausted her.

Some time later, they tried again. They cranked up the top end of the bed and she was able to see more. She was lucid now, up to a point. Her memory was still a void.

She was in a small, clinically clean private ward, with partly closed venetian blinds, two easy chairs, a TV attached to the wall, a bedside table with some kind of con-

4

trol panel. A glass jug of water. Facing her on the wall was a framed print of figures moving through a field of poppies, one of them holding a sunshade.

I can remember that this painting is by Monet, she thought. Claude Monet. I can remember a nineteenth-century artist's name, so why can't I remember my own?

The black man had a stethoscope hanging from his neck. He wore a short white jacket over a blue shirt and a loosely knotted striped tie. He was very much the junior doctor wanting to give reassurance, in his twenties, with a thin moustache. His voice had a Caribbean lilt.

"Feeling any better yet?"

She said, "Yes." It came out as a whisper.

He seemed not to have heard. "I asked if you are feeling any better."

"I think so." She heard her own words. *Think so.* She wanted to sound more positive. Of course if her voice was functioning she had to be feeling better than before.

"I'm Dr. Whitfield," he told her and waited.

She said nothing.

"Well?" he added.

"What?"

"We'd like to know your name."

"Oh."

"You're a mystery. No identity. We need to know your name and address."

"I don't know."

"Can't remember?"

"Can't remember."

"Anything about yourself?"

"Nothing."

"How you got here?"

5

"No. How *did* I get here?"

"You have no recall at all?"

"Doctor, would you please tell me what's the matter with me?"

"It seems that you've been in an accident. Among other things, you're experiencing amnesia. It's temporary, I can promise you."

"What sort of accident?"

"Not so serious as it might have been. A couple of cracked ribs. Abrasions to the legs and hips, some superficial cuts."

"How did this happen?"

"You tell us."

"I can't."

He smiled. "We're no wiser than you are. It could have been a traffic accident, but I wouldn't swear to it. You may have fallen off a horse. Do you ride?"

"No . . . I mean, I don't know."

"It's all a blank, is it?"

"Someone must be able to help. Who brought me here?"

"I wish we knew. You were found yesterday evening lying unconscious in the car park. By one of the visitors. We brought you inside and put you to bed. It was the obvious thing. This is a private hospital."

"Someone knocked me down in a hospital car park?"

He said quite sharply, "That doesn't follow at all."

She asked, "Who was this person who is supposed to have found me?"

"There's no 'supposed' about it. A visitor. The wife of one of our long-term patients. We know her well. She wouldn't have knocked you down. She was very concerned, and she was telling the truth, I'm certain."

"So someone else knocked me down. Some other visitor."

"Hold on. Don't go jumping to conclusions."

"What else could have happened?"

"Like I said, a fall from a horse. Or a ladder."

"In a hospital car park?" she said in disbelief, her voice growing stronger as the strange facts of the story unfolded.

"We think someone may have left you there in the expectation that you would be found and given medical attention."

"Brought me here, like some unwanted baby—what's the word?—a foundling?"

"That's the general idea."

"And gone off without speaking to anyone? What kind of skunk does a thing like that?"

He shrugged. "It's better than a hit-and-run. They just leave you in the road."

"You said this is a private hospital. Where?"

"You're in the Hinton Clinic, between Bath and Bristol, quite close to the M4. Do you know it? We've had car accident victims brought in before. Does any of this trigger a memory?"

She shook her head. It hurt.

"You'll get it all back soon enough," he promised her. "Parts of your brain are functioning efficiently, or you wouldn't follow what I'm saying. You can remember words, you see, and quite difficult words, like 'foundling.' Did you go to school round here?"

"I've no idea."

"Your accent isn't west country. I'd place you closer to

London from the way you speak. But of course plenty of Londoners have migrated here. I'm not local either." He smiled. "In case you hadn't noticed."

She asked, "What will happen to me?"

"Don't worry. We informed the police. They took a look at you last night. Made some kind of report. Put you on their computer, I expect. You can be sure that someone is asking where you are by now. They'll get a report on a missing woman and we'll find out soon enough. Exciting, isn't it? Not knowing who you are, I mean. You could be anyone. A celebrity. Concert pianist. Rock star. Television weather girl."

The excitement eluded her. She was too downcast to see any charm in this experience.

Later they encouraged her to get out of bed and walk outside with one of the nurses in support. Her ribs felt sore, but she found no difficulty staying upright. She was functioning normally except for her memory.

She made an effort to be positive, actually summoning a smile for another patient who was wheeled by on an invalid chair, some poor man with the sallow skin of an incurable. No doubt the doctor was right. Memory loss was only a temporary thing, unlike the loss of a limb. No one in her condition had any right to feel self-pity in a place where people were dying.

Before returning to her room, she asked to visit a bathroom. A simple request for a simple need. The nurse escorting her opened a door. What followed was an experience common enough: the unplanned sighting in a mirror of a face that turned out to be her own, the frisson of seeing herself as others saw her. But what made this so

8

unsettling was the absence of any recognition. Usually there is a momentary delay while the mind catches up. This must be a mirror and it must be me. In her case the delay lasted until she walked over to the mirror and stared into it and put out her hand to touch the reflection of her fingertip. The image was still of a stranger, a dark-haired, wide-eyed, horror-stricken woman in a white gown. She turned away in tears.

In her room, Dr. Whitfield spoke to her again. He explained that her condition was unusual. Patients with concussion generally had no memory of the events leading up to the injury, but they could recall who they were, where they lived, and so on. He said they would keep her under observation for another night.

The loss of identity was still with her next morning. One of the nurses brought her a set of clothes in a plastic container. She picked up a blue shirt and looked at the dirtmarks on the back and sleeves. It was obvious that whoever had worn this had been in some kind of skirmish, but she felt no recognition. Jeans, torn at the knee. Leather belt. Reeboks, newish, but badly scuffed. White socks. Black cotton knickers and bra. Clothes that could have belonged to a million women her age.

"Do you want me to wear these?"

"We can't send you out in a dressing gown," said one of the nurses.

"Send me out?" she said in alarm. "Where am I going?"

"The doctors say you don't need to be kept in bed any longer. We've kept you under observation in case of complications, but you've been declared fit to move now."

"Move where?"

"This is a private hospital. We took you in as an emergency and now we need the bed for another patient."

They wanted the bed for somebody who would pay for it. She'd been so preoccupied with her problem that she'd forgotten she was literally penniless.

"We're going to have to pass you on to Avon Social Services. They'll take care of you until your memory comes back. Probably find you some spare clothes, or give you money to get some."

On charity. She hated this. She hoped another night would restore her memory. "Can't I stay here?"

She was collected later the same morning by a social worker called Imogen who drove a little green Citroen Special with a striped roof. Imogen was pale and tall with frizzy blond hair and six bead necklaces. Her accent was as county as a shire hall. "I say, you were jolly fortunate landing up there," she said as they drove out of the hospital gates. "The Hinton is *the* clinic to get yourself into, if you're in need of treatment, that is. I don't like to think what it would have cost if you hadn't been an emergency. What's your name, by the way?"

"I don't know."

"Still muzzy?"

"Very."

"I'll have to call you something. Let's invent a name. What do you fancy? Do you object to Rose?"

The choice of name was instructive. Obviously from the quick impression Imogen had got, she had decided that this nameless woman wasn't a Candida or a Jocelyn. Something more humble was wanted.

"Call me anything you like. Where are you taking me?"

10

"To the office, first. You'll need money and clothes. Then to a hostel, till you get yourself straight in the head. They told me you cracked a couple of ribs. Is that painful? Should I be taking the corners extra carefully?"

"It's all right."

The doctor hadn't strapped up the damaged rib cage. Apparently if your breathing isn't uncomfortable, the condition cures itself. The adjacent ribs act as splints. Her sides were sore, but she had worse to worry over.

"I'm an absurdly cautious driver actually," Imogen claimed. "Do you live in Bath, Rose?"

Rose. She would have to get used to it now. She didn't feel like a flower.

"I couldn't say."

She thought it unlikely that she lived in Bath, considering it made no connection in her mind. Probably she was just a visitor. But then she could think of no other place she knew.

They drove past a signpost to Cold Ashton, and she told herself it was the sort of name you couldn't possibly forget.

"Ring any bells?" asked Imogen. "I saw you looking at the sign."

"No."

"The way we're going, down the A46, you'll get a super view of the city as we come down the hill. With any luck, some little valve will click in your head and you'll get your memory back."

The panorama of Bath from above Swainswick, the stone terraces picked out sharply by the mid-morning sun, failed to make any impression. No little valve clicked in her head.

Imogen continued to offer encouragement. "There's always a chance some old chum will recognize you. If this goes on for much longer, we can put your picture in the local paper and see if anyone comes forward."

She said quickly, "I don't think I'd like that."

"Shy, are we?"

"Anyone could say they knew me. How would I know if they were speaking the truth?"

"What are you worried about? Some chap trying his luck? You'd know your own boyfriend, wouldn't you?"

"I've no idea."

"Stone the crows!" said Imogen. "You do have problems."

They drove down the rest of the road and into the city in silence.

At the office in Manvers Street, Rose—she really was making an effort to respond to the name—was handed twenty-five pounds and asked to sign a receipt. She was also given a secondhand shirt and jeans. She changed right away. Imogen put the old clothes into a plastic bin liner and dumped them in a cupboard.

She thought about asking to keep her tatty old things regardless of the state they were in. Seeing them dumped in the sack was like being deprived of even more of herself. In the end she told herself they were too damaged to wear and what were clothes for if you didn't use them? She didn't make an issue of it.

Then Imogen drove her to a women's hostel in Bathwick Street called Harmer House, a seedy place painted inside in institutional green and white. She was to share a room with another woman who was out.

"How long do I stay here?"

"Until you get your memory back—or someone claims you."

12

Like lost property.

Imogen consoled her. "It shouldn't be long, they said. Chin up, Rose. It could happen to anyone. At least you've got some sleeping quarters tonight. Somewhere to count sheep. You're luckier than some."

Welcome to the Island of Morada—getting there is easy, leaving . . . is murder.

Embark on the ultimate, on-line, fantasy vacation with
MODUS OPERANDI.

Join fellow mystery lovers in the murderously fun MODUS OPERANDI, a unique on-line, multi-player, multi-service, interactive, mystery game launched by The Mysterious Press, Time Warner Electronic Publishing and Simutronics Corporation.

Featuring never-ending foul play by your favorite Mysterious Press authors and editors, MODUS OPERANDI is set on the fictional Caribbean island of Morada. Forget packing, passports and planes, entry to Morada is easy—all you need is a vivid imagination.

Simutronics GameMasters are available in MODUS OPERANDI around the clock, adding new mysteries and puzzles, offering helpful hints, and taking you virtually by the hand through the killer gaming environment as you come in contact with players from on-line services the world over. Mysterious Press writers and editors will also be there to participate in real-time on-line special events or just to throw a few back with you at the pub.

MODUS OPERANDI is available on-line now.

Join the mystery and mayhem on:
- America Online® at keyword MODUS
- Genie® at keyword MODUS
- PRODIGY® at jumpword MODUS

Or call toll-free for sign-up information:
- America Online® 1 (800) 768-5577
- Genie® 1 (800) 638-9636, use offer code DAF524
- PRODIGY® 1 (800) PRODIGY, use offer code MODO

Or take a tour on the Internet at
http://www. pathfinder.com/twep/games/modop.

MODUS OPERANDI—It's to die for.